PAOLA SANTIAGO
AND THE
SANCTUARY OF SHADOWS

ALSO BY TEHLOR KAY MEJIA
Paola Santiago and the River of Tears
Paola Santiago and the Forest of Nightmares

PAOLA SANTIAGO

AND THE

SANCTUARY OF SHADOWS

TEHLOR KAY MEJIA

RICK RIORDAN PRESENTS

𝒟𝒾𝓈𝓃𝑒𝓎 • HYPERION   LOS ANGELES NEW YORK

First Edition, August 2022

1 3 5 7 9 10 8 6 4 2

FAC-004510-22168

Printed in the United States of America

This book is set in Janet Antiqua Std/Monotype
Designed by Tyler Nevins

Library of Congress Cataloging-in-Publication Data
Names: Mejia, Tehlor Kay, author.
Title: Paola Santiago and the sanctuary of shadows / Tehlor Kay Mejia.
Description: First edition. • Los Angeles ; New York : Disney/Hyperion, 2022. • "Rick
Riordan presents." • Audience: Ages 8–12. • Audience: Grades 4–6. • Summary:
"Thirteen-year-old Paola Santiago must return to the void to rescue her best friend Dante
and face her biggest foe yet: El Cucuy, the lord of nightmares"—Provided by publisher.
Identifiers: LCCN 2021045623 • ISBN 9781368076876 (hardcover) • ISBN 9781368078115 (ebook)
Subjects: CYAC: Fear—Fiction. • Supernatural—Fiction. • Mexican
Americans—Fiction. • LCGFT: Novels. • Paranormal fiction.
Classification: LCC PZ7.1.M46915 Paq 2022 • DDC [Fic]—dc23
LC record available at https://lccn.loc.gov/2021045623

Reinforced binding
Visit www.DisneyBooks.com
Follow @ReadRiordan

To everyone still with me at the end.
Thank you for this incredible journey.

CONTENTS

ONE

Poor Patrick

"You got this, Pao!"

"Take him down!"

"On your left!"

Paola Santiago barely heard the noise of the small crowd as she faced down her opponent. He was already missing an arm, his head was tragically lopsided, and he moved in the jerky, unpredictable way Pao had come to associate with drunk people—or toddlers who really needed a nap.

Despite his erratic movements, Pao tightened her grip on her Arma del Alma, a long, shining staff with a viciously bladed end. *Let your opponent come to you*, said her father's voice in her head. *Let them expend their energy circling and crossing the space and striking. Be still water, ready to ripple or wave. Wasting nothing.*

Her opponent had almost reached her, and every part of Pao screamed that she should strike now—leap across the space and finish the job of severing his wobbling head. But instead she waited like still water, until finally, *finally* she was allowed to rush forward and stab through the neck. Then she heard the satisfying *crunch* that meant his head had hit the ground.

Pao felt no remorse, only victory, as she lifted her sweaty

face, pushed her bangs back, and waited for her well-deserved accolades.

"Oh no!"

"Poor Patrick!"

"Someone get some tape, stat!"

Three Niños rushed past Pao in a blur as she groaned, sinking onto the concrete floor. Her magical staff was already shrinking of its own accord into a travel-size magnifying glass she could fit in her pocket.

"Well, *I* thought it was impressive," said a voice from behind her, and Pao turned with a smile to see her best friend Emma Lockwood approaching with a water bottle, her eyes dancing with laughter.

"These milk drinkers wouldn't know impressive if it cut off *their* heads," Pao grumbled, taking the water gratefully and chugging half of it before dumping the rest on her sweaty neck.

"If you wanted the Niños to be on your side, you probably shouldn't have named the sparring dummy," Emma said as they surveyed the scene.

The ragtag group of kids and teenagers who called themselves Los Niños de la Luz were already on her side, Pao knew. And, as her town's protectors against the monstrous creatures of the void, they were important allies to have.

Not just for their warehouse headquarters, either. Though it was pretty awesome. The rafters in its ceiling were nearly thirty feet above their heads. The glossy concrete floor was painted and taped with complicated diagrams of footwork, advances, and retreats, all color-coded according to types of creature. Best of all, it was in a part of town far from any prying eyes. Ideal for monster-hunting practice.

Of course, at the moment, the only creature in sight was an old dummy on a rolling cart. And he was currently missing a head.

"Patrick," Pao said, rolling her eyes at her own folly. "What kind of a name is *Patrick* for a monster anyway?"

"Hey, there are a lot of Patricks in the world," Emma replied. "I'm sure at least *some* of them are monsters."

Pao couldn't argue with that, so she got to her feet and walked over to a section of school gym bleachers that her friend Naomi had "liberated" from Silver Springs High. Then she flopped down, her muscles burning from a long day of training.

"How do you feel?" Emma asked, her eyes x-raying Pao. They looked even bluer than usual against her pumpkin-orange sweatshirt. Despite the fact that it was still over a hundred degrees in Silver Springs, Emma was determined to show her fall spirit.

Pao thought about changing the subject to actual pumpkins, or costumes, or Halloween baking or crafts, all subjects she knew would distract the girl in front of her. But she'd never been able to lie to Emma, or avoid her questions for long, so she told the truth. As much of it as she could bear to say out loud, anyway.

"I'm frustrated," she said, kicking her white sneakers against the bench. "I'm restless. I can take Patrick's head off fifteen times a day, and it's not gonna get us any closer to rescuing Dante."

At the sound of their ex–best friend's name, Emma went quiet for a moment, and Pao knew she was remembering things, too. Things like the trailer laboratory the two of them had found in the middle of the Oregon forest last winter. And the man inside, who'd been Pao's long-lost father and not her father all at once.

Pao had told Emma everything, of course. All the gory

details Emma hadn't seen while she waited outside the trailer. About finding out La Llorona was not only the ghost-deity Pao had defeated in the void, she was also Pao's *grandmother*!

That part had taken a little explaining. See, after drowning her three children in the river, La Llorona had found a way to bring them back to life by merging their souls with those of living victims. Her twisted experiment had only worked on her second son, Beto, which, Pao discovered, was her father's true identity.

Only, the experiment (like most things La Llorona did) had gone pretty horribly wrong. Beto had run away in horror from his mother, changed his name, and tried to bury his past. But over time the soul his was bound to—a boy victim of La Llorona's named Joaquin—started to become more dominant . . . and resentful.

Eventually, Joaquin had hatched a plan to use Pao's connection to the void to tear open its fabric and let out every loathsome creature inside to feed on the living. Luring her to the forest by using Dante as bait . . .

Working with Beto, Pao had managed to free Joaquin's soul, put an end to his awful plot, and get her friends back to safety. All except Dante, who, fed by his own jealousy and anger, had gone willingly into the void and remained there.

Even with the Niños' centuries of knowledge about the void and its inhabitants, her father's memories of Joaquin's machinations, and Pao's own growing desperation to smash her way into that terrible place by whatever means necessary, they still hadn't managed to rescue him. It had already been eight months.

"We're going to find him," Emma said at last, putting a hand on Pao's shoulder. "You said yourself that whoever is keeping Dante wouldn't want to give up the leverage they have over you by killing him, so it's just a matter of—"

"Of finding a way in," Pao said, almost to herself. She had fallen asleep repeating that truth to herself over and over every night since January. But the months kept going by, and Pao's faith in her own understanding of the situation was flagging by the day.

Joaquin had told her, while tied to a chair in his trailer lab, that the void wanted her, La Llorona's granddaughter, who had twice defied its soldiers, who had snatched three living souls from its depths and was determined to take a fourth. But if the void wanted her so bad, why hadn't it shown her how to enter it again? Why wasn't it using Dante to lure her back?

She hadn't had a single vision of its ghost-riddled depths since she'd returned from Oregon. Not one. And she couldn't help but wonder why her dreams, the connection that had allowed her to save her friends and family before, had deserted her now, at this crucial juncture.

Though Pao didn't exactly *want* to be the descendent of an evil ghost woman who had drowned countless children, or to belong, in part, to the spooky, monster-ridden place that had given her power, she couldn't help feeling a little abandoned.

Not that she could ever admit that to Emma. Or anyone else.

"It's my dad, mostly," Pao said when the silence had stretched out a beat longer than she could stand. "He wants to act like I'm just this normal kid, like I shouldn't be getting involved with paranormal stuff, even though I *saved his life* by getting involved with it. I wish he would just let me be who I am."

Before Emma could get to one of the fourteen solutions to this problem she had undoubtedly brainstormed in the past ten seconds, Pao's stomach grumbled, and they both laughed.

"Come on," Emma said, getting to her feet, the bleachers groaning under her bright green sneakers with the rainbow laces. "Let's get out of here. Ice cream? Pizza?"

As much as Pao wanted to hold on to her frustration, to sit here and stew, the appeal of a pizza was pretty undeniable. "Okay," she relented. "But first I have to talk to the biggest jerk in Arizona. Wait for me outside?"

"I'll be the one with the sparkly purple bike."

When Pao opened the door to the warehouse's attached office, Franco was sitting in front of what appeared to be a super-old computer, but Pao knew it was an invention of her father's—a machine that could read magical signatures and measure the intensity of the energy they gave off.

Hopefully the computer couldn't measure the waves of irritation coming off Pao, because she thought the strength of them would probably break it.

"Franco," she said when it became clear he wasn't going to acknowledge her presence beyond a wary glance. "Find anything new?"

"I'm sure Beto would have told you if we had," he said curtly.

"I . . . He's not really . . . I'm asking you," Pao stammered, feeling her face heat up. You'd think that living with a man who'd been studying the paranormal for *both* of his lives would have put her at the forefront of the Niños' activities, but Pao had been relegated to perpetual trainee. Which meant fighting dummies and having her questions constantly brushed aside.

Franco didn't answer at first, just stabbed the buttons on the field unit in his hand a little harder than Pao felt was necessary. But she'd learned from months in this grumpy boy's company that he could never resist the urge to talk about his work for long, so she waited, counting down from ten in her head.

When she got to six, he pushed back from the desk with a huff. "The whole map's a blank! I thought the thing in B.C. was an anomaly, but *every* known entrance to the void that we've mapped in the past fifty years is gone. Just disappeared."

Pao stilled at the mention of Canada. It had been their first trip after they returned from saving Beto. An expedition to the only known void entrance on the West Coast—besides the Gila River one Pao and her friends had destroyed the summer before. Based on Pao's dreams, Beto and Franco had been sure the machines were misreading things, that the void entrance would be there even though no evidence of it could be seen.

They'd all been so hopeful, she remembered. So sure they would get through. That they'd bring Dante back, and this whole nightmare would be over. They'd prepared for months, and Pao had brandished her Arma del Alma without a doubt in her mind, the still-chilly March winds cutting through her sad excuse for a winter coat.

Most of the Niños had been forced to stay behind, their status as lost, escaped, forgotten, or otherwise fugitive children making it difficult for them to travel, so Pao, her father, and Franco (who'd been a smug teenager for a hundred years now) had made their way through the snowy woods outside British Columbia to find . . .

Nothing.

No liminal space. No monsters. No evidence—besides a

black scorch mark on the ground—that there'd ever been a portal to the malevolent underworld there.

To cover his disappointment, Franco had tried asking the locals living near the void entrance about what had happened, but everyone they'd approached had, frustratingly, clammed up instantly at the sight of them. They all categorically denied that they'd ever seen, heard, or experienced anything strange.

That was when, Pao remembered, Franco had started looking at her differently.

And maybe it was also when her dad had started his all-training/no-telling-Pao-anything protocol.

Now Pao wanted to growl like a feral animal, or at least hit something that wasn't headless Patrick. Instead she waited as Franco looked at her with that distrustful, suspicious expression. She tried to avoid it by studying the walls covered in maps, notes, and theories that had been crossed out one by one.

"Any chance it's the instruments malfunctioning?" she asked, just to break the horrible silence between them that seemed to be growing fangs by the second.

"It's not the *instruments* that can't be trusted," he said coldly, turning his back in clear dismissal, and Pao left the office feeling like she always did after an interaction with Franco—like she was somehow contaminated. Like she'd failed to live up to even his low expectations of her.

"Pipsqueak?" The voice drifted across the massive parking lot before Pao could turn the corner that would lead her to Emma. The sky beyond the warehouse was almost dark, the days getting shorter now that winter was on its way again.

"Hey, Naomi," Pao said, not bothering to disguise her bad

mood. Naomi, the queen of bad moods, could hardly hold it against her.

"Isn't it past your bedtime? Papi Precioso must be waiting."

Pao rolled her eyes as she approached. Naomi was sitting on the concrete steps out front, smirking down at her.

"What? Trouble behind the white picket fence?" Naomi's tone was teasing, but after the two of them had traveled hundreds of miles together, traversed a haunted forest, and fought more than one warped fantasma together, Pao could tell there was a grudging respect beneath her casual mocking.

"It's fine," Pao said, shaking her head. "Just sick of being treated like a baby all the time."

"I've been saying it since the beginning, tourist," Naomi said, eyeing Pao with that surprisingly adept intuition of hers. "Once you cross over, it's hard to go back to normal life."

Pao was quiet for a long minute, appreciating the fact that Naomi did not insist on filling every moment with chatter. Emma, as much as Pao loved her, had never met a problem she couldn't immediately offer *several* solutions for, and sometimes Pao just needed to stew.

"It's just . . ." Pao said at last. "Dad expects me to be so grateful he's here. He says I don't need to worry anymore, that he and Franco can take care of everything. But where would either of them be if I hadn't taken charge? Why does he want to force me back into a life I don't fit into anymore?"

Naomi got to her feet, offering Pao a high five as she turned toward the warehouse door. "Look, Beto's not a bad guy, from what I've seen. But you know how I feel about Franco, and about men and their *I've got this under control, little girl* crap in general.

If you want to go after hero boy yourself, you know I'm on your right."

"Thanks," Pao said, not trusting herself to say more. The fact that Naomi would be willing to follow her out into the fray again, even after all that had befallen them on their last attempt to join forces, meant more than Pao was willing to admit at the moment.

And Pao would have taken her up on the offer, she realized. In a heartbeat. If only she had any idea where to begin.

TWO

"Why Don't You Let the Adults Handle This?"

Full of pizza *and* the massive ice-cream sundae Emma had insisted they split, Pao made her way back to the Riverside Palace after dark, feeling marginally more cheerful than she had before the infusion of bread, cheese, and sugar.

Her spirits flagged slightly, however, at the sight of the dark windows of apartment K. Señora Mata—Dante's abuela and Pao's crotchety, erstwhile spiritual guide—had been moved to a care facility for seniors over the summer after a nasty fall had left her with a badly sprained wrist. Her memory hadn't improved, and though Pao visited as frequently as her school and ghost-hunting training allowed, it had been months since the old woman had one of her lucid spells.

And then there was Dante, the boy who had never returned to the apartment they'd shared. He'd been the only constant for so long in Pao's uncertain life. They'd gone through everything together—missing parents, losing teeth, the awkward transition from elementary to middle school. Then had come the strange boy-girl feelings she'd been afraid would ruin their friendship. . . .

But they hadn't. Nothing had, until the green mist. The supernatural quest his abuela had set them on. The final rift.

Joaquin and the void had been able to worm their way into Dante's mind and steal him away.

Sometimes she could remember it like it was yesterday. The hard look in his eyes, and the way he'd swung *his* Arma del Alma (a shining and wildly destructive club he'd inherited from his abuela) at Pao like she was just as much his enemy as any monster they'd fought together.

She knew, in her heart of hearts, that most of Dante's anger toward her was the result of evil outside influences. But were the changes in him *all* due to that? She would never know until she found him.

Pao was turning away when she saw it—just a flicker of movement, a stretching shadow, maybe a flicker of green light from around the corner. Her heart began to pound, her palms to sweat, the pizza to churn in her stomach. Was this the sign she'd been waiting for? Finally? She extended her Arma del Alma automatically, finding that the weight of it in her palm steadied her. Tiptoeing, eyes wide and scanning for anything unusual, Pao crept across the front of the building to the place where she'd seen the disturbance, ready for anything.

A loud *clang* made her jump, but she pressed forward, and for a second, she was sure she saw Joaquin's twisted face, the flashing of the trailer lab's buttons and switches. She closed her eyes and screamed at the top of her lungs, a reaction she couldn't have controlled if she'd wanted to.

"Paola? Is that you?" Footsteps. The staff was shaking in her hand. It was all she could do to drag in a breath, hiccup it out, and repeat.

"What's the racket?"

"Did you hear that?"

"The neighbors," Pao said, forcing her eyes open only to see her dad running up to her, a look of concern etched on his now-familiar features. The wide brown eyes, the unkempt hair, the lines that barely betrayed what he'd seen and done in his exceptionally long life. But this was no time to wax nostalgic about her father's face. "Dad," she said, still panicked, needing him to understand. "We have to get the neighbors out of here before he . . . before . . ."

Pao trailed off, looking into the alleyway where she was sure she'd seen lights. Shadows. Glowing eyes. Instead she saw a roof rat—a big one, in her defense—staring at her from over the rim of a trash can.

"Are you all right, mijita?" her dad asked, putting a hand on her shoulder and turning her gently to face him.

Confused and embarrassed, Pao saw his gaze move to the staff she'd extended for any neighbor to see. She shrank it at once and shoved it back into her pocket. "I just . . . thought I saw . . ." She trailed off. There was no way to explain the feeling she'd had. That she was somehow back in the woods. Or that Joaquin was here, a fantasma again. The complete lack of control she'd felt . . .

"Let's get you inside," Beto said, unable to mask the pity and worry in his eyes.

Pao scowled at the ground and scuffed the dirt with her sneaker. "I'll be right behind you. I just need a minute."

Beto hesitated, then finally nodded. "Don't be too long."

Alone again, the muttering neighbors having retreated behind their closed doors and blinds to make her their nightly chisme, Pao took deep breaths of the night air and tried to force her heart to slow down, her face to cool, her thoughts to stop racing.

"It was just a rat," she said under her breath. "What's wrong with you?"

The last thing she needed was her mom coming out looking for her next, so Pao blew out her last deep breath noisily, double-checked her pocket for the magnifying glass on its handy key chain, and pushed open the door to apartment C.

She'd clearly interrupted her parents talking about her, because they both looked up quickly from where they were sitting on the couch. The too-wide smiles on their faces told her they'd just agreed not to overwhelm her with questions.

An ugly feeling began to spread through Pao. A feeling that she would have preferred walking into an empty apartment with a fire-hazardy number of candles left burning. A feeling that maybe she hadn't really known what she was wishing for all those nights when she'd drifted off to sleep dreaming of two parents who would notice her.

"Niña!" Beto exclaimed, as if he hadn't just found her brandishing a legendary weapon at a common household pest in a dark alley. "Welcome home!" He motioned for her mother to scoot over and patted the empty cushion between them. "Join us! How was your training? Did you speak to Franco? I haven't been able to get over to the warehouse yet today."

With all the misplaced adrenaline still coursing through her body, Pao wanted to scream or punch something. Instead, she took his lead.

"Training was fine," she said, dropping her bag on the floor and slumping onto the couch. "Franco is a jerk. He says you guys are looking for more magical signatures."

"We've been working on it day and night, mi amor," her father said, reaching out to touch her shoulder in what was obviously supposed to be a consoling way. But Pao didn't want to be consoled.

"Well, what can I do?" Pao asked. "I don't think Patrick needs his head whacked off one more time, so there's gotta be something more useful I can . . ." She trailed off at the dubious expression on his face. An expression that said he didn't think she was ready, and her scene in the parking lot had only proved it.

"Look!" she said, getting back to her feet, too agitated to sit. "I'm not losing it, okay? I know that's what you think. I'm just *frustrated*. My brain has been in mystery-solving, monster-hunting, fantasma-dispatching mode for over a year now, and I'm *good* at it. So why won't you just let me help?"

Beto didn't immediately answer. He just looked at her with that pained, worried expression for several long moments while Pao felt like an insect under a microscope.

"Dante was my friend," she said, trying to sound less heated and more like a normal girl who wouldn't go full warrior woman on a rodent in a parking lot. "And it's my fault he got taken. I can't just sit around and wait for someone else to find him."

At this, Pao's mom leaned forward as if to speak, but after one of those annoying silent adult conversations that only involve eye contact, she stood up and kissed Pao on the forehead. "I'm going to leave this to you and your papá." But, unable to resist, she added, "We just want you to be safe. Especially after . . . all that's happened. We're lucky to be a family again, and we don't want anything to get in the way." Maria walked down the hall to the bedroom she now shared with Beto.

Pao's dad picked up the reins. "Niña, I need you to understand that I don't keep you 'out of the action' so to speak because I do not trust you. I do it because the past year of your life should never have happened. You should not have been left alone to face so much, so young." He paused here, his face full of emotion, and Pao—as much as she wanted to interrupt—found herself waiting for him to continue.

"I left you and your mother when you were small because I wanted to protect you from my past, my identity," Beto said when he had collected himself. "I thought if you could grow up with your mother, and without my demons at your dinner table, you'd have a chance to be the child I never got to be." He dabbed at his eyes before meeting Pao's again. "But fate found you, despite my best intentions, and it changed you. I came back, Paola, because I want to make sure that it never has a chance to do that again. That you have a chance to heal."

"But I *love* it!" Pao said, unable to hold her tongue now. "I love scientific research and solving mysteries, and helping people, and even fighting. I love the Niños, and my Arma del Alma, and—"

"And you love seeing monsters around every corner?" her father asked knowingly. "You love your heart racing and your palms sweating and your mind telling you that you're in grave danger even when you're not?"

Pao was trapped, as he must have known she would be.

"There will be *time*, Paola," he said, reaching forward to take her hands in his. "Time to grow into an adult who can handle these situations. Who has training and knowledge and the wisdom to apply them both. I will help you with that. But these episodes of yours—and don't insult me by pretending this was the first—are simple proof that your mind was not ready for the horrors it has faced, and to expose it to more would be a grave mistake."

"So, you're benching me," Pao said flatly, pulling her hands away. "Until when? Until I graduate from monster-killing school and do an unpaid internship? Come on! Dante is in danger *now*! You need me *now*!"

Beto's expression turned from emotional to businesslike so fast Pao almost checked him for possession by an accountant or a school principal or something.

"I understand your worry for your friend, and your desire to be involved, Paola," he said. "But hear me when I say that Franco and I have spent decades studying these phenomena and fighting their corporeal forms. You are hardly leaving your friend in incapable hands."

The message was clear: Dante was better off with two old dudes chasing after him than with Pao at the helm of the operation.

"Why did you even bring me to Canada, then?" Pao asked, mutinous. "Why not just leave me at home to do my homework or something?"

At this question, an unreadable look crossed her father's face. "I had thought . . ." he began, hedging. "Perhaps the connection with the void that brought you to me would prove useful. But it was wrong of me to rely on a child," he added hurriedly.

"It was my mistake, Paola, no fault of yours whatsoever. I'm *glad* the void's visions no longer trouble you."

But Pao had already stopped listening. He'd spoken the truth at last. Beto thought of her as just a kid who jumped at shadows and overreacted to roof rats, and she didn't even have her spooky dreams anymore. She was useless to him.

"Mi amor," Beto said, oblivious to the way Pao's insides were turning to stone. "It should be a relief to be free of these visions, these responsibilities. A relief to be thirteen! Trust me, it does not last forever."

The only thing Pao was *relieved* about was that this conversation had come to an end.

Be thirteen? she repeated to herself, curled up in bed with Bruto some time later. What did being thirteen even mean anymore?

As Bruto snored, his paws and ears twitching, Pao tried to picture her life as if none of this had happened. If Emma had never gone missing, and La Llorona had stayed a myth, and her father had disappeared in one of the normal ways fathers disappear all the time. If Dante hadn't been tempted by the void. If all her friends weren't immortal ghost hunters.

There was a big fat nothing where that future should be. Emma would probably still have come out to her parents, joined the Rainbow Rogues, made new friends. Pao and Dante . . . It hurt too much to imagine it. Would they still be awkwardly holding hands? Pretending to his soccer buddies they liked each other *like that* when they both knew it didn't feel right?

Would Pao's mom have married her recent boyfriend, Aaron? Or someone like him? Would they have moved into some bigger house, left this place and all its memories behind?

Pao shook her head, dispelling the horrible vision. Pao had found the thing she was best at. The place she belonged. And now that place was full of adults who thought they knew better, Pao's dad was pacifying her with training sessions against dummies, and she was supposed to hang out at Pizza Pete's like a normal kid.

But she wasn't a normal kid. And the "adults" who were supposed to be in charge had had months to find Dante, but the window to apartment K was still dark, and somewhere, the void was holding on to him, waiting for Pao to come and get him.

The streetlight was too bright through the window, and she needed to close the blinds. Pao threw her covers off with a groan, causing her now-massive chupacabra pup to *ruff* in his sleep. He didn't awaken until she let out a yelp, sure she'd seen a Mano Pachona in the closet. But it wasn't a hairy disembodied hand that stole people—it was just the furry monster-foot slippers Dante had once gotten her as a present.

She stayed perfectly still for a minute or more as Bruto looked up at her balefully, already dozing off again in the absence of any threat. All was quiet in the house. Beto hadn't heard a thing.

Get it together, Santiago, she told herself as she climbed back into bed. *We have work to do.*

THREE

Tarot Cards Aren't So Bad—No, Wait, Maybe They Are

Pao woke the next morning with a familiar sense of disap-pointment already rooting into her stomach.

Another dreamless night.

He's probably right about you, said a new, snarky voice in the back of her mind. *Without your dreams, you're not even special— just a kid with a stick, and those are a dime a dozen.*

Pao lay there for a long time, squeezing her memories like a lemon in a juicer, trying to remember anything, but there was just a blank expanse where once she had woken up with clues. Information only she could have known. A way forward.

On the floor beside her bed, Bruto whined like he knew how miserable and out of place she felt. Despite her mom's strict instructions to the contrary, Pao patted the bed, the universal signal for *please jump up on this piece of furniture you're not sup- posed to be on.*

But Bruto didn't jump up. He continued to look at her like she was his favorite flavor of doughnut, but he didn't obey.

"C'mere, buddy," Pao said, patting again, harder this time. "Come on up."

Bruto didn't come on up.

The tears that had been threatening since last night broke through at last. "Fine!" she said, tossing a pillow on the floor. "I get it. You don't need me, either." And, turning her back on her beloved beast, Pao sobbed until she was out of tears.

Only when she'd been quiet for a while did her mom tap lightly on the door. Knocking was a new phenomenon in the Santiago house, and Pao was still often surprised by it. "Come in," she said through her stuffy nose, wiping her eyes hastily, though she knew her mom would be able to tell she'd been crying anyway.

"You okay in here?" Maria asked, crossing to the chair beside her makeshift desk and sitting down.

In the light streaming in from the window, Pao recognized that her mom was getting older. She was still beautiful, but she looked a little tired, too.

"I'm fine," Pao said. "Bruto won't listen."

Pao's mom quirked an eyebrow, as if to indicate that she doubted this was the whole story, but she was polite enough not to pry.

"Where's Dad?" Pao asked when the skeptical silence had stretched as long as she could stand.

"He went out," Maria said, a little evasively.

"I know he only goes one place," Pao said. "You don't have to hide it from me." Apparently she wasn't even mentally stable enough for him to *pretend* to involve her anymore.

"He wants to fix this for you, Paola," her mom said, her voice surprisingly non-patronizing, like she was addressing another adult and not some sulky kid. "He feels responsible, you know?"

Pao couldn't help it—she rolled her eyes. "Yeah, but I don't need to be protected from everything! I want to fight. I want to save Dante like I saved Emma. Like I saved *Dad*."

Pao's mom looked sad and understanding all at once. "He doesn't forget how much you've done," she said. "He feels ashamed that you had to do it in the first place."

"I know. He told me all this already," Pao muttered, aware of just how much like a whiny little kid she sounded. "But some things you're *meant* to do."

"I agree," Maria said, nodding, and Pao almost fell off her bed in surprise.

"You do?" she asked.

"I do. Beto thought he was protecting you, Pao, but that doesn't change what you've had to overcome. You deserve all the credit for that. You've accomplished more than most adults in your short time, and it's changed you. We can't pretend you're the same little girl you were."

"Yeah!" said Pao, unnecessarily loud, excited to have an ally for once. "He's been gone all this time, and I'm not four years old anymore. So how do we make him understand that?"

Maria chuckled. "If I knew that, Paola, I would have had a very different life."

Pao felt a little deflated. She'd thought her mom had come in here with a plan to get her dad to understand, to convince him to let Pao do what she did best.

"Sometimes you just have to be patient with people," her mom said, getting to her feet. "And with yourself."

For the first time in recent memory, Pao didn't want her to go. Maybe it was Beto getting to her, but she felt like this once she might appreciate some parental advice. Maybe she couldn't ask her mom why she wasn't having the dreams anymore, or where Dante was, but she . . .

And then it dawned on Pao like the sun shining right in her eyes. She *could* ask her mom because her mom could ask someone else. Or some*thing* else.

Ignoring the feeling that she was losing some ancient battle, Pao jumped out of bed in her too-short pajamas and said the last thing on earth she'd ever expected to say to her mother:

"Mom? Could you read my tarot cards?"

Seated at the kitchen table, in the very place where she had once accused her mom of being the source of all superstition against Mexican American people in the Southwest, Pao felt distinctly uncomfortable.

Sure, Pao had fought ghosts with a magic weapon and watched a man's face switch between two separate consciousnesses, and there was a chupacabra asleep in her room . . . but tarot cards had always been, in Pao's opinion, the height of woo-woo dorkiness. The thing that definitively marked science-minded people like her as separate from people like her mom.

Desperate times call for desperate measures, she told herself as her mom picked out a deck in the other room.

When Maria reentered the kitchen, Pao could tell she was doing her best to act nonchalant, like her daughter hadn't just validated her spiritual practices for the first time in her life.

If she'd been rating her mom's performance, Pao would have given it a four.

"Okay, so . . . what do I do?" Pao asked when her mom had settled across from her and her *no big deal* expression was in danger of cracking to reveal tears, or a beaming grin, or, worst yet, the intro to a Mother-Daughter Moment.

"Well," her mom said, blinking a little too rapidly. "First you have to think of a question. Preferably something open-ended. I find the cards work best when you're asking for clarification or guidance, but that's just my personal practice. The question is up to you."

This was good, Pao thought. Maria had hit her stride with the spiel. Now Pao could have been anyone across the table. It was much more comfortable this way.

"Okay," Pao said, nodding. "That's easy." There was a long pause during which Pao's mom seemed to be trying to x-ray her brain through the overlarge glasses she'd taken to wearing.

"Oh! Well, obviously you don't have to share the question with your reader . . . uh, me . . . if you don't feel comfortable! Just focus on it while I shuffle and tell me when to stop."

It took Maria a few moments to start actually shuffling the cards, and Pao could tell that her mom was still hoping to hear the question—the all-important reason Pao had broken the tarot taboo at last.

And it wasn't that she didn't *want* to share, Pao thought, closing her eyes like she'd seen some of her mom's clients do. It was just that she didn't want to answer the many, many questions that were sure to follow.

So instead, Pao focused as hard as she could on her query. She needed guidance all right, and clarification, and elucidation, and anything else she could get.

How do I make the dreams come back? she thought, remembering the way she'd felt on the riverbank under the stark white sky. Or in the forest, the trees pressing in all around her as she searched for her father . . .

"Stop," Pao said when she was immersed in the feeling of the dreams.

The shuffling sounds ceased. Pao kept her eyes closed.

"Okay, now say when," her mom said, and Pao did, opening her eyes to see Maria laying out the cards in what looked like a giant plus sign. One card at the center, four more surrounding it.

When the spread was complete, her mom stared at the cards a long time—long enough that Pao started fidgeting beneath the table. Maybe Pao hadn't thought hard enough about her question. Maybe her question didn't have an answer. Maybe her mom had just learned way too much about her. . . .

Or maybe tarot cards were just as pointless as Pao had always imagined.

"First of all," her mom said at last, cutting into Pao's patented thought spiral. "There's a lot of major arcana here. That means you're dealing with some big stuff."

"You can say that again," Pao muttered.

"The central card here is the Moon, so that's all about your instincts, your intuition, maybe even your dreams. But there's a sense of melancholy with the Moon, as well, a danger of going too deep into another world."

Okay, Pao thought. *Spooky*. But she just nodded, and her mother went on.

"Right now, the Moon is below the Ten of Pentacles"—Maria pointed to the card on top of the plus sign showing two people looking at each other surrounded by ten golden coins—"which is the major obstacle in your reading." She furrowed her brow.

"This is usually a positive card, so it's a little odd to see it as an obstacle, but it's also a card about legacy, maybe even inheritance. The resources that come as a result of who you are and who your family is . . . Any of this resonating for you?"

My instincts and intuition and dreams, blocked by my family legacy, Pao thought. Not bad. But wasn't that backward? Shouldn't her connection with La Llorona and the void have made the connection *stronger*?

"Yeah . . . maybe," Pao said at last, not wanting to disappoint her mom, but not sure it was making much sense. "Does it say what I should, you know, do about it?"

"That's the next section," her mom said, gesturing at the three remaining cards, under the Moon at the center like a bowl.

"Cool," said Pao, though she could already feel herself checking out, putting up the walls that had always protected her from taking this stuff too seriously.

"In the past, you have the Hierophant," her mom went on, seemingly oblivious to her daughter's inner turmoil. "He's the structural center of the deck—traditional, educated, maybe a little rigid in his beliefs. . . ."

"Is that the card talking, or you?" Pao asked with a smirk.

"It's always both," her mom said with a smile. "This card means that in the past you adhered very strictly to a certain set of beliefs and expectations and didn't allow a lot of room for anything new."

"And the next card?" Pao asked pointedly, not wanting to dwell on the mistakes of her past any longer than necessary.

"The next card is the present." A little frown line appeared between her mom's eyebrows as she studied it. "It's the Lovers card. Which doesn't mean what you think it does!" she said hurriedly, as Pao's eyes were drawn in horror to the image of the naked man and woman she had always been so embarrassed by as a child.

"Mom!" she said, pushing her chair back, ready to flee and pretend this had never happened.

"Just listen before you run away, Paola," said Maria in an unmistakable mom voice. "There's nothing wrong with the human form—we don't have to be ashamed of it. But in this case, I don't think the card refers to any sort of . . . intimate . . ."

"MOVING ON!" Pao shouted.

"All right, all right! The Lovers card speaks of perfect harmony, duality, but also of the end of innocence. A discovery made on a journey that forces one out of childhood and into adulthood, and the way those two phases of life balance each other out."

Pao's face began to cool, just a little.

"Again, though, the card is reversed, which means you're having trouble digesting whatever lesson it is that you're supposed to learn. It feels like this goes back to the Moon and the Ten of Pentacles over here. Like whatever this legacy piece is, it's blocking the synthesis you need to happen in order to move forward."

Pao's head was swimming. She didn't know what she'd expected when she'd asked for this reading. When she was little and had watched her mom consult tarot cards for others, it had always seemed a little magical. But this wasn't magical at all—it was just confusing. And there was that naked guy, just smiling up at her like this wasn't all terrible.

"Okay," she said, trying to keep these thoughts off her face. "Well, thanks, Mom. This has . . . given me a lot to think about."

"Wait," Maria said before Pao was all the way out of her chair. "There's one more card. It's the future. The likely outcome if you stay on the path you're currently on."

"Oh, right," she said. "Well, let's hear it, then."

This time, Pao's mom looked like she was the one regretting the reading, but she soldiered through anyway. "It's the Tower," she said, her voice a little shaky. "Which is another commonly misunderstood card. There's nothing to be . . ."

But Pao wasn't listening anymore. Instead, she was staring at the card. A tall tower stretched up into a black sky as a lightning bolt cleaved it in two. Pieces of the structure were falling, flames were coming through the topmost windows, and a human figure was plummeting down, down, down. . . .

Pao thought she could hear her mom explaining that the tower just pointed to a transformation that required a sacrifice. That it had to do with letting go of what didn't serve you. But to Pao, the falling figure had Dante's face, and she knew more surely than ever before that she had to save him. Her father was wrong to try to keep her out of it, no matter how jumpy and useless she'd recently become.

If Pao herself couldn't sort out what was keeping her separated from her power and her potential, Dante was going to be lost forever. And not just Dante . . . He was just one little figure amid the burning wreckage of the tower. The void, with its plethora of monsters, was there behind the fabric of reality, calling to Pao and repelling her all at once. The Lovers. Duality. The Tower. Destruction. And Pao was suspended at the center of it all, waiting as everything built to its final peak.

"I gotta go," she said, standing abruptly, dimly aware that her mom was still speaking in that same concerned *it's not so bad* voice Pao had never believed even as a little kid. "Sorry, Mom. Thanks, but I forgot I have something to do."

In her haste, she knocked over the chair, but she couldn't stay, couldn't hear her mom tell her to just be a kid, that everything was going to be fine. Pao had tried that before, and she'd almost lost Emma that way. She wasn't going to lose Dante now. Not even if her dad was back and Franco thought he was king of the world.

It was all up to her.

FOUR

More Problems Than an Antigravity Beanbag Can Solve

Pao was halfway to Emma's house before she even realized where she was going. The sun beat down on the long-sleeved black T-shirt she'd worn to bed, and she was starting to sweat as morning inched toward afternoon.

Images inspired by the tarot cards still tumbled around in her mind, and as much as Pao wanted to let go of them and get back to the business of smashing monster skulls, she couldn't stop seeing them: a cascade of mysterious women and smirking naked people and lightning bolts striking Dante first, and then herself, and then Emma, and then her mother, and then . . .

"Paola, dear! We weren't expecting you!" When Mrs. Lockwood greeted her at the door, her voice was detached and personable, but not friendly. Pao knew she still blamed her for Emma's disappearance last year, even though country-club politeness demanded that she pretend otherwise.

"Sorry, Mrs. Lockwood," Pao gasped out as her pulse began to slow from the walk up the hill. "I just need to see Emma, if that's all right."

"She's packing for a trip with the Rogues right now. I'm sorry, dear. If you'd only called first . . ."

Pao's heart sank. Was Mrs. Lockwood really going to turn her away? "Oh," she said, trying to hide her disappointment and horrified to feel her chin beginning to tremble. "Well . . . if I could just . . ."

"Mom, what are you doing? Let her in!" Emma's voice came from the long hallway behind her mother. Relief coursed through Pao as her friend approached, dressed in a sky-blue sweater covered in fluffy clouds, and dark blue wide-leg corduroy pants.

"How many times do I have to tell you Pao's not to blame for what happened last year?" Emma said to her mother as she reached the door. Her hands were on her hips, and her eyes were narrowed. Funnily enough, Pao thought, she looked a little like her imposing mom in that moment. "And furthermore," Emma continued, "placing blame on Pao, a member of a less privileged ethnic group than yours, is revealing your implicit bias."

Pao was taken aback by this display to say the least. She never would have dreamed of speaking to someone like Mrs. Lockwood that way.

Emma's mother looked abashed—and a little weary—as she backed away from the door. "You're right. Of course, honey," she said, smoothing Emma's hair. "It's a new world. Us old folks have got to catch up."

"Age isn't an excuse for outdated beliefs," Emma said, a little more gently now. "But I appreciate your willingness to learn."

"I'll leave you two to it, then," said Mrs. Lockwood. "And, Paola, dear, I apologize for my . . . implicit bias rearing its ugly head. You're always welcome here."

"Thanks, Mrs. Lockwood," Pao managed as the older woman

disappeared down the long tiled hallway to the living room. "You don't have to do that for my benefit, you know," she mumbled to Emma after her mother was gone.

"I know," Emma said, her face softening. "But it's important for me not to let other members of my privileged community escape uncomfortable moments—especially my family. If you'd prefer I not do it in front of you, though, I fully respect that boundary!"

"It's okay," Pao said, finding it really was. "You're kind of a marvel, Emma Lockwood."

Emma's cheeks turned a little pink. "Well, I don't expect you walked all the way out here just to watch privileged-and-out-of-touch family theater, so what's up?"

Suddenly, everything that had happened this morning came crashing back down on Pao's shoulders, and she felt exhausted again.

"I'm not really sure why I'm here," she admitted. "I had a weird morning with my mom, and I'm . . ." She lowered her voice. "I'm still not dreaming, and I'm worried I'm just failing everyone. I have to find a way to connect to the void again, or according to my mom's tarot cards, the world is going to end and kill all of us in the process, so . . ."

There was no harm in leaving out the part about the rat she'd thought was a twisted fantasma, right? Or the Mano Pachona slippers? Or the hundred other heart-racing moments she'd had in the past few months?

She had to preserve *some* dignity.

Emma stood perfectly still for a moment, taking in all Pao had said. Then she put her arm around Pao's shoulders. "Let's go to my room. If you let Maria read your tarot cards, things must be worse than I thought."

Emma's room was half the size of Pao's entire apartment. The carpet was a blue that matched her sweater, and the fluffy faux-sheepskin rug underfoot was impossibly soft. Her bed was queen size, the accent wall behind it painted in rainbow tones that brightened the peachy pale paint on the rest.

Her desk stood in the corner, a shiny silver laptop open on top, and across her bed was a purple duffel bag covered in badges and patches.

"I always forget how nice your room is," Pao said, flopping herself into Emma's pink "antigravity" beanbag chair and feeling the beads envelop her until she was at least partially weightless.

Emma perched on the edge of her bed, pushing the white canopy netting aside and peering down at Pao. "You could come over more often, you know."

"I know," Pao said, closing her eyes, trying to let the fancy chair take her problems along with her body weight. "It just feels like there's always something."

Emma was quiet for an uncharacteristically long moment, and Pao thought she could feel the other girl's eyes on her, but when she opened hers to meet them, Emma was up, folding a lavender sweater and putting it in her bag with a thoughtful expression on her face.

"What's all this for again?" Pao asked, with the nagging feeling that she was supposed to know already.

"The Rainbow Rogues' fall volunteer road trip," Emma said, her voice a little distant. "We're going to New Orleans to volunteer with America's WETLAND Conservation Corps, learning about the ways wetland loss impacts world ecology. I'm hoping to convince the mayor that Silver Springs should be a WETLAND partner city!" Her enthusiasm ramped up as she went, and Pao felt a twinge of . . . was it jealousy? That couldn't be, right?

It was just that, while Emma was a little advanced in a lot of areas for an eighth grader, *she* knew exactly what it meant to be thirteen. Pao, her head in the world of void entrances, spectral grandmothers, and tarot symbols, sometimes felt like she was on a different planet than her best friend.

"The trip sounds amazing," Pao forced out after a too-long pause. She was sure Emma could tell her heart wasn't in it because she pulled up a second beanbag chair beside Pao and sat down.

"You don't have to say that. I know it's unfair that I get to go off on some trip while you're here dealing with all the consequences of my mistake."

"*Your* mistake?" Pao asked, bewildered. "How is Dante being gone *your* fault?"

"This is *all* my fault," Emma said quietly. "I'm the one who wandered off after Ondina, the one who got taken into the void. . . . I'm the one who set all this in motion, Pao. I was ignorant of your cultural mythology and disrespectful of the very real reasons to stay away from the Gila, and we've all almost died multiple times because of it. Now I'm off to save some wetlands that aren't anywhere near the biome I should actually be taking responsibility for and leaving you and the Niños to clean up after my disaster."

For a minute, Pao could feel the weight of all Emma had

said, the burden her friend had been carrying this whole time. They'd talked about it before, of course, Emma's feeling of responsibility for what they'd gone through at the river, but Pao hadn't known she was still struggling with it.

"Emma," Pao said, sitting up, looking her best friend dead in the eyes. "La Llorona is *my* grandmother. *My* father was being held hostage by the soul of a boy who was sacrificed. *My* dreams drew me to the void, *my* family, *my* . . ." Pao trailed off, thinking of the tarot reading in a new light. "My inheritance. I know accountability is, like, the first pillar of restorative justice or whatever, but you can't take all this on yourself."

Momentarily, at Pao's mention of accountability and restorative justice, Emma's dazzling smile broke through, but then her face settled back into seriousness. "I didn't mean to center myself," she almost whispered. "I know it isn't about me, not really, but I just want to help, and I feel useless. Like I'm dragging you down."

"No," Pao said, leaning forward. The tiny fairy lights on the wall were pinprick reflections in Emma's shiny lip gloss. "You've got it backward. Some days you're the only thing propping me up."

The silence stretched on for a moment, their eyes still on each other's, and in the background music, some girl was singing a sad song while playing guitar. Absurdly, Pao thought of that terrible card her mother had pulled. The Lovers. The end of childhood innocence. Perfect harmony and duality.

"So," Emma said at last, looking away a second after Pao had decided to. "Tell me about the tarot and your mom and everything." It was a little forced, which confirmed for Pao that she hadn't imagined the charged moment between them. She filed it away like the result of an experiment for future hypothesizing.

"It was . . . terrible," Pao said, looking at her hands in her lap as she explained. The disappointment of another dreamless night. Her mom's excuses for her dad shutting her out of everything. And then the reading itself. Her instincts blocked. The lightning cleaving the tower in two.

For reasons she wasn't really sure of, she left out the Lovers card.

"Wow," Emma breathed. "It sounds like your mom is amazing, but I can understand why what she said upset you."

"It didn't really *upset* me," Pao said. "It just didn't make sense. The void basically *is* my inheritance. My grandmother was La Llorona! Wouldn't that bring me closer? Instead, it's booted me out, and I don't know why!" She tugged at her braids in frustration. "But apparently, if I don't *find out* why really soon, the giant lightning bolt is coming to destroy everything I love."

Emma didn't speak immediately, but her eyes were doing a very familiar bugging-out thing that meant Pao was missing something obvious, and Emma didn't want to patronize her by pointing it out.

"What?" she asked with a sigh. "Whatever it is, just say it."

"I don't want to presume to tell you your own story . . ." Emma said in a voice that indicated she was *bursting* to do exactly that.

"*Someone* should," Pao said firmly. "And if you can do it in a less batty way than with a bunch of cards, I'm giving you full permission."

"Well, it makes *sense*, doesn't it?" Emma said without a beat of hesitation. "Your ancestry *would* bring you closer to the void if you weren't afraid and traumatized by it!"

"What do you mean?"

"I mean your grandmother was . . . well, not the nicest of people—"

"She literally drowned children as a hobby," Pao cut in.

"Right," Emma said. "But not just *any* children! She killed your *father*, Pao, and your aunt and uncle, and she tried to kill Dante and me, not to mention you! She terrorized and traumatized you like she has everyone in your family for three generations, and *lots* of people's families before that! As a person who's trying to come to terms with a *lot* of colonization and genocide and slavery in my own ancestry, I can tell you it doesn't integrate easily."

"But I'm not like her!" Pao said, nonplussed. "I'd never kill children, or drown myself to stop feeling guilty, or *any* of that stuff."

"I know you wouldn't. But has it ever occurred to you that since you found out about your connection with her, you've been desperate to emphasize the ways you're different? That maybe if you don't start accepting the parts of you—not the murdering, obviously!—that are like her, you'll never be able to access her world the way you used to?"

Pao didn't answer right away. She just sat there mulling over what Emma had said, trying to make sense of it amid the images on the cards that were still overwhelming her. Finally, she shook her head.

"I see what you're trying to say, and I appreciate it, but what I really need is a shortcut. Something that'll make me dream. Something I can take that'll just . . . wake up whatever part of me is in control of the visions and help me find Dante. I can deal with all my other complicated family crap after he's home."

She could tell that Emma wanted to say more, probably about how true healing from trauma wasn't linear and couldn't be rushed, but right now Pao didn't have time.

"Can you help me find something like that?" she asked when the silence stretched on.

Finally, the tension seemed to ebb out of Emma a bit. She smiled. "Of course. Witchy stuff is so in right now, and as hollow and appropriative as it is to co-opt religious rituals from other cultures for purely aesthetic purposes, I—" She stopped short at the impatient look on Pao's face and pulled out her phone. *"Herbal potion for lucid dreaming DIY,"* she said aloud, emphasizing every word as she typed.

FIVE

Implicit Bias Training

It didn't take them long to settle on a site called Bruja Alexa's Home Herbalism, and while Pao could tell Emma wanted *very badly* to finish her diatribe about the commodification of "witchy" culture by the social media generation, instead she used a piece of narwhal stationary from her desk to write down the ingredients they needed.

"Passionflower, skullcap, kava kava, ginger, blue lotus, blue cornflower . . ." she read. "Oh, and they should be *organic or wildcrafted* when possible." Emma rolled her eyes but didn't elaborate.

"My mom has all that stuff," Pao said, her skin crawling at the thought of going back to her apartment after that tarot reading. "But I . . . don't think I can . . ."

"Say no more," Emma said, hopping up. "This is a real two-birds–one-stone situation, actually." A pained look crossed her face momentarily.

"I know," said Pao. "No birds were harmed during the usage of that phrase."

Emma smiled sheepishly and then asked, "Isn't there a *botánica* in town?" in that adorably overpronounced accent of hers.

Pao stifled a smile of her own. "There is," she replied. "On Second Street, by the check-cashing place. It's where my mom gets most of her stuff."

"Perfect," Emma said, crossing to the door without another word and calling to her mom.

"Emma . . ." Pao began warily. "I'm not sure it's the kind of neighborhood your mom . . ."

"Implicit bias eradication in action," Emma said, beaming as her mother made her way up the hallway.

"What's up, honey?"

"Mom," Emma said, turning on her model daughter voice, "Pao and I need a few things for a school project. Would you mind running to the botánica on Second Street and picking up these things for us?" She smiled sweetly as her mother visibly balked.

"I'm not sure I even know where . . ."

"It's on Second, by the check-cashing place," Emma said with perfect certainty, like she went to that part of town every day.

Pao felt sure Mrs. Lockwood's eyes were going to pop out of their sockets, and she tried to make sure she was hidden from view—for who else could possibly be responsible for precious Emma's knowledge of such lowbrow haunts?

But to her credit, Mrs. Lockwood's feathers seemed to settle, and she held out her hand for the list. "This is for a school project?"

"Well, for the Rogues," Emma lied smoothly. "We're doing a project on the roots of modern herbalism."

"None of this is . . . dangerous, is it?" she asked, squinting at the list.

"It's basically Sleepytime tea," Emma assured her. "And, Mom?" She smiled again. "Don't do that thing where you clutch your purse, okay? Second Street and the botánica are part of our community."

"Implicit bias, right?" Mrs. Lockwood asked with a nervous little chuckle.

"That's right," Emma said, ushering her out and closing the door.

Pao just shook her head and laughed.

"Sleepy yet?" Emma asked, perched on the end of her bed in her sun-and-moon pajama set. She had insisted that Pao sleep over, even though Emma had to leave early in the morning for her trip. *You shouldn't be alone after drinking that stuff, just in case.*

Pao shook her head, feeling anxious. Would the tea work? Would she wake up tomorrow morning with a plan to get Dante back at last? Or would it be just another in a long list of disappointments? "Maybe if we lie down?"

They did, Pao on the left side of the bed, Emma on the right, a laptop perched on a pillow between them playing the last episode of *She-Ra and the Princesses of Power*, which they'd seen a hundred times before. The bad guys were vanquished. The two heroines kissed. . . .

At this point, Emma usually gave Pao her spiel about the importance of queer representation in media, but tonight when Catra's and Adora's lips met on-screen, she was uncharacteristically quiet. Pao couldn't help noticing certain similarities in a much more up-close-and-personal way than usual.

Adora was Emma, of course—she even looked like her, with

her long blond hair and her sparkling blue eyes. Always standing up for what was right, always giving others chances long after most people would have given up. And wasn't Pao a dead ringer for Catra? Her haunted past and ancestry, her tendency to be a loner, to lash out at the people closest to her . . .

But deep down she was good, wasn't she?

Wasn't she?

Pao was standing outdoors somewhere. It was pitch dark, and she couldn't see her surroundings at all.

A field, maybe? It didn't matter. No time to focus on trivial details. There was too much to do and too little time to do it in. Her every thought was urgent, motivated by some pulsating fear. Of retribution? Punishment? Whatever the case, Pao knew that if she didn't accomplish her task, all would be lost.

She could feel the fabric of the void. Her current location was unimportant as she reached outward with some extra sense and tested the surface of what looked, in her mind's eye, like a dark, swirling soap bubble.

A rainbow-colored oil slick seemed to cover Pao's vision.

No. It was someone else's vision she was sharing.

All was quiet in the cactus field along the Gila. It was quiet, too, in the Oregon forest where once there had been an anomaly.

An opportunity lost.

She felt a stab of irritation at the thought of it. The snare had come so close to working! How brutally they'd been punished for the failure.

But this plan would make up for it, and she would be instrumental to its success. She would be rewarded above all others.

Back to the task at hand. She had closed the opening to the Canadian forest herself—there was no trace of it now. For a moment, she saw the entire West Coast as though lifted from an elementary-school geography map. The oil slick across it was unbroken, solid, impenetrable.

She ranged eastward with that strange extra sense, knowing she was looking for something—feeling for it almost, like using the fingertips of a massive, far-reaching hand to grope for a hole in the universe's coat pocket.

Nothing for a time, and then . . .

As if a hangnail had caught a loose thread, she felt an unraveling. An opening large enough to walk through. It was a lake, surrounded by mountains, the water disturbed, boats on the bottom, lost. The urgent feeling demanded that she stop now and get back to he who was waiting, but she had to be cautious and check for other openings first. She could not afford another mistake. Not with an enemy on her trail.

So she stretched farther, her consciousness dancing along the oil slick until she felt another snag. This one was easy to identify—the cliff face was familiar to her, and with her portals, she wouldn't even have to climb it. But she had the nagging sense that these two openings were not the only ones left, and so, despite the fear and haste pounding in her every cell, she allowed herself to remain in the searching state until, at last, she found it. The final rift. A cornfield, a church's tall spire casting its long shadow. The caw of birds, and then nothing.

She held the locations in her mind. The lake—that's where she would go now, and then to the cliff, and then to the church in the cornfield. A stab of anxiety pierced her thoughts. What if the enemy beat her there? What if she was thwarted again? He would blame her, and she would not survive the process. . . .

But the girl and her friends hadn't made it to the northern woods in time, she reassured herself, even though they'd known the location. These other openings would be a mystery to them, and that would slow them down.

A flash of the enemy's face: light brown skin, wide brown eyes, eyebrows furrowed in concentration, long dark hair in two braids. Pao recognized it as her own. Her confusion was sharp, and foreign to the mind she was sharing, and for a moment, the two were aware of each other, just barely. Like the feeling of déjà vu, or that nagging sensation you get when you think you recognize someone from somewhere.

But then a voice sounded, loud and clear, as if the speaker were standing right next to her, though the nondescript dark field was empty.

"RETURN TO ME."

And with those words, the awareness, the confusion, the memories, and everything else was drowned in a deluge of fear so visceral it made her entire body tremble. There was no thinking or deciding, only the act of stepping forward, the absolute *need* to return that instant in the forefront of her mind as ghostly green shapes sprouted from the earth and rotated around her in a strange dance.

She felt the void's breath on her face, and then nothing.

SIX

To Portal or Not to Portal

Pao awoke in Emma's bed as abruptly as though cold water had been thrown on her. The laptop screen glowed, asking if they were still watching *She-Ra and the Princesses of Power.* Pao blinked at it groggily, the return to her own mind happening slowly at first, then all at once.

She sat up, careful not to shake the bed too much. Emma was asleep, facing away from Pao, her arms wrapped around an extra pillow, her back rising and falling steadily beneath her pajama top. Pao matched Emma's breathing, low and slow, until she felt it was safe to get up without waking her.

Everything looked so different now that Pao was back in her own mind. Nothing was ominous or swirling or oil-slicked. The pounding, visceral, bone-deep fear that had driven whoever (or *what*ever) she'd been in the dream was gone, replaced by her own constant anxiety, buzzing a little louder now, like a persistent fly.

Pao held on to the images of the rifts—for she was now sure that's what they were, rifts in the fabric between the world she lived in and the void—surprised to find that they hadn't slipped away upon wakening. The lake—there was no way she could get to that one soon enough, not when it was the first one on the dream girl's list. The cliff face—that could have been anywhere. There hadn't been any clues to help her find it. She put it out of her mind as she gently lifted the laptop from Emma's bed and padded as quietly as possible toward her desk.

The glare of the monitor was harsh on her eyes as she brought up Google, typing in any keywords she could remember from the last location. *Old. Church. Historical. Cornfield. Crows.* Maybe something would come up. But of course, she wasn't that lucky. Even the first page of search results was a charming mixture of horror movie trailers, corn maze ads in the Midwest, and Christian-alternative Halloween celebrations.

Pao knew she should give up, but the image was still so strong in her mind, like she was still inhabiting the perspective of the strange, terrified girl from her dream. The unique silhouette of the building with its adobe arches and rounded apex. The cross on the spire, black against the heavy clouds, reaching toward the heavens. The cornfields surrounding it for miles. The desolate calls of the crows.

Without much hope, Pao toggled over to the Images page, scrolling through page after page of cornfields and churches, and then, with a bolt of electricity that sizzled all through her, she saw it—a small, pixelated photo, but there was no mistaking the silhouette. The article it was attached to was eight years old, from some tiny paper in a place called Santuario, Texas. *Fitting,* Pao thought, pleased that she recognized the word from her erstwhile attempt at Duolingo. Or it may have been from Señora Mata—the old woman had said it often enough.

Sanctuary.

The church, according to the article, was hundreds of years old. A forgotten relic of another time, nearly swallowed by a cornfield that was part of a massive agricultural tract owned by a corporation somewhere. The article said they'd been planning to tear it down for years, but it still stood. The girl in her dream had been sure, and so was Pao.

A quick second search showed her that Santuario was outside San Antonio—nearly fifteen hours away from her current location, and that was *if* she had a car.

Why does the fight between good and evil so often rely on a middle schooler getting ahold of a bus ticket without parental supervision? Pao wondered, frustrated. She thought of last winter, when Johnny had chauffeured her and Naomi in a stolen red Karmann Ghia while El Autostopisto stalked them across state lines.

But she couldn't go to Naomi this time, Pao thought. There was too much risk that Franco would find out, take over, and tell her dad. And Beto absolutely could not be part of this. Not after what he'd said.

So she would go alone—and now, she decided. Before anyone could stop her. She had to reach the void entrance in the cornfield before the dream girl could close it. Her haunted inheritance might have abandoned her, but tonight she had stolen a little of its magic back, and she didn't need to be told twice that it might be the only help she got.

The only help she *or* Dante would get.

Pao closed the laptop, grabbed an old windbreaker she knew Emma hated out of the closet, and made as quietly as she could for the door, safe in the assumption that none of the Lockwoods' newly installed floorboards squeaked. She'd be gone before Emma woke up, and it was better that way, she told herself, though she paused before leaving to look at her honey-colored hair sprawled out across the pillow.

Be thirteen, her dad had told her, and Pao had resented it at the time, but on the precipice of yet another trip into the terrifying unknown of the magical underworld, with her friend's life (and possibly many others) hanging in the balance, Pao thought she might have given all the pink Starbursts in the world to crawl back into bed, fall asleep, and wake up in the morning to Mrs. Lockwood's whole-wheat blueberry pancakes. . . .

But that wasn't what her life was meant to be, Pao thought sadly as she turned away and slipped through the door. Maybe after she got Dante back. Maybe when the void was no longer a threat. Maybe when . . .

A guttering snore shook her out of her thoughts. Down the hall, Mr. and Mrs. Lockwood's door was open. Pao held her breath, grateful not to see any light coming from the room. It was long past midnight, and Pao knew she should leave a note or something, that they'd worry. But Emma was a spectacular liar, and she would know where Pao had gone—or at least what she had gone to do—and she'd cover for her.

Emma could always be counted on.

Another twinge of wishing she could stay, and then Pao was at the back door, easing open the sliding glass and padding out into the massive, shadowy backyard—complete with pool and high privacy fence.

Pao knelt on the sprinkler-damp grass and touched her fingers to the ground, hoping devoutly that none of the Lockwoods would look out the window to see their overnight guest disappear into a sinister-looking ring of tiny, dancing, glowing green figures, like paper dolls connected by the hands. But then the Lockwoods were gone from her consciousness, as was the grass itself, and the pool, the sultry night air of Silver Springs, and everything but the shining seed that was Pao's image of the church in the cornfield. Santuario, Texas. The third void entrance on the list. The one she would get through in time.

She had to. Though she hadn't had any luck summoning a portal since she'd come back with her father, she was confident that tonight would be different. Tonight she had the memory—stolen though it may be—telling her where she needed to go and reminding her how the void magic felt. Tonight she had no other choice.

Pao concentrated so hard she felt she might actually erase herself and every other place but that church and that cornfield just from the sheer force of her will to get there. She focused until she was sure she could hear the wind whispering in the cornstalks and the caw of a lonely crow. . . .

But when she opened her eyes, she was just a thirteen-year-old girl in a borrowed windbreaker, kneeling on a rich family's lawn in the middle of the night. There was no cornfield, no adobe-walled church with its devout cross reaching for the sky. There was no green light, no invitation from Pao's ancestor to join the family she'd never wanted.

There was nothing.

"No," Pao said under her breath. "No, it has to work. It was supposed to work!" She closed her eyes again, straining so hard she thought she felt something pop in her neck.

"Take me," she whispered to the no-show paper dolls. "You remember me, don't you? I'm Paola Santiago. I'm . . . her granddaughter."

As she said the words, she saw *her* behind her closed eyelids, worse than any nightmare. La Llorona, with her waxen features twisted in a scream, her clawlike hands reaching for Pao's throat. A spike of panic went through her like she'd grabbed an electric fence, and she lost the vision of the church. Lost her balance, even, tumbling over onto the grass and pushing herself up with shaking hands.

There were tears on her face, and she wiped them away fiercely. She wasn't going to let fear get in the way. Not when her father had decided it disqualified her. Not when Dante was counting on her. Not when lightning was waiting to strike.

One more time, her fingertips touched the ground, and she closed her eyes again, ignoring her pounding heart and the cold sweat beading on her forehead despite the heat of the night. "Santuario," she said under her breath. "The old church. Take me there, please."

But her shaking wouldn't stop, and little though she liked to admit it, Pao couldn't help flinching when she felt herself entering the trancelike state. What if La Llorona was waiting for her there?

Down the street, a neighbor's dog barked loudly, and Pao nearly jumped out of her skin. Shaking all over now, she lowered herself to the ground, hopeless. She couldn't do it. She couldn't make a portal. And the dream girl was going to close all the void entrances before Pao could make it to one of them, and Dante was going to die, and it was all going to be her stupid, scaredy-cat fault.

"Pao?"

She leaped to her feet reflexively at the sound, her hand already darting to the magnifying glass in her pocket before she identified Emma, walking across the lawn in her slippers, her fuzzy hair a halo catching the kitchen light.

"Sorry," Pao said, hastily wiping her tears on the back of her hand. "Did I wake you?"

"No," Emma said, rubbing her eyes, looking suddenly like a little kid. "I woke up thirsty and you were gone, and I thought . . ." She seemed to realize what was happening for the first time, her eyes brightening as she took in the scene. "Did it work? Did you dream?"

Pao nodded, not sure she wanted to confess the extent of her failure to the most competent person she knew. "It worked," she said finally. "I know where the rift is. But it doesn't matter because I'll never get there in time."

For once, Emma seemed not to have an immediate solution. She sat down on the edge of the concrete patio leading to the pool, her purple-painted toenails sparkling in the grass. Pao—without even deciding to—sat down beside her.

"Were you trying to make another portal?" Emma asked at last, her eyes steady on Pao's.

Pao nodded again, and another silence enveloped them. Her continued presence in the yard was proof enough that she hadn't been able to manage it. "It's *her*," she said, her voice cracking. "Every time I try to travel, to call on who I am, I see La Llorona. Her face, and her hands . . ." Pao shuddered. "She takes over everything, and I lose my focus, and . . . And it's not just her. I see them everywhere—Joaquin, the Manos Pachonas, the ahogados, El Autostopisto. . . ."

Emma put one of her hands on both of Pao's shaking ones. For a minute, the caring gesture was more powerful than Pao's despair. "It's not your fault," Emma said.

The simple statement fit like a key into some horrible lock in Pao's heart, and suddenly she was crying.

"Nothing any of them did is your fault," Emma went on, "and the fact that you don't want to be like them isn't your fault. And these circumstances forcing you to confront it all again and again when you're still traumatized by it aren't fair or normal at all. I need you to know that."

Even after Emma had finished speaking, Pao kept crying. Emma squeezed her hands, and when Pao could finally sit up straight, she knew from the look on her best friend's face that Emma didn't think any less of her for this display. She may have even admired it a little.

"It's in Texas," Pao said, sniffling. "A church in a cornfield outside San Antonio. And the person, or *thing*, that's closing the entrances is going to be there soon, and I can't travel without getting Franco or my dad involved, and even if I could—"

"San Antonio, huh?" Emma interrupted with that glint in her eye Pao knew so well. "I might have a way to get you there by tomorrow night. There's just one catch. . . ."

"What is it?" Pao asked, breathless with hope.

"You have to like classic campfire songs with updated gender-neutral pronouns."

SEVEN

Peppy Poppy and the Field Trip from Hell

Emma fell back asleep almost immediately, but Pao lay awake for hours, watching the sky gradually lighten beyond the massive bay window.

She told herself that she wasn't tired, that she was just anxious about the journey to come, but in reality, every time she closed her eyes, she saw La Llorona, and her heart leaped into her throat. She just couldn't fall asleep again and let her mind be vulnerable.

So when Mrs. Lockwood knocked on Emma's door at six thirty, Pao was both restless and exhausted. Plus, she looked like the human version of a tamale that had been reheated too many times.

"Are you okay?" Emma asked as she searched through her closet for clothes Pao could borrow. "I mean, I know last night was a lot, but—"

"I'm fine," Pao said, a little more curtly than she'd meant to, and Emma fell silent.

Pao knew she should apologize, but she absolutely couldn't talk about her family and her pain and her generational trauma with Emma right now. If Pao was going to do what needed to be done, she had to keep all that stuff where it belonged—stuffed into a little box in her mind that she'd hopefully never need to access again.

Unless you want to make a portal, or find out what the weird dream girl is up to, or—

Pao shoved this know-it-all version of her subconscious into the box, too, and smiled at Emma tentatively when she offered Pao a full backpack.

"Thank you," she said, holding Emma's eyes, seeing the hurt there and hoping her best friend would find it in her heart to understand. "For everything, really."

"What are best friends for?" Emma asked, smiling back. "Plus, it's kind of cool to be along for the adventure for once! I'm usually just sitting here coming up with cover stories for you, or . . . well, being held unconscious in a weird chamber in an underworld palace or something. So this is a first!"

Pao's stomach dropped as a vision of Emma in danger suddenly popped into her mind. "Yeah, it'll be great." She would have given almost anything to leave Emma here, safe in her mansion, while Pao took on all the danger herself.

Anything but ask her dad or Franco for help, anyway.

And as for the cover story, Pao had texted her mom in the middle of the night with the lame excuse that she would be staying with Emma for a few days to work on a school project with her. She slipped in something about taking her dad's advice. Trying to be thirteen.

If only it were true.

In any case, Pao figured that by the time Maria called Mrs. Lockwood—if she *ever* called Mrs. Lockwood—the bus would be well on its way to Texas, for better or worse.

"Emma, you'll be late!" came Mrs. Lockwood's voice from the front of the house. "We need to get going!"

"Ready?" Emma asked.

Pao just nodded, her stomach now squirming uncomfortably. Despite the dream, she felt more cut off from the source of her power than ever, from the thing that made her more than just a random eighth grader with a magic stick. And this time she didn't even have the Niños on her side. . . .

For a moment, she panicked as Emma headed for the door, oblivious. *Maybe I should go to the warehouse instead after all,* thought Pao. She didn't have to tell Franco or her dad, but she could enlist Naomi's help, couldn't she?

And she would have, if the urgency she'd felt in the mind of the dream girl wasn't still present in her own, like a ticking clock that grew louder every time Pao was idle. She'd already lost too much time, and she wasn't about to give up her only ride because she was too scared to be on her own. That was exactly what her dad and Franco expected her to do—act like some useless child who couldn't handle things by herself.

She would prove them wrong this time.

Shouldering the backpack, Pao followed Emma determinedly out the front door to where Emma's mom was waiting with breakfast bars and water bottles, the car engine already running.

"Thanks, Mrs. Lockwood," Pao said before sliding into the back seat.

"Uh, Pao, honey . . ." said Mrs. Lockwood, looking confused. "Shouldn't you be getting home now?"

"She's coming on the trip with me!" said Emma brightly. "Isn't that great?"

"When did—"

"We worked it out at the last minute," Emma continued without missing a beat. "The Rainbow Rogues believe it's important for all kids to have enriching extracurricular experiences, not just members. Don't you agree, Mom?"

Pao kept her face blank, letting Emma do what she did best as her mother nodded, still looking confused—but now maybe a little ashamed for asking, too.

"Yes, we certainly wouldn't want her to miss it," Mrs. Lockwood said.

They arrived at the school parking lot ten minutes before the bus was due to take off, only to find a dozen kids with a plethora of hair colors swarming around, bidding their parents good-bye, loading their luggage underneath the bus, and greeting each other enthusiastically.

Two adults with clipboards—the chaperones, Pao guessed— were frantically trying to take attendance. Pao hoped Emma had a plan for getting the name Paola Santiago added to the list at the last minute.

Right now, though, Emma was busy with other things. Four Rogues—three girls and a boy—descended on her the moment she and Pao got out of the car.

Pao tried not to feel immediately left out as they started shouting out nicknames and inside jokes, but when a short, black-haired girl with porcelain-pale features and a pixie cut stepped up to Emma and said "Hey, Adora," Pao couldn't help but bristle. She-Ra was *their* thing, wasn't it? Or had Emma been watching it late into the night during sleepovers with this girl, too?

Emma glanced nervously at Pao before giving the girl a high five. "You all remember Pao, right? She's been my best friend since I moved here, and she decided to come on the trip with us!" There was an edge to her voice, like she was glad to have Pao along but not sure anyone else would be.

Pao got tepid hellos from the Rogues she had met last year, during her one doomed attempt to get along with the group for Emma's sake. But the black-haired girl (or the *other* Catra, as Pao had already christened her) narrowed her eyes.

"I thought this was a Rogues-only trip," she said, glaring daggers at Pao.

"Come on, Kit, you're not really going to begrudge WETLAND another volunteer," Emma said, inching closer to Pao. "Plus, Pao actually joined the Rogues early last year—she just had to step away because of other time commitments."

Yeah, like chasing fantasmas up the West Coast, and rescuing my dad from a soul-stealing maniac, and finding out my grandmother is a legendary child drowner, Pao thought, wishing she could say it all out loud just to see the look on the other Catra's face.

Kit immediately changed tactics when Emma defended Pao, smiling too sweetly through her purple lipstick. "Oh, *totally!*" she said. "It's actually great you already know people, Pao, because *Emma*"—she stepped forward possessively and linked her arm through Emma's—"and I already agreed we'd sit together on the bus ride, right?"

Emma's face flushed. "I *did* say I'd sit with her," she said in a low voice to Pao that absolutely everyone could still hear. "But that was before I knew you were coming, so I can totally—"

"Don't worry about it," Pao said, pasting on her own toothy, fake smile and aiming it straight at Kit. "We just spent the whole weekend together. I don't want to monopolize your time *too* much."

She barely had time to watch Kit's grin wilt before one of the chaperones, a college-student-type person, stepped up to the group. She was tall and lanky, with big glasses that kept sliding down her nose, pants that looked like they were made out of random pillowcases, and a sweater that could very well have been taken from a sofa back at Señora Mata's nursing home. The overall effect was a little nutty, but Pao got the impression the chaperone was well liked by the way everyone turned attentively toward her, so she kept her comments to herself.

"Hello, everyone," she said in an overly enthusiastic tone better suited for a kindergarten classroom. "My name is . . ." The counselor paused, as if trying to remember. "Poppy! My pronouns are she and her! I am an intersectional feminist who enjoys reducing my carbon footprint and using my white privilege in a way that promotes allyship with marginalized communities!"

Pao looked around surreptitiously. Was this a normal way to introduce oneself at a Rainbow Rogues event? Because Pao didn't think she could come up with that many four-plus-syllable words that meant she thought she was better than other people.

I bet Kit *could,* she thought, throwing a dark look over to where the girl was still arm in arm with a sheepish-looking Emma.

"Uh, hey, Poppy," Emma said. "We're just about ready to head out. Also, remember my friend I told you about? Pao? Well, she decided to come along with us on the trip! She already got her parents' permission and everything."

Well, not exactly. Pao's mom had texted Pao a thumbs-up emoji. As for her dad . . . would he be upset when Pao returned with Dante in tow and a thrilling tale of how she'd managed to single-handedly retrieve him from the malevolent clutches of the ghostly underworld? Probably. But that was a future Pao problem.

Pao held her breath, waiting for Poppy to turn her away or ask for some paperwork.

"Sooooo cool!" Poppy said, her eyes wide as she clapped her hands together. "The more the merrier, right! Go, WETLAND WARRIORS!"

"Okay, great," Emma said, her smile faltering. "And I also brought that article from my mom's *Environmentalism Today* magazine I was telling you about. It's—" But Poppy walked away before Emma could finish, like she hadn't even heard her. She was clapping and cooing at another group of decidedly not five-year-olds before anyone could call her back.

For a minute, they all looked at each other, even the animosity between Kit and Pao forgotten. Pao was sure something was off about the counselor. Shouldn't she have asked to see a permission slip? Or speak to Pao's parents? Shouldn't there have been hostel or hotel or campground arrangements to make? And did she always act like a camp counselor on steroids? Pao was starting to think something was seriously wrong, but then everyone else burst out laughing at the same time.

"Oh my god!" said a kid with crayon-red hair. Pao thought her name might be Robin. "Remember how loopy she was that time she had a cold? Ten bucks says she took a decongestant this morning."

"Or maybe more than one. Who wouldn't?" Kit said, finally letting go of Emma's arm to bend over in paroxysms of hysteria.

"I mean, come on, a three-day bus ride with you guys? I'd be popping 'em, too." She pantomimed swallowing pill after pill.

"I didn't think she looked cold-medicine loopy," Pao said, her skin still crawling like something supernatural was about to burst out of Poppy's forehead and devour them all. "She kind of seemed more . . . body snatched."

They all turned to look at Pao, their cheeks still pink from laughing—even Emma's, who now had her arm linked through Kit's again. Pao thought for a moment they were going to take her seriously, ask what she thought was going on—not that she would have known what to say if they did. But instead, they all fell out laughing again, this time at her expense.

"Body snatched?" said Kit, laughing louder and harder than anyone, tears now smearing her raccoon eye makeup. "I guess Emma's friend has been bingeing *X-Files*. My *dad* had a real-alien-encounters phase, Emma's friend. Maybe you should yuk it up with him instead."

Almost everyone was laughing again, except for Emma, who was red in the face and looking decidedly torn. Pao ignored the rest of them, disregarded the heat in her own cheeks, and looked right at her best friend, who hadn't let go of Kit's arm.

"I think I'll take my chances at the bus station," Pao said, knowing Emma could hear her, and turning around to make for the parking lot entrance.

"Pao, wait!" Emma called, disentangling herself at last and chasing her to the curb, where they were out of earshot of the rest. "I'm sorry, okay? I don't know why Kit's being like this. She's probably just—"

"It's not about *Kit*," Pao interrupted. And it wasn't, though

Emma's eyes said she didn't believe her. "Look, this is why I left the Rogues in the first place, okay? I'm not like them, and they don't like me, and whenever I'm around, I'm just forcing you to choose between us all the time, and it's not fair. To you."

Emma looked pained, but she didn't deny it. Instead, she said, "I get it, and I know it's awkward, but I want you here, and once they all get to know you, I think they will, too, okay? Plus, it's not like you're just coming along to hang out. You have a mission, right? Just let me help get you there."

It was the ticking clock, the haste she'd borrowed from someone else's mind in a dream, that made Pao agree. "I really do think there's something weird about your counselor," she said as they headed for the bus. "*Kit* doesn't have to believe me, but I have a weird feeling about Poppy."

"I believe you," Emma said immediately, but again, there was something reserved in her expression.

"But . . . ?" Pao asked with more edge to her voice than she'd intended.

"No but! I just want you to consider that maybe you're a little shaken up from last night—and that would be totally justified!" she added hurriedly. "You might be dealing with *actual* PTSD from everything that's happened to you. Hypervigilance can be one of the symptoms, and—"

"And you *don't* believe me," Pao cut in, shouldering Emma's tie-dyed backpack again. "Good to know."

This time, Emma didn't run to catch up. The other chaperone, a red-haired dude with the name KYLE stitched on the front of his ASU jacket, stood by the bus door and flashed brilliant white teeth at everyone who boarded. Peppy Poppy sat in the first row of the mini charter vehicle—outfitted with reclining seats and an onboard bathroom because the Rainbow Rogues were clearly *very* well funded. Poppy's smile stretched unnaturally across her face, but it didn't reach her eyes.

Pao walked all the way to the back and sat against the window, putting Emma's backpack in the aisle seat to prevent anyone from sitting next to her—as if anyone would have. She told herself it didn't bother her when Emma and Kit sat together a few rows ahead, or when Kit scooted closer to her and held out one of her earbuds so they could listen to the same song together. Once, Emma glanced back at Pao, but Pao looked out the window, and the bus rumbled to life, pulling out of the parking lot and onto the highway out of town.

Santuario, here I come, she thought.

EIGHT
Dude Ranch Showdown

Four hours into the drive, Pao was exhausted, her sleepless night catching up with her, and her mood was plummeting. Emma and Kit were still talking and giggling in their row, and Pao's whole vision of spending this time with Emma, doing whatever else she'd cooked up in her delusional, She-Ra–influenced sleepover brain, had officially imploded.

At this rate, she'll probably just pretend not to notice me when we get there, Pao thought bitterly. *I'll sneak off toward Santuario myself and she'll get to have a cozy volunteer weekend with* Kit.

As awful as the thought made her feel, Pao knew that was exactly what *should* happen. Emma wasn't tangled up in all this the way Pao was, or even the way Dante had been. Emma's relatives were the normal kind of weird, and there was nothing stopping her from being thirteen.

Nothing except her friendship with Pao.

It was evening when they stopped for the day, and Pao had thought of at least a hundred reasons why it would be better for her to go on alone. She told herself it wasn't about Kit, or being jealous that Emma had other friends while Pao had none.

No, the sooner Emma realized this was the world she belonged in—not the haunted, terrifying one Pao kept dragging her into—the sooner she'd be safe and happy, and Pao could stop worrying about getting her killed all the time.

And Pao would be just fine. Really. She'd survived losing one best friend—she was an old pro at this by now.

To keep Emma safe, Pao had faked being asleep every time Emma had glanced back or walked past, and when they'd stopped for snack breaks, Pao had pretended to be on the phone until the bus engine started again. More than once, Pao thought Emma was going to force her to admit she wasn't sleeping and she had no one to call, but every time Pao caught that determined look in her eye, Kit was there to distract Emma with one of those magnetic elbows of hers and pull her off in another direction.

It was for the best, Pao thought, again and again. So then why did it feel so bad?

The first overnight of the trip was at a dude ranch outside of Van Horn, Texas. It had seemed like an absurd but almost fun idea when Emma had first told her about it, but that was before Kit and the rest of the Rogues and the sketchy chaperone, and before Pao had decided *totally selflessly* to distance herself. Now? It sounded like hell. And coming from someone who had basically *been* to hell, that was really saying something.

"Okay, everyone!" said Perky Poppy when they disembarked. "We'll be staying in these cabins here. There are four bunks in each—split up as you see fit!"

No room assignments? Pao thought. No archaic separation by gender? Some of the other Rogues were exchanging surreptitious high fives and making whispered plans for after-hours debauchery, but to Pao, this was just another red flag on a list of them. She knew what Emma would say, what her *father* would probably say: She was tired and suspicious from all the times seemingly normal things had tried to kill her. But still, hadn't her intuition been right enough times to make it worth listening to?

The Rogues were heading off to the cabins, already grouping up. If the chaperones weren't going to pay attention to what they were doing, Pao thought she'd be better off just sleeping by the campfire. It wasn't like it'd be the first time she'd slept outside on her way to a magical rift. And tomorrow this would all be over. They'd be in San Antonio, and she'd be back where she belonged—on a seemingly futile, haunted quest. Alone.

But just then Emma, Kit, and the tall redhead Pao thought was named Robin approached, looking significantly less critical than they had at the beginning of the trip. "We're gonna go explore, check out the horses and stuff," Emma said to Pao's shoes while the other girls stood by. Pao could tell this was her way of trying to make amends, squashing the squabble like they had so many other times, whether it was over a borrowed sweater that wasn't returned, a broken telescope, or a forgotten phone call.

And Pao wanted to give in, really she did, but Kit was still standing so close, and Pao felt a weird tightness in her chest she'd never had when she'd thought about Emma and the Rogues before. She'd always assumed that what she and Emma had was different, more meaningful. They were *best* friends, while these were just extracurricular buddies.

But the way Kit looked at Emma, and the way Emma blushed and didn't seem to mind all the arm-linking, made Pao wonder:

If a best friend trumped a school friend, what did a *girlfriend* do to a *best* friend?

They were all still waiting for her answer about the horses, Pao knew, Kit and Robin looking bored and Emma still unable to meet Pao's eyes.

"I think I'll stick around here," she said finally, with a lump in her throat as she thought of her dad's advice to *be thirteen* again, and what it would be like if she could. Just go off and giggle with these girls she was supposed to have so much in common with.

"Have fun," Kit said, rolling her eyes and nudging Emma. "Maybe you can get Poppy to share some cold medicine. See what this *body snatching* stuff is all about."

"Kit, don't," Emma said with a hint of irritation, and Pao's heart skipped a beat. But a minute later, they were turning around, walking off into the flat, grassy farmland and leaving Pao on her own.

It was always like this lately, Pao thought. She wanted to be alone, and she pushed everyone away so she could sulk, but the second whoever she'd been mean to was gone, she felt lonely and miserable. Served her right.

In front of the dude-ranch cabins, chaperone Kyle and a pasty white kid with spiky teal hair and super-baggy clothes were building a fire. Pao thought she recognized the kid as Alex, a Rogue Emma had once described as loving metalworking and dumpster diving and abhorring the gender binary.

It wasn't a lot to go on. What was she supposed to do, walk up and say, *Hi, I'm Pao. I hear you like garbage food?* And when was the last time Pao had talked to an eighth grader who wasn't either an immortal child outlaw or someone she'd known half her life?

Luckily—or unluckily, she wasn't quite sure—Alex headed into one of the cabins before Pao could come up with something vaguely normal to say to them. She felt relieved and then felt stupid for feeling relieved, and she flopped down in an Adirondack chair, wondering if there was a void beast that sucked your ability to overthink *everything* out one of your ears—because right now, if one appeared in the twilit field of the dude ranch, she wouldn't even fight back.

"Someone's got a case of the Monday blues!" came an obnoxiously high-pitched voice from behind her, and Pao closed her eyes, swallowing a scoff with considerable effort. She didn't answer, but of course her silence didn't deter Peppy Poppy, who perched on the log next to Pao with a massive, vacant smile. "So, what's eating you, Suzie Q?"

"More unresolved trauma than most people experience before high school," Pao muttered, halfway hoping Poppy hadn't heard.

"Ohhh, I know your type," Poppy said, poking Pao in the shoulder as if they had a preexisting relationship that supported that kind of thing. "You're smart and sad, right? That's what makes you way too good for fun."

Pao, forgetting her plan to be as boring as possible until Poppy left her alone to find a kid with easier-to-solve problems, spluttered with indignation. "You don't know me!" she said, turning to look at Poppy. "I'm not sad! I'm not too good for fun! I'm just—"

"Different from everyone?" Poppy asked. "Above them, right?

Because you have a rough family life and you haven't figured out how to be thirteen?"

Had Pao imagined it, or had Poppy's vacant eyes flashed strangely when she'd mentioned Pao's family? Unbidden, Emma's dismissal of Pao's suspicions came back to her. *PTSD*, she'd said.

"Something like that," Pao replied, staring too intently into Poppy's eyes now, waiting for the flash to happen again so she could have some proof. If this dumb, happy college girl was evil, Pao would get to prove Emma wrong.

"I have news for you, pumpkin!" Poppy said in a singsong voice, reaching out to tweak Pao's nose—a gesture she escaped only narrowly. "*No one* knows how to be thirteen! The people who seem like they do are just . . . pretending!"

Though she didn't want to, Pao considered this. She couldn't say she knew that many "normal" kids, but was it possible they all felt just as confused and left out as she did?

An image of Kit flashed in her mind. Her brazen confidence, her loud clothes and makeup, the way she seemed so comfortable grabbing Emma's arm, declaring who she was, what she liked and what she didn't.

There was no *way* that girl felt as left out as Pao did, and Perky Poppy wasn't going to convince her otherwise.

"Even her," the smiling bobblehead in question said, as if she'd plucked the thoughts right out of Pao's head. "Whoever you pictured when I said that? She feels just like you do."

Pao looked out across the endless field in the direction Emma and Kit and the others had gone. If it was true that everyone was just faking it, couldn't she fake it, too?

Sure, said the snarky little Pao in the back of her mind. *Fake it until one of your demonic dead relatives kidnaps the next person you get close to. I bet some badly applied black eyeliner will* totally *get you out of that one.*

"A piece of advice?" said Peppy Poppy just when Pao had almost forgotten she was there. "Tell Emma you like her. She's just biding her time with old Raccoon Eyes. Every time you're not looking at her, she's looking at you. Oooooh, I just love romance, don't you?"

Poppy did indeed seem to love romance, because she was glowing as she said this. Like, really glowing. In fact, even before Pao could digest the implications of what this counselor had just said, she realized that the darkness around them now was far from natural, and the vacant eyes that had so annoyed Pao were now shining green and pupil-less. Peppy Poppy's smile stretched feral and rabid over her razor-sharp, pointed teeth as she stood up from her stump, reaching a height of at least seven feet. Her features were waxen and strange.

"I knew it!" Pao said, self-righteousness trumping fear for the moment as adrenaline flooded her brain. She reached for the magnifying glass in her pocket, transforming it effortlessly into the long, shining spear that had been created just for this purpose. "No field-trip chaperone would *ever* let kids pick their own cabin assignments. It's literally against the laws of nature!"

As she said this, she swung the staff, but Poppy didn't need a weapon to counter. Foot-long talons had grown from the place where her lime-green-painted fingernails had been moments ago, and she swiped them at Pao, who dodged them as she had dodged the nose tweak just moments ago. Pao lunged before Poppy could recover, the bladed end of her spear flashing in the green glow of the monster's eyes.

"I'm Paola and I'm so sad," Poppy screeched through her

twisted mouth in a, frankly, offensive impression of Pao. *"No one help me! No one save me! I like being alone!"*

"Shut up," Pao grunted, jabbing with her spear just like she'd jabbed at Patrick's raggedy, often-headless form. "That's not even my biggest problem!" Her spear connected with Poppy's arm under her weird, grandma-y afghan sweater, and the sensation was horribly familiar. The crunching, shattering, frozen ooze feeling of a void creature's flesh giving way to an Arma del Alma's blade.

"What if killing's all I'm ever fit for?" Poppy said, still in that horrible voice, one of her arms now dangling from a strip of ghostly flesh as she continued to advance. *"What if I'm never normal?"*

"Seriously, this is why I never confide in anyone," Pao returned, sliding under a swipe from Poppy's single set of remaining claws to jab the creature in the back of the knee. This time Pao saw green ectoplasmic goo drip from the wound into the dirt. How long did she have before someone heard them? Before one of the Rogues . . .

Her question was answered before she could finish asking it, and in a voice that made her stomach drop.

"Pao!" It was Emma, and she was close. Much too close. "Poppy? What's happening!"

NINE
Boffering Saves the Day

"Stay back!" Pao called, willing her best friend to listen.

Poppy's horrible feral smile stretched wider still. *"You can't save her,"* she said in a horrifying mashup of her perky field-trip-chaperone voice and the grating, metal-on-metal tone Pao had come to associate with void creatures. *"As long as she loves you, she'll be in danger."*

Pao, pretending like these words didn't cut her to the core, lunged again. Poppy danced out of range again as the voices of the Rogues came closer. "Stay back!" Pao called again. "She's dangerous!"

Poppy lashed out with her talons, and Pao barely stumbled out of range this time. Her arms were so much longer than Pao's, and she wasn't the slightest bit winded. Even with the length of Pao's staff, how long could she keep Poppy at bay?

How long could she keep her from hurting one of the other kids? And was the other chaperone a monster, too?

"You can't protect them forever," snarled Poppy, again seeming to take the thoughts right out of Pao's head. *"They're mortals. Silly, fragile creatures. They die from tripping and falling—seriously, they do! Seventeen thousand of them a year in this country alone—it's ridiculous! Best not to get too attached."* Another lunge, and

this time Poppy didn't miss. The razor-sharp claws tore through Pao's sleeve and sliced open her forearm. Blood spurted from the wound and dripped down her arm, making her grip on the staff slippery.

"I *can* protect them." Pao grunted, stepping forward into her strike to give it power like her father had taught her. She caught Poppy off guard, and her blade bit into the fantasma's good shoulder. "It's what I do."

Poppy staggered for a moment, assessing her injuries, and Pao wiped her hand forcefully on her jeans, getting ready to strike again. But just then a strange flash crossed the mutated girl's face again, like a spark of inspiration, and instead of lunging forward to meet Pao's attack, she turned abruptly and darted away.

Right toward Emma, Kit, and Robin, who hadn't run far enough.

"No!" Pao shouted, running full pelt after Poppy, who had much longer legs and the strength of the void within her.

Pao wasn't going to make it in time. *"Run!"* she shouted to the girls at the top of her lungs, unable to see in the dark whether Emma and the rest of them had realized what was happening in time to get a head start. "RUN!"

Eyes narrowed, head down, staff pressed aerodynamically against her body, Pao ran faster than ever before, her long, sleepless night dragging at her heels. She was right behind the creature, and there was some commotion ahead. . . .

She saw it before her brain could really register it. Armed with a shovel and a rake that had been leaning up against a fence, Kit was actually *fighting* Poppy. Emma and Robin, Pao could now see, were a safe distance away. Emma was watching with wide eyes while Robin hid her face in her hands.

"Get back!" Pao cried to Kit, out of breath, her staff already swinging. "She's too dangerous! I can take it from here!"

"No way!" Kit called, dealing a clanging blow to Poppy's head with the metal shovel. "This is the most fun I've had on a Rogues trip in . . . ever!"

Pao's next swipe missed, but Kit got in another hit, an expert sweep to the ankles that would have impressed even Naomi. It brought Poppy's mutated form to her knees. Pao, shaking off her disbelief and her irritation at Kit's refusal to obey orders, realized it was now or never. Poppy had expected to use these girls as bait, but instead Kit had held her own, and now Pao had a clear shot.

Recalling the anatomy unit in last year's science lab, and hoping this fantasma makeover hadn't rearranged Poppy's insides too much, Pao ran up from behind just as the creature struck a desperate blow—blocked by Kit's rusted rake head. Pao plunged her Arma del Alma between what she devoutly hoped were the correct ribs.

There was a second of stillness, then two, before a horrible, earth-shattering shriek—like the call of a thousand eighth-grade girls who'd all just found out they didn't get the lead role in *Annie: The Musical*. Then Poppy melted into green ooze on the ground in front of a very mortal girl, singeing the dry grass for a meter around.

Pao faced Kit over the scorch mark, acutely aware of her own torn shirt, the blood dripping steadily from her sleeve, and the mythical, shining weapon dangling from her hand. For a minute, they just stared at the green ooze burning and seeping its way into the ground. Then they both spoke at once:

"I knew Poppy was a bit much, but what the *hell*?" said Kit.

"Where did you learn to fight like that?" asked Pao.

"Boffering club, obvs," said Kit, who didn't look the least bit traumatized by her field-trip chaperone—a girl she'd seemingly known for a while—turning into a void creature who was eventually murdered right in front of her. "We meet every Wednesday after school."

"What's . . . *boffering?*" Pao asked as Emma and Robin climbed over the fence to join them, both looking impressed and anxious in equal measure.

"What's *boffering*, she asks," Kit said, staring at Pao in disbelief before pointing at the Arma del Alma. "How about *what's that thing?* And why was Poppy twisted and glowing and violent? And why didn't *you* seem surprised by any of it?"

"Pao, I'm so sorry!" Emma cried, skidding to a stop amid the group, clutching her side and panting. "You were right, and I called you paranoid, and you could have died, and I'm so sorry!" Seeming to disregard the fact that they hadn't spoken to each other throughout the long, awkward bus ride, Emma flung herself forward and wrapped her arms around Pao, who barely caught her.

"It's okay," Pao said, her cheeks heating up as Emma held on a little longer than normal. For a ridiculous second, she flashed back to the chaperonely advice Poppy had given her before she became a murderous servant of the void. About Emma and the feelings she definitely, *definitely* didn't have for Pao.

"Anyway!" Kit said, causing Emma to let go of Pao abruptly, and a little guiltily. "Answers? I think you were about to give them to us?"

Pao glanced at Emma, who was already looking at her as if

to ask, *What the heck do we tell them?* But there was no time to coordinate a story, so Pao took a deep breath.

"Look," she said. "The world isn't . . . exactly the place it seems to be. I mean, it is, but it has a lot more ghosts and monsters than most people know about. I'm part of a group of people who, like, find them and take them out, and right now I'm hijacking your field trip to get to a town outside San Antonio where I have some . . . ghost-hunting stuff to do. So, sorry to crash, and thanks for your help. Whatever boffering is, you were pretty awesome."

Pao found it didn't cost her as much as she would have thought to say this. Even to Kit. There was something bonding about turning a sentient creature to goo, as she'd discovered to her amazement with Naomi, the Queen of Snark, last year. Apparently even *this* girl wasn't an exception to that rule.

"I *knew* it," Kit was saying already, while Robin's eyes stayed as round as quarters. "I mean, come on. There's no way life is just *normal*, right? And this is so cool. Even you were pretty impressive, Straight Girl." She twirled the rake in her hands. "So, where's the next one? Is it Kyle?"

Straight Girl? What was that *about?* Pao wondered. But instead of stopping to ask, she said, "There is no next one, okay? Not for you. I appreciate your help and everything, but I can handle it from here." It felt good to say this, even though Pao's hands were still shaking from the fight, and the bus would probably get turned around as soon as Kyle and the driver found out what had happened—if they weren't monsters, too, that is—and they were still hundreds of miles from Santuario, and Pao was running out of time.

"Um, Pao?" Emma said in a small voice. She was standing close enough that their elbows almost touched. "Maybe we should let them help? I mean, we're kind of out of options, and Kit was pretty good in the fight, you have to admit. Plus, Robin's the only one of us who can drive, and if we want to get to Santuario before that dream girl closes the void entrance, we should get moving."

Pao had already opened her mouth to say *absolutely no way* when the last part of Emma's plea finally reached her prefrontal cortex. "You can drive?" she asked Robin, letting all the rest slide for now. "Like, legally?"

"I have my learner's permit," Robin said, looking less nauseated now, though her voice still wobbled a little. "My dads didn't put me in kindergarten until I was six, so I'm older than most of the kids in our grade. They didn't want my creative spirit dampened by the introduction of too many rules that pandered to the lowest common denominator."

Pao didn't really understand what any of that meant, so she repeated the question. "You can *drive?*"

"Yeah," Robin said, her voice barely above a whisper. "I practice every Saturday."

Suddenly, the silhouette of the mini charter bus against the twilit sky seemed much more prominent than it had even a minute ago.

"I don't suppose your dad drives a *really big van* or something like that, does he?" Pao asked.

"He drives a Prius?" Robin said, each word taking her voice up a few notes.

"Close enough."

TEN

What Do the Backstreet Boys and Driving a Bus Have in Common?

It was truly remarkable the lengths normal people would go to ignore the supernatural.

Pao, Emma, Kit, and Robin trudged across the field back to the cabins, expecting at the very least to have some awkward explaining to do to Kyle and to the other Rogues, but there was no sign of the chaperone, and the other eight kids were either sleeping off the long day of driving or on their phones with earbuds in.

"I thought the Rainbow Rogues were some kind of radical collective that prefers face-to-face communication to the toxic disconnect brought on by our generation's reliance on technology," Pao said with an eye roll when they'd checked all four cabins.

"That's a real-expectations-versus-reality-type thing," said Kit. "There's the mission statement, and then there's, like, a long day on a bus."

"Fair enough," Pao said. "At least we don't have to worry about anyone freaking out—yet." Emma's group sat around the fire, all looking to Pao for guidance. "We need to find out where Kyle is, and the bus driver, and the dude-ranch guy, and make sure they don't suspect anything before they go to bed. As soon as everyone's asleep, we hit the highway and just hope we can make it far enough to ditch the bus before the cops catch up with us."

It sounded so simple, she thought, when you said it like that.

"How are we going to get the key from the driver?" Emma asked.

"I've got an idea about that," said Pao.

"Knock him out cold?" Kit asked eagerly.

"No, something a little more . . . subtle."

"This is all assuming I can even drive the bus," Robin said, looking absolutely panicked while Kit seemed excited and Emma vacillated between the two. Pao, for her part, felt like a kinder-garten teacher on the first day of school with these noobs.

"Are we totally sure we shouldn't call the Niños or your dad or someone?" Emma asked Pao for the third time.

"No," Pao said emphatically. "They won't believe us, or they'll send us home and take over everything. We can handle this."

"Wait," Robin said. "There are adults with actual driver's licenses that know about this stuff and would come take over so we could go home? I'm super confused as to why we're not going with that completely reasonable option."

Emma looked at Pao, her expression saying she was glad Robin had said it so she didn't have to.

"I'm with Straight Girl on this one," Kit said before Pao could retort. "Getting someone's dad involved sounds like a real buzzkill. Come on, grand theft auto? A chance to take out our adolescent angst on some tangible enemies for once? Why aren't we more excited?"

"Easy for you to say," Robin muttered. "You're not the one who has to drive the bus."

In the end, they agreed to split up, Kit and Robin to examine said bus—to see if they could get inside it, for starters—and Emma and Pao to look for the adults. "We meet back here in no more than thirty minutes," Pao said. "And if you see a sign of anything weird at all, you run. Got it?"

"Got it," Kit and Robin said in unison. But the way Kit twirled the rusted rake with that gleam in her eye made Pao very nervous.

The owner's house was half a mile away from the cabins, for privacy, and Pao and Emma decided to head in that direction. From the bleary eyes and stubble Pao had noticed on the bus driver earlier, she had the feeling he was more likely to be having a whiskey at the dude's house than touring the property. She hoped Kyle was with them and not lurking somewhere in the dark, planning an ambush.

"It's pretty," Emma said after ten minutes of awkward silence, the only sound their footsteps in the rustling grass.

"Hm?" Pao asked, distracted by her spiraling thoughts of how very many ways this plan could go wrong.

"The ranch," Emma said, gesturing at the fields, the horses, the river in the distance. "It's pretty."

"Oh, yeah," Pao said, forcing herself into the present moment with considerable effort. "I never really understood the horse thing, though—they kind of freak me out."

Emma smiled. "I used to ride in Montana before we moved," she said. "I know, very WASPy, but I liked it. There's something kind of humbling about knowing they could hurt you but they're working with you instead."

Under normal circumstances, Pao would have teased her about it, but after the day they'd had, she wasn't sure she had the right to. Plus, she could almost feel Poppy's words swirling between them. *Just tell her you like her. . . . I've seen how she looks at you. . . .*

It was ridiculous, Pao thought, glancing at Emma sidelong while she was busy looking out at the horses. Emma was her best friend, nothing more. And Pao had liked Dante. Didn't that make her . . . straight? Kit seemed to have taken it as a certainty without even asking.

But you never really liked Dante like that, said the infuriating little Pao in the back of her mind. Even you admitted you just acted that way because you thought you were supposed to.

But not being into one guy doesn't necessarily mean you're into girls instead. And even being into girls wouldn't necessarily mean this girl, Pao retorted inwardly before realizing that she was arguing with herself and also that she had much more pressing concerns than an identity crisis brought on by a monster chaperone she had impaled with a spear.

Sure, she'd been jealous of Emma and Kit, but only because she was afraid of losing her best (and only) friend to some too-cool-for-everyone girl who would probably never accept Pao. There. Problem solved.

"I see it," Emma said, pointing up ahead at the dude's house, which was just coming into view, its lighted windows standing sentry against the gathering darkness. "Think they're inside?"

"Only one way to find out," said Pao, smiling at Emma just to prove nothing had changed.

When Emma smiled back, Pao's stomach did a feeble back-flip, but this wasn't the moment to think about that.

· · ·

By the time Pao knocked on the door to the ranch owner's house, she'd put every thought about Emma into the tiny little box where she placed all her inconvenient feelings, and she was ready to lie to adults.

After a minute or so, a woman Pao assumed to be the dude's wife answered the door, looking like every white grandma in any movie Pao had ever seen. "Hello, dears," she said to complete the aesthetic. "Is there something I can do for you?"

"Yeah," Pao said, doing her best to seem like a teacher's-pet eighth grader who'd been sent on an errand by a chaperone instead of killing one. "I was just wondering if our bus driver is here?"

"And Kyle?" asked Emma. "Our chaperone?"

"Mr. DiLorenzo and my husband, Jimmy, are out back by the fire, swapping war stories," the old lady said. "Haven't seen anyone else. Would you like me to go fetch 'em for you?"

"Y—" Emma began, but Pao cut her off, improvising.

"No, that's all right," she said with her best teacher's-pet smile. "Can you just give Mr. DiLorenzo a message from Poppy? One of the kids is sick and needs to sleep alone in the cabin Mr. DiLorenzo was going to use. So, Mr. DiLorenzo's gonna have to sleep on the bus tonight." Pao looked up anxiously as if at some imaginary storm clouds. "Poppy wanted us to let him know to get a blanket in case the temperature drops. I just hope he's feeling better from his pneumonia last month. . . ."

Pao waited a beat, then two, and finally said, "Well, thanks! Cool place you got here."

She grabbed Emma's arm and turned to leave, counting down from five in her head.

Three, two . . .

"Wait a minute, dear!" Granny was on their heels, wringing her hands. "I can't have the poor man catching a cold! He'll sleep in our guest bedroom tonight, and I won't take no for an answer, not when he and Jimmy are getting along so well."

"Oh!" said Pao, as if she had not even expected—much less been counting on—this reaction. "Well, if you're sure . . . Would you mind grabbing the keys from him? We still have some luggage on the bus. Our chaperones need to get in there."

Five minutes later, the two girls were on their way back to the meeting place, Mr. DiLorenzo's keys jingling on one of Pao's fingers.

"How did you know she would make that offer?" Emma asked when they were out of earshot. "That was a pretty big risk. I mean, what if he'd really ended up sleeping on the bus?"

"Then we would have had to hope he was a deep sleeper," Pao said, tossing a smirk over her shoulder that said it had never even been a possibility.

"So, is this what it's always like?" Emma asked, wringing her hands in an unconscious imitation of Granny. "Getting attacked in random places, lying to adults on the fly . . ."

Pao wasn't sure what the right answer was here. She had a feeling Emma wouldn't want to hear it, but the truth was, she'd almost perfectly described every one of these harebrained adventures, so Pao just gave a noncommittal shrug. "I hope the other two didn't get into any trouble. . . ."

But Kit and Robin were (miraculously) exactly where they were supposed to be when they returned to the fence, and better yet, they'd been productive, too.

"We found Kyle. We told him Poppy's cold got a lot worse

and we were taking care of her in our cabin," Kit said. "He took charge of the other three cabins, and lights-out is in five."

"And he just . . . believed you?" Pao asked.

"Perks of a largely decentralized leadership structure," Kit said with a shrug. "Besides, I'm totally Kyle's favorite."

"Yeah, right," Robin said with a scoff. "We both know E-Money is Kyle's favorite. She's *everyone*'s favorite."

Even in the almost total dark, Pao could tell Emma was blushing. "It's a privilege thing," she said. "Being white and straight-passing and affluent, not to mention, like, very femme, makes me more palatable to a wide audience."

"That, and you're adorable," Kit said offhand, just as Pao asked, "What's *straight-passing*?"

"It's like when someone from one ethnicity passes for another, but in this case, it's the queer community," Emma explained. "Though I might be a lesbian, all the rainbow shoe-laces in the world won't stop strangers from identifying me as straight."

"But doesn't that boil *everything* down to appearances?" Pao asked, confused. "I mean, who cares what you look like? It's about who you *are*, right?"

"Of course!" Emma said. "To you it is. But it's good to be aware of the privilege you carry in the wider world so you can best use it to benefit members of your community who are less supported by a cisgender, white, straight default."

Pao nodded slowly, thinking she understood, but she was still stuck on the idea of *straight-passing*. Could someone pass even to themselves? The question was there, on the tip of her tongue, but she couldn't quite bring herself to ask Emma. Not now, after what Poppy had said . . .

And definitely not in front of Kit.

"As interesting as Queer 101 undoubtedly is," the Kit in question was currently saying with a fake yawn, "can we get back to talking about bus stealing and monster killing?"

They all looked at Pao eagerly, and suddenly the exhaustion of her previous sleepless night and the long bus ride and the fight for her life made themselves abruptly known. But they had no time to lose. She could nap on the bus.

"We'll wait an hour, until everyone's asleep, and then get going," Pao said. "In the meantime, let's check out the bus." She jangled the keys in her hand.

"It'd better not be a stick shift," said Robin. "I can't drive manual."

"Don't worry—the modern ones are automatic," said Kit. "You'll be fine . . . as long as you don't have to park, reverse, or make any sharp turns."

"Are you okay?" Emma asked Pao quietly, while Robin and Kit climbed aboard to examine the dashboard.

"I'm fine," Pao said tersely. "Just want to get on the road."

"Pao, I'm really sorry I didn't believe you about Poppy," Emma said in a rush, like she'd been holding on to this sentiment ever since she'd seen their feral chaperone try to take a chunk out of Pao. "You were right, and I should have trusted you. More than that, I shouldn't have made you doubt your instincts or claimed it was PTSD. Can you please forgive me?"

"Yeah," Pao said a little hoarsely, shrugging. "It's no big deal."

"It *is*," Emma insisted quietly. "I wanted to come along to support you, and so far all I've done is the opposite, which has probably made you feel really isolated. I'm going to do better, I promise."

For a second, Pao considered telling Emma that she wasn't wrong. That it wasn't only real-world monsters plaguing her. Poppy's stupid college-kid advice was still haunting her, stopping her from getting closer to Emma without questioning too much. So instead, she just shrugged again and said, "It's okay. Let's just get going," and stepped onto the bus, leaving her best friend looking slightly deflated behind her.

Soon all was dark and quiet on the ranch. No one bothered the girls as they tossed their luggage into the front seats and settled in—all sitting as close to Robin as possible to give her emotional support. She looked ashen and clammy, and Pao privately thought she was more likely to throw up on the steering wheel than use it to successfully navigate them onto the highway. But she kept that unhelpful thought to herself.

"Hands at ten and two," Robin was muttering to herself. "Adjust your mirrors. Check your blind spot. Use your blinkers. . . . What am I forgetting?"

"Headlights?" Emma said nervously, glancing out the windows at the long dirt road barely lit by the half-moon.

"No headlights!" said Kit and Pao at once from opposite sides of the aisle.

"It's a dead giveaway," Pao explained when Robin's complexion took on a delicate hint of green. "We'll have to navigate the road by moonlight, keep the lights off until after we pass the house."

"Okay," Robin said in a shaky voice, running through her checklist again before sticking the key into the ignition and jumping badly when the bus beeped in response.

"It's okay," Emma said, getting up out of her seat next to Pao and standing beside Robin in an uncharacteristic violation of bus safety protocol. "Just pretend this is the Prius and you're out for an evening driving lesson with your dad. What would he say to you?"

Robin just shook her head, her mouth clamped shut, her eyes too wide.

"Is there anything special you guys do together when you practice?" Emma asked again, her voice quiet and gentle and patient even as the ticking clock in Pao's sleepless brain grew louder and louder.

"Backstreet Boys," Robin mumbled, barely opening her lips.

"What's that?" Emma asked as Pao fought the urge to roll her eyes.

"My dads were into boy bands when they were my age," Robin said a little louder. "Pops always puts on the Backstreet Boys when we drive, to lighten the mood."

Kit's phone was out in a second, illuminating her face as she scrolled through a page of music videos. "Good thing my parents have the reception-even-in-the-middle-of-nowhere plan," she said under her breath before the notes of a song Pao had never heard began to play from the tinny speaker. "And that they even have oldies like this on the internet."

But Robin didn't seem to care how old or corny the song was, or how bad the sound quality. The second her beloved Backpack Boys began to sing in sugary five-part harmony, the color returned to her cheeks, and she reached down to take the bus out of park.

"That's it," Pao said. "Nice and slow here."

Every bump was a catastrophe. Every clunk or groan of the engine was going to get them spotted, chased down, and arrested for stealing school property and driving without a license while the sinister dream girl closed the last of the void entrances and Dante was lost forever. . . .

Slowly, painstakingly, Robin coaxed the bus down the long driveway until the house was in view. There were so many things Pao wanted to say, so many words of caution, but instead she held her breath along with the rest of them as the small, metallic-sounding voices joined in what Pao considered embarrassing late-'90s pop harmony. The music seemed to steady Robin's hands on the wheel, her foot on the gas pedal. . . .

Pao watched the house with eagle eyes for a lighted window, an open door, a drunk Mr. DiLorenzo shaking his fist as the dude-ranch proprietor ran out behind him with a shotgun. . . .

But none of those things came to pass, and as the Backstop Boys burst into the last iteration of the chorus they'd already sung five times, the bus tires met the highway, the road empty as Robin clicked the headlights into blazing life and turned left toward San Antonio.

Pao couldn't help it—she joined in with the others when they closed out the song at the top of their lungs, led by Robin, the incessant repetition having taught them all the words:

"I never wanna hear you say . . . I WANT IT THAT WAY!"

They dissolved into a fit of giggles the minute the song was done, and Pao felt like her bloodstream was full of sparkling cider, her head light and dizzy with relief as they drove a respectable five miles below the speed limit along the empty, arrow-straight highway.

And just when she thought she couldn't feel any better, Emma flopped into the seat next to her (even though there was an equally empty one next to Kit) and leaned her head on Pao's shoulder.

ELEVEN

The Road to Santuario Is Paved with Identity Crises

The euphoric feeling lasted at least a hundred miles. Pao, Emma, and Kit took turns visiting Robin in the driver's seat, but the older girl really seemed to have found her confidence. Not that Pao was an expert or anything, but she thought Robin was driving down a perfectly straight highway with no other traffic or obstacles as well as almost anyone could have.

And so, deprived of anything to worry about in the immediate present, Pao's thoughts shifted to the future. To Santuario, and the church in the cornfield. To the mysterious mind of the girl from her dream, and the race against time, and Dante. Always Dante.

If he were here, Pao thought, and things were normal, he'd be getting Pao all jacked up on sugar. And insisting on discussing the finer points of the newest superhero movie to distract her. Emma was good for problem solving and support, but Dante had been holding off the worst of Pao's overthinking freak-outs for a lifetime.

Despite how weird things had gotten in the end, or how awful, she missed the old Dante. The one who really knew her.

"Granola bar for your thoughts?" Emma asked, offering Pao one of those dry, crumbling field-trip staples from the bottom of Poppy's tote bag.

Pao took it gratefully, using the feeling of maple-flavored gravel in her increasingly dry mouth to avoid answering. But Emma was patient, and soon Pao had washed the thing down, officially out of excuses.

"I was thinking about Dante," Pao finally said, choosing honesty for once. "Worrying about whether we'll make it in time and all that."

"We will," Emma said automatically. "And then . . . I mean, once he's back, it'll all be okay, right? Now that you know he was being controlled by the void and stuff, you guys can just . . . go back to the way things were."

Pao shook her head, sensing there was more to this question than was immediately apparent. "The void just magnified what was already there," she said, voicing thoughts she'd run through until they were as smooth as river rocks. "The jealousy, the anger, the feeling that I wasn't good enough to be the hero? That was all Dante. I don't know if there's any going back for us. For *any* of us," she added, thinking of those innocent days on the Gila riverbank. Before the three of them had known about the other world existing alongside theirs. Before disappearances and adventures and stupid demon chaperones and their weird advice had made everything a confusing mess.

Pao hoped there would be something good on the other side for her and Dante. But no matter what, it wouldn't be the same as what they'd had before. . . .

"I think I need to try it again," she said now, wanting to

change the subject before she was forced to give voice to any of these feelings. "The sleep tea or whatever."

"You're not tired enough already?" Emma asked nonchalantly, and Pao had the feeling her best friend knew exactly how much (or little) she'd slept since showing up on her doorstep two days ago.

Pao shook her head, letting her frustration show. "It's La Llorona again," she said. "And Joaquin. The monsters. Every time I close my eyes, they're there." To Pao's great relief, Emma did not say anything about PTSD this time, she only nodded sympathetically. "It's like they're jamming the signal to the real dreams," she said. "And the tea is the only override."

"How much farther to Santuario?" Emma asked, glancing at Pao's phone while she checked the map.

"Another four hours at least," Pao said. "Ten, if Robin doesn't get better acquainted with the gas pedal soon. She does know you can be pulled over for going *under* the speed limit, too, right?"

Emma stifled a giggle. "I think she's the best option we have."

Pao had to agree, repressing a sudden image of Kit in the driver's seat, her eyes barely visible over the dashboard, the speedometer creeping toward one hundred as she brandished her rake out the window and cackled.

"Good point."

"Should be enough time to take a peek beyond the veil, anyway," Emma said, and Pao could hear the herculean effort at a casual attitude in her voice. "I'll keep watch if you want, wake you up if it seems like it's getting too intense?"

Pao, so used to dealing with things like this on her own,

already preparing to isolate herself from the others once again, was caught off guard by the offer. "You wouldn't mind?" she asked, looking at the granola bar wrapper in her lap instead of at Emma.

"I'd be glad to," Emma said, smiling before turning toward the front, where Kit was hanging on the driver's seat bothering Robin. "Hey, Rogues? Pao has to do some ghost-hunter stuff before we get where we're going, so we're gonna head to the back of the bus."

"Oh, suuure," Kit said. "*Ghost-hunter stuff.* I didn't know that's what the kids were calling it these days."

Pao watched a blush progress across Emma's face as she felt her own cheeks heat up. "It's not like that," she said, a little more forcefully than necessary. Kit's eyes widened, and so did Emma's.

"*Aggressively* Straight Girl. Got it," Kit said. "Good luck with your secret and *strictly hetero* back-of-the-bus stuff."

She should have been glad Kit had dropped it, but as they made their way down the aisle of seats, Pao could sense that Emma's thoughts were somewhere else, the closeness so recently regained between them gone.

After adding the tea leaves to Emma's lukewarm water bottle, Pao shook it, willing the leaves to infuse even though the water wasn't hot and they didn't have all night. When the liquid looked sufficiently greenish through the plastic, Pao unscrewed the cap with trembling fingers, hoping Emma wouldn't notice her fear. But her friend's eyes were fixed somewhere out the back window, like Pao wasn't there at all.

"Look," Pao said, not *just* to stall the moment when she'd have to succumb to the vulnerability of sleep. "About what I said . . . I . . ." Usually Emma could be counted on to bail Pao out of her more awkward, stumbling sentences by finishing them for her, but this time it seemed she was on her own. "I didn't mean to act like I think it's . . . bad . . . the idea that . . . I mean, the back of the bus, or . . ."

Finally, Emma seemed to take pity on her. "You don't want to be wrongly identified. I totally get that."

But she didn't get it, Pao thought. Pao wasn't worried about being *wrongly* identified. It was more like being *prematurely* identified. To have some part of her that still felt nebulous and unfixed and strange pinned down by the mocking words of a girl who spoke them out of jealousy.

Only how was she supposed to explain that to Emma?

"You and the other Rogues are all so sure," Pao found herself saying almost against her will. She just knew she couldn't stand the look of hurt on Emma's face. She'd rather tell the portion of the truth she *did* know than let Emma believe Pao somehow disapproved of her. "Your labels, your identities, your community. And Kit . . . she wants me to be this or that so she can have something to tease me about, but I'm . . . not ready."

The distance in Emma's eyes was gone. In fact, Pao thought she had never seen into them so clearly. Emma was here, *right* here, seeing her in a way that almost felt scary. "You don't have to be ready," she said. "Not today, not ever, if you don't want to be. Not for Kit, not for me, not for anyone but yourself."

Pao nodded, the green-tinged water in the bottle sloshing with the rocking rhythm of the bus, and she felt like they were in a little bubble, just the two of them, where it was safe to say anything.

"Sometimes I think—" Pao began, but just then the brakes squealed and the two of them slammed into the seat ahead of them, the water splashing all over Pao's hands and Emma's lap.

"Sorry! Tumbleweed!" Robin shrieked from the front as the bus righted itself between the yellow lines.

Pao looked at Emma, her heart beating like a jackhammer for a variety of reasons, and then they both burst into the kind of hysterical laughter only a near-death experience can bring on. "If she keeps that up, there won't be any more weird leaf juice to drink," Pao said, still hiccupping with barely suppressed giggles.

"Kind of like solving one problem to create another, isn't it?" Emma said, wiping her eyes.

"Story of my life," Pao said, tipping the bottle back and draining it—leaf bits and all—before she could lose her nerve.

Maybe it was the actual plant matter she'd consumed, or just the sleepless nights, but Pao found herself becoming drowsy almost immediately. Emma wordlessly passed her the puffy cloud sweater, and Pao balled it up into a pillow, reclining against the bus window and stretching her legs out in front of her.

She felt absurd, like a vampire lowering herself into a coffin, and she kept opening her eyes just a slit to see if Emma was looking back at her from the seat ahead. But after two or three checks her eyelids became too heavy to open, and finally, with the knowledge that Emma was watching over her, Pao let herself drift off to sleep.

It was cold when she opened them again, and she was standing in the center of what looked like a shallow blast crater, the ground blackened in a four-foot circle around her, snow falling heavily. She was exhausted—a weariness that made her chest feel hollow and her limbs rubbery. But there was no time to rest. She had closed the entrance—and this one had been a fighter; the smell of burned hair hung in the air. She longed to rest, but that terrible urgency still drove her, the timer on a bomb ticking down to utter destruction.

The rifts she could handle. That was the goal, after all. But her own life? She was rather attached to existence, and she'd do whatever it took to make sure hers continued.

Brushing herself off, taking one last look around to make sure there were no witnesses, she remembered what this closing had cost her and prayed the next one wouldn't be so difficult. *The enemy is in motion, and if that girl reaches any of the locations before they are sealed off . . .*

There it was again—the cold spike of fear driving into her heart, and this time, it was accompanied by an image. Malevolent pupil-less green eyes, a face swathed in shadow, a cruel laugh echoing as if from the bottom of a stone well. He would call her back to him if he suspected hesitation, caught even a whiff of failure. He had not been generous before, and there was little reason to suspect that would change. . . .

She shuddered, pulling dark sleeves down over her scars, proof of his former displeasure. *I cannot disappoint him again.*

The snow had nearly covered the scorch marks now. Around her, with the barrier dissolved, the sounds of wildlife could be heard creeping back into woods previously deemed haunted. She shuddered again. *Life*, the way they all clung to it, the way they feared what came next. What a waste.

Her knees hit the ground before her eyes closed, and she quieted her mind, the sounds of the snowy forest, even the thumping of her own useless heart. Every cell in her body strained for one location, the only image allowed through the iron barrier around her thoughts. A lakeside. A dense wood. A wood cabin eroded by insects and time.

It was the next step on a winding road only *he* could see the end of. She would have to trust that there was glory there for all of them—but mostly for her. He had promised.

Around her, the ghostly green shapes unfolded, spinning and whirling until the scene around her dissolved and even the chill was gone. She walked into the green light and then she was gone, too.

On the bus, Pao awoke shivering. She was drenched in sweat, and her body ached like she'd just done one of those terrible weight-room circuits in PE. It took her a minute to register where she was, *who* she was. The determined, terrified consciousness she had been inhabiting was slower to let go this time.

The bus, she remembered. Robin driving. Kit. Emma now in the seat beside Pao, her eyes round with anxiety. One of Pao's hands was warmer than the other, like someone had been holding it. It was this, along with the attending butterflies, that brought Pao firmly into the present.

"You're back," Emma said, her voice high and restrained. "I'm sorry. I tried to wake you, but . . ."

"No, it's good," Pao said, trying to ignore the clammy, sticky feeling across her skin, to struggle upright so she didn't feel so faint. "I saw what I needed to see. She's . . . going to the lake. She just finished closing the void entrance at the mountain, but it made her weaker. If we can get to Santuario today, I might have a chance to get through."

It should have made Pao feel better, the knowledge that they were still on track, that there was hope. But she couldn't feel anything but the cold emptiness that had inhabited the other girl.

"Who is *she*?" Emma asked in a whisper. "Did you see?"

"No," Pao said, sitting up now, dizzy and frustrated. "I can't see anything. It's like I *am* her, so all I can see is what she does. I don't even know myself when I'm in her thoughts. But she's in a hurry, and she's scared . . . really scared."

"Of what?" Emma asked, glancing furtively up the aisle at Robin and Kit, who were laughing at something.

The image intruded into Pao's thoughts just as it had the dream girl's. The pupil-less green eyes. The shadows both sharpening and obscuring his features. The laugh that had sent a cold spike through her chest and was currently causing Pao's heart to speed up.

"I don't know." But that wasn't the whole story, and Emma seemed to know it, her wide eyes still locked on Pao's. "It's someone . . . someone who's giving her orders. All I saw were glowing eyes. But whoever he is, he's bad news."

Emma was silent this time, and it was a mark of the seriousness of the situation that she didn't ask fourteen follow-up questions. Pao was grateful for the moment of quiet, to digest all she had seen, to think about what was coming next.

The man—she was sure, somehow, that it was a man—with the glowing eyes had sent this dream girl to close the void entrances before Pao could reach them. But he couldn't be doing *all* that just to keep her from getting to Dante, right? What did it matter if one thirteen-year-old boy was a prisoner of the void or out playing soccer with his friends? There was no way this could all be about Pao and her middle-school life.

Then what is *it about?* asked the other part of Pao's brain. The logical, scientific part that had never stopped trying to pick everything apart and see how it worked. If her hunch was correct, if the green-eyed man was after something more than just Dante, more than thwarting Pao, then what would she be walking into when she finally reached the church in the cornfield?

Pao had been so fixated on getting there before the dream girl that she'd barely stopped to wonder what would happen when she did. In her mind, it had been a blur of carving a path through monsters and fantasmas with her Arma del Alma until she reached the void, and then finding Dante and taking him home.

But with her glowing phone screen saying there were only two hours to go before they reached Santuario, her half-baked plan seemed worse than childish. It seemed reckless, dangerous. And now she had Emma and two tourists along for the ride.

You should have called your dad, said the critical little voice in her head. *You should have let the Niños handle it.*

I've handled things like this before, Pao thought back. *I didn't need them then.*

You weren't alone then, said the voice again, snarky and condescending. *You had Dante with his magical club, and Marisa, Ondina, Naomi, Estrella. . . .*

This jab Pao couldn't brush aside. It was true that she'd rarely acted alone, that there had always been someone stronger, or more knowledgeable, or with a cooler weapon, to back her up, help her through.

And now? Pao glanced guiltily at Emma, who was almost undoubtedly choking back all her questions to give Pao space. Pao had dragged her into this and somehow also ended up with Kit and her decidedly non-magical rake and Robin with her not-quite-a-driver's-license. If they died, it would all be because Pao had been too stubborn and proud to ask for help.

But Dante's life was at stake, also, she couldn't forget.

And anyway, it was too late now, she thought as the bus barreled east toward the church and the cornfield and their fate. The dream girl had already closed the first opening. She was on her way to the second. Even if a miracle happened and she was somehow waylaid there, Pao had seen inside her mind, the urgency, the fear. Nothing would slow her down for long.

"You okay?" Emma asked in a small voice, snapping Pao out of her thoughts.

"Yeah," Pao said automatically. "Well, no, but yeah."

"I know what you mean," Emma said, holding her gaze.

"Look, Emma," Pao began, tugging on the end of her braid. "Whatever this is, I think it's bigger than Dante, and you Rogues are—well, no offense, but you're not exactly the Niños de la Luz. You haven't pledged your lives to eradicating ghosts and protecting magical rifts." It was a miracle, Pao thought, that Emma hadn't interrupted yet, but she seemed determined to hear her out before she protested.

"What I'm saying," Pao continued after a frustrated exhale, "is that I think you should drop me off in Santuario and get these girls home. I can't ask you to face this for me."

"Are you finished?" Emma asked, and Pao nodded. "Good. Because you're not *asking* me to face anything. You're my best friend, Pao, the most important person in my admittedly small universe. Do you really think I could live with myself if I went home and left you alone with this?"

"I can—"

"I know, I know. You can take care of yourself," Emma said with an affectionate smirk. "But answer me this: Would you walk away knowing *I* was heading off to face something dangerous? Leave me without help or protection just because I said I was fine?"

With a sinking feeling in her stomach that told her she wasn't gonna win this one, Pao shook her head. "I guess not."

"Exactly," Emma said. "Which is why I'm not going to, either. I'll give Robin and Kit the option of turning around after you and I get off, but I think we both know Kit isn't going anywhere."

Pao rolled her eyes. "Stuck to you like glue, isn't she?" she said without thinking.

Once again, Emma's cheeks went pink. "It's not like that," she said quietly. "At least, not for me."

"Oh, cool, yeah. Or . . . not *cool*, but . . . you know what I mean."

"Yeah," said Emma with a smile. "Despite your best efforts, I know what you mean."

Was it Pao's imagination, or had someone turned off the gravity in here? She felt like she might float right out the window. Was she going to examine the reason for this newfound weightlessness? Absolutely not. But on a journey to the void, Pao had learned, you had to take whatever buoyancy you could get.

Emma leaned against the window again, and Pao followed suit . . . just in time to see a green highway sign as they passed it.

SANTUARIO, it read. 115 MILES.

TWELVE
So, When You Say a *Murder* of Crows . . .

Santuario, Texas, was a ramshackle place that seemed to consist primarily of tumbleweeds and cornfields.

An unnatural hush—ending the one-girl karaoke show Kit had been putting on for the past half hour—settled over the bus as they trundled past a WELCOME sign that was rusty, slightly crooked, and peppered with holes of mysterious origin.

They had more sinister things ahead of them than some drunk cowboy with a shotgun, Pao thought, which was either comforting or terrifying, depending on how you looked at things.

"So, where's this church?" Robin asked in an unnaturally high voice.

Emma and Pao exchanged a look. A *we're gonna have to figure out a way to get her home soon* kind of look.

"My Maps app says four miles outside of town, down this road!" Pao said, her voice so upbeat she could have been auditioning for *Poppy the Homicidal Chaperone, Part Two.* "We'll be there super soon!"

"And . . . not to ruin a good time with a plan," said Kit, sounding a little less aloof herself, "but what exactly are we supposed to do when we get there?"

Pao was going to tell the truth: She had no idea, but she really hoped something would come to her when she arrived. That had been good enough to get the job done the last two times she'd been forced to confront the unknown, so why not now?

Because there's no one in your dreams or real life telling you what to do this time, said her inner snarky voice. *Because these sorry saps actually believe* you're *going to tell* them *what to do.*

The silence had obviously gone on too long, because Emma leaned forward in her seat and said, in a much more believable upbeat voice than Pao's, "See, Pao has these . . . dreams, but they're not really dreams. They're more like instructions. That's what she was doing in the back of the bus—"

"*Napping?!*" said Robin, the bus lurching forward as she stomped on the gas in her panic. "We thought you two were going over some secret monster-killing plan back there, or—"

"Or at *least* swapping spit," Kit said, waggling her eyebrows. "But sleeping, wow, that really *is* boringly hetero." But her cavalier attitude was wavering, noticed Pao, who didn't understand how she hadn't clocked Kit from the start. Kit's relentless mocking was clearly just a defense mechanism. A way to distract people from her own insecurity.

Even her, Poppy had said. *The girl you just thought of? Totally faking it.*

"Enough," Pao said, standing up with a silent prayer that Robin would keep her foot steady on the gas this time. "Listen, when we stop up ahead . . . you two are gonna let us out and take off. Head for the San Antonio airport, ditch the bus there, and call your parents to let them know you need to get back to Silver Springs. Tell them the bus was hijacked but you managed to escape. Your parents can buy you a plane ticket or come get you."

"We can't ask you to be part of this," Emma agreed. "I could even use my emergency credit card to—"

"Yeah, right!" Kit said indignantly, standing up to face Pao with two spots of color high on her cheeks. "You're not using us for my fierce rake-combat skills and a ride and then ditching us before anything cool happens!"

"Nothing *cool* is going to happen!" Pao said, losing her patience now. She could feel it in the air—they were close to where she needed to be. There was no time for this. "Only incredibly *dangerous* things. If I'm very lucky, they won't literally kill me, but I can't say the same for you. You're civilians. *Tourists.* You'll only get in the way, so go home."

Kit's eyebrows drew together, and she folded her arms across her chest in a way that told Pao she absolutely was *not* going to take this lying down.

"Kit . . ." said Robin's tremulous voice from the driver's seat. "Maybe we'd better listen to them. I mean, this isn't sneaking backstage at a concert. It's actual monsters, and I . . . I think I'd like to go h— AAAAHHHHH!"

The bus jerked suddenly and catastrophically to the left as the sound of shattering glass caused them all to duck. There was no righting the bus this time. The vehicle went over the double line into the (thankfully empty) other lane, then its front left wheel slid into a ditch, and the rest of the bus followed. There was screaming, broken glass underfoot, the awful tumble of seat-belt-less chaos, and then stillness.

With her heart beating loudly in her ears and her palm

bleeding from a shard of glass, Pao was the first to rise. The bus hadn't fully tipped over, but the floor was at an extreme angle beneath her feet. "Emma?" she said. "Kit? Robin?"

"Here . . ." came Emma's voice as she pushed some luggage off her legs and pulled herself to standing on one of the crooked seats. She was pale and shaken but seemed unhurt.

"I'm so sorry!" Robin said from up front. "I'm so, so sorry! It hit the windshield, and I thought . . . I'm so sorry!" Her words failed her then, giving way to hiccupping sobs.

"Kit?" Pao called again.

There was a groan from the stairs by the door. Emma fought her way down the aisle, holding on to the seats for support, with Pao on her heels.

"What was that you said . . . ?" began Kit as they reached her, her arm bent at a strange angle and her forehead striped with a cut. "About us taking the bus to the airport?" She stretched out her hurt arm, wincing, but then wiggled her fingers and laughed hoarsely before coughing herself quiet again.

Pao was about to break Kit's arm for real, she really was, but in the next second, another violent *thud* made them all jump. This one hadn't broken the windshield, but it was unmistakably a bird. A big black one.

"It was a *crow*," Robin said through labored breaths, hoisting herself out of the driver's seat, her eyes too wide. "That's what hit us before. . . . It was like—"

Crash! A window on the side of the bus that was pointing to the sky broke. This time the bird made it into the bus, one wing held limp like Kit's arm as it flapped and screeched wildly. They all screamed, huddling together in the little stairwell as the thing stalked toward them unevenly.

"Open the door!" Kit said. "Open the door before it eats us!"

"It's not going to eat us," Pao snapped. "It's just—"

Another smashed window, another chorus of screams. Someone's hand was squeezing the life out of Pao's upper arm, but the girls were so tangled together she didn't know whose it was. Now there were two creepy crows coming up the aisle, broken and bleeding but still moving forward like they were drawn to the huddle of girls.

Only when they were close enough did Pao notice their eyes. Their glowing green eyes.

"On second thought, yeah, let's open the door," she said in a rush, trying not to let on how definitely bad this was. They were too squished together for her to transform the Arma del Alma, and anyway, she needed more space to maneuver, and if these crows were from the void, then Kit's hysterical comment might not be so far off.

"Robin, open the door!" Kit screeched.

"Um, I'm not *actually the bus driver!*" Robin said back in a sort of strangled whisper-yell. "I don't know anything about this stupid hunk of metal!"

"Fine! I'll just do it myself!" Kit said, clambering over the rest of them with an elbow to Pao's chin. But there was no time to chastise her now, not when Pao had to keep her eyes on the murderous birds and their strange, limping gaits, and those eyes. . . . Those terrible eyes that had never promised anything but destruction . . .

"Where. Is. The. Stupid. Button," Kit was saying, the accompanying sounds telling Pao she was smashing every switch-shaped thing she could see.

"Anytime now, Kit," Pao said warningly. The crows were only two seats away, and Pao didn't like the new ominous scratching sounds coming from the top of the bus.

"I'm TRYING!" Kit grunted, just as the glass door Pao was pressed up against gave way with a pneumatic hiss and Robin, Emma, and Pao climbed out and fell into an unceremonious heap on the ground.

"Ow!"

"Ugh!"

"Cannonball!"

A second later, before anyone could recover, Kit had jumped out the open door as well, flattening them all just as they'd started to get to their feet.

"Do you *have* to be like that?!" Pao said irritably once she'd finally untangled herself, brushing the dirt off the knees of her jeans as Robin and Emma continued to separate their hair and clothes and limbs. Only Kit seemed unscathed. Even her arm seemed better.

"Be like what? A genius you're totally glad to have on your monster-hunting team?"

"Emma?" Pao said, her eyes never leaving Kit's.

"Yeah?"

"Hold me back," Pao said calmly.

"Look out!" Robin screamed before anyone could act. Emma grabbed Pao's shoulder and forced her to the ground as two more crows swooped low overhead, talons flashing, green eyes laser-focused on the group of girls.

While lying on the road, Pao took stock of where they'd crashed. They were next to a massive cornfield with dead, bleached stalks at least eight feet high. The bus had flattened the area where they were currently cowering, but there was no seeing beyond the stalks.

Pao turned to look at the bus, desperate for a place to take shelter from the birds, wondering if there was anything salvageable inside, anything they could use to defend themselves. What she saw made her heart sink and her stomach do a series of nauseating cartwheels. The bus, wheels half in and half out of a massive ditch on the side of the road, was barely visible under the absolute swarm of winged black creatures currently jostling for space on its surface. Fortunately—or unfortunately, as the case may be—its headlights were still on, so the girls could see more than a foot in front of them.

The others were still checking out their surroundings (Kit and Emma) or covering their face in fear (Robin). Pao, for her part, began to back away slowly from the bird-infested bus, too aware that every single toxic green eye seemed to be trained right on her.

Why weren't the crows moving? Pao wondered. What did they want? Was this part of the void's protection?

"Rogues?" she said as calmly as possible. "I think we need to move."

One of the birds cocked its head and made a low squawk that seemed to travel through the flock like the wind through the cornstalks.

"Good thinking, O Fearless Leader," said Kit sarcastically, still facing away from the bus. "We exist only to follow you." She turned toward Pao, her hand already halfway up in what was sure to be some irritating mock salute. That's when she caught sight of the one hundred birds and her smirk died on her face.

"Like I said"—Pao kept her voice as level as possible—"I think we need to move."

"Move, yeah, definitely," Kit said. "Uh, where to, boss?"

"Anywhere there aren't birds?" Pao said, already starting to walk in a westerly direction, toward where the map had said the old church would be. But finding a place free of birds was a much more difficult task than she'd imagined. The things were *everywhere*. Coating the bus, perched on every dry stalk, swooping and chattering and settling as they watched the girls' slow, nervous advance through the corn.

Now that Pao had some breathing room, she pulled out her magnifying glass and transformed it into the long, glinting staff with the viciously bladed end, just in case the birds decided to do more than watch—which, if Pao knew anything about approaching a void entrance, they definitely would before long.

Emma, always prepared, pulled out a flashlight to light their way. They walked for five minutes or so with absolutely no end to the birds in sight. There had to be thousands of them, Pao thought deliriously. She'd never seen so many of anything. . . .

"What do we do if they attack?" Robin asked, her thoughts aligned with Pao's, though the trembling in her voice made Pao feel almost brave by comparison.

"That's what this is for," Pao said, brandishing her staff in an attempt to make Robin feel better.

"And *this*!" Kit called from a few yards to the left, flourishing the rake she'd somehow managed to drag out of the bus.

"Oh god," Robin said, her hands flying to her face again. "Oh god."

"It's okay, Robin," Pao said. "I've definitely dispatched worse things than a few void crows in my time. You're in good hands."

"It's not that! It's just . . . I'm a vegan!" Robin said, still peeking through her fingers. "I don't condone animal cruelty, even in survival scenarios! And crows have shown signs of near-human intelligence, so we can't—"

"I promise you," Pao said, cutting her off as the birds chattered to one another as if to prove Robin's point, "these aren't your average crows. They're monsters from the void, and they're probably here to stop me from reaching the entrance."

Robin showed every sign of being close to another panic attack, so Pao stepped closer. "Look at their eyes," she said. "Have you ever seen a normal bird with glowing green eyes?"

"N-no," Robin stammered.

"Okay, then," she said. "If they attack, I'll do what needs to be done. But I promise, there will be no unnecessary loss of bird life, or any other kind. We're gonna have to move a little faster now, though. Are you good with that?"

"I almost stayed home from the trip with a stomachache," Robin said in a near whimper. "My dad said instincts are one thing and anxiety is another, but LOOK AT THIS!" She waved her arms at all the crows shifting restlessly on their stalks.

"Robin, I really need you to get it together," Pao said. "You have me and a really cool weapon to protect you, but only you can decide to be okay."

One of the crows took flight abruptly in a whirl of feathers, causing Robin to let out a little shriek.

"Okay, Robin?" Pao asked, louder this time.

"Okay!" Robin picked up the pace, and they were on the

move again, Pao swinging the staff in an attempt to show the crows they'd be stupid to attack, not entirely sure whether it was working or the birds were just biding their time.

By this time, ten minutes had passed, and the landscape hadn't changed. Pao wanted to check the map again, but she was sure her phone wouldn't get reception here. They'd just have to keep . . .

"Wait!" Kit called. "I've seen that bent cornstalk before! I think we're going in circles!"

"No way," Pao called back. "We've been moving in a straight line! All the corn just looks the same!"

When Kit replied, her voice was farther away. She'd stopped. "No," she said as Pao groaned loudly, doubling back. "This one has my blood on it, see? I'm the one who bent it. . . ."

Pao stabbed at a low-flying bird and bent down to examine the stalk, which looked newly broken and did indeed have bloody fingerprints on it right at Kit's arm level.

But if they weren't going in circles . . .

Suddenly, Pao was flashing back to a haunted cactus field and a riot of hysterical laughter as she walked in a straight line away from Dante only to find herself beside him again. And another time, in a frozen forest a thousand miles north, where she and Naomi had carved their initials into a tree. They hadn't walked in a circle, but that didn't mean they hadn't ended up back where they'd been.

"It's a liminal space," Pao said, almost to herself. And then: "A LIMINAL SPACE!"

All three of the others looked at her like she'd lost it, and maybe she had, because she was smiling so big her face hurt.

"That means we're close! And the entrance is still open! Liminal spaces protect the void entrances—they make it so no one can find their way through! It means we're right on top of the place!"

"Great!" said Kit. "Now how do we get through?"

Pao's excitement died almost instantly in her chest, leaving a hollow feeling behind. The truth was, Pao didn't have an answer to this, either. The first time, she'd kicked a flashlight in anger and its beam had ended up being a key to the void's magical signature. Emma's flashlight was just the normal hardware-store variety. The second time, a group of duendecillos had emerged from the forest at just the right moment. . . .

Pao looked around her. Kit was holding a rake with a broken handle. Robin was crouched beside Kit, breathing in and out and counting as she did. Emma was alert, her eyes trained on Pao like a straight-A student awaiting the details of a project worth a third of their grade.

Pao knew it was supposed to be up to her to tell them what to do, but she had absolutely no idea. Again. "We just have to keep moving!" she said. "Eventually the way will . . . reveal itself! Come on, let's go!"

Not only was this absolutely not true, it was actually futile to keep moving in a liminal space—you'd just tire yourself out and get nowhere. But Pao knew things would be easier if the rest of them didn't mutiny. She was going to have to at least pretend they were doing something constructive if she wanted to keep up morale.

And for a while, it worked. The other girls dutifully trudged through the whispering cornstalks after Pao, all pretending not to notice the thousand pairs of sinister eyes staring down at them. Though privately Pao felt that the birds were just taunting her at this point.

But maybe a miracle will happen, Pao thought as she marched forward. Maybe for once, the liminal space would just . . . yield to her. *Come on. Just yield. Just* yield.

The first three times they passed the broken cornstalk with Kit's bloody fingerprints on it, the Rogues had the good grace to pretend they hadn't seen it. Pao could tell Emma was ready to pass it a fourth time, her eyes fixed determinedly forward, but Pao could keep up the charade no longer.

"Stop!" she called to Emma. Kit had already halted to stare a little squeamishly at her own blood. Robin was putting on a brave face, but a cornstalk she had plucked was drooping, and her lower lip was trembling. "You all, I . . . I'm sorry, but I don't know what to do."

"Let's go back to the bus!" Kit said, and her voice had an angry, disappointed edge to it that was far different than her boastful teasing. "Back to the highway. It'll be light soon. And if there's nothing to kill, we might as well wait for help."

"We can't," Pao said in a hollow voice that was barely audible over the racket the crows were making. "Once we're in the liminal space, the only way out is through, and I don't . . . know how to get through."

She had never been great at admitting she didn't know the answer to something, but this time the words practically stuck in her throat, burning like a hot marshmallow she'd swallowed too fast.

None of the other girls spoke, and Pao couldn't bring herself to look at their faces. She looked at the staff in her hand instead. The shimmering, iridescent surface, the mythic blade she'd had found when she'd showed compassion to the fantasma she'd dispatched. She'd been so sure then. Unaware of her true identity, and determined to do what was right.

And I had help, she thought, remembering the way Señora Mata had risked her life to portal back to Raisin Valley, saving toddler-aged Dante from his father's grim fate and giving Pao the clue she needed to dispatch the mutated ghost man who had haunted the dusty town for decades.

But there was no such help now, and she had no one to blame but herself. She could have told Franco, or even one of the less offensive Niños, like Naomi or Marisa. She could have told her dad. She felt a pang as she thought of him—she'd only just gotten him back, and now she had gravely disappointed him at best and lost him his daughter at worst.

Would the birds try to kill them? Would they be able to fight them off?

I don't even deserve this thing, Pao thought, looking down at the weapon again. It was the weapon of a hero, and Pao wasn't a hero. She was the granddaughter of one of the most evil villains in history. She was tainted, toxic, impure.

You act like you're some kind of savior, but you're not, Dante had once said, and he'd been right.

Pao let the weapon slide out of her hand and onto the ground. Without her intention to give it form, it changed back into the magnifying glass—but not the pocket-size, key chain version Pao had been carrying around this past year.

This was the golden, ornate-looking glass she had first pulled out of the flower, and it had landed on its side.

I should just leave it there, Pao thought with a kind of desperate sadness. *Maybe a* real *hero will find it. . . .*

But just then, as she was giving it a long, last, self-pitying look, she caught sight of something strange through the lens—a line of shining gold, like sunlight painted on the ground with a brush.

"Um, hello?" Pao said, bending down to pick up the heavy instrument, then peering through it properly. "Remember when I said I didn't know where to go? I may have been a little hasty. . . ."

And then, as if they needed to hear her every word, each crow weighing down a cornstalk went deadly silent.

"Which way?" Emma asked, and this time, Pao knew.

"This way," she said confidently, setting off to follow the light before she realized only one set of footsteps was following her. "Kit, Robin, come on, we have to move."

"And we're supposed to believe that *now* you know what you're doing?" Kit asked, dropping her rake with a *thud* and lowering herself to the ground. Robin followed suit. They were both clearly exhausted.

Pao wanted to scream. They did *not* have time for this, and she was about to tell Kit exactly that when Emma stepped up beside her, a hand on Pao's shoulder, her eyes narrowed.

"I'm sorry," she said to Kit. "Do *you* have some hitherto unshared knowledge of how to get out of a haunted cornfield and access a magical void? Because if not, it seems like Pao's plan is the best one we have. So, you can either come with us"—she linked her arm through Pao's in a gesture of solidarity—"or you can stay here and change your names to Birdseed. Either way, *we're* going."

Kit's expression had gone from insolent to shocked during the course of Emma's uncharacteristic outburst, and Robin had stopped hyperventilating at last, getting to her feet and crossing over to them on shaky legs.

"I'm with you," Robin said with grim determination. "We've made it this far."

And with Robin on board, Kit couldn't do anything but follow.

THIRTEEN
A Dream Without a Dream

Pao led the way, her feet following the glowing line through the corn like it was painted on a school floor to show the kindergartners how to get to lunch. They appeared to be going the same direction they had been before, but this time they didn't pass the bent, bloodstained cornstalk. This time they went on, twisting and turning through the corn on a path so convoluted Pao knew they never would have made it if it hadn't been for the magnifying glass.

Her magnifying glass, Pao thought, feeling a sense of fierce pride to counteract the despair that had almost overtaken her. The Arma del Alma had chosen *her*. That meant she was different from La Llorona, different even from her father. She was good, and she would prove it. She would get Dante back.

She was nearing the end of her self-pep talk, hope blazing in her chest along with the sunrise, when all at once the crows began to fly up from their perches on the corn.

"Uh, fearless leader? This doesn't look so g— OWWW!" Kit squealed in pain as the first one dove at her, and soon her screams were joined by others. The first peck Pao took on the cheek told her the crows meant business. Before, they'd only been trying to intimidate the humans into staying away from the entrance. But now that the girls were on the right track, the demon birds were ready to stop them by any means necessary.

"We just have to keep . . . moving . . ." Pao grunted as two more birds tore at her arms with their talons. She could feel a trickle of blood flowing down her cheek. "They don't want us getting near the entrance—they're protecting it, which means we're close!"

Pao looked back to see Emma and Kit still on her heels. Robin had fallen behind and was batting away a bird. "Get off!" she screamed. "Get off me!" Professional boffer though she was, Kit couldn't get an angle on the crow, so Pao transformed the magnifying glass and took a swipe—along with a chunk of Robin's hair.

"Sorry!" Pao said, helping Robin up from where she'd fallen and urging her forward. "I can't use the staff and the magnifying glass at the same time, and we need the directions, so we're just gonna have to run through the crows. Wave your arms, stay in motion, and holler if you really need a bailout, okay?"

Her friends were much worse for wear, but they all nodded with the grim determination of monster-bird-fighting veterans, and Pao felt a swelling of pride for all of them.

"Let's go!" Emma called, wiping blood across her face unknowingly and charging ahead as Pao shrank the staff again and ran for it.

It was four more minutes—though it felt like an eternity—of pecking, clawing, shrieking chaos before they caught sight of the church. Robin lost another chunk of hair, Kit and Emma were both bleeding freely from various wounds, and everyone's eyes were wide. Pao had taken the brunt of the beating, with several more scratches on her face and arms, and a nasty gouge in her left leg.

"There!" Pao called. "The church! That's where we need to go! Just get inside!"

With their destination in sight—the whitewashed adobe building looking even smaller than it had in the pictures—she transformed the Arma del Alma again, staying as close to her friends as she could while she swung the blade at the crows. She didn't even care how many she hit, she just wanted to keep them from snatching an eyeball or worse before her friends reached safety.

"What if it's locked?" Robin shrieked.

"It isn't!" Pao called back, not sure how she knew this but not stopping to wonder.

They leaped up the few stairs one by one, and Kit grabbed the massive, tarnished door handle and tugged hard. As Pao had predicted, it swung right open, and without even looking at what was inside, all four bleeding, exhausted girls forced themselves through the door and slammed it shut behind them.

Outside, Pao could hear the *thud-thud-thud* of crow after crow hitting the door, the scratches of hundreds of talons, and the settling of wings on the roof above them. But inside, they were mercifully safe. She didn't even have the energy to make it to the rough-hewn wooden pew a few feet in front of her— she just slid down onto the ground as if her bones had been removed and lay there, cheek on the cool stone floor as she caught her breath.

"We made it," Emma said at her side, but suddenly her voice was far away. Though Pao was awake and the church's high ceiling was still visible, she found she could *feel* the dream girl, like a second set of thoughts beside her own, a second heartbeat, a second set of aching, exhausted muscles.

The dream girl was *weary* in a way Pao felt in her very soul. She was standing beside a lake, a few ripples at the center all that remained of the void entrance that had once been there. Despite the fact that she had closed it, the fear and urgency thrumming inside her drowned out any sense of relief or feelings of fatigue.

There can be no rest. Not when his enemies are on his heels and all could be gained or lost in an instant. There'll be no rest until afterward, when I'm honored above all his disciples, when I can promise him that there will be no more interference and their path is wide open. . . .

If that path closes, there'll be nothing but fear and pain. He told me never to consider that outcome. Not even to hold it in my mind, for the mind is powerful and can bring about its worst fears. And that, of course, is how he stays in business.

So, with the exhaustion of someone who had lived a thousand lifetimes, the dream girl buried her fears once more and focused every writhing, shadowy filament of her soul on the final location. Where she would close one path forever and open another wide.

With two minds, like some kind of distorted double image, Pao saw the room she was sitting in. The chapel with its aged and cracking white stucco walls, the roughly carved pews, the stained-glass window, small and round, its colors faded from time and sunlight. The dream girl focused on the room with all her might, reaching forward, her reaction time slowed by her weariness but still as effective as an expensive instrument.

As the dream girl reached into oblivion, Pao came back to herself fully, her heart racing, adrenaline pushing all her own weariness aside. She gasped, "She's coming," to the bewildered crowd. She pushed herself to her feet, extending the staff so abruptly she almost skewered Kit's arm.

"What? Who?" Kit asked as Emma turned her wide eyes on Pao.

"When?"

"*Now,*" Pao said, still not knowing who the rift-closer was, or what terrifying force was compelling her, but understanding the most important thing—which was if she didn't find the void entrance and Dante before the dream girl arrived, all would be lost.

"How can I help?" Emma asked, and Pao's heart squeezed in her chest at the way her best friend, still bleeding from several places, her sweater torn and her hair twisted and tangled, was willing to put aside her exhaustion, too. To be there for Pao, always.

"Keep them safe," Pao said. "I have to look for the rift entrance."

"How will you—" Emma began, but even as she asked, Pao could feel it. Like a radio station that had been on at low volume in a noisy room, unnoticed, but unmistakably there. The hum of the void. Pao's mind and body bent toward it even as she told herself it wouldn't feel like going home.

"I'll find it," she said. "Just . . ."

"I won't let anything happen to them," Emma said, and Pao didn't have the words for how brave she looked, or how strong. Pao just stepped forward and embraced her, a fierce sort of gesture that left Emma looking a little dazed when she let go.

"If I don't come back soon," Pao said, the buzzing getting louder, the urgency from the dream girl's mind crowding her thoughts, "take them to the airport. Get them home."

It was a mark of the seriousness of the situation that Kit didn't protest being kept out of the action, and Pao knew it.

"I will," Emma said, her eyes still blazing.

Pao nodded once and turned away, feeling that she had already lingered too long and there would never, ever be enough time for all she wanted to say to this girl.

The church's altar was small, and Pao could already tell the rift wasn't near there. The low buzz was muted, like it was somewhere deeper inside the structure. As skeptical as Pao was of her connection to the void, the one that had caused her and her family so much pain, she couldn't help but follow it now. It was something primal. Instinctive.

She saw a small door, one that in a normal church might have led to a closet or a storage room or something, but this one was different. The wood had a strange quality to it, a shimmer you could only see at certain angles. As Pao pushed it open, she took one last glimpse back at the Rogues. Kit was handing out a heavy silver candlestick and a lumpy, scepter-like object and instructing the other two in the rules of boffing combat.

If she was lucky, Pao thought, and her hunch was correct, the dream girl would be coming for the entrance, and Pao. She wouldn't be concerned with a bunch of candlestick-wielding tourists with rainbow shoelaces. Or at least Pao hoped not.

Before any of them could look over at her, Pao was through the door. It swung shut behind her, blotting out all noise as swiftly and completely as if she'd stepped into a tomb.

FOURTEEN

My Own Worst Enemy

Pao had been right. It wasn't a closet.

A set of stone steps led down, and she followed them without hesitation, trying not the let the choking panic take over, telling herself the Rogues would be okay, that she would find Dante without losing someone else she loved. . . .

Or even someone I can barely tolerate, she added, thinking of Kit.

The stairs went down and down and down, curving or taking a sharp angle from time to time. The walls were made of the same stone, and after she'd been descending for at least two minutes, Pao noticed it was damp down here, probably because she was so far underground.

She tried not to feel claustrophobic, to focus instead on the hum she didn't want to admit was welcoming as it grew louder and louder the closer she got to the void. Her staff was a comforting presence in her hand, even though holding it became more awkward as the stairway narrowed.

Just a little farther, Pao told herself, choking on a giggle when she remembered the first time she'd ever approached a void entrance. She'd been in a haunted cactus field that time, and she'd had a floppy, hilariously disobedient chupacabra puppy along for the ride. *I'll get home to you, boy,* she thought desperately as the stairs narrowed further still, her elbows brushing the damp walls at this point.

And then, just when Pao thought she'd soon be out of air, the descent was over. The stairs leveled off at the threshold of a rectangular room no bigger than Pao's mom's bedroom back home. A torch burned on the wall, which Pao found curious. Who would be coming down here to replace a torch? And why weren't they here now to use the light?

But her thoughts of the torch were lost when Pao entered the room properly and saw its main feature.

There were double doors in the room's north wall, and they weren't closed all the way. Through the crack Pao could see a pulsing, swirling, distinctly supernatural material that she'd only encountered once before. A massive bubble of it had encased La Llorona's infamous underwater palace. A full-body shudder coursed through Pao at the memory, bringing back her nightmares, her sleeplessness, the shadows that seemed to lurk around every corner.

I'm not like you, she thought to the specter of her grandmother that would never leave her alone. To the mad eyes of Joaquin looking through her father's face, promising her death and worse.

"I'm not like you!" she said aloud this time, needing to hear it as much as she needed to say it.

As if in response, the light in the room changed, bathing the walls in green.

"That's exactly your problem," said a chillingly familiar voice.

Pao's thoughts raced to identify the voice as she turned, as if in slow motion. There was no way. There was *no way.*

But there *was* a way, because when Pao had rotated around, she was looking at a girl she had seen a million times before. A girl who had stared back at her from the mirror every morning for her entire life.

She was looking at herself.

"Surprise!" said the shadow version of Pao, who was brandishing a staff of her own, long and metallic, but hers was made of some shining black stone streaked with malevolent green.

"How . . . ? What . . . ?" Pao stammered, even as her own staff swung around automatically.

"Geez, he told me I was a copy of you, but I've never made that gaping fish face, so it must not be true." Even as she spoke, the dream girl was edging around, trying to place herself between the real Pao and the doors to the void. Pao could almost see the scene from her oil-slicked perspective, and she wondered where the girl's usual fear was, the crushing terror that had previously characterized every moment of her thoughts.

"So, it was you," Pao said, using her age-old tactic of forcing the villain to reveal their plan as a distraction. "On the mountain, and by the lake. You're the one who's been closing the entrances. And you've been wearing my face."

Suddenly, a puzzle piece clicked into place. Canada. Franco's suspicion, her father's wavering faith in her. When they'd questioned the locals, had they gotten a description of Pao and concluded she was somehow sabotaging them? It would explain a lot. . . .

Shadow Pao's eyes were suspicious as the two girls circled each other like cats. "How did you know about that?"

Pao smirked, putting on a show even as her mind raced furiously to understand what a clone of her was doing in this church, why it *existed* in the first place. "You think you're the only one who knows things?" Pao asked. "That's cute. But since you're just a copy, I guess I can't expect you to understand."

She was hoping to upset Shadow Pao enough that she'd confess something important. Something that would help the real Pao make sense of all this.

Unfortunately, Shadow Pao seemed to shake her doubts loose at precisely that moment, and this time, she stepped closer. "He said you'd try to confuse me. In fact, he told me not to talk to you at all. He said to just kill you and be done with it."

"Funny," Pao said, still miles from understanding, realizing in this moment that she'd have to fight before she got any answers at all. "He told me the same thing."

"Lies," hissed Shadow Pao, and now, for the first time, Pao could see differences between them. In the way the other girl's eyes narrowed, the way her face became sharp and angular and cruel in her rage. "He told me you would lie. That you would say anything to protect that feeble human boy of yours. He told me you were an embarrassment to your ancestor. To all of us."

"What do you know about Dante?" Pao asked, advancing, the blade end of her staff now pointed forward, though she had no idea what she was going to do with it. How connected was Pao to this other version of her? What would happen if Shadow Pao died? Was that even possible? Would real Pao have time to find out?

"*Danteeee*," the other girl said in a screeching imitation of Pao's concern. "The master told me you would do anything to get him back. But I'm here to tell you that, as long as I'm standing, you'll *never* get through those doors."

"Guess we'll have to do something about that whole you-standing thing, then, won't we?" Pao said, and she lunged, not surprised to be parried. Her staff glanced aside, and Shadow Pao's eyes burned green, her face—*their* face—stretching and twisting into a horrible mask just like the Poppy copy's had.

"I was curious about you," Shadow Pao said, her voice sounding normal though her twisted mouth never moved. She began circling again. "It's why I didn't kill you while you stood there gaping. I wanted to know how much of me was in you. . . ." It was her turn to strike this time, that green-laced obsidian staff jabbing toward real Pao, its deadly point barely missing her ribs before she danced away with steps her father had taught her and then blocked it with the butt of her own weapon.

"Hate to break it to you," said Pao, grunting with the effort, "but now that your face looks like that, I don't think we have much in common at all."

With Beto's voice in her mind guiding her moves, Pao launched a furious assault that Shadow Pao could barely keep up with, slashing and jabbing and moving inexorably forward. At last, with a frustrated shriek, Shadow Pao swept Pao's leg out from under her and brought a stop to it.

Pao was back on her feet in an instant, her training kicking in, her body knowing the steps to this dance even while her mind was preoccupied.

"Don't you know who you are?" Shadow Pao asked as she spun gracefully, her staff coming down in a punishing arc Pao could barely counter in time.

"I know who I want to be," Pao said, the force of the blow ringing through her staff and rattling her bones, making her feel unsteady and weak for a moment before she recovered. "If you want the perfect-granddaughter-of-the-void role, it's all yours."

"And all I have to do is let you through to your boyfriend, right?" Shadow Pao taunted. "You must really think I'm stupid."

"No," Pao said, shaking out her arms before launching another attack. "Just evil. Tends to limit your options."

"Oh, does it?" asked Shadow Pao, ducking low to avoid the swipe as if she were doing the limbo at a school dance. Before Pao had finished her follow-through, her shadow was lying on the floor, then pushing up with all her strength and kicking Pao hard in the chest with both feet.

"Why do you want to stop me?" Pao asked, slumped against the wall she had hit hard. "Who are you working for?"

"You don't want to know," Shadow Pao said under her breath. "You'd never survive an encounter with my master." She looked more deranged than ever now, her frozen features tinged by the glowing green light encasing her staff as she crouched over it.

"Master, huh?" Pao asked, panting. "That's how I *know* you're not me. I have what my mom and teachers affectionately call a *serious problem with authority.*"

"The world will be his before long," Shadow Pao said, fear mixed with awe making her voice sound oddly simpering. "I will not be the only one of us who calls him master then."

"Not if I can help it," Pao said, something solidifying in her mind. This girl, as much as she might look like Pao, was nothing but a void creature. There was no reason to hesitate.

She made a run at Shadow Pao once more, righteous anger burning through her, as well as the knowledge that Dante was close. So close. She could finally get to him and make this right once and for all.

Except the other girl was no longer there.

Pao cast around, feeling stupid and probably looking even stupider, alone in the room where she'd just now been fighting a snarky copy of herself.

"You limit yourself." The voice came from above, and Pao looked up to see herself wraithlike, cloaked in green light, hovering near the ceiling of the stone room. *"You limit yourself because you cannot admit what you are."* Shadow Pao's voice was layered now, like El Autostopisto's had been when he took the form of multiple victims at once. Her glowing eyes were the only source of light in the semi-darkness.

The ceiling wasn't high here, and Pao's staff was long enough to reach, but her hands had begun to shake, and cold sweat was coating her palms.

"You waste precious time justifying, twisting your actions in your mind so you can deem them *good* or *bad*," Shadow Pao went on, holding her staff in one hand and a fistful of green flames in the other. "You're so determined to suppress who you are that you throw every scrap of power away."

"I don't want power," Pao said automatically. "I just want to do what's right."

"What's *right*," Shadow Pao jeered. "And you're the person to judge that, are you? You deserve to decide what's good and what's bad? I'm here to tell you those things are made up. The only reality is the tools at our disposal, *Paola*, and what we choose to do with them." With this she flicked her wrist and the fistful of green flames became a ring that encircled Pao, burning hot and bubbling like acid all at once, eating a circle into the stone floor as Pao stood there gaping, her staff useless at her side.

"I'm you, you know," Shadow Pao said, lowering herself to the ground again and walking straight through the flames as if she couldn't even feel them. "Down to the very cellular structure. There's nothing I can do that you couldn't if you were brave enough. . . ."

As if to prove it, she stepped forward suddenly, surprising Pao, who stumbled back too close to the flames. "Ow!" she cried as the heel of her shoe began to melt.

"It burns because you won't accept you're made of the same substance," Shadow Pao said relentlessly, walking forward farther still so that Pao had nowhere to go. "The flames are of the void. So is this staff. So am I. And so . . ." She was so close now that Pao could see her reflection in those venomous eyes. "Are you."

There was no weird ghost psychology about it—Pao was burning. She could feel the heat licking her ankles and the backs of her calves. Her heart raced along with her mind, which was screaming something like *BLADE IN FRONT, FLAMES BEHIND!* over and over, drowning out all reasonable thought.

Dante needs you, she told herself, trying to cut through the noise. *Emma and Kit and Robin are upstairs. Your parents are at home worried sick. You have to get back to them. You have to find a way.*

"Your *friends*, your *parents*, the people you're *responsible* for . . ." said Shadow Pao in a singsong, mocking voice. "Don't you ever get tired of convincing yourself to do the 'right thing'? Don't you ever just want to hurt someone because it would feel good?"

"No," Pao said, hating the small, whimpery quality of her voice. "I'm not like you, and I'm not like *her*. I would never hurt anyone."

"But you *have* hurt people, haven't you?" The gleam in Shadow Pao's eye said *I have you and you know it*. "You've teased them and mocked them and made them worry. You've pushed them away and left them out. You've hated them for no good reason. You've felt envious and angry and mean. Stop trying to fight it! You're not good! You're just like me!"

All that was true, Pao had to admit. She'd said terrible things to Dante, been jealous of Emma and Kit, run away from home three times . . . and without having to be possessed by an evil soul like her dad once was.

Pao felt a strangled sob escape her throat. The heat was boring through her skin, and the pain was intense. All-consuming. It was time to accept that she was going to die here. Die before she got the other girls home safe. Die before she ever figured out how her dad fit into her life. Die before she could ever convince Dante that she was good.

In the haze of pain and grief and letting go, Pao thought she would lose it all. Soon the pain would take everything, burn it away until she was nothing. Perhaps it would be better that way. . . .

But then a tiny spark lit in the back of her mind. If she was evil, would she care so much about her parents? About Emma and Dante? And what about Bruto? He was supposed to be a monster, too. A void creature. But he was good. And he had chosen her. . . .

The pain receded, just a little. She could feel the flames, but no longer as an adversary. She checked her legs surreptitiously for injury, held up a hand to see if it was shaking.

It was steady. Her skin was intact and un-blistered by the flames, which she now vanished into thin air with a snap of her fingers. The fire was a tool she could control. And if it was a choice between harnessing this power and death, she would do what she needed to do.

Without thinking, without wondering if it was right or wrong, Pao lunged forward with her staff, feeling the blade connect with the shadow girl's wrist, hearing her hiss of pain. As Shadow Pao recovered, real Pao snapped her fingers again, bringing a wall of flame to life between them.

It wouldn't stop her clone, but maybe it could distract her for long enough.

The doors to the void were right there, ready to open and swallow Pao whole, but she found she couldn't go through. She couldn't leave this monster here in the same building as her friends.

So Pao walked through the flame wall instead, kicking out the moment Shadow Pao was in reach. Real Pao swiped the other girl's legs out from under her and would have cut her in half with her arma if the shadow hadn't rolled out of the way just in time.

"That's what I'm talking about," said Shadow Pao, but her bravado wasn't as convincing as before, and Pao could once again sense the terror she carried. The crushing dread of failure, of what her mysterious, shadow-shrouded master would say if she came back to him empty-handed . . .

"You really should let go of that," Pao said, laughing, a reckless thrill running through her. "The fear of what he'll think. Maybe we're more alike than I thought."

"How d-dare you?" Shadow Pao spluttered, stepping forward and striking again. She missed the mark wildly, leaving herself wide open for Pao to deliver a slice to the upper arm that did not bleed red. Instead, the same green goo that had flowed from Peppy Poppy's wounds began to soak her shirt, and she looked down at it with revulsion.

"This is like the part in *Pinocchio* when he finds out he's not a real boy, right?" Pao said, no longer afraid, tasting victory in the air around her, which suddenly seemed alive with possibility.

She spun Shadow Pao around and kicked her hard in the back, sending her sprawling into the wall opposite the void doors, her obsidian staff spinning out of her hand and across the ground.

Pao stepped up to her, holding her shining spear to the other girl's throat. Shadow Pao's eyes went wide, acknowledging her loss. But even in these last moments, a smirk twisted the clone's pointed features. "This means nothing," she said. "I might not live to see it, but what he's planning . . ." She coughed, a wet-sounding thing that sent more green goo spattering the floor between them. "Let's just say you should try to enjoy the last few days of humanity."

"What do you mean?" Pao asked. "Tell me! Who sent you? What's he planning?"

Shadow Pao just laughed, a hollow, dispassionate sound that seemed to hold all the exhaustion in the universe within it. "Just kill me and be done with it."

"You know, I don't think I will."

"Oh gods, not more of this good-girl stuff." She actually rolled her eyes. "To the victor go the spoils, and all that."

"I don't like killing someone unless I've got a really good reason," Pao said, shrinking the staff and pocketing it. "Besides, if this master guy wants you so bad, maybe I'd be better off trading you for my friend." It was a tactic she wouldn't have even considered an hour ago, but now, as she grabbed Shadow Pao's arm and hauled her up, it seemed like a great strategy.

"You can't take me back there," Shadow Pao said, starting to panic. "Seriously, just kill me—it'll be better for both of us."

"Shut up," Pao said, dragging her toward the doors, pulling them open and standing there for a moment contemplating. It was time to go into the void. She knew that. But her palms had begun to sweat again as the fear she'd thought she left in the flames had returned as sharp as the scent of pine in the Oregon forest, or creosote in a haunted cactus field. . . .

There was something in her way, something more than just a spooky copy of herself. It had been in her way for months, keeping her from using portals and cutting her off from her dreams. . . .

The Ten of Pentacles, she remembered suddenly, like her mother was in the room with her. *The Moon. Whatever this legacy piece is, it's blocking the synthesis you need to happen in order to move forward.*

Even Emma had seen it, the fear that kept Pao from accessing the other world . . . a world she'd been born to be a part of.

"I don't want to be like them," she said in a voice no louder than a whisper.

Shadow Pao laughed again, and the laugh became another

coughing fit. "Then just don't," she said. "You humans waste too much time worrying about things you'll never understand."

Maybe she was right, Pao thought. Dante was inside the void, and whether or not she'd ever be good enough to prove to him that she wasn't La Llorona, that the Santiago legacy hadn't infected her, this was the choice in front of her—to stay here and be afraid, or to use her power to do the best she could.

Pao closed her eyes. She focused on the people who loved her. Those who saw her for all she was instead of breaking her down into parts and judging her for what they found. She held their images in her mind like stars in the night sky, their light guiding her way.

With all of them beside her, she stepped through the strange, viscous shell protecting the entrance and left this world for another.

FIFTEEN
The Obsidian Tower

At first, Pao felt weightless, and the darkness pressed in on her tightly, like it was sealing her. A little vacuum bag of Pao leftovers floating through space.

But she wasn't alone in the bag. Shadow Pao was here, too, and they were smooshed together so tightly as they hurtled through the place between worlds that Pao thought she was dreaming again. Their thoughts were layered on top of one another (hers mostly of Dante and what lay ahead; Shadow Pao's filled with the face of the guy bossing her around, with his glowing eyes and that awful, grating laugh) until eventually Pao wasn't sure which belonged to whom.

And then, just when the weightlessness and the thought parade had begun to make her seriously nauseated, the pain began—so abruptly that it shocked her. It was like someone was opening her chest to perform heart surgery with no anesthesia. She was screaming, she was sure, the sound echoing inside her mind, inside this bubble still moving inexorably forward. Or downward, maybe.

"Stop!" Pao yelled again and again. "Make it stop!"

This is what you deserve, said a chorus of voices. *This is the consequence of killing La Llorona.*

"I didn't kill her!" Pao sobbed, the pain going on and on and on. "I was good, *I was good!*" But the longer the pain went on, the more blurred the lines between good and bad became.

Good? came the voice again. *Just another word for* obedient.

"Stop, please," Pao panted, her voice too worn out to scream. "I'm sorry. I'll do better, I'll *be* better, just make it stop!"

She could see Dante swimming in front of her, scorn and disgust in every line of his face. *You're not a hero,* he spat. *You're the bad guy. You could never have been anything else.*

And then La Llorona herself was there, her twisted, waxen features, her mouth open in its perpetual scream. Next came Joaquin, with his mad eyes, and the chair, and the swirling mass of the anomaly he'd created to loose the creatures of the void on the living.

"Stop," Pao said. "Please, I'm not like them. I'm not."

Oh, but you are, said the judgmental eyes of her tormentors. She had walked through the green fire. She had used the tools of the void to gain the upper hand. When circumstances forced her to show what she was made of, she had chosen the same path they all had.

"I'm sorry," she sobbed. "I'm sorry."

The pain went on and on. The void didn't seem to care about her remorse. How had entering it the first time been as easy as forgiving herself? Forgiving her mother?

Because you were better then, the awful voices said. *More innocent, more pure.*

"No," Pao said aloud, even though she knew the criticism was coming from inside her. From the self-hatred she'd carried ever since she'd discovered who she was. *What* she was. "I just did what I thought was best. . . ."

La Llorona reappeared, her words swirling around Pao. *I did it because my children would have suffered,* she said, her voice plaintive and sad. *I did it because I loved them.*

Then Joaquin was back, too, in his teenage fantasma form here. *I did it because they killed me,* he said. *I did it because I deserved revenge.*

Through Pao's haze of pain, a ray of understanding broke through, weak at first but then strengthening gradually. They hadn't done evil deeds because they *decided* to be evil. They'd done them out of selfishness. They'd believed that their wants, needs, and hurts were more important than other people's lives.

Power and privilege are just tools, Pao remembered— something out of a Rogues' tirade Emma was fond of delivering. *Good is what you do, not who you are.*

Pao wasn't destined to be evil because she was descended from people who had done evil things. She wasn't evil because she had the ability to access the void through portals and dreams. She wouldn't be evil unless she forgot what she owed to the world and used her tools to uplift herself at the expense of others.

And hadn't she done the opposite? Every time she'd had the chance? She'd freed the tortured souls of La Llorona, Ondina, and Joaquin. She had released them with love, not anger . . . and each one had achieved peace at the end. She'd done whatever was necessary to keep her friends, family, and town safe.

If she could use the neutral tools that were part of her inheritance to right wrongs and protect other people, how could that be bad? Maybe the concepts of good and evil were for lazy people, she thought, as the pain receded further.

When Pao opened her eyes again, La Llorona, Joaquin, and even Dante were gone. She was alone in the bubble with Shadow Pao, who looked so much smaller and more helpless than she had in the midst of their fight.

"You were right. I'm no different than you," Pao said, looking her clone full in the face for once. Shadow Pao was unmoving, her stare glassy. "I just made different choices."

Even while frozen, Shadow Pao was able to give the impression of rolling her eyes.

"I'm not going to stop making different choices than you," Pao said, the pain all but gone now. "And, if given the chance, I'd kick your butt again any day of the week. I'm not scared of you anymore."

Shadow Pao looked like she wanted to speak, but before she could, light flared to life between them, a pulsing purple ball of luminescence that grew in brilliance and size until Pao was forced to cover her eyes with her hands as everything around her and within her was erased by its intensity, its heat. . . .

When the light faded and her feet touched the ground, Pao's legs were shaking. She wasn't sure if she had traveled for minutes or hours or days. She only knew she was in a massive field, the dark green sky ominous with lightning streaking above her, and she was alone.

The silence pressed on all sides, eerie and watchful. Pao cast around for her shadow self, thinking she might prefer her company over this nothingness. But she was gone. Had Shadow Pao landed in another area of the void? Pao wondered. Been summoned home by her supposedly all-powerful master?

Pao stopped short of calling out, not wanting to attract

anyone's attention just yet. She still had vivid memories of the yard of ruins outside La Llorona's glass palace and all the monsters that had haunted it. She and Dante had fought their way through tooth and nail, only to be betrayed by Ondina in the end.

Even Ondina (her ghost aunt?) wouldn't have been an unwelcome sight right about now, Pao thought. There was a long way to go until Pao reached the obsidian tower at the top of the hill, and what she would find when she got there would be—

Pao stopped her thoughts in their tracks, like Wile E. Coyote skidding to the edge of a cliff in pursuit of the Road Runner. What had she just been thinking?

An obsidian tower. She could see it as clearly in her mind as if she'd always known it. And she knew how to get there, how long it would take, and—

Pao's brain snapped effortlessly into hypothesis mode—even though the theory in question was so distasteful she kind of wished she could slow down the process. Something had happened in that bubble when she'd confronted Shadow Pao.

Pao had felt it when she decided to control her own choices, not to be afraid of her clone. She'd seen the disgusted look on Shadow Pao's face, predicted the snarky comment she'd been about to make before the purple light came to life and swallowed them both.

But what if the light had done more than swallow them? What if it had . . . *digested* them? Boiled them down to their shared common denominator, which was, of course, this body. Frantically, desperate to prove herself wrong, Pao began the process of examining her own mind, her memories. There was the sleepover at Emma's, the episode in the yard following the weird sleep potion, her knees on the cold stone as she awaited her assignment and—

Nope, Pao thought, zeroing in on that last memory. It stood out like the zebra in the lineup of fruits and veggies in a *Highlights for Children* magazine. Pao had never been to this part of the void before, never knelt on shining black stone and received an assignment from someone with a clear, pitiless voice. A voice telling her to close all the void entrances, to speak to no one and trust no one, to expect pain and misery if she failed . . .

And yet the memory was there, as clear as the strange look in Emma's eyes when Catra and Adora had kissed on-screen. It was like Pao had undergone the moment of kneeling herself, complete with the simultaneous feelings of terror and determination.

Green lightning shot across the eerie purple sky. There was no rain, of course. It was a dry storm. The kind that lit up summer nights and made the hair on your arms stand on end.

Beneath it, Pao tried to stop herself from panicking at this intrusion. To realize Shadow Pao's memories were a tool like anything else. But these memories were seriously unpleasant. Nothing like arguing with someone else's little sister, or eating a flavor of ice cream you didn't like and enjoying it, or having a dog that obeyed basic commands.

It was hard not to slide back into believing the worst about herself when she could literally remember kneeling before the shadowy man (even Shadow Pao hadn't known his true identity) saying *Yes, my lord* and plotting to thwart Pao's attempt to reenter the void and rescue Dante. . . .

At the very least, it was confusing, and standing in the middle of this awful, lightning-struck field trying to process it all was doing nothing more than making her bait.

Power and privilege are tools, she reminded herself. Shadow Pao was gone, thanks to real Pao. And those memories residing in her brain didn't mean that Pao had done those things or made those choices. It just meant that she now had new insight into what was going on here.

If Pao could use the information to save Dante, to prevent the devastation the tarot card tower had promised if she didn't begin to reconcile her ancestry, then she was using it for good. Right?

Good is what you do, not who you are, Pao repeated to herself, trying to focus on her surroundings again. The field was empty, but she knew the direction the tower was in. It was where he would be, the man with the face she couldn't see, the one who had given all the orders.

But nowhere in either set of Pao memories was Dante's location. She was just going to have to head for the place with the dark stone walls and hope she could find him there. Hope he was still alive.

Pao knew from her shadow self's thoughts that there were two guards stationed at the tower door, and she always portaled into the field, never into the tower itself. As she walked toward the place she knew from her stolen memories, the pointed top slowly revealed itself as she got closer.

No one else's memories could have prepared her for the sight of the obsidian tower in its entirety. The structure was at least a hundred feet high, the surrounding field barren and unguarded. It was easy to see why. On every jutting balcony, at every window, was an archer with a bow.

And these archers weren't human.

They were ghostly warriors twice as tall as Pao. Monstrosities that looked like fantasmas and skeletons somehow rolled into one—and, of course, armed to the teeth. Their blank gazes ruthlessly scanned the field, but Pao wasn't fooled for a second into believing they couldn't put an arrow through someone at any range.

So why hadn't they shot at her? Why didn't they seem concerned by the fact that she was making her way slowly toward their lord's tower like she didn't have a care in the world?

It was their indifference, as well as the other Pao's memories jostling for space with her own, that catalyzed her plan. Shadow Pao and real Pao had been identical, and Pao now had every memory the other girl had made since the moment she'd stepped out of a weird incubation chamber somewhere in this tower. So what was to stop her from pretending she *was* Shadow Pao, coming home with the void closed and the enemy thwarted for good?

Maybe, if she could convince the strange shadow lord of this tower that she was his minion, he would tell her where Dante was and she could get him out before the man was the wiser. . . .

Pao had never passed a longer five minutes than she did crossing the remainder of the field to the tower's door. At any moment, she expected an arrow through the eyeball, or the clattering sound of ten bone warriors rushing forward to tear her limb from limb. At the very least, some kind of siren or alarm, declaring her an intruder, putting the tower on high alert.

But despite the way every turn of a bone warrior's head jolted her nerves, and the crawling sensation across her skin that said someone inside was aware of her approach, none of these fears materialized, and Pao continued her way toward the door unobstructed.

At least for now.

She was within ten yards of the only door. Then she reached it. *They're going to stop me*, Pao thought as she drew level with the guards. *They* have *to stop me, don't they?* But they let her pass without a glance.

It's because you belong here, said another inner voice, the one that had driven every hateful, critical thought she'd directed at herself since her fight with Dante in Raisin Valley last winter. *It's because they know your kind.*

Good is what you do, Pao thought to counteract the voice. *All we can do is make the best choice we're equipped to make in the moment and—*

Once again, Pao's inner monologue came to a halt. She was standing in an entryway made of the same obsidian as the outside of the tower, a perfectly round room containing two massive cages with dull steel bars. Was Dante . . . ? No, she thought with disappointment. Both stood empty.

"Not much of an interior decorator," Pao muttered under her breath. At least La Llorona's palace had been, like, scary-magnificent instead of just scary. The only other feature in this room was a staircase made of (shock of all shocks) obsidian, and it led up. "Here goes nothing," said Pao, her heart in her throat, aware of her complete aloneness in a way she'd never been before.

She climbed the stairs until she reached a second floor, then a third, all perfectly round and set with cages completely devoid of captives.

For Pao, who was used to being overwhelmed by enemies in situations like this, the quiet was even more disturbing. Her every nerve seemed to be firing, awake to the possibility of danger, poised to defend against attacks that didn't come. It was like that time in the alley when she'd drawn her Arma del Alma on a roof rat. She wished she could draw it now, take comfort from its familiar presence in her hand. But Shadow Pao's staff had been as black as the tower walls, and as far as Pao knew, it was still lying on the floor of the church basement in another world. The swirling brilliance of her own weapon would be a dead giveaway, and she couldn't afford a misstep now.

Not when she was so close.

Another uncomfortable peek into Shadow Pao's memories had shown her several previous marches to the top of this tower—another twenty-two floors past more rooms filled with more empty cages before she reached the place where this nameless void lord resided. Pao flinched from the memory. Every time she tried to access memories of the guy who was pulling the puppet strings, or even just the top floor of this place, the fear was so sharp it felt like she'd been burned.

One unknown is better than all unknowns, Pao told herself, and she continued to climb.

If Pao had hoped to settle into the steady monotony of climbing stairs, like she was doing some PE challenge in which she could zone out and think about a science experiment instead, she was sorely disappointed.

Every empty cage could have been Dante's. Every gleam of torchlight dancing in the glasslike stone could have been a monster, or a bone guard, or the lord of the tower himself finding her out. *Hypervigilance*, Emma had called it, and it felt terrible.

The twenty-fifth floor of the tower came both before and long after she was ready. Her legs were burning, her lungs barely keeping up a shallow wheeze. Even the muscles in her butt were sore. But the fear from Shadow Pao's memories had begun to creep in, too, and before she walked through the final doorway, Pao stopped, closing her eyes and composing herself.

Shadow Pao had been under orders to close all the void entrances. She had closed the first one—which hadn't been easy. The mountain air had been freezing, and when she'd tried using the phrase her master had taught her, the one every void mouth would obey without question, the rift had started an avalanche before she could get all the words out. She'd tumbled a mile down the mountainside and had to portal back to the top.

And then there was the lake with its haunted cottage and surrounding woods thick with fantasmas that didn't respect her authority. She'd had to fight through a particularly nasty band of them before the lake itself had created a whirlpool that had nearly drowned her, and then . . .

The church had been next, Pao thought. Obviously she wouldn't be able to relay an experience there because the closing had never happened. What could she say instead? That the crows had attacked? That much was true. But what would the church have done to protect its entrance?

The whole thing had come crashing down around her, she decided. All the aboveground church stuff had fallen through to the basement, where she'd been nearly buried alive in rubble. And there'd been no sign of the girl and her friends at all.

That was plausible, right? Pao silently asked her warped reflection in the obsidian door. He would believe it. And if he didn't?

Well, at least running down the stairs would be easier than walking up.

Pao took a deep breath, steeling herself for what was to come. She tried to push away all her own memories, to become Shadow Pao so completely that even this all-powerful man in his ridiculous tower would be fooled.

Her thoughts of Emma had to go first, of course. Her goofy, crooked smile, the way she chewed on her lip when she was thinking hard. Most of all, the way she made Pao feel. Safe, happy, a little giddy, like there was a swarm of butterflies—

Her thoughts were abruptly cut off by a wave of cold dread. The kind of fear that made your stomach drop through the ground, caused a cold sweat to break out on the back of your neck, squeezed your heart and increased your pulse. The kind of fear you felt in a nightmare, or on the worst day of your life.

The kind of fear Pao was too well acquainted with but would never, ever get used to.

"Are you coming in, Falsita? Or are you planning to keep me waiting all day?"

SIXTEEN
The Lord of Nightmares

The door opened before Pao could obey the terror coursing through her and flee. Run down the stairs and past the bone guards, all the way back to the world she was supposed to be in, somehow.

There was no escape from what was coming. Pao knew from the memories that her shadow had been afraid, too, and there was no stopping the fear. Not once you had made it this far into the tower. Not when you were this close to *him*.

It had been pointless to try to forget the things that made her Pao. She knew that as she stepped through the door, something compelling her to move even though every cell in her body was screaming at her to go the other way. There wasn't room for Emma, or She-Ra, or science, in here. There wasn't room for anything but icy-cold dread.

"Come, now, you know I won't bite."

She walked forward—because her instincts and the memories told her it was obey or die—into a room larger than the ones below it, a room where a man sat on a massive, throne-like chair that was facing away from Pao.

The throne rocked slightly, and each time it moved, a

horrible, grating, grinding sound filled the room. But that was nothing compared to the sound it made when it began to turn around.

Kneel, came a command from somewhere—her memories, or her instincts, or the very walls around her. Pao obeyed it without hesitating, casting her eyes down at the floor, the space she was staring at and the horrible sound of the rotating chair the only things in her world. She didn't know who else was in the room, what other dangers could be lurking there. It was just the horrible sensation of every nerve on fire and every alarm bell in her head screaming at the danger. Enough that she might go mad if she didn't find a way to escape.

The chair stopped moving. The seconds ticked by in silence. Then Pao heard a pair of shoes taking their owner's weight, and she opened her eyes a fraction to see shiny red boots, the swishing hem of a long black cloak. They moved closer, and Pao's nerves—already on overdrive—ramped up to a level she hadn't even known existed. A level far beyond anything she had felt in the glass palace, when she'd believed Emma was going to die, or in the trailer, when she thought she had killed her own father. . . .

Nothing compared. Nothing came close. This was a fear that could gnaw away the edges of your soul. Erase you until there was nothing left.

"Rise," said the voice, and up close it was a thousand chittering insects, or the cry of birds from far off. It was the distant screams of people running, burning, dying.

Pao obeyed, her legs straightening awkwardly, the shaking worse.

"S-sir," she said in a voice barely above a whisper, knowing that despite the fear she had a job to do. She had to lie. To survive just a little longer until she could flee this place. "It is done."

"You refuse to look on the beloved face of your master?" he said in that voice again, buildings collapsing and cars colliding and lightning striking and someone screaming again, far away.

Pao could not raise her head. She just kept staring at the same spot on the floor. There were lights moving in its shining surface, and shadows swirling.

"Look at me." A hundred children screaming. Closer now.

Pao couldn't. She couldn't.

And yet she did.

He wasn't tall—no taller than Pao's mother, anyway. His long black cloak was something out of a Dracula movie, lined with red satin. He wore it over a dark pin-striped suit.

But Pao didn't linger on any of that. She didn't dwell on the crudely cut windows around the room, slits that barely let in the light from the purple sky outside.

All she could see was his face.

Beneath black hair gathered into a waist-length black ponytail, it wasn't fixed like a person's face, with features moving into expressions. In fact, it was nothing like a face at all except that it occupied the same place one was supposed to.

When Pao looked at it, she had the vague impression it was a blank canvas, or a projector screen, and across it was playing every fear she'd ever had, every fear *anyone* had ever had. Fully detailed things that were worse than just images. They imprinted on her soul, causing her stomach to twist and somersault, her pulse to race so fast she was sure her heart would explode.

This man was a walking bad dream, and finally Pao's nerves had suffered enough. She knew why she was here, what she had to do, the consequences if she didn't. But she turned around anyway, a scream lodged in her throat, the shifting, mercurial nightmare of the tower master's face still burning in her memory, and she ran for the door.

A bone warrior appeared before Pao could blink, his empty eye sockets boring holes into her as she skidded to a stop to avoid crashing into him.

"No," she whispered. "I can't . . . I have to . . ."

"As fleeing is an occupational hazard of reporting to El Cucuy," came the voice from behind her, "I won't toss you out the window this time. But I won't be so lenient again."

Of course, Pao thought, floating outside of herself to the world of children's stories and folktales. To the hundred warnings from her mother she'd scoffed at. El Cucuy. The bogeyman. The monster under the bed. The lord of nightmares himself.

Something worse than fear began to spread from the place in her brain where his words had made contact. A helpless desperation that made her body feel heavy and her mind slow. She would never get out of here. She had been cavalier to come in the first place, resting on luck and laurels that she'd earned alongside more talented friends, and now she was alone and she was going to die.

And, worse than that, leaving this place by any means would be a relief.

"You say you were successful," he said, a casual plague of locusts descending. "All three void entrances have been closed?"

"Yes," Pao said automatically, because survival was ingrained in her so deeply she knew she could not fail to answer his questions. "I closed the mountain mouth first, then the lake, and then the church."

"Come, come," he said, turning away, momentarily relieving Pao of the terror of his ever-shifting face. "You know how I like details. Tell me how it *scared* you. . . ."

"The mountain collapsed before I could speak the words," Pao continued robotically, following the script she'd made for herself. "At the lake, the fantasmas were feral. They'd forgotten their allegiance. I killed them first."

"Good, good," he said, facing her again. The images flickered faster—snakes writhing, spider legs twitching, human mouths screaming. "They've been unattended for too long. The weapon I gave you was satisfactory, I assume."

"Yes," Pao said, suddenly aware of a major flaw in her plan. "But I lost it at the third location." *Please,* she thought. *Please believe me.*

"The church," he said. "An old favorite of mine. My human subjects are always too willing to spread fear and judgment there. And were you bothered by the girl? Her friends? Your little doppelgänger has caused us no end of trouble recently."

"N-no," Pao managed. "I must have beat her there. I never saw her."

"Pity," said El Cucuy, beginning to pace the room. "It would have been helpful to have her out of the way sooner rather than later. She's proved crafty one too many times. Luck, of course, and the failings of schemers weaker than me."

Don't punish me, Pao thought desperately. *Don't punish me for not killing her.*

Killing me? she wondered. The semantics weren't important just now. The details of Shadow Pao's punishments had been obscured by the clone's fear, but anything that could cause that much terror was nothing Pao wanted done to her.

"No matter," El Cucuy said after an agonizing minute of silence had passed. "We'll get her in the next phase. We'll get them all. Come, you've shown me what you can do—now let me show you what *I've* done."

Abruptly, he was sweeping past her, his cloak brushing against her exposed arm, sending the skittering feeling of a thousand centipede legs down to her fingertips. Pao slapped at her skin helplessly, knowing there was nothing there, her mind overreacting to every fear trigger like it was life or death— because here, it could be.

"Are you coming, Falsita?"

"Yes, master," Pao said. Her mind was clearer now that he had left the room, and she glanced around, memorizing the place. It was sparse, the black stone walls their own kind of ornament, but on a table near his throne there was a strange object on display.

It looked like a Rubik's Cube made of dark metal and swirling with purple void essence. Pao could only look at it for a single second before terror clutched at her belly again, causing her skin to crawl and a scream to build in her throat.

"I'm losing patience," came his voice from the stairway, and Pao scurried out.

"Apologies, my lord," she said as she came to a halt behind him. "I suffered a small injury on the mountain—it's made me slower."

"Is that so?" he asked, turning his face on her again before she'd had time to steel herself. The impact was immediate, the way fear clawed at every inch of her. "Well, we can fix you up in due time. We must keep our tools sharp, mustn't we?"

"Yes, my lord," Pao said. But deep inside, at last, she felt something other than terror. A small rebellion had stirred when he called her his *tool*.

Paola Santiago was no one's tool.

As she followed El Cucuy back down to the landing below, she allowed herself to keep this flicker of self-righteous revolt, to let it burn in her heart like a candle in a storm.

"This way," he said, his voice a sword leaving its sheath, determined, deadly. "I think you'll like this."

"I'm sure I will," Pao said, privately thinking anything that could make the lord of nightmares sound this self-satisfied was something she was definitely NOT going to like.

He stopped in front of a blank stretch of obsidian wall and pressed his hands to it. It was the first time Pao had seen his fingers—pale, long things that looked like the legs of albino spiders, nails too long and caked with what looked suspiciously like blood.

Pao looked away, revolted, but she heard a panel in the wall give way with an ominous groan. She turned to see El Cucuy step into a dark-glass chamber, his cloak swirling behind him like a shadow.

"Come," he said, snapping his fingers at her with a sound like a gunshot.

Pao wanted to duck, every cell in her body rebelling against the idea of standing that close to him and putting herself at the mercy of those terrible claws.

Dante is waiting, she thought. She wouldn't let him down. Not after everything she'd been through to get here.

So she stepped into the glass enclosure, which was barely big enough to hold the two of them, and swallowed the dread trying to claw its way through her skin as the stone closed in front of them.

El Cucuy snapped again, sending all the hair on Pao's arms standing, and without warning, the glass prism began a free fall toward the ground.

This time, Pao couldn't help it. She screamed. The descent went on and on, and for a moment, she was afraid he'd found her out, that he'd brought her into this glass cage to drop her to her death.

He was the lord of the void, Pao thought. He could probably just disappear into thin air. But she couldn't. And outside the ground was getting closer, reaching up to meet them, promising a swift and miserable end to one of the worst days Pao had ever had (okay, among the top five, anyway). Her screams continued, intensifying as the ground grew closer, and then stopped abruptly as somehow, miraculously, the glass cage continued to fall into the earth itself. Like the soil wasn't even there.

"I love that part," El Cucuy said, and Pao glanced at his face reflexively, forgetting the horrors she had found there before.

It was as if he was feeding on her fear. The strange, ever-changing images that crossed his features were clearer and sharper, and they lingered longer. Before she looked away, Pao thought she recognized, for a brief second, the wide, empty sky that had hung above the Gila in her earliest childhood nightmare.

At last, when Pao's ears had popped three times, when she

could feel the pressure around her increasing by the ton, the glass cage eased to a stop, and the wall slid open.

Pao found she couldn't move at first. The ride had turned her knees to jelly, and her terror hadn't loosened its viselike grip on her heart for a moment. She was weak with it. Desperate and hopeless at once. And now he had her underground, a million miles below the earth's surface. She doubted very much she could start the elevator on her own, so if he discovered her true identity down here, she was doomed.

"If I didn't know any better," he said, his voice low and dangerous, a swarm of wasps coming ever closer, "I'd say you aren't as eager to witness my accomplishment as I am to show it to you."

"Very eager, my lord," Pao said, forcing herself to move forward on legs that shook violently with every step. "What new horror will we be unleashing on the living?"

She had borrowed the language from Shadow Pao's memories, but the nausea they created in the pit of her stomach was all hers.

"Convincing," El Cucuy said, and though Pao didn't know how, considering the arrangement of his bizarre face, she thought he was smirking. "Just up this way."

They were in a cavern, the granite walls shot through with veins of obsidian. The tower itself seemed to be built on top of some kind of mine, but it was eerily empty, like the rest of this corner of the void.

Pao followed in El Cucuy's wake, trying not to think about the way his footsteps sounded like thunderclaps or the slithering of his cloak like so many hissing snakes. She tried instead to master her fear as they walked through the cavern toward a strange electric buzzing a ways off.

They came to another door, this one in a rock wall, with two more bone guards standing outside it. The skeletons didn't stir as El Cucuy pressed his hand against the shining stone and waited for the panels to slide apart.

"Obsidian," he said in a hiss. "Incredible magical connectivity, did you know that? Amplifies like a dream. In here, Falsita, watch your step."

Now, more than at any other moment in this nightmare, the terror reared up in Pao like a frightened horse, warning her with all its might not to enter this room.

But she had no choice. She had come alone, and she had to do this alone, so when he beckoned, she followed again, allowing the door she did not know how to open to close behind her.

The cave-like room was low ceilinged and claustrophobic, making Pao's already-shallow breaths come shorter and sharper. But it wasn't the room itself that made it something out of a sci-fi horror comic. It was the smoked glass prisms lining the walls—which went on for what seemed like miles. A long, narrow tunnel through the mine filled with them.

And inside each one, Pao realized as she stepped closer without permission, was a person in suspended animation.

"Tell me," El Cucuy said, beginning to stroll down the line. "What do you think of my new pets? Now don't feel left out— you'll always be my favorite. In fact, I modeled some of this batch after you. The old ones could barely hold a conversation, let alone open or close a door into the void."

"They're . . . more copies?" Pao asked, peering into the glass to see curly hair, or a stubborn chin, freckles scattered across the bridge of a nose. Suddenly, here in this cave, she could finally see Shadow Pao's origin clearly. Understand the sensation of being born from a tank like this one.

A tank that looked suspiciously like . . .

"I got the idea from a rogue fantasma who seized a little too much power," El Cucuy was saying now, as he continued to walk down the line. "Poor woman was half-mad when she created the technology. It was all destroyed, of course, when that little brat and her friends brought down the palace, but with the remnants of her inventions and what was left of the girl's next act of sabotage, I was able to create these."

La Llorona's prisms, designed to transfer the soul of a living person into a fantasma, to bring the dead back to life. Joaquin's tech, which was going to tear open the void. El Cucuy had somehow managed to salvage the worst parts of both from the scraps Pao had left behind.

"So many . . ." Pao breathed as she continued to take in the scene with mounting horror.

"And there will be more still by the time the veil thins enough to unleash them," El Cucuy said, his voice the proud snarl of a predator with its mouth coated in blood. "As one of my two earliest experiments, I thought you'd be pleased."

Pleased, Pao thought, dizzy with dread. "Some of these people are still alive in my world," she said carefully. "How did you manage to . . . copy them?"

El Cucuy waved his hand dismissively. "There are more ways to brush the void than death. All we need is an impression. There are those who have traveled inside, of course, like your own model. But near death will do it, as will a significant trauma. Even a bad dream will suffice."

Anyone, Pao thought. *He could do this to anyone.*

"And did . . . the boy have a part to play in this as well?" she asked, knowing she was pushing her luck, but feeling in her bones, in every nauseated rotation of her stomach, that she couldn't be Shadow Pao for much longer. She had to find Dante and get out of here as soon as possible if she was going to do it at all.

"The boy, yes. My first source of inspiration. Don't hold that against me, Falsita—it was just a matter of proximity. We don't often have live subjects waltzing into our lairs, after all." They had been walking what seemed like a mile through the shining tunnel, and still Pao couldn't see its end. "I can't keep him here with the other copies, of course—he's useless now. Mind utterly destroyed. But see what he's given us?"

El Cucuy stopped some ten paces ahead and gestured at a cluster of tanks. Pao was still reeling with the casual way he'd dismissed Dante. *Useless. Mind utterly destroyed.* It couldn't be true. It couldn't! Pao stopped, sweat dampening the neck of her shirt, causing her palms to go clammy and cold. She did not want to see what was in the tanks, but she also could not stop herself from tiptoeing forward.

Please, no, she thought again and again. *Don't let it be . . .*

But there he was. And not just one of him, but three, four, five . . . More than Pao could count. She wanted to laugh and sob and throw up all at once. To see him after all this time, to finally see him, but to know it wasn't truly him. Just some cheap copy made for some monster's sinister purpose . . .

"He should be honored to be involved in such important work," Pao said, hoping El Cucuy would interpret the trembling in her voice as awe instead of anger. But she was angry. And the angrier she got, the less afraid she was. "Maybe he should see. Maybe his mind isn't as far gone as you think."

"You doubt me," El Cucuy said, his voice skittering across the obsidian floor like tossed ice chips. "The boy is gone. Perhaps some lingering affection for him remains from your predecessor. We will have to eliminate that in the future models, of course. Once we've taken over, once the land of the living is entirely subsumed by the dead, there will be no limit to what we can achieve."

So that was it, Pao thought. Joaquin's plan again, but in much more capable hands. She should have known better than to think she had thwarted it for good. And El Cucuy wasn't just going to open the gate and see what happened—he had built an army of copies, an army of *shadows* ready to do his bidding.

"Perhaps I can bring him back to his senses," Pao pressed, every part of her tensed against the fear of retribution. "He cared for the girl, even loved her. Maybe believing she is here to rescue him will rouse him into usefulness."

When El Cucuy peered at her this time, Pao looked back, separating her need to survive from the rest of her, which was currently writhing and cringing with terror. The candle in the storm stayed lit, and she didn't turn away.

For a long minute, they stared at each other, as Pao watched in his face everyone she'd ever loved being killed off by the evil power of this place. *The Tower cleaved in two by lightning,* Pao remembered. If only she could show her mom how accurate her tarot reading had been . . .

And all the while, El Cucuy stared at her like he was x-raying her soul.

"An intriguing proposition," he said at last, like a police officer's car door shutting with a firm snap. "But I have a more immediate use for you, Falsita. It's why I brought you here. Did you think I was really just showing off? That you're important enough to be worth sharing my plans and accomplishments with? How quickly the ego grows when one walks among the living."

It was here when the real fear began to creep in. The fear she'd been feeling so far had felt like something foreign injected into her blood, like the time she'd taken a stimulant as part of her sleep doctor's plan to rid her of nightmares and her heart had raced for half a day.

If I'm scared now, Pao thought, the wheels turning, the variables shifting, *what was I before?*

"Anything my lord requires of me, I am at his disposal," Pao intoned as her thoughts continued to churn. "I'm only honored to have had the chance to serve you by thwarting the girl who shares my face, by closing the doors to—"

"Enough groveling." The images on his face were speeding up again, flickering impatiently from one to another so fast that Pao could almost tune them out. "Time grows short, and I need all the copies I can get before the veil is thinnest. Your work is done."

Pao's heart was pumping so hard she felt sure he'd be able to hear it banging against her ribs. She had to get out of here. But the door was closed and the elevator was inoperable without El Cucuy along for the ride. She was out of options.

El Cucuy had turned his back to her, and she didn't understand what he was going to do until she heard the hiss of a tank opening. "Think of how many more useful soldiers you will give me," he said.

"Can a copy be copied?" Pao asked, desperate to buy herself some time. "Won't it be risking the integrity of the new ones? Faults could multiply. . . ." She trailed off, terror choking her as he turned back to her. On his face she saw images of herself being forced into the prism screaming and kicking. Then her sleeping face through the warped glass. Unconscious as her DNA was copied to create more Shadow Paos who would have no one to save them.

"It's a risk I'm willing to take," he said, his voice sounding like chain saws through bone as he gestured to the open tank, so sure she would obey.

Pao didn't tell herself to run—the impulse was as much a part of her as her love for science and her hatred of cheese tamales. She was a survivor, through and through, and just as it had in La Llorona's lab, running would buy her a little time to think.

"What is this?" His voice was a serial killer's in the confession room, bored, amused.

Pao was halfway down the corridor, heading back to the door she couldn't open, guarded by skeletons she couldn't hope to defeat. She still hadn't heard his footsteps behind her, but it was only a few seconds before she understood why. All around her, the obsidian walls came alive with images. El Cucuy's face was projected on every surface, reflecting strangely off the tanks, a hundred close-up pictures of Pao's worst fears playing again and again as her heart threatened to beat out of her chest and her legs turned to jelly. She collapsed, the stone floor biting into her knees even as it, too, showed the nightmares.

I need to get to Dante, she thought in her terrified delirium. *I need to get us home.*

There was no way. Even the green lights flickering on the floor told her that. She was a prisoner here.

But the lights were growing into figures, and suddenly Pao understood. They weren't part of the nightmare. They were an invitation to depart, if she could just let go of her fear.

El Cucuy's images shifted again, showing Pao her own face from dreams long past—green-eyed and feral as she dragged Dante into the void. Her head on La Llorona's twisted wax body, claws stretching out in front of her, Emma falling to the floor, slashed and helpless.

If you use her gifts, you're just like her, said the worst part of Pao's mind, the part that had taunted and betrayed her all the way here. *If you step into that portal . . .*

But she had listened to that voice enough. El Cucuy hadn't followed her down the hallway because he didn't think he had to. He believed he could count on her fear to subdue her, to bring her back in line. But Pao had a candle in the storm, flickering, close to dying out, but still burning after all.

She pictured Dante, their best moments together, the times when she'd felt the closest to him: his hand snapping to hers like a staticky sock, his voice ringing out across the void as he battled monster after monster trying to get to her. Even his cruel words didn't deter her. Good was a choice you made, and Pao had chosen.

El Cucuy was shocked into inaction. He had to be, and Pao would take advantage of it. She had no other choice.

"Take me home," Pao said loudly, performatively, hoping to trick him one last time. But she held her true destination in her heart, and the glowing paper dolls, once a nightmare themselves, surrounded her, dancing and twirling in a way that felt welcoming this time. The green light swallowed the nightmares, both real and imagined, and Pao was whirling through space.

But not toward home. Not yet.

SEVENTEEN
Reconciliation

The first thing Pao noticed when she rolled out of the portal was that she was no longer underground. The air wasn't fresh and she was still in the tower, but at least the awful pressure of being so far down inside the earth was gone.

She straightened up as fast as her legs would allow, dazed and a little loopy from her first portal travel in almost a year. That's when she realized her awful, pervasive fear was gone, too. Her adrenaline was still pumping like she was being chased by the king of dread through a tower in the magical underworld, but the terror he had manufactured to make her feel hopeless and desperate was mercifully absent.

"Pao?"

Her heart, so recently her own again, leaped into her throat at the sound. The voice was weak and ravaged and barely recognizable, but when Pao turned, she saw him behind the bars of a cage. He was no longer the vessel for Joaquin's anger and spite, as he'd been the last time they were together, he was just . . .

Dante. The boy from upstairs. Her first best friend. Her family.

"It's me," she said, not caring if he saw the tears in her eyes. "It's me."

She stepped toward the cell, wanting to touch some part of him—an elbow, a pinkie finger—just to make sure he was real. But as she moved closer, he recoiled, his eyes distrustful, all the hope gone.

Suddenly her feelings crashed back in, memories of the hurtful words he'd spoken in the vineyard, and every time she'd lain awake wondering if he'd meant them. Was this proof? Did he really think she was a monster, even now?

"You're not Pao," he said scornfully. "You're just another copy. Don't think you can trick me." He slid down the wall until he was sitting on the ground, utterly defeated.

But Pao, by contrast, had never felt lighter.

"It's me, you idiot!" she said. "The *real* me, I swear! Look!" She held out her arms before realizing that of course Shadow Pao had looked exactly like her, so this wouldn't help. Dante didn't even dignify her performance with a response.

"Shoot," she said. "Duh. Um . . . Okay, ask me something. Ask me something only the real Pao would know."

Dante seemed to consider this, but for way longer than they had time for.

"Seriously, anything," Pao said. "But El Cucuy is coming, like, *soon*, so if you could think of a question faster than you usually come up with a Scrabble word, that would be really, really good."

Hope flared in Dante's eyes, and in a flash, he got to his feet again and crossed to the bars until they were face-to-face. "When was the first time you beat me at *Mario Kart*?" he asked, and Pao groaned aloud.

"Really? I thought it was gonna be something meaning-ful! After everything we've been through together, *that's* the question? I mean, fine, I'll never forget whupping your butt—it was after Thanksgiving dinner, your abuela had fallen asleep in her chair, and we were playing in your room. I was Princess Peach because her little voice annoyed you, and—"

"Pao?" Dante asked, cutting her off, his eyes filling with tears. "It's really you?"

"It's really me," she said. "Now let's get you out of here."

"You came back. . . ." He was showing signs of really committing to this crying thing, and Pao needed him to be at least mostly functional, so she reached through the bars and punched him on the arm.

"Of course I came back," she said. "Now let's go before he—"

But even as she said it, Pao could feel it returning. The terror gripping her heart. The low light in the room began to flicker, and Pao knew the truth before Dante said it in a harsh whisper.

"He's coming back. Pao, you have to run!"

"I'm not going anywhere without you!" she said fiercely, gripping his hand through the bars. "I'm gonna portal in there, and then we're gone. Just—"

A high, cold laugh filled the room, bouncing off the walls until it sounded like a hundred men laughing, not just one. Nightmares images began playing on the obsidian stone. Dante sobbing over Pao's dead body, his last hope of rescue gone. Dante falling from the top of the tower just like the image on her mom's tarot card . . .

Pao closed her eyes, ignoring the pictures, and the green figures rose and started to spin around her again. She hoped this was the last time she'd have to portal *into* a cell. . . .

But nothing happened. The bars were still solidly between Dante and herself.

No! Pao thought. *No, no, no, no!* She'd been so sure it would all be easy, that they'd be out of there in seconds.

"The cell's programmed," Dante said. "Only my DNA is allowed inside. Just go, Pao. Run. Save yourself."

The nightmares were creeping in around Pao's consciousness, overwhelming her again. She had to focus on what needed to happen. She couldn't let El Cucuy win, not when she'd been through so much to get to Dante. Not when they could both die if she didn't figure out how to do it.

"Do you trust me?" she asked Dante as the sound of thunderous storms—the kind that had caused flash floods during her childhood—pounded against the walls all around them.

"What?" Dante called.

"DO YOU TRUST ME?"

"YES!"

"Then close your eyes and stand still," Pao said, doing the same even though every nerve in her body was screaming at her not to let her guard down in here of all places.

Instead of thinking about El Cucuy and the fact that he could burst into this room at any moment, Pao focused on the portal itself. Its dimensions. Its energy.

She had spent so long abhorring these supernatural powers, worrying they would make her like her murderous grandmother. But now she honed in on the portal as a means of safety, of rescue. Portals had brought her mom and Emma to her in the woods. They had brought Señora Mata back in time to save toddler Dante. They had saved her father's life.

Now she needed this one to save Dante's.

So she fed her gratitude for this tool into the dancing green shapes around her, tried to love it for what it did instead of what it meant, who it connected her to. *Portaling is something you do,* Pao told herself, and she willed it to grow, to expand, to push past the bars with its incorporeal nature and wrap around Dante, too.

"Whoa, what's happening?" Dante asked, panicked, and Pao smiled through her weariness. It was working.

"Trust me," she said. "Please."

The nightmare images were blotted out by the green glow, and a humming sound drowned out the screaming, the skittering, the drowning. Pao could feel it when Dante was in the circle with her, as sure as if she'd been holding on to his arm, and that's when she knew it was time.

"Take us to Santuario," she said quietly, and then to Dante: "Hold on!"

The portal's buzzing and crackling reached a fever pitch as it worked to transport them even with the space between them created by the bars. The lights spun and still El Cucuy didn't appear, but his anger roared with the sound of an apartment building on fire, the screams of people trapped inside. His own screams went on and on, shredding every one of Pao's nerves until she was screaming, too, forgetting the portal, forgetting everything but her fear, and then . . .

And then, like a switch had been flipped, they stopped. *Everything* stopped. There was silence, and motion, but for the first time, Pao could appreciate that traveling by portal was something like being in a womb. All potential energy. Safe and whole and in between.

After that, her knees were hitting stone, and something

warm and solid had fallen into her lap, and before she was aware of what was happening, she was being hauled to her feet and crushed within an inch of her life.

"You came back," said Dante's hiccupping voice. "You saved me."

She hugged him too, for once not thinking about what their embrace meant, just squeezing until she was sure one of his ribs had cracked. "Sorry it took me so long," she said.

For a while, there was nothing in the world but the two of them, like when they were small. Two kids playing on a shag carpet in an apartment that smelled of arroz con pollo and fresh tortillas. For the first time in all these months, Pao felt like she had come home.

"I've had a lot of time to think," said Dante when they stepped apart. "And I need to apologize. I said some terrible things. . . ." His teary eyes searched hers for understanding.

"Yeah, you did," Pao said. She couldn't help wanting him to squirm a little, to know how much he'd hurt her. "But I know that wasn't you talking. Or at least *all* you."

He nodded vigorously. "Something, like, took over my brain, and I was so angry all the time, and this weird guy was showing up in my dreams telling me you were my enemy, and I just . . ." He trailed off.

Pao had wanted to hear this apology for a long time, and so she let herself enjoy it. She knew that eventually they'd have to drag it all out, and it could even get messy. But right now, in this moment, she was just glad he was alive and back with her.

"Believe me, I know," said Pao. "I'll explain it to you when we get home. You can meet my father, and—"

"Your father's back?" Dante asked with raised eyebrows. "That's great! Right?"

"There are pluses and minuses," Pao said, wincing slightly as she imagined how Beto would react to her latest escapade.

She was about to tell Dante more when a throat cleared behind her, echoing in the high-ceilinged stone room.

Pao turned to face Emma, Robin, and Kit, who were sitting in a row on one of the church pews looking thunderstruck (Emma), overwhelmed (Robin), and skeptical (Kit).

All Pao wanted in the world was to run up to Emma and tell her how relieved she was not to have died in El Cucuy's tower, how glad she was to be in the same room with her again. But the Pao who would have done that wasn't the same version Dante had left behind, and she felt stuck, not sure which version to be. . . .

It was like two (three?) parts of her life had collided, and she wasn't sure how to make all the pieces fit. But before she could make her tired, fear-ravaged brain come up with a solution, Emma was on her feet, flying across the church to grab both Pao and Dante in an awkward and teetering yet somehow perfect three-person hug.

Maybe it isn't possible for a hug to take you back in time, but in that moment, it sure felt like it did. For a brief second, Pao wasn't in some creepy church in a cornfield surrounded by killer birds hundreds of miles from home. She was on the sun-drenched bank of the Gila River, and monsters were just part of the embarrassing experience of living with her mother. Pao was obsessed with algae as a fuel source, she was hanging out with her two best friends, and they were all safe from everything except the prospect of cheese tamales for dinner.

"I missed you guys so much!" Emma said, sniffling suspiciously, and Dante pulled back a little, using the arm that wasn't hooked around Pao's shoulder to ruffle Emma's hair.

"You finally got taller," he said, and she choked back a laugh, or a sob.

"And you finally got a clue," Emma said.

It was this comment that made them slowly let go of one another, reclaim their own limbs, and morph from a six-armed nostalgia monster into three separate, awkwardly shuffling eighth graders standing in a church.

Kit cleared her throat, and Pao was forced to look up and acknowledge her.

"Hi, yeah, is anyone gonna explain the random boy I think was in my sixth-grade science class showing up looking—no offense—really haggard in the middle of this creepy church, or are we just gonna have to figure it out for ourselves?"

Pao rolled her eyes, but more affectionately this time. Maybe it had only been a few hours since she'd left this place, but melding with Shadow Pao, meeting the king of dread in the flesh, confronting all her worst fears, and stealing Dante back from the jaws of death had really given her some perspective.

"We'll have time to explain later," Emma said, and Pao saw that her face was giddy with relief, the way it looked when a really tough test was finally over—times a million. "Dante's back, so it's all over, right? All we have to do now is figure out how to get home . . . and . . ." She lost steam quickly, presumably at Pao's expression, or Dante's.

"Yeah . . ." Pao said, glancing at Dante guiltily. "About that . . ."

EIGHTEEN

How Many Grumpy Toddlers Does It Take to Portal Home?

"So, you're telling me this . . . Cuckoo Clock guy made the Poppy Copy, *and* a copy of you, and a *bunch* of copies of you, and he's about to unleash a ton of undead repeats on the world of the living, and . . . we're the only ones who know?"

"El *Cucuy*," Pao said wearily to Kit. "And yeah, that's basically the gist of it."

"I'm sorry, *who* are they?" Dante asked Pao for the second time as they stood in a circle arguing—or, as Emma put it, *having an informational discussion in which a lot of differing opinions are given space to breathe.*

"They're from the Rogues," Pao said wearily.

"Okay, but what are they doing *here*? And why are we telling them things?"

"I'm sorry, Crypt Keeper Junior, but *you're* the one that just appeared out of literally nowhere," Kit said, narrowing her heavily lined eyes at Dante. "We've been here since the beginning, okay? We helped fight off Poppy, and we literally *drove* these two here in a bus that crashed because of demon crows, so I don't think our legitimacy as, like, accomplices should be in question here."

"Since the beginning," Dante scoffed, looking at Pao as if to say, *Can you believe them?*

Kit actually hissed, baring her teeth like a cat, and Robin seemed to be shrinking.

Pao sighed, stepping between Dante and Kit before someone threw a punch, devoutly grateful for the moment that Dante didn't have his spectacular and devastating weapon on hand.

"Kit, Dante's been through a lot these past few months, so we're gonna cut him some slack. And, Dante, Kit and Robin are . . ." She steeled herself, barely believing she was going to say this about *Kit*, of all people. "They've actually been surprisingly helpful, and we're not really in a position to be turning down allies right now, so let's play nice, okay?"

Neither Dante nor Kit seemed to want to back down—in fact, they were still glaring at each other as if Pao hadn't spoken at all.

"Y'all?" Pao said. "I'm always up for a good feud, as you both know, but we do have a *bit* of a ticking clock on this thing, so maybe we can table it?"

"Speaking of which," Emma said, interjecting as it became clear Kit was going to retort. "My mom's been texting and calling." She held up her phone screen to show the unanswered messages. "She must have heard by now that some of us went missing from the trip. I want to tell her we're okay, but—"

"Don't!" said Pao. "And turn it off so she can't track us. The last thing we need is more people coming here and getting hurt."

"But how exactly are the five of us going to take on an army of the undead led by the most fearsome fantasma in history without anyone else getting hurt? Just out of curiosity . . ."

Pao laughed, a humorless, barking thing that made Kit and

Dante finally stop glaring at each other. "Listen, I know I've been slightly . . . allergic to enlisting help in the past—"

"Understatement!" Dante said, hiding the word poorly in a cough at the same time as Emma said, "You think?" with a smirk that made Pao's stomach flip even as she leveled her own best glare at them both.

"OKAY," she said. "I've been stubborn and idiotic, and it almost got us all killed! Happy?"

"Not-unless-you-say-we're-going-back-to-get-help-from-the-Niños-and-your-dad," Emma said all in one breath like she was trying to get it all out before she lost her nerve.

"We're going back to get help from the Niños and my dad," Pao said dutifully, feeling in her heart that it was the right decision. "If El Cucuy wants to go to war, we'll be ready for him. All of us."

"I'm in," said Kit, twirling the broken rake she still refused to part with. "I know I haven't been there *since the beginning*"—she pulled a face at Dante—"but any chance to do something cooler than math homework and I'm there."

"Thanks, Kit," Pao said, doing her best to smile in a way that wasn't half a grimace.

"You know I'm here for whatever happens," Emma said, her eyes never leaving Pao's. "And not just as the 'guy in the chair.' I want to make a safer world for y—for everyone," she finished, her cheeks turning the same pink as her windbreaker in a way that made Pao wish she knew what Emma had been about to say.

"I want to help, too," Dante said. "If you'll have me after everything I did. This was basically my fault to begin with, but if you let me stick with you, I promise not to be a—"

"A dumb jealous meathead?" Pao offered.

"A typical man refusing to let a woman have the spotlight?" Emma chimed in.

The old Dante probably would have snapped at them for ganging up on him, but now he smiled. "Yeah," he said. "All that."

"Happy to have you back," Pao said, clapping him on the shoulder and then pulling away quickly when he started reaching for her hand.

Everyone shuffled around awkwardly after this until Robin, who was sitting in the pew behind them, surprised absolutely everyone by standing up, a serious expression on her face, and saying, "I'm with you guys, too. Whatever happens. I know I've been a bit of a . . . well, a total chicken up to now, but my therapist is always saying I need to push the boundaries of my comfort zone, and what better way than this, right?"

"Robin," Pao said, strangely moved by this pledge of loyalty from a girl she'd been *sure* was heading for the nearest exit as soon as physically possible. "You were *not* a chicken! The way you drove that bus? None of us could have done that. I would have gotten us killed for sure."

"Me too," Emma said, her eyes wide.

"I definitely could have done"—Kit began, but changed tack swiftly when Emma elbowed her hard in the ribs—"SO much worse," she finished, wincing. "Like, exponentially worse."

"*That* I think everyone can agree on," Pao said, and somehow, they were all laughing. Despite their differences. Despite everything that lay ahead.

It's probably good we're laughing now, she thought grimly. Because once El Cucuy opened the void, no one would be laughing for a long time. Not unless they could find some way to stop him. And this time, Pao knew she couldn't do it alone.

"All right," Pao said, rubbing her hands. "We don't know exactly when the veil between us and El Cucuy's world will be thinnest, but we know he was counting on having Dante in a cell *and* the element of surprise, so we can bet he's not gonna dally now that he has neither."

"Not to mention that people on this side are bound to be looking for us by now, too," reminded Emma.

"Yeah, we're fugitives, right?" Kit said, her eyes flashing excitedly.

"The bus is too messed up to make it home," Robin said in a voice that was trying really hard to sound regretful but was definitely more relieved. "Otherwise you know I'd *totally* be down to drive again."

"Yeah," Pao said. "What I have in mind is . . . both faster and much weirder than a bus ride, so you all are gonna have to trust me a little."

Four pairs of eyes swiveled her way, most of them looking wary or skeptical.

"Okay, you're gonna have to trust me a lot?"

"You're going to try to make a portal again, aren't you?" Emma asked, and Pao knew she was thinking of the scene in her backyard when Pao had broken down crying.

"Unless anyone else has a plan to get us back to Silver Springs in, like, thirty seconds, that's probably our best bet, yeah."

"She can do it," Dante said.

Pao appreciated his confidence, even if she didn't totally share it. "Thanks," she said, her cheeks heating up. "But last time was . . . a life-or-death situation. I always work better with adrenaline. Doing it in this quiet room will be—"

"BOO!" Kit screamed suddenly, throwing her arms wide and making everyone jump.

"What the heck?" Pao yelled.

Kit shrugged. "You said adrenaline, right? I just figured I'd lend a hand." Her Cheshire cat grin said she'd had no intention of being helpful, and Pao barely fought the urge to tell her she could find her own way home.

"Right," Pao said through clenched teeth instead. "If no one else has any great ideas, I'm gonna try it. The closer together you can stand the better, probably. You'll see a circle of lights, and—"

"*Now?*" Robin asked, all the courage she'd mustered to join the fight suddenly gone.

"Unless you want to wait here for El Cucuy to rip open the void," Pao said, trying not to sound testy. "I have a bunch of vague half information and no idea how to stop him, so the sooner we get back to the Niños and my dad, the better." She took a deep breath. "Any other objections?"

No one spoke up, and Pao was relieved. She just wanted to be back in Silver Springs, with all of Franco's lab equipment, and Marisa's understated brilliance, and her dad's decades of theories and experience, and even Naomi's snark. Pao knew she'd been stupid to do this alone, and it was time to rectify that mistake as quickly as she could.

"Huddle up, okay?" Pao said, stepping forward. Emma joined her almost immediately, putting a hand on her arm and sending goose bumps chasing across her skin. Robin stepped in next, then Dante, putting his hand on Pao's other arm. Kit remained outside the circle, glaring at Dante.

"Oh, grow up," Emma said before Pao could intervene, stepping forward and pulling Kit bodily into the cluster.

"Okay, just . . . stay still, I guess," Pao said, feeling nervous all of a sudden, like she was about to give a report in front of the class. She knelt, forcing Dante and Emma to let go of her arms, touched her fingers to the floor, and closed her eyes.

I want to go home, she thought. *Take us—*

"So how does this work, anyway?" Kit asked loudly.

Pao groaned. "Well, it definitely *doesn't* work if you interrupt me while I'm trying to focus."

"Sorry!" Kit said. "I didn't realize we were in church!"

"We're *literally in a church*," Pao said.

"Oh, you know what I mean. It's an expression!" Kit said, throwing up her hands. One of them "accidentally" hit Dante's shoulder on the way down.

"Watch it," he snarled.

"Come on!" Pao said, her legs starting to go numb from crouching on the floor. "Do you want to get out of here or not?"

They fell silent, and Pao could practically feel Emma glaring all of them into submission. Pao closed her eyes again, feeling the stone beneath her fingertips, picturing home with all the detail she could muster, letting her need to get there well up from her heart and spread into her fingertips, into the floor. . . .

"HOLY HECK, WHAT *WAS* THAT?" asked Kit.

"Please, I really want to get home . . ." said Robin.

"Are you okay, Pao?" asked Emma.

"NO, SERIOUSLY, THERE WERE GREEN THINGS COMING OUT OF THE FLOOR!"

"WOULD YOU JUST SHUT UP?" Pao stood up and walked to the nearest window. She leaned against it, staring outside to where the sky had started to ease toward evening. Wind rippled through the cornstalks. The crows had left.

How are you supposed to save these people when you can't even make a portal with a mild distraction present? asked the hyper-critical voice in the back of her mind—the one that always seemed to be most active at times like these.

Kit is hardly a mild *distraction,* Pao retorted mentally, glancing over to where she and Dante were standing toe-to-toe, having an intense whispered argument that had Robin cowering again.

Emma was approaching on Pao's left. How she managed to look this pretty even after a bus accident, a demon crow attack, and almost a whole day of trying to keep Kit from doing something stupid, Pao had no idea.

"You okay?" she asked again, leaning against the wall next to Pao, looking out the window herself.

"I'm fine," Pao said. "It's just . . . a lot."

"Kit's not helping, either."

"Does she ever?"

"She was pretty handy with that rake, I guess?" Emma said with a stifled giggle. "But I think the cons outweigh the pros overall."

"Just . . . if I can't even make a stupid portal to get us home, how am I going to stop the literal lord of nightmares from taking over the entire world of the living?"

"One step at a time?" Emma said. "Sorry, I'm a little out of my depth in terms of pep talks here."

Pao laughed. "Nah, *one step at a time* was pretty good."

"Okay . . . how about *you're not in this alone*? Too cliché?"

"No, that helps, too," Pao said, letting herself meet Emma's eyes, where she found a calm she usually only felt when she looked at the stars. And then she had an idea. "Hey, you babysit sometimes, right?"

"Sure," Emma said, a little line appearing between her eyebrows. "Why?"

"What do you do when you have to get something done and a bunch of toddlers are making a mess of everything?"

"Well . . ." Emma said slowly, her eyes sliding out of focus like she was picturing it. "It usually helps to get them involved. Give them a little job to do that makes them feel like they're part of things. Like, if I have to fold laundry, I'll give them all the hand towels and let them try to fold, too. They're not *really* helping, but it keeps them busy while you do the real work. . . . But why exactly are we talking about babysitting?"

"Oh," said Pao, a plan already forming in her mind. "We're not."

"Okay," Pao said, back in the center of the circle on her knees while the others stood around her. "I figured out why it's not working. If we all want to travel, we *all* need to be focused on our destination, not just me."

Kit looked like she was going to interrupt, but Emma stomped on her toes just in time to prevent it.

"So," Pao went on, "I need you all to close your eyes and *silently* focus on the thing you're most looking forward to getting back to in Silver Springs, okay? A person, a place, an activity, doesn't matter what. Just focus hard."

"Mine is—" Kit began loudly, but Pao cut her off.

"In your head only! If you say it out loud, it's . . . less potent," she invented wildly. "Our memories are more powerful than the language we use to express them."

She glanced at Emma, who mouthed, *Good*, and gave her a thumbs-up.

Kit, miraculously, had her eyes—but, most important, her mouth—tightly closed.

"Great," Pao said, closing her own eyes, trying for a third time to feel the grit of the stone floor beneath her fingers. Of course, none of the people present could create a portal even if there were a million-dollar cash prize at stake, but the quiet made it possible for Pao to reach out. To imagine Silver Springs, her mom, Beto, the weird multicolored rug in their living room.

And maybe it was the feeling that everyone around her was concentrating, too, but this time it came easily. She could see the green light through her closed eyelids, feel the arms of the dancing dolls reaching up and the air brushing against her face as the figures began to spin around them.

Take us home, Pao thought, and then she had the familiar sensation of stepping forward and being embraced by the dark womb. It was working! They were finally going—

A high, cold laugh interrupted Pao's celebratory musing, chilling her to the bone. Around her, where there should have been nothing but darkness and pressure and movement, there was light. A bright white background on which too-familiar scenes were now being projected.

"You thought you could travel through my world after you stole from me, you entitled little brat?" The voice came from everywhere and nowhere, sounding like long fingernails scratching down a windowpane, the click of a cell door being locked, a shout from the end of a long tunnel echoing, echoing.

"Stay with me," Pao said to her friends, the people who had trusted her to take them home. She reached out in this strange nothing space to make sure they were still there. She touched arms and shoulders, but the white was so bright, she couldn't tell if he had taken anyone.

Suddenly, she saw Emma gone again. Dante back in his cell. The void tearing open along the seam, disgorging clone after clone, and the nightmare lord shepherding them all to the homes of her loved ones.

"Let us go!" Pao said, a sob catching in her throat. "Please, let us go."

The terrifying images shifted faster in response. Bruto dead, his sightless eyes staring up at her. The Riverside Palace in flames, her mom screaming from inside. Spiders coming out of the bathtub drain, crawling across her legs . . .

They're all counting on you, said the snarky voice inside her. *And you're too scared to take them home.*

"I'm not too scared," Pao said, though her body was shaking and her voice was weak and feeble. She had been foolish to cross into the void, to make this portal in the first place. She had underestimated El Cucuy's powers, and if she couldn't find a way to undo it, she was going to kill them all.

Take me home, Pao thought once more, closing her eyes against the nightmares, focusing on the beat of her own heart instead of the sounds of burning and screaming and crawling and dying. *Take me home.*

NINETEEN

You Know How They Say You Can't Go Home Again?

The next thing Pao knew, she was facedown on the bank of the Gila River. She rolled over to see the sun painting a brilliant display across the Arizona sky she would never get enough of.

Pao gulped in the air, reveling in the feeling of her body, solid and here. She had done it! She had broken free. And then, from her left, came a cough, a brushing of hands against jeans. She waited to move her head, hardly daring to hope. . . .

Now holding her breath, Pao turned to see Dante and Kit (the latter scowling furiously) untangling their limbs after having fallen on top of each other, and Robin standing over them looking awestruck at the landscape in a way Pao found deeply relatable.

But where was Emma?

"No," Pao said, struggling to get to her feet. She could feel the ground beneath her shoes and the sun on her face, hear Dante and Kit squabbling behind her and the river rushing by. This wasn't just another nightmare. "Emma!" Pao screamed at the top of her lungs.

This can't be happening, Pao thought. She couldn't have lost Emma just when she'd gotten Dante back. She couldn't face the end of this adventure—possibly the end of the world—with the same problem she'd had at the beginning. Emma, gone.

But it isn't the same problem anymore, Pao thought. Because her feelings for Emma had changed. She knew it as surely as she knew she was breathing. Losing her two years ago meant losing a best friend, a partner in comics and nail polish and silly jokes.

Losing her now? It was more. It was—

"PAO!"

With her heart in her throat, Pao ran toward the voice, not caring that she was tripping over rocks and being stabbed by cactus spines. "EMMA!"

When they met each other halfway, it was with the kind of fierce collision that leaves a mark inside and out. "I thought you were gone," Emma said breathlessly. "I thought . . ."

"I thought so, too," Pao said, grabbing a fistful of her sweater as if with that one gesture she could hold Emma on this earth forever. "But I would have cut everything in the entire void apart until I found you."

"I know," said Emma, pulling back, smiling, her cheeks pink from running. "You already did it once."

This time, instead of looking away, Pao held Emma's gaze. She wanted to memorize her face. Those few freckles across her nose, the way her irises were lighter in the middle and darkened as they reached the edges.

"Pao?" Emma said, a little hitch in her voice.

"Yeah?"

"There's something I should tell you."

"Okay." Pao's heart was beating so fast. Because of the running, sure, but not just that.

Emma took a deep breath. "I've been waiting to say it for a while," she said, clearly stalling.

"Okay . . ." Pao said.

"Okay, here goes. Pao, I—"

"Dang, Lockwood! Don't scare us like that!" Dante's voice came booming across the desert, and he wasn't alone.

The spell was broken. Emma pulled away from Pao as Dante and the other two girls barreled into the moment, bringing the real world with them like El Cucuy's trailing cloak. "Yeah," Emma said with a nervous chuckle. "I let go too early, I guess. Don't worry, I'm aware of the one-friend-lost-in-the-void-per-adventure rule. Not planning on breaking it."

Dante laughed, but Kit was looking suspiciously between Pao and Emma, like she could see an invisible thread connecting them, and she didn't like it.

Pao was still dizzy from the portal travel, the cold brush of El Cucuy's presence as they'd passed it, and the terrifying thought of having lost Emma again. On top of all that, a restless feeling was bubbling up inside her, telling her she was both desperate and not at all ready to hear what Emma had been about to say.

"So, I think we're about a mile out of town," Dante said in his hero-boy voice, which grated a little on Pao's already-jangling nerves. "We should get a move on to the haunted cactus field, check in with the Niños."

"The Niños haven't lived there for a year," Pao said irritably. Shouldn't he have known that? Pao and Dante had spent a rather memorable night together in the Niños's deserted camp last winter after all. "They're in a warehouse now, south of town. It'll take longer to get there than home, so I think it would be better to check in with my dad first."

Again there was the flash in Dante's eyes that Pao assumed meant he resented her authority. But it was gone as soon as she noticed it, and he was smiling again, his hair—longer now, after his months-long stint in El Cucuy's prison cell—flopping into his eyes like old times.

"To the Riverside Palace it is!" he said, taking a large step west, away from the river, before he caught himself and stopped. "Lead the way, Captain."

"Thanks," Pao said, trying not to stare at him too long. It wasn't that she minded this exuberant, friendly Dante, it was just that she'd expected him to be more . . . messed up, after nearly a year in a terror palace being tortured and copied into oblivion.

Hadn't El Cucuy said his mind was destroyed?

She shook herself. When she was questioning even the *good* things, she knew it was time to take a break from her spooky thoughts.

Plus, they had a bit of a walk ahead of them. She'd hoped the portal would drop her right into her living room, but she'd panicked when she'd heard El Cucuy's voice and seen the swirling nightmare images. She must have pulled out too soon.

Pao wanted to ask the others if they'd seen him, too, but based on their excited chatter and obvious relief to be home, she had to assume the answer was no.

"So, um," Robin said, jogging to catch up to Pao, "is the war starting . . . right away? Or would it be okay if, after we see your dad, I go home and see mine? Just to tell them I'm okay?"

Pao considered this for a long moment, the sun setting behind them as they walked toward the outskirts of town. Robin, no doubt, lived in one of the big houses in Emma's neighborhood.

Pao didn't think these dads would be super thrilled to find out that Pao had involved their precious daughter in stealing and illegally driving a charter bus, leaving her fellow Rogues stranded, then almost getting killed by a murder of mutant crows, traveling through space/time in a very untested and definitely dangerous way, and agreeing to fight in a war against the lord of nightmares and a bunch of his lab-engineered shadow soldiers.

But what was she going to do? Pao asked herself. Refuse to let Robin go home? Forbid her from telling her parents what was happening? They'd find out soon enough, when the void was ripped open and people started getting murdered by clones. Maybe the days of keeping the worlds separate were over.

"Yes, you can go home after," Pao said wearily. "Tell your dads whatever you want to tell them."

Robin beamed.

"But, Robin?" Pao asked as the older girl continued with a new spring in her step.

"Yeah?"

"If they don't believe you . . ."

"I'll be back anyway," Robin promised, and Pao could tell by the look on her face that she meant it. "Even if I have to steal the Prius."

Pao smiled. "Thank you."

"Thar she blows!" Dante called, pointing to where the Riverside Palace had just become visible over the low hill. "I can't wait to see my abuela. Even a lecture sounds pretty good right about now. . . ."

Emma looked sharply at Pao, whose stomach was slowly sinking down into her left sneaker. Of course Dante didn't know that Señora Mata had lost her memory entirely. That she'd been living in a nursing home for months. It suddenly seemed so stupid and so villainous of Pao not to have warned him about this that she didn't even know what to say.

This was going to be the last straw, Pao thought. The thing that finally revealed the depth of his mental and emotional scarring. The thing that broke the Happy Dante facade for good.

She already missed it.

"Dante, I—" she began, before words failed her. He would be no better than an orphan, Pao thought. With Señora Mata unable to care for him, he'd end up in foster care. He'd . . .

"What is it?" he asked. "Pao, what's going on?"

"Dante," she said again, stepping toward him even though her body was remembering the way he'd once swung at her with his club in a blind rage. "Your abuela . . . You remember how her memory was failing? Well . . ."

"She's dead, isn't she?" he said, all the goofy relief gone in an instant, his eyes urgent and serious.

"She's not!" Pao said quickly. "She's just . . . She was having trouble on her own. She had a bad fall, so we had to find her an assisted-living home. My mom helped. It's a really nice place, and we visit her all the time!" She was rambling now, delaying the moment when she'd have to hear him say it was all Pao's fault, that if it wasn't for her, none of this would have happened. "She doesn't always remember us, but she's having a great time, beating all the other old ladies at poker and—" Abruptly, she ran out of energy to pretend this was anything more than a tragedy. "I'm sorry. Dante, I'm so sorry."

For a long time, he said nothing. The whole desert seemed to be holding its breath. Then he walked purposefully toward

Pao, and for a brief, wild moment she thought he might attack her again. Instead, he hugged her. A bone-cracking embrace only a few seconds long. Just enough time for her to become thoroughly confused.

"Thank you for getting her the help she needed when I couldn't," he said. "I'm just so glad she's alive."

"But—" Pao began

Dante held out a hand to stop her. "Let's get through the war first—we can work out the rest after. I assume it'll be okay if I crash on your couch until it's over?"

"Of course," Pao said, still feeling like she'd been hit with a frying pan and had little birds twittering over her head. "Of course."

"Cool," Dante said, rubbing his palms together. "Let's get going, then, or we'll be finding crash pads for a lot more orphans than just me."

This cavalier approach chilled Pao even more than anger would have, but Dante was already making his way over the rise, and she thought she'd better be there when he knocked on the door of her apartment, so she hurried to catch up, with Emma, Robin, and Kit on her heels.

Riverside Palace always looked strange to Pao when she returned to it from somewhere else. Maybe it was the fact that it was eternally weird. The dusty-pink-and-green exterior, the massive sprawling cactus in the parking lot, the apartment with the roof caved in that no one had ever bothered to repair.

"People actually *live* here?" Kit asked, her jaw dropping as they made their way into the parking lot. "I thought it was like . . . a cautionary tale."

"Nice," said Emma. "Real nice, Kit."

"It's not much," said Pao, thinking of every old cheesy movie in which someone had said exactly this. "But it's home." There was a reason for cliches, after all.

"I'd come in," Kit said as Pao began to approach apartment C. "But I don't think I've had my latest tetanus booster."

"Fine by me," Pao said coolly. "There's zombie roof rats in the dumpsters. Tell them I say hi."

Somehow, when Pao made it to her front door, Kit was closest behind her.

Pao took a deep breath before opening it, turning around to face the rest of them before she did. "It's probably best if you just . . . let me do the talking," she said. "My parents are kind of unique, and—"

But, of course, the door flew open before she could finish, her mom standing there with her flyaway hair pinned up halfway with a pencil, and Beto behind her with his phone to his ear, his mouth hanging open.

With a bark that was all bass, Bruto came barreling into the mix next, not seeming to care who he knocked over on his way to leap onto Pao and start licking every inch of skin he could reach.

"It's okay, buddy," Pao said, smiling so wide it hurt her face. "I'm here, I'm here."

"I'll need to call you back," Beto said, dropping the phone as both sets of her parents' eyes flew almost comically from Pao to Dante, back to Pao, and then to Dante again.

"Hey, Mom and Dad," Pao said sheepishly, Bruto now pressing against her shins so hard she was teetering over. "Look who I found. Surprise?"

TWENTY

Being Left Out Is Even Worse Than Being Grounded

The hugging came first, an avalanche of it. Pao's mom hugged her with tears in her eyes, then moved on to Dante—who was very nearly as tall as her now—then back to Pao, then to Emma, and then to Dante again for good measure. Bruto stayed right in the thick of everything, nearly tripping everyone who moved.

Wordlessly, Maria ushered the group into the living room and managed to find places for all of them to sit. When she'd finally recovered the use of her voice, she said, "Mrs. Lockwood called us first thing this morning. She told us you went on a volunteer trip with Emma?" Here she glared at Pao. "Why didn't you tell me . . . us?"

"Yeah, about that, Mom—"

"And then the charter bus was *stolen*? At some ranch in *Texas*?" With each line, Maria's eyes bulged a little more.

Pao nodded and opened her mouth to explain, but her mom didn't give her a chance.

"When four kids were discovered missing, we thought you'd been . . ."

"We *thought*," said her father, speaking up for the first time, "that you'd been abducted. We . . . Everyone was crazy with worry." He gestured to Dante. "But now I see that you were up to something, Paola. Doing exactly what I told you not to do."

"But I succeeded, so we're good now, right?" Pao asked hopefully.

Everyone fell silent. Pao could tell her father was trying to gauge how much of their unusual world he could divulge in front of Robin and Kit, and that he was both horrified and passionately curious about how she'd managed to retrieve Dante.

For a minute, Pao was sorely tempted to pretend that Kit and Robin were still clueless just to avoid the lecture her dad was clearly brewing up. But, of course, Kit—who'd been silent since the mention of the zombie roof rats—could never let anything be easy.

"No need to hold back the supernatural talk on our account," she said, lounging in Pao's mom's favorite chair, looking like she'd just gotten out of a movie instead of a portal through the void. "Robin and I are old hands at this now, see?" She brandished the rusted rake head like it somehow proved something besides her own unhinged nature. But Pao's father just turned to Dante.

"There's no doubt we're all glad you're back among us, hijo." Then he said to Pao's mom, "We need to get these children home. Now. After that, Pao and I can have a long talk about respecting rules, and I'll determine the appropriate punishment."

"Wow, someone forgot to tell this guy the patriarchy's over," Kit said under her breath. Everyone ignored her.

"Actually . . ." Pao said, finding herself less relieved to be home than she'd imagined, and pretty ticked off at the way her dad was behaving in front of her friends. "These *children* have just been through a bit of an ordeal, and I told them you'd have some answers for them, so before we go *sending* them anywhere, maybe you'd like to hear what we have to say."

Maria stepped between Pao and Beto. "I'm sure your friends would like to get home to their families and—"

"It's El Cucuy," Pao blurted out. Part of her wanted to shock her parents a little, if only to make them listen. "He's in the void, in some terrible tower—just like the tarot card you showed me, Mom. He was keeping Dante prisoner there."

Maria gasped.

Dante nodded, sitting on the edge of his seat. "For months."

"El Cucuy is there as we speak," Pao went on, "making copies of every human he's been able to get close to in the last thousand years or so."

"What do you mean, 'copies'?" Beto asked, his scientist's curiosity kicking in.

"Like clones. Well, more like shadows."

"What was he going to do with them?" her dad asked.

"Not *was*—*is*. When the 'veil is thinnest'"—Pao made air quotes with her fingers—"he's going to tear open the void, just like Joaquin was planning to, and sic his army of shadow soldiers on the living."

The silence was absolute save Bruto's indignant huff. It was probably an awkward moment for some of the non-Santiagos in residence, but Pao didn't drop her father's gaze to find out.

"My friends helped me," she persisted when he didn't immediately proceed with his assumed plan to ground her for the rest of her life. "They helped me fight off a twisted chaperone—one of El Cucuy's copies—and get through the liminal space in Santuario, and they stood guard while I battled the shadow version of *myself* and went into the void to rescue Dante. *They* helped me get back home. While you and Franco and everyone else were just sitting in your precious lab wondering why your machines weren't working right, me and a bunch of *kids* got the job done. Just like I said we could. So I'd like it if you treated *us* with a little respect."

Beto's eyes had widened when Pao mentioned the battle with her shadow self, and they'd continued to widen through-out the rest of her monologue until she could see the white all the way around his irises. Now he gazed around at the rest of them—Dante, who was sitting at Pao's right; Emma on her left; and Kit and Robin, who were sharing an armchair and looking a little taken aback. It was like he hadn't noticed them before.

Pao had to admit she'd felt pretty much the same way when she'd first met Robin and Kit, so she tried not to judge her father too harshly. But when it had been a whole minute with no reply, Pao began to bristle again.

"Well?" she asked, taking a step toward her father, who was now looking a little ashen. "Don't you have anything to say?"

"Paola . . ." her mom chastised. She was looking at Beto, too, concern painted in every line of her expression.

Whether it was the worry on Maria's face, or some internal mechanism clicking into place in his own mind, he focused on Pao at last.

"The copies," he said. "You're sure?"

"I saw them with my own eyes," Pao replied, trying not to lose heart at the haggard, gaunt look on his face. Was this about the war to come? El Cucuy's plan? Or was he just remembering his mom's horrific experiments?

"You still have your Arma del Alma?" Beto asked in what Pao considered to be an odd change of subject.

"Yeah, of course," Pao said, nonplussed, already reaching for it in her pocket. But her father held out a hand to stop her.

"Good." He patted his own pockets and looked around the room distractedly, like he'd lost something. "Good. And you were all there, too, you say?" Beto asked, looking around again at Pao's friends. "In Santuario? In the church?"

Emma, Robin, and Kit nodded. Dante stayed quiet. Everyone knew where *he* had been.

"Then we need to get all of you to the Niños' headquarters immediately."

"Wait," Pao said. "Aren't you gonna tell us what this means? *What we're going to do, maybe?*"

"Yes, yes," Beto said, pacing around the room, sticking seemingly random objects in his pockets. "We'll talk at the warehouse. Let me just find my things. . . ."

He was in another world now, and Pao knew there was no use talking to him. He didn't have a lot of practice being a dad, or the leader of a war effort, but he did well enough at acting normal that sometimes Pao forgot he'd lived alone in a tin can in the woods for a decade, his only company the sinister interloper who was stealing his memories.

Instinctively, Pao looked at her mom for an explanation, but she was shadowing Beto, asking him questions in hushed Spanish that Pao couldn't understand.

"Is he . . . okay?" Emma asked. It was the first thing she'd said since they walked through the door, and when Pao turned to face her, she saw that Emma was scared. Like, more scared than she'd been during the fight against Poppy, or the episode with the murder of murderous birds, or even the portal travel.

"He'll be fine once he solves his mental jigsaw puzzle. I think," Pao said. "How are *you*?" Pao was suddenly super aware of the fact that Emma had wanted to tell her something important, and that she'd almost done it, and it hung between them now like something tangible in the air.

"I'm okay," she said in a small voice. "I'm worried about my parents . . . what they'll think about all this. Whether they'll be safe."

"When we get to the warehouse, we'll make a plan," Pao said, trying her best to be reassuring. "We'll keep them safe, okay? Everyone in Silver Springs." It sounded good, she thought, as promises went. Even if she had absolutely no idea how she was going to keep it.

"Thanks, Pao," Emma said, her face visibly relaxing. Like she believed Pao could keep an entire town safe when she'd barely gotten the five of them back here in one piece.

"Is everyone ready?" Beto asked, rushing into the living room with his hair a mess and a leather bag slung across his shoulder. Who knew what it contained.

"Um . . ." came Robin's timid voice from behind them. She was still sitting in the armchair, Kit beside her. "Mr. Santiago? Pao said it would be okay if I went home . . . to see my dads? I definitely want to help with the war and everything, but I should just check in . . . first. . . ." She trailed off when she saw that Beto was already shaking his head.

"If the lord of nightmares has decided to open the void, there are precautions we must take before anyone can leave this group," he said, somehow both vague and authoritative at once. "We'll rendezvous at the warehouse first; then we'll make arrangements for contacting your families."

He had barely looked at her, and Pao could see Robin's lower lip start to tremble. "O-okay," she said. "It's just . . . Pao said . . ."

"I'm afraid Paola was not in any position to be granting requests," Beto said, casting a severe look at his daughter. "We are at war, Roberta, and we must take every precaution."

"It's *Robin*," Pao said fiercely. She was really starting to regret coming home first, letting her stupid, childish belief that her parents would have all the answers get in the way of what she owed to the people who'd decided to follow her.

"It's okay," Robin said, shrinking back into the chair again, tears welling in her eyes. "I'll just call them. They'll understand."

"No contact," Beto said brusquely. "Not yet, anyway. Now let's get going. I've already sent word to Franco—they're expecting us."

Pao looked at her mom again, but whatever her father had said to her in Spanish seemed to have done the trick. She was going along with his plan, even though her eyes were wide and fearful. "I'll be here, mijita," she said softly. "But for now, I think it's best to do as your father asks."

All Pao could do was shrug helplessly as they were all shunted back out into the October evening, their heads spinning, somehow more confused and less reassured than they'd been when they were entirely on their own.

TWENTY-ONE

"Why Don't You Let the Adults Handle This?" (Remix; Feat. Runaway Robin)

They made their way across town in Beto's old Volkswagen Beetle like it was a clown car—Pao's father driving, Dante in the front seat, and Emma, Kit, Robin, and Pao in the back with Bruto wedged under their feet (Pao had flat-out refused to leave him behind), trying not to feel awkward as laps were occupied and limbs overlapped and shoulders were squished together.

Pao attempted to focus on the impending doom ahead and not the fact that Kit, as the smallest person present, had ended up on Emma's lap. *Emma said it wasn't like that,* Pao reminded herself. And then: *Why would you even care?*

The warehouse parking lot was empty in the dusk, and they climbed out in a rush after being forced into such close quarters for twenty minutes. None of them had spoken the entire time. Impending doom had a way of shutting people up.

Beto made to hurry inside the building the moment they were all free of the tiny car's confines, never looking at Pao or any of them, just barking, "Follow me," over his shoulder and trusting that they would.

He just wants to get to Franco, the real *expert,* Pao thought bitterly as she watched him walk away. She didn't know why she'd expected anything different. Franco, who'd been sitting in his stuffy little office going over figures and staring at computer screens. Franco, who'd been planning for *months* and doing absolutely nothing while Pao had singlehandedly (okay, almost singlehandedly) traveled halfway across the country, entered the void, tricked El Cucuy into giving up Dante, and *discovered a plot for world domination.*

But of course, Franco would be the first one to hear whatever theories her father had come up with about Pao's information. Of course.

"Come on," Pao said irritably, scratching Bruto's ears to keep her temper under control. "Let's get in there. I at least want to hear what they're telling each other, even if they won't tell it to me."

"Pao?" Robin's eyes were red, a telltale sniffle betraying her tears. "I really just want to go home. Just to make sure my dads are okay, to tell them I'm alive. Can you convince him? Please? I promise I'll be back to help."

Whether it was Pao's desire to keep the promise she'd made to Robin, or her even greater desire to rebel in this small way against her father, Pao spoke in a low, quick voice. "There's a bus stop on this street, in front of the 7-Eleven," she said. "Go. I'll cover for you."

Robin's face sagged with relief, her eyes filling with tears again. Unexpectedly, she stepped forward and hugged Pao briefly, and Pao surprised herself by returning the embrace. "Come back, okay? We need you." She turned to Kit next. "You can go, too, if you want," she said. "Check in with your parents. He can't keep you here."

Kit rolled her eyes with a little less gusto than normal. "They probably haven't even noticed I'm gone. And anyway, I'm not missing the good part, so let's just get on with it."

Robin hugged Kit and Emma good-bye, gave Dante a sort of weird half handshake, half high five, and darted off toward the bus stop. Pao watched her father carefully until he reached the warehouse door. He didn't turn around until Robin was already out of sight, and Pao exhaled in relief as he called, "Come on, come on, there's no time to waste," without even seeming to realize that one of the five children he'd transported here had just vanished into thin air.

"We better go in," she said, ushering the others forward, Bruto trotting obediently at her heels. There was a heavy, gloomy feeling around the group that hadn't been present in the church, or even amid the dive-bombing crows. They weren't in control anymore—they were just along for the ride. And from the look on Beto's face, it was going to be quite a ride.

"You kids need to go into the training room and wait," he said when they were all congregated, still not noticing Robin's absence. "I'll consult with Franco and meet you all there to . . . go over the plan. We'll send someone to sit with you in the meantime."

"Are you talking about a *babysitter*?" Pao said, her voice shooting up at least an octave on the last word. "You can't be serious. Whatever you have to say to Franco, I want to hear it. I've just been to the void and *faced* El Cucuy. I got Dante back! You can't shut me out!"

"Mi amor," Beto said, meeting her eyes for the first time since she'd told him about the El Cucuy's master plan. "It's not a matter of shutting you out. It's a matter of keeping you safe until we have all the information."

"I'm the one *with* the information!" Pao shrieked, truly at her wit's end. "Don't you want to hear what I know? What I *saw*?"

"Yes, yes," Beto said patronizingly. "In due time."

"In due time," Pao muttered. And then: "Fine, have it your way. Come on, Bruto." She banged through the flimsy door and stalked through the office without a word to Franco, who was, as predicted, sitting in front of his dumb computer screen looking like he'd done nothing but stare at it since she left.

She kept going through the bunk room, where the Niños' hammocks hung at various heights, and into the garage section, where Pao had recently beheaded poor Patrick. How had that only been days ago? It felt like a year.

The color-coded tape was there on the floor, lines her father had laid out to *encourage proper fighting form* in the undisciplined newest Niños learning the ropes, but Pao was now beginning to suspect were actually for her benefit alone. Something to keep her busy, since she clearly couldn't be trusted with anything real.

Nothing had changed, Pao realized. Even after she'd gone to hell and back, he was still treating her like a little kid who'd gotten in trouble.

"AAAAAARRRGGGHHH!" Pao screamed out of sheer frustration, causing Bruto to flee to the other side of the room and curl up in fright, his eyes never leaving her. Emma jumped a little, but Kit somehow looked impressed. Dante was standing a little apart from them, his gaze trailing back to where Pao knew her father was now confiding in Franco.

She expected them to ask her what the heck she was doing.

Instead, before she knew it, Kit was screaming, too. And then Emma joined in. Pao screamed again, and she couldn't deny it made her feel better.

"Cacophony as catharsis," Kit said, a little hoarsely when she had finished her high-pitched, batlike shriek. "Didn't think you had it in you."

This time, Pao noticed, she didn't say *Straight Girl*.

"You show up," called a voice from across the garage, "you take our jobs, you scream at the top of your lungs while we're napping. Remind me why we let you in here again?" Naomi was crossing the practice space with a sly—if somewhat sleepy—grin on her face, and it was all Pao could do not to sprint over there and hug her in relief.

Bruto, however, had none of the same reservations. He bowled into Naomi with the power of an Olympic gymnast's vault.

"Does this make you our babysitter?" Pao asked when she got closer.

"Hung up my babysitting hat when this tourist I rescued from a chupe in the wasteland went and got herself promoted to actual fantasma killer," she said, scratching Bruto's ears. "Good to see you, by the way. Hey, non–hero boy, looks like you were finally sprung. Anyone care to fill me in?"

"We just got back . . ." Pao started, not waiting for Dante to say hello. He and Naomi had never been on the best of terms, and this was urgent.

Naomi's sardonic smile faded quickly as Pao told her the saga of her trip to Santuario, the battle with Shadow Pao, and El Cucuy's promise to tear the void wide open.

"My dad said he contacted Franco before we came over," Pao said. "He won't let any of us leave because he 'doesn't have all the information yet.' I just assumed Franco would have told you all what was going on. Or at least you and Marisa . . ."

"He didn't tell us anything," Naomi said, storm clouds gathering in her expression. "Well, not me, anyway, and as far as I know, Marisa's not even here. Franco said there was a call about a fantasma in a barn about twenty miles from here, and she went—"

"When was the call?" Pao asked, starting to get a suspicion she devoutly hoped was wrong.

"About a half an hour ago. She asked me to come with her, but I decided to chill here. Wait, why?"

"Because that was exactly when my dad supposedly let Franco know we were coming," Pao said. "Does Franco know you didn't go with Marisa?"

"I don't think so. . . ."

"He was trying to get rid of you both," Pao said. "Get you out of the way so he could scheme with my dad without any leadership scuffles, I'll bet you anything."

"The timing *is* pretty sus," Naomi agreed. "But what could they be talking about that they wouldn't want us to hear?"

"I don't know," Pao said grimly. "But if they want to keep it from all of us, it can't be anything good."

"What do we do?" Naomi asked as Kit and Emma watched their conversation like a tennis match. Dante continued to edge toward the door, where Franco and Beto had closed the blinds.

"I have an idea," Pao said, the pieces coming together slowly. "How many of the other Niños are here now?"

"Almost everyone, I think," Naomi said. "They're all back in the courtyard eating pozole right now."

As good as pozole sounded at the moment, Pao knew they didn't have much time. "Let's go there now," she said. "If we tell the other Niños what we know, my father and Franco won't be able to keep us all in the dark."

"It's worth a shot," Naomi said with a shrug. "Although I was kind of hoping the plan involved punching Franco's stupid face."

"Later, if I have anything to say about it," Pao replied, picturing it with perhaps unnecessary enthusiasm.

Pao told her friends what they were up to, and Dante volunteered to stay behind in case Beto or Franco came out asking questions. Pao decided to leave Bruto with him, because the chupe often lost his mind around pork.

Whether Beto had forgotten to send someone to "mind them," or they'd just gotten lucky, no one stopped Pao, Naomi, Emma, and Kit as they made their way to the courtyard.

There were twenty or so Niños in the courtyard, little kids (who appeared no older than eight or nine) all the way up to the older teenagers, who shepherded the younger ones around, making sure they had enough to eat and their scuffles didn't turn too brutal.

Sal waved with enthusiasm from a nearby bench, his cheeks bulging with soup. Pao waved back, feeling another spike of fear when she imagined him fighting El Cucuy's monsters alongside them.

Some of the younger Niños were really decades older than they looked, but others—like Sal, who had rescued Pao on her first paranormal excursion, thereby earning a special place in her heart—were still just kids.

She had to save them. She couldn't trust anyone else to do it for her.

Pao remembered the way she'd felt during the few days she'd spent in the Niños' camp last year. When she'd been a cog in this machine, keeping herself and others safe, deferring to leaders when necessary but considered a valuable part of things herself—even when she'd only been a tourist.

"You miss it?" Naomi asked, stepping up beside her and correctly interpreting her expression.

"All the time," Pao said. "More lately, since my dad seems determined to box me out of every decision."

"I learned this lesson the hard way, and he will, too," Naomi said. "Paola Santiago doesn't stay where you put her. Even if you try to tie her there." She smirked, and Pao returned it, remembering the night Marisa and Naomi had literally bound her to a cot to keep her from going off to the void on her own.

Pao held out her hand to Naomi, who boosted her up onto a plastic picnic table. Then Naomi went to stand with Emma and Kit, who looked at the older girl—with her undercut curls bright white in the twilight, and her black patched uniform—like she was the most awesome thing she'd ever seen.

"Hey, Niños!" Pao called from the tabletop. A few kids looked up—the rest were so used to shouting by now that they tuned it out.

"Oi! Shrimps!" Naomi called through cupped hands, and everyone snapped immediately to attention. She hopped up onto the table herself with an alarming crash and looked out on the now-attentive crowd. "Our favorite honorary Niña de la Luz has something to say to you all, and I suggest you listen, hmm?"

A few of the smaller kids nodded, but most just waited. Now that Pao had the spotlight, she found her throat was dry, her hands a little sweaty. But then Emma caught her eye from the ground and gave her a thumbs-up, and Pao smiled, forgetting her nerves.

"Niños," Pao said, her voice clear and ringing, "I've just returned from the void, and I have news for you from El Cucuy, the lord of nightmares."

If anything was going to get the attention of a bunch of fantasma hunters, this was it. Everyone was looking now, whether they were staring at Pao in rapt attention or checking Naomi's face for proof that it wasn't a hoax. Within seconds, her grim expression had done the trick.

"I went into the void to rescue my friend," Pao said once the mess yard was silent. "I thought it'd be an easy in and out— I've been into the void before—but what I saw there was even worse than a kid in a cage." She paused for effect, and it worked. The Niños were hanging on her every word. "El Cucuy is inside the void right now, creating an army, and when the veil thins enough to be torn open, he's going to unleash it on us all."

There was a wave of shocked muttering, and a voice could be heard above the din. "Someone's gotta tell Franco and Marisa!"

Pao looked at Naomi for something. Permission? Reassurance? Whatever it was, she got it in the form of a nod and turned back to the Niños. "Franco knows," Pao said, not bothering to stop herself from scowling. "My father told him almost an hour ago, and they're in the office right now, holed up and plotting without us. He sent Marisa on a pointless errand to get her out of the way, and we don't know why. But what we do know is it isn't right to keep this from you guys. You're the Niños de la Luz. If you all can't stop this, who can?"

Once again, her words had the desired effect. Some of the Niños were getting to their feet, expressions of righteous anger painted across their features. They were proud, they were angry at being left out, and Pao wasn't alone with either of those feelings anymore.

"What are we gonna do?" one of them called to Pao, and she felt a thrill at being deferred to . . . before she realized she didn't know what to tell them.

Doing everything alone is how you got yourself into this mess in the first place, she reminded herself. *There's nothing wrong with asking for help.*

"That's where you come in," Pao said. "I found the void entrance, fought a shadow version of myself, and made it into El Cucuy's lair. I tricked him into telling me his plot. But now I . . . *we* need a plan that will keep Silver Springs and everyone in it safe. A plan that will send El Cucuy and his shadow army back to the void for good."

She waited for them to call her a fraud. To ask why she was even here if she couldn't save them. But instead they looked excited, energized, and hopeful, putting their heads together not to whisper about her lack of capability, but to plan. To help.

"Did you really do all that stuff?" came the voice of one of the younger kids. "Fight your shadow and trick El Cucuy?"

"Of course she did!" called Sal around another mouthful of pozole. "Pao's the best!"

Pao couldn't help it: A sheepish grin stretched across her face despite it all.

"Cool," said the kid, and then more voices were chiming in, impressed but also boastful. Sharing their own fantasma-hunting

stories until the courtyard was filled with such lively, hopeful chatter Pao thought her heart might burst. She had a whole community willing to help. People who believed in her, and trusted her, even if her father and Franco hadn't bothered to acknowledge everything she'd done.

They were going to be all right. They were going to—

"What is going on out here?"

Pao abruptly crashed back to reality, a cold chill running through her when she heard Franco's voice. The smiles faded from almost every face as his shadow stretched long across the courtyard, darkening soup bowls and shading faces. Pao didn't turn. She didn't want to give him the satisfaction.

"I asked what's going on," he said, and Pao could hear the clunking steps of his boots as he drew nearer. "You tourists were supposed to be waiting in the training room, and the rest of you—" He stopped abruptly as his eyes fell on Naomi. He was in front of them now, glaring, but Pao still refused to meet his eyes.

Tourist, she thought. She'd show him a tourist.

"You were supposed to go with Marisa to the haunted well," he said to Naomi, every word clipped, his face a mask, giving nothing away.

"Slept right through it," Naomi said with a very convincing yawn, stretching her muscled arms high over her head. "Can you believe that? And good thing I did, too, because it turns out this *tourist* had some information that was pretty damn relevant to all of us. What do you make of that, Franco?"

Before he could answer, one of the Niños shouted, "El Cucuy's coming, and we have to help make a plan!"

And another: "He's got an army of shadow soldiers. Why didn't you tell us, Franco?"

"This is supposed to be a collective, isn't it?" Naomi asked in that bored drawl of hers. "A collective of fantasma hunters, no less. Seems like something our leader should have shared with us."

"It's . . . complicated," Franco said in a low tone clearly intended only for Naomi's ears, though Pao could hear him perfectly. "I had to get all the information before—"

"Before you even told us the truth?" Naomi said, not bothering to lower her voice at all. "Before you let us know there's a threat to us, and our friends, and the entire town we're supposed to be protecting?"

"It's for your safety," Franco said. "All of you. There are things you don't understand."

"Things you think you're better equipped to handle than us?" Naomi asked. "That's not really how leadership of Los Niños is supposed to work, Franco, even if you *were* our leader, which technically"—she put her finger and thumb to her chin, pantomiming thinking hard—"you're not, right? Our leader is Marisa, and you sent her away on a job—which seems like pretty convenient timing, now that I think of it."

Franco's face was flushing, splotches of purple appearing high on his cheekbones as he scanned the crowd for their reaction to Naomi's words. Some of them were watching with rapt attention, their jaws hanging open. Others looked angry, their brows furrowed, their mouths set in hard lines. "I'm a hundred years old!" he yelled. "I have perspective, understanding that—"

"All in favor of waiting until Marisa gets back to make any

decisions, say sí!" Naomi called out, putting her own hand in the air as way more than half of the Niños called "Sí" along with her.

"That's not . . . I don't . . ." Franco spluttered, but then a larger shadow than his darkened the courtyard entryway, and Pao didn't need to look to know who it was.

"What's the meaning of all this?" Beto asked, his voice soft and authoritative, not blustering and puffed up like Franco's. The effect was immediate. Even among a bunch of immortal ghost hunters, a real adult with wrinkles on his face and silver wings in his hair was intimidating.

His sharp eyes took in the scene, from Franco's flushing cheeks to Naomi's folded arms and jutting chin, all the way to Pao, defiantly standing on the tabletop and facing the crowd.

"Paola, come down from there."

"No," Pao said. "The Niños deserve to know what's going on! I know you've been on your own a long time, *Beto*, but here we do things together, not on our own."

"You foolish child." His voice was so quiet, his words so hurtful, that Pao was instantly rattled. "You have no idea what you're toying with, and this little stunt isn't going to make it better." He stepped forward with purpose, and Pao was a mouse in the leonine intensity of his gaze.

He took her by the arm and pulled her down. Not hard enough to hurt, but hard enough that she didn't have a choice. When she was safely on the ground, Emma rushed to Pao's side. The look on her face was unfathomable, but her solidarity was clear.

"I understand you fancy yourself a hero," Beto said, his love for Pao warring with his irritation at being undermined. "And you have behaved heroically in the past; there's no doubt about that. But another display like this, going over my head, jeopardizing this entire mission with reckless impulsivity, and you'll be going back home to sit with your mother until this is all over. Do we understand each other?"

"You can't send me anywhere," Pao said, wrenching her arm out of her father's grasp and turning to face him, toe-to-toe. "Because wherever I am, *that's* where the void will be opening." She didn't know what made her say it. Perhaps it was a combination of her own deductions, Shadow Pao's memories, and the imprint left on her by El Cucuy's laboratory in the void. But as the words left her lips, she knew they were absolutely true. She would have bet anything in the world on it.

Beto was rattled; she could tell. He gazed at her for a long minute before saying, "Come with me, Paola. There are precautions we must take, and then I'll need to hear the rest of what you know *in detail*. Do we have an understanding?"

Pao didn't answer, just whirled around to Naomi before he could grab her again. "Keep trying to think of a plan," she whispered. "I'll be back as soon as I can."

Naomi gave her a little salute and the shadow of a wink. Satisfied, Pao turned back to her father. "*Now* I'll go," she said.

He didn't bother to respond, just ushered Pao, Emma, and Kit back inside, leaving the rest of the Niños staring after them.

TWENTY-TWO

The Key to Good Leadership Is Keeping Busy

The first thing they saw when they returned to the garage was Dante, sitting alone on the bleachers, staring off into space. Bruto had gotten as far away from him as he could and curled up against the far wall by the door. He huffed reproachfully at Pao when she entered.

"I thought Dante was supposed to be our lookout," Emma whispered to Pao. "What's he doing?"

"I don't know," Pao said, a little anxious alarm going off somewhere deep inside. Had his behavior earlier just been a result of adrenaline? Could this be the crash she had been waiting for?

Useless. The word rang in her head. *Mind totally destroyed.*

"Sit there," Beto said, gesturing to the bleachers beside Dante, not seeming to notice that he was barely present.

One thing at a time, Pao told herself, and then turned to her father. "Tell us what's going on," she demanded. "What were you and Franco talking about in the office? Since I'm the one who found out about El Cucuy's plot, I should be able to help make a plan. I'm not useless, and I'm not too young. Let me help!"

"You *will* be of help," Beto said. "Hand me your Arma del Alma, Paola."

"What?" Pao said, nonplussed. "No way." The idea of being without her staff when at any second the void could open its awful, gaping maw and cough up shadow soldiers into this world was too terrible to contemplate.

"I only need it for a moment," Beto said impatiently, reaching out his hand. "I won't even require the weapon itself, only its magnifying glass form for the time being."

The image of the golden trail winding its way through the cornfield returned to Pao, and her desire to keep the arma in her possession doubled. She reached into her pocket automatically to reassure herself it was still there.

Except it wasn't.

Trying not to let her father see her panic, Pao checked her hoodie pocket and all four of her jeans pockets before she was forced to admit to herself—if not to her impatient, overbearing father—that it was gone.

"Paola," he was saying, oblivious to her distress. "Wielding an Arma del Alma is a privilege, and it is to be used for the good of your team. Right now, yours is in danger, and if you refuse to help, what was that little display outside for?"

"Do you know how I *got* my Arma del Alma, *Dad*?" Pao asked, her temper flaring, making her forget for a moment that the arma in question was nowhere to be found. "I traveled back in time through a void portal in a dream and rescued a toddler version of my best friend from a fantasma that was terrorizing an entire town. I released that mutated sucker by finding his family and honoring them, even though their patriarch tried to literally murder me, and I was *rewarded* with this weapon. For being out in the world helping. So if you think I'm gonna let you use it while you keep me out of everything, you got another think coming."

Beto just blinked slowly for a few long seconds. He didn't have much practice in being a parent, Pao knew, and she was banking on it, because if she'd ever dared to talk to her mother that way, she would have been grounded from this and all future wars. Beto, on the other hand, looked at her like a complex lock on a door he needed to open, and when he spoke, it wasn't to punish her.

"You've behaved admirably, Paola," her father said, and for a moment, his eyes glowed with genuine pride. "Had you not risen to the occasion, we wouldn't be facing a breakthrough of this magnitude. The chance to rid ourselves of El Cucuy for good. But there's no reason for you to do it all yourself. Not when Franco and I are here with our—"

"Your decades of experience," Pao said. "Yeah, I've heard. And working together *is* the best way forward. I know that. But . . . when was the last time you actually *fought* a fantasma, Dad? When was the last time you did anything but research and hypothesize?"

Beto didn't answer. He looked taken aback to say the least.

"The other Niños might not have your experience, but they can fight. And so can I. You have to let us help!"

"We don't have time for this," Beto said. His tone was pleading. "Paola, the Arma del Alma, *please*."

A little thrill of fear went through Pao before she stuck out her chin and said, "Not unless you tell me what you need it for."

"To . . . assure me that we're moving forward in the right way."

"Oh, that really clears things up," Pao said. "Thanks."

"There is no need to be rude," Beto said. Then he lowered his voice. "I will tell you what I know, I promise you. But I can't do it now. Not in . . . present company."

He looked so desperate and frazzled, so afraid, that Pao would have given it to him. *If* she'd had it. It almost made her glad she didn't.

All of this must have shown on her face, or else her father knew her better than she thought he did, because after a long moment of silence, he asked, "When was the last time you had it?"

"At . . . the apartment," Pao said with a heavy sigh, knowing there was no point in lying now. "Before the ride over here. I'm sure I had it then."

"And you just noticed it missing?"

"When you asked me for it," she said, and beside Dante, she could see Emma looking worried and Kit looking confused. "I . . . I never leave it anywhere. I can't imagine—"

"All of you, turn out your pockets," Beto barked at her friends.

"Dad!" Pao shrieked. "What are you doing? None of them would have—"

"Your pockets, now," he said as Pao stepped forward.

"You don't have to do anything," she assured them. "Dad, these people helped me. They brought Dante back with me. You can't just accuse—"

"Paola!" Beto said, turning to face her again. "It is time for you to accept that you have a less-than-perfect understanding of what may be happening here and to *trust me* for once. Can you do that? Because I need to make sure that none of your companions . . ." He trailed off, his eyes drifting upward like he was counting in his head. "There were four," he said when his eyes met hers again. "Three girls and the boy besides you. Where is the other one? With the garish hair? Where is she?"

"I . . . let her go home," Pao said, suddenly not sure that had been the right decision after all. Beto's fear had sharpened, she could see it on his face. "I promised her she could, and I didn't see why . . ."

But Beto was already turning away from her, facing Franco. "We have to find the girl, immediately. If we don't . . . We have to find her." He turned back to Pao, to Emma and Kit. "If you care for your friend, for her family at all, you will tell me where she went. There's no time to waste."

"I don't know where she lives," Pao said, hearing her voice as though from far away. If Robin was in danger . . . if something happened to her because of . . . Robin hadn't even wanted to go along. She'd just been trying to be a good friend. Bruto sidled up to Pao and licked her hand to alleviate her distress. "She said she was going home. To see her dads. She was really upset. . . ."

"*I* know where she lives," Kit said. Beto took another step toward her, but Kit's eyes darted to Pao first. She was asking permission, Pao realized, and Beto seemed to realize it, too, because when he looked back at Pao, it was with a new expression. Some new light that hadn't been there before.

"I don't have time to explain how absolutely vital it is that we find her," Beto said to Kit, entreating her. "If she was in the church in Santuario, if Paola transported her by portal . . . she could be in immense danger, and the only way we can keep her safe is if she's back here."

But still, Kit looked to Pao, who felt the weight of responsibility settle heavily on her shoulders. She had led before, by necessity, but this time someone was choosing to follow her. Robin had chosen, too, she remembered. She'd promised to rejoin them, to be part of the fight.

Pao had to honor that by keeping her safe, and right now this was the best way.

"Tell him," she said, and Beto's shoulders sagged with relief.

"She lives on Skyview in a white house with a porch swing," Kit said. "I'm not sure the exact number, but I can show you if—"

"You'll need to stay here," Beto said, already shaking his head. "All of you. Franco and I will fetch the girl and bring her back to safety. In the meantime, Paola, as their leader, you must watch over them, ¿entiendes?"

Pao nodded, her mind racing. Was it really necessary for *both* Beto and Franco to go after Robin? Even though El Cucuy's shadow soldiers could be coming through at any moment?

She didn't have the answers, but she was absolutely sure more was going on than met the eye. They needed information, and a plan. But first, the only thing Pao and her dad could agree on: Get Robin to safety.

"Dad?" She jogged up to him and Franco.

"Yes, niña?"

"She . . . didn't even really want to be part of this. Not at first, anyway. If something happens to her, it's all my fault and . . ."

Beto took Pao's face between both of his big, warm hands. "Whatever happens, I will make sure she's safe."

"Promise?" Pao asked, wishing for a moment that she really was the little girl she felt like when he looked at her like this.

That she *could* just go home and be thirteen like he wanted, and let the grown-ups handle everything.

"Lo prometo," he said, kissing her on the forehead. "Now I must go before any harm can befall her."

"Robin," Pao said, feeling the crushing weight of worry on her chest again the moment he let go. "Her name is Robin."

Beto looked for a moment like he was going to say something, but instead he shook his head a little sadly and took off at a lope for the open warehouse door. When it closed, echoing through the huge, mostly empty room, Pao had never felt more alone.

Bruto whined, nudging her hand with his cold nose, as if he could sense her thoughts.

"Hey," Emma said, sneaking up behind her and bumping shoulders. "It'll be okay. He'll get Robin back. He might be a little . . . intense, but he seems efficient, if nothing else!"

Pao thought of the way he had looked when she'd found him in the forest lab, his eyes inhabited by an evil spirit, his face lit by a panel of instruments as he prepared to use Pao to open the void. . . .

"I just wish I knew what was going on," she said, shaking her head as if to dislodge the image. "How are *you* doing?" She turned to Emma, looking—really looking—into her tired blue eyes.

"I don't understand why we have to stay here. Does your dad think we got infected or something?"

Pao shrugged. "I don't know. For the first time, I don't even have a theory." She scrubbed at her eyes with the heels of her hands, trying to stave off her exhaustion. "Do you want to call your parents, or . . . ?"

"I texted them when you were addressing the Niños," Emma said a little sheepishly. "I told them we were back in town and your dad would be dropping me off soon. I didn't say anything else, because I just . . . don't even know what I'd tell them right now."

"Me neither," Pao said, wishing her father had left them some instructions, at least. What if El Cucuy—

"It's Dante I'm worried about," Emma went on, cutting off Pao's thoughts. She nudged Pao around until she was facing the bleachers instead of the door. "He hasn't said a word since he volunteered for—and then totally failed at—guard duty. He's just staring at that wall like he's trying to read something on it."

"Dante, reading?" Pao said with a weak attempt at a smile. "That's how you really know something's wrong."

Emma smiled, too, and even though it was exhausted-looking, it still made Pao's stomach do a backflip. She remembered the look on Emma's face back in the desert, when she'd wanted to tell Pao something important.

Pao hadn't felt ready to hear it at that moment, but things had changed since then. Something had happened to Pao when she was standing on that table, the Niños looking at her like she knew what she was talking about. Then Kit had deferred to her, and even her *dad* had seemed to grudgingly respect her role as leader to her friends. All this had made Pao feel like she was grown-up enough to decide who she was. That she was strong enough to make people listen.

"Emma—" she began just as Emma said, "Maybe you should—"

They both stopped, giggling. "Go ahead," Pao said, hoping Emma would tell *her* to go ahead instead.

But she didn't. Emma just charged forward, like saying this sentence was a serving of steamed broccoli she just wanted to scarf so she could move on to dessert. "Maybe you should talk to him," she said, looking over at Dante again. "You're probably the only one who can get through."

Pao deflated a little at the idea of talking to Dante. "I don't know what to say," she admitted, following Emma's gaze, looking at him slouched in the bleachers, staring at the wall.

"What was it like in the tower?" Emma asked. "Like, *really* like."

"It was awful," Pao said, remembering the cage, the nightmares, the way they'd taken over the walls, the bars, the very air. She tried to relay all this to Emma but felt sure she'd fallen short of the real experience.

If she was lucky, Emma would never have to find out.

"Dante's probably traumatized beyond belief," Emma said, a hint of pity in her voice. "Eight months in a cell like that? What's weirder than how he's acting now is how he was acting normal before this."

"He was probably just relieved to be free," Pao said from experience. "Sometimes adrenaline is the only thing that keeps you going. Knowing that you're a step from danger, that there's something you've gotta do, somewhere you need to be. When you get to a safe place, that's when it all hits you."

"See why I said you'd be the best person to talk to him?" Emma asked, her smile more genuine this time. "You're kind of amazing, Paola Santiago."

Pao could feel her cheeks heating up, and she didn't know what to say, but Emma didn't seem to expect anything. They just stood there grinning for too long, considering the end of the world was, like, super nigh.

"Go," Emma said, bumping Pao with her shoulder again. "I'll be here."

"Promise?" Pao said for the second time in five minutes.

Emma just smiled again.

"Come on, boy," Pao said to Bruto, but his hackles were up the instant he realized where she was going. He absolutely would not go any closer to Dante.

"He probably smells the void on him," Pao said, unconvinced by her own theory. "Can he stay with you?"

In response, Emma scratched his ears, causing him to close his big eyes and sigh.

Pao made her way across the warehouse feeling like her sneakers were full of lead. "Hey," she tried when she reached Dante, plopping down beside him, the bleachers creaking. "You okay?"

The Dante from earlier would have shrugged it off. Made a joke. This one just shook his head.

"Anything I can do to help?"

"Día de los Muertos," he said so quietly she could barely hear him.

"Huh?"

Dante sat up, looking at her dead on. "Día de los Muertos is when the veil is the thinnest."

It was so obvious it felt like a slap in the face. The day when the dead could visit the world of the living. It was a holiday intended for living family members to honor their dead ancestors, but of course it could work in a sinister way as well. The veil didn't know who it was letting in or out.

"I'm so stupid," Pao said aloud. "It makes sense—it makes total sense. God, they're gonna revoke my Mexican card for not thinking of that one." Dante still hadn't responded, but Pao went on, thinking out loud. "This is great, though! Here I was thinking it was gonna be any minute, but Día de los Muertos is still, like, ten days away!"

Dante laughed hollowly, immediately puncturing Pao's hopefulness. "You could have a year," he said, his voice seeming to echo like in her nightmares, "and it wouldn't be enough. Eternity wouldn't be enough. You have no idea what he's capable of."

"Seems like maybe you could help us with that one," Pao said. "I know it must have been awful. . . . I'm not asking for a play-by-play, but anything you can tell us would help. Anything at all."

But he only shook his head, his shoulders slumping again, his eyes sliding out of focus.

"I'm here if you need anything, okay?" Pao said, not expecting a response. She grabbed his shoulder and squeezed because she didn't know what else to do.

Feeling guilty for leaving him, she crossed over to the doorway, where Naomi was standing half in and half out of the training room, keeping an eye on the courtyard and the warehouse with her head on a swivel.

"Dante knows when the attack is going to be," Pao gasped out when she reached the older girl. "He just told me."

Naomi raised her eyebrows, which for her was basically the same as throwing a parade.

"Día de los Muertos," Pao said excitedly. "That's ten days away. We have time to make a plan, to evacuate the town if we need to. To call in reinforcements, even."

"That's good news," Naomi said in her usual unimpressed way, but Pao knew her well enough by now to recognize the way her shoulders relaxed just a little. "But we still don't know what we're gonna do in ten days."

"I've been thinking about that," Pao said. "How many weapons do you guys have stored away here?"

"Not as many as we should," Naomi said. "We lost a lot in the battle against El Autostopisto, and Franco's been taking some apart to experiment on them. We have enough to outfit most of us who are in fighting shape. And maybe five to ten more."

"What about allies?" Pao asked. "Is there anyone who would come and fight with us against the shadows?"

Naomi shook her head slowly. "Look, living in a haunted cactus field and dealing with the secret forces of the supernatural world doesn't exactly ingratiate you with the neighbors, if you know what I'm saying."

Pao nodded, trying to find a silver lining. They were outnumbered and outgunned, facing the possible extermination of their entire town and potentially the world. . . . "Well," she said, "we've faced worse odds before, with less time to prepare, and we came out okay, right?"

"That's the spirit," Naomi said flatly.

"Of everyone here, how many are *in* fighting shape?"

"Most of us," Naomi said. "A little rusty after eight months of sitting around here, but we can come together when we need to."

"So, I guess we should start with training?" Pao said. "Brushing up on the basics, sparring . . . And maybe we also need to find somewhere safe for the ones who are actually little kids?"

"You said the void is going to open wherever *you* are?" Naomi asked, looking a little afraid for the first time.

"I think so," Pao said, although it was more than just a guess. She felt it in her bones. El Cucuy had to tear his hole into the world somewhere, and she had thwarted him, tricked him, and delayed his attempt to destroy the world of the living twice now—as well as alerting the Niños to his third try. She knew he wanted to get back at her for all that and make sure she couldn't stop him this time.

"I think you're right about training," Naomi said. "Even if the newest kids can't learn much in ten days, the rest of us can brush up, and it'll give everyone something to do besides sit around waiting."

Pao was about to volunteer to lead some sparring sessions when she remembered her Arma del Alma was missing. She'd been so concerned with Robin and Dante, and then carried away with planning, she had momentarily forgotten. But the loss of it hit her as hard as the first time, like a part of herself was missing, and she said as much to Naomi.

"I'll get everyone organized," Naomi said. "And hey, if it's here, we'll find it. No one in this lot is a thief."

"Thanks," Pao said, checking her pockets again, like maybe it had reappeared out of thin air. They were empty, though, and she felt hollow at the thought that it was really gone.

"Oi!" Naomi called out into the mess yard. "Drills in five. Everybody arm yourself and meet in the training room. When this bogeyman gets here, we won't be *picking our noses, José.*" She charged out into the yard, followed closely by Kit, who had barely taken her eyes off the older girl since she'd first appeared.

"I'm Kit," she was saying. "I'm in a boffing club at school, which means I'm pretty great with a weapon."

"That isn't a weapon," Naomi said, barely pausing to look. "That's a rake."

Pao could hear Kit arguing as they made their way outside. Feeling unmoored without a weapon or a task of her own, Pao turned back to the room.

Dante was still sitting in the bleachers, staring at the same wall like he was trying to put a hole through it. Emma was with Bruto by the door, rubbing his belly as he threw baleful looks at Dante.

The Niños began to file in from the mess yard, all lively chatter and playful roughhousing, just like Pao remembered. Naomi got them in line as she was harassed with endless questions from Kit. Patrick was wheeled in from some dusty corner, headless, but still something they could hit hard, which was always helpful.

They were settling into a groove. Preparation gave them something to do besides focus on the long odds of the conflict. This, thought Pao, must be at least half of what it meant to be a leader—just finding something to keep everyone busy.

She'd almost enjoyed a full fourteen seconds of peace, too, when all hell broke loose again.

TWENTY-THREE

An Especially Neutral Memory

At first, it was just the warehouse door banging open. No one even flinched but Pao, who recognized her dad right away. Behind him was Franco, and between them . . .

"Robin!" Pao cried, stealing Kit's attention from Naomi at last.

Emma joined them halfway across the warehouse, Bruto at her heels, but before they could reach their friend, Franco yelled, "Stay back!"

And that's when Pao realized what was really happening.

Robin's face was streaked with tears, and her wrists seemed to be *tied* together in front of her. Franco was still shouting at them to keep their distance, but Pao's ears were barely working— everything sounded like it was underwater, so powerful was the rage crashing over her.

Her father's face was set in a grim expression. One Pao knew all too well.

This is for the greater good, it seemed to say, but all Pao could see was Robin's hunched shoulders and her unmistakable fear.

"What are you *doing*?" Pao screamed, pushing past Franco to stop in front of her father, forcing him to either run her over or face her. "Why is she tied up like this? You said you were going to keep her safe!"

"I'm keeping us *all* safe," Beto said in a tone that asked Pao to understand. To trust him despite the way this looked. "Please, Paola, let me do what I need to do."

"I believed you," Pao said, standing her ground. "I believed you when you called me a leader, when you said you would help us. Robin didn't *do* anything, so let her go!"

"This is not Robin," her father said at last, in a fierce whisper only the four of them could hear. "Do you understand me? That's why it was so imperative that we keep the five of you isolated. To test . . . to make sure . . . It's too much to explain." He tossed up one hand in exasperation. "We're running out of time."

"We have ten days," Pao said, not bothering to lower her own voice. "Dante said the veil will be thinnest on Día de los Muertos, which gives us until next Friday and gives *you* plenty of time to tell me what the heck you're doing with my friend."

Beto laughed, a hoarse bark that held no joy whatsoever. "You really think he will wait until then? Now that one of his soldiers has crossed to the land of the living?" He shook Robin's bound wrists, causing her to cry out in pain.

"Stop it!" Pao said, her voice high and shrill. "She is not a copy!"

"She *is*," Beto said. "Franco detected a void signature in the desert *just* where your portal landed. A powerful one. We thought it was a fantasma, but then you showed up at home and it all became clear. El Cucuy sent a shadow back with you, Paola, because you were reckless and traveled before you had my say-so. Now we need to secure it. Get out of the way, Paola. Now."

"How do you know it wasn't me?" Pao asked desperately.

"The void signature. I mean, I'm part . . . whatever, too, right?"

"You think I don't know what a partial void signature looks like?" Beto asked. "It was you *and* a copy, I am sure. Now, please, let us through."

He pushed past Pao, who found Robin's watery gaze. "Pao, help me, please," she said. "I don't know what he's talking about! They grabbed me at the bus transfer station on my way home, and they won't even tell me what I did wrong. Please help!"

"I will get you out of this," Pao promised. "I'm so sorry, Robin. So, so sorry."

"What the junk is going on here?" Kit asked when Pao turned around. She was holding her rake menacingly, her raccoon-eye makeup smudged but somehow more intimidating that way. "I'm sorry, Pao. You've turned out to be pretty badass, but if he doesn't let Robin go, I'm gonna have to brain him." She slapped the rake head into her palm. "And Naomi says my form is *excellent*, so—"

"I don't know what's going on," Pao admitted, cutting off Kit before she could go any further. "I wish I did. He seems to think Robin's a copy, but he won't tell me how he knows, or what he's going to do with her. I . . ." A hopeless feeling was starting to well up in Pao. If Beto really wouldn't listen, what could she do? He wasn't a fantasma she could dispatch, or a monster that would bleed green and disappear into a cloud of vapor.

He was her father. And she loved him. But he was wrong.

Beto and Franco almost had Robin to the door of the office. She was no longer struggling, just walking with lurching steps as they steered her inside. Bruto followed for a hopeful moment, wagging his tail, but they shooed him away.

"This'll do for now," Pao heard Franco say just before the door closed behind him, "but we'll have to move her somewhere more secure before long. If my assumptions are correct, these things are deadly strong and . . ."

"What are they planning?" Emma asked, looking nauseated. "She's . . . She has a four-point-oh grade average and teaches ceramics to seniors at the nursing home. She would never hurt anyone. . . ."

"She would if she was a copy." Dante had come up behind them so silently that all three girls jumped at the sound of his voice.

"She's *not* a copy!" Kit snarled, spinning around to face Dante with her rake held at chest height. "I dare you to say it again."

Dante barely glanced at her or her weapon. He seemed to have eyes only for Pao. "The copies are loaded with as many of the original's memories as possible," he said. "Remember how I thought you were one when you came in to rescue me? They're *that* convincing before they start attacking."

"We fought one," Pao said, remembering Poppy. The way she'd been all smiles and field-trip enthusiasm until the moment she'd decided to kill Pao. The way she'd stretched tall, her eyes glowing green, her face going waxy and white.

"I had no idea it wasn't Poppy," Emma said through the hand she'd placed over her mouth. "I mean, she was a *little* off, but nothing that couldn't have been explained by too much coffee."

"*You* knew," Kit remembered, pointing the rake at Pao now, who barely resisted the urge to slap it out of her hand. "You knew something was fishy about Poppy, didn't you? Robin's normal. So why can't you just go in there and tell them it's the real her?"

"It doesn't work like that," Pao said. She wanted to sleep, or cry, but leaders couldn't do either when something this awful was happening. "It's . . . complicated. I don't know how I knew Poppy wasn't the real Poppy. I'd never met her, and I had nothing to compare her to. I just sensed something was off and . . . I was also probably having a massive PTSD episode or something at the time, so it was really just a lucky guess."

Lucky guess? Kit mouthed to Emma.

"We have to get her out of there," Emma said, that blazing look Pao loved in her eyes.

"We *have* to make sure she's not a shadow," Dante argued, a different kind of fire in his face, which scared Pao a little. "You don't understand. If she's one of his copies . . . If she opens the void . . . we're all going to die."

"We're all going to *fight*," Pao corrected. "But there has to be a way to find out whether she's the real Robin or not."

"It won't be easy. El Cucuy engineered the copies to pass as their real selves. He wants to create utter chaos, force people to distrust one another, to turn on their own loved ones because they don't know whether they're real or not. It's the secret weapon within the weapon. He'll need fewer soldiers if we're all too scared to kill them."

"So how did you know it was me?" Pao asked. "Some question about the first time I beat you at *Mario Kart*? How did you know he wouldn't have had my clone programmed with that memory?"

"Because that experience didn't matter to you," Dante said, his cheeks flushing. "But it did to me. El Cucuy makes sure the copies have memories of all the big emotional moments, but he can't give them everything. It's the little details that will give them away."

"Cool. Does anyone know anything about Robin that absolutely does not matter to her?" Kit asked, twirling her rake again in a way that made Pao want to hit her with it.

"I don't really know her that well," Emma said. "I feel bad about it, but she only joined the Rogues at the beginning of the year, and I guess I didn't take the time to get to know her as well as I should have."

"To be fair, it's not like you could have known that trivial details about Robin's life would one day be the key to saving the world," Pao said, knowing Emma had a tendency to beat herself up about things. "I'm sure you were planning to get to know her better."

"I was," Emma said in a voice barely above a whisper. Pao grabbed her hand without thinking and squeezed, grateful when it made her smile. "Kit? You know her pretty well, right?"

"I mean . . . I've known her since fourth grade," Kit said, shifting uncomfortably.

"Great," Pao said, letting go of Emma's hand to rub hers together. "So tell us some small detail of her past that only the real Robin would remember, and then we'll . . ." She trailed off. Kit was already shaking her head.

"Look, I don't know if you guys have noticed this, but I'm not, like, the *best* listener." Only through herculean effort did Pao refrain from rolling her eyes. "I don't have a face that screams, *Confide in me.*"

"I don't think it's your *face* that's the problem," Pao muttered, earning an elbow in the ribs from Emma.

Kit, as if to make her case, didn't seem to have heard. "Sure, I've known Robin a long time. Our parents are friends, we live in the same neighborhood, whatever. But like . . . I don't know some deep personal thing about her that can fix the problem here."

"Come on," Pao said. "There has to be *something*. The color of her favorite stuffed animal from elementary school, or a food that she hates?"

"Food she hates won't work," Dante chimed in, really earning his stripes as the group downer. "People feel really strongly about food memories made early in their lives. El Cucuy would have caught that."

"Fine," Pao said, exhaling sharply. "A food she feels especially *neutral* about, then."

But Kit only shrugged. "Sorry," she said. "Nada."

Pao threw up her hands. If this had been Emma or Dante, she would have had a million questions that could irrefutably prove who they were. How selfish could Kit be?

"She really loves her parents," Kit said, her eyes straying longingly back to where Naomi was trying to get the younger Niños to practice their drills. "Maybe Pops One or Pops Two will know."

"Oh, sure," Pao said, actually rolling her eyes this time. "We'll just walk up to their front door and be like, 'Hi, Mr. and Mr. Long, we accidentally took your daughter Robin too close to a malevolent magical rift on our recent field trip and think she may be a copy of herself made by El Cucuy, the lord of dread. Could you share a trivial fact about her past so we can decide whether or not to kill her? Thanks!'"

Kit shrugged again. "Sounds pretty good to me."

Pao groaned.

"You know, getting her parents involved isn't the worst idea . . ." Emma said thoughtfully. "I mean, who else would know this stuff? And if El Cucuy is going to tear open the void and murder everyone, I guess they'll find out about the supernatural soon enough, right?"

Pao considered this. She hated the prospect of getting more tourists involved. Especially parents, who might do something idiotic, like involve the police.

"Worth a shot," Dante said, looking at Pao. They were all waiting for her to decide, trusting her when she wasn't at all sure she deserved it.

"Okay, I'll ask my dad and Franco," Pao said at last. "I mean, they have to be worried they're wrong, right? They'll jump at the chance to prove she isn't a copy. . . ."

"Yeah," Kit said with a bored yawn. "Two old men who think they're experts about this stuff. They'll be *dying* to find out they're wrong."

They weren't.

"Absolutely not," Franco said through a crack in the door. He wouldn't open it all the way, and no matter how high Pao tried to stand on her tiptoes or how much she craned her neck, she couldn't see around him.

"But, Franco," Pao said, as patiently as she could, Bruto's tail thumping against her legs as she cajoled. "What if she's not a copy? What if you have an innocent, scared fifteen-year-old girl in here waiting to be vaporized because you made a mistake?"

"We didn't make a mistake," Franco said through clenched teeth. "She fled the scene before we could round you all up and

check you for authenticity. She took your Arma del Alma knowing it was the *one way* to distinguish between the copies and
the originals. She's not your friend, and you're wasting my time."

"So she has my Arma del Alma?" Pao asked, her heart leap-
ing into her throat. "She's the one who took it? Have you already
used it on her? Have you—"

"We don't have it. She must have ditched it somewhere when
she was out on her little joyride," Franco interrupted. "Now if
that's all, I have—"

"That's *not* all," Pao said, horrified. "You don't even know
she took it? Then where's your proof? Why are you keeping her
here?"

Franco looked back and forth, his eyes shifting in a way
Pao was absolutely certain made him guilty. Then he said, "We
don't have to share every detail of our operation with a *child*.
Go practice your drills. We'll be updating everyone very soon."

And he closed the door in her face.

Pao banged on it again, the glass rattling, the blinds jumping
and crashing on the other side. But she couldn't see anything,
and no one opened the door this time. "Robin!" Pao yelled when
her father's and Franco's names were worn out. "Don't worry!
I'm gonna get you out of there!"

But as she walked away, she had a sinking feeling that was
going to be a lot harder than making a promise through a
closed door.

It took only a few minutes to catch the rest of them up on what
Franco had said. Naomi had joined the group, and by the time
Pao finished talking, the other girl was gritting her teeth.

"He's a dead man," Naomi said. "Running this place like his

own private lab, no respect for the group. It's antithetical to the whole mission of Los Niños de la Luz and he *knows* that. He just wants to use our resources for his own cause. He always has."

"My father isn't helping," Pao said, shaking her head. "He lived alone in the woods for way too long. He's totally forgotten that you need *people* to fight, not just theories and hypothetical junk. I mean how far did that get him out in the woods? He was two seconds from letting a vengeful spirit literally use his body to tear open the void until I showed up."

"Too true," Naomi said, reaching across to bump fists with Pao. "But what are we gonna do about it . . . now? Because if they feel like what they're doing will advance the cause, end things for good, they won't care about what happens to that girl."

Pao took a deep breath, closing her eyes to think. Her usual approach (namely smashing in with no real plan and trying to handle everything on her own) wasn't going to work here. She needed something with more nuance. She needed something that would really work.

She needed her mother.

TWENTY-FOUR

Mother Knows Best and Other Popular Folktales

Before Beto or Franco had opened the office door again, Maria Santiago came bursting into the warehouse with two very confused-looking middle-aged men trailing behind her.

She had been willing to accept Beto's authority when her daughter and a missing boy had appeared, decrying the end of the world, but Pao's mom had been a law unto herself for much longer than she'd had a husband around calling the shots, and the idea of a little girl being held prisoner in some musty office without the comfort of her parents was where she drew the line.

Or at least, that's what she had said on the phone to Pao.

"Where is he?" she asked now, with an expression Pao had associated with extreme danger since before she could remember. *"Where is he?"*

Pao pointed wordlessly toward the office door. A hush had fallen over the Niños, their weapons at their sides. Naomi had already told all the kids who could be recognized to hide, but even the rest were used to living out in the desert, in a liminal space where no one could find them. The idea of strangers coming in was understandably terrifying to most of them, but they had no choice today. Not if they wanted to save Robin.

"Beto, you open the door this instant!" Maria was now saying in a ringing voice that had too many times summoned Pao home after dark. Pao crept up close, trying to be as unnoticeable as possible so she could hear what they were saying.

"Robin?" called one of the men with her while the other one sobbed noisily. "Robin, sweetie, are you in there? It's Dad!"

"BETO! NOW!"

The door opened just a crack, and this time, it was Pao's father who peered out. "Maria?" he said, his eyes bleary. "What are you doing here? I told you to stay home."

"You *told* me you were coming here to keep our daughter safe," Maria said, and Pao could almost see flames sparking out of her eyes. "You *told* me not to worry. You *didn't* tell me part of your plan was to tie up a fifteen-year-old girl and keep her from her parents while you did *experiments on her.*"

"Experiments?" said one of Robin's dads, his hands against his cheeks. "What kind of experiments?"

"Who is *that*?" Beto asked, exasperated, now peering around the doorframe to see Robin's dads huddled behind Maria like the sheer force of her anger could shield them from this strange place.

"The girl's parents, Beto," Maria said. "They're here to help."

"She said that . . . might not be Robin in there?" one of the men said, turning to Pao. "That this might be some kind of imposter? And that ghosts are real? I'm so confused, honestly."

"Personally, I consider myself a witch," said the other, his glasses perched on his nose over a bushy beard. "But some of the stuff she's saying is *beyond* crystals and tarot cards and the occasional meditative spirit-guide quest, okay? We're in *way* over our heads here."

"It's okay," Pao reassured them. "It's good that you're here."

The witch dad started crying again, and the other one rubbed his arm consolingly. Beto and Maria were still furiously arguing through the door.

"Paola says the girl's parents can ask her questions and prove whether or not she's an imposter. Well, they're here. And unless you have a better plan, I think we ought to do what she says, Beto."

"Paola is a child!" he said. "She doesn't understand what's truly at stake! Maria, I need you to trust me, please."

"I trust our daughter," Maria said simply. "And either you let us in to see the girl or I'll force my way in, and I can't imagine you'll enjoy a woman humiliating you in front of your little friends."

Pao couldn't help it—despite the dire circumstances, she grinned. How had she never realized how seriously amazing her mom was before?

"You're making a huge mistake," Beto said, but he opened the door wider and stepped aside.

"Oh my god, Robin!"

"Why is she tied up like this?"

"That's it, I'm calling the police."

"Wait," said Beto, pinching the bridge of his nose. "There's so much you need to understand, and the police won't help—they'll only muddle things and put people in greater danger."

Pao made her way into the room to see Robin, her wrists tied to Franco's desk chair, a strange helmet on her head. Her eyes were wide and fearful; then they filled with tears as her dads rushed forward and knelt beside her, tugging at the ropes.

"Please," Beto said, putting his hand on the shoulder of the bearded man. "I mean your daughter no harm. The trouble is, we're not convinced this *is* your daughter. She may be a copy made by a paranormal entity attempting to enter this realm."

Robin's dads were still clutching at her, but both were now staring slack-jawed at Beto like they hadn't retained any of what he'd said.

"He's telling the truth," Pao said, stepping up and kneeling between Robin's dads. "And it's all my fault. I'm so sorry. I went along on the Rogues' field trip, and along the way, another one of the copies—Poppy, the trip chaperone—attacked us. I thought I could stop it on my own, and Robin was the only one who knew how to drive, so she helped me. If she was copied . . . if this isn't really her . . . it's because she helped me. Because she wanted to do the right thing."

"This is absurd," said the non-bearded dad in a sort of horrified whisper. "This is our baby girl, and we are taking her home right now."

"If you do that," Pao said, "and we're wrong, she could kill you in your sleep. She could open a portal to the underworld and let out thousands more copies that will overwhelm Silver Springs first, and then the world."

The non-bearded dad made to speak again, but the witch dad stopped him, a hand on his arm. "How do we find out?" he asked.

"Jonathan, you are *not* seriously entertaining these lunatics. We need to bring the FBI in here, or . . . whoever's in charge of kidnappers and child torturers, and get this place *shut down* before—"

"I'm sorry," Jonathan the witch said, holding out a hand.

"We're *not* calling the FBI! Or anyone in law enforcement! With this many people of color here? It could endanger the lives of any one of them. There has to be another way to solve this, Todd."

"I'm all for community care instead of carceral justice, and you know that, but these people have our daughter *tied to a chair!*"

"Okay, okay," said Jonathan, turning back to Beto. "I'm assuming there's some way to find out whether this is the real Robin or not, so just tell us what to do."

Beto was going to speak, but Pao stepped forward. "You need to ask her something only the real Robin would know. Not anything big—our enemy can program the copies to remember emotional moments. Something trivial. Inconsequential."

"What color was your fifth birthday party dress?" Jonathan asked immediately.

"Birthdays won't work," Pao said. "They're too emotionally charged. It has to be something even less important than that. Something the enemy wouldn't have thought to transfer over."

For a moment, everyone in the room was silent; then Todd stepped up. "What did you call the neighbor's cat when we lived in the loft downtown?" he asked, looking Robin right in the eye.

In that moment, Pao knew. Before she even answered the question. This *was* the real Robin.

"Sparkles," she said in a whisper, her eyes brimming over with tears. "I called him Sparkles because his collar had rhinestones and sometimes they refracted the light like a disco ball."

Todd's eyes filled with tears, too, now, and Jonathan was on his knees again. "Oh, honey," he said. "It's you; it's really you."

"Untie her," Pao said to Beto. "She doesn't have the Arma del Alma, and she answered the question. She's not the copy."

"That doesn't prove anything!" Franco was saying. "The thing with the cat could have an emotional subtext that flagged it as high priority for the replicating process. We don't know the context—we can't just let her go!"

"We don't tie up children and hold them hostage in *my* warehouse," came a voice from the door, and Marisa, the true leader of Los Niños de la Luz, walked in looking thunderous. "Let her go, Franco, or suffer the consequences of disobeying me."

"Marisa, you don't know what you're doing," he said dismissively. "Let me—"

"Let her *go*," Marisa repeated, and this time, before Pao could even adjust to her slim navy coveralls or her hair—in its two strawberry-blonde French braids again—she had crossed the room and pinned Franco to the wall by the throat.

"Nice," Pao said, and from just outside the office door, she heard Naomi chuckle.

And then Robin's dads were untying their daughter, and she was falling into their arms, and they were all sobbing, and Pao's mom was behind Pao, squeezing the life out of her, and she didn't even mind. Franco was gasping and choking as Marisa let go of him in disgust, and for a moment, Pao felt like everything was going to be okay.

"You did well, niña," Beto said, approaching Pao and her mom. "The way you talked with the girl's parents. With respect and empathy but also an understanding of what needed to be done. Those are the qualities of a real leader."

Pao still felt mutinous, but when he stepped forward to hug

her, she let him. "I know the version of me in your head is still, like, four years old," she said, peering up at him. "But I've grown, okay?"

"I'll remember that next time. But for now, if the girl wasn't the copy, we need to find out who is."

"And for that we need my Arma del Alma?" Pao guessed.

"Yes," Beto said, and the fact that he was speaking freely, giving her the information she had asked for, meant more to Pao than she could explain. "The lens shows the absolute truth. If you look at one of his shadow soldiers through it, it will reveal their true form."

Pao thought of Peppy Poppy, her twisted face, her glowing green eyes. And Pao's own shadow self, the way she had changed at El Cucuy's bidding. The glass would show them that more quickly and effectively than a thousand questions from a loved one.

And someone had stolen it. Someone Pao had brought here through the portal.

Someone who wasn't Robin.

"I need to talk to Emma and Kit," she said decisively as her mom spoke in hushed tones with the Misters Long while Robin rubbed her wrists and clung to her dads. The last thing Pao wanted was to believe that one of her friends was a copy. That she'd be forced to . . .

Well, she'd burn that bridge when she came to it.

"*I'll* talk to them," she repeated to her father. "Alone. And no tying them to chairs or anything. Not until we know something for sure."

"Understood," said Beto, and Pao wanted to believe him,

wanted to think he'd finally begun to trust her. But part of her knew that no matter what he promised, he would do what he thought was best when the time came.

"Okay," she said with a sigh. "Stay here. I'm going."

Bruto met her at the door and padded beside her as Pao approached the girls, dreading what was coming.

What if it's Emma? asked her cruel inner voice. *What if that's what she wanted to tell you?*

It's not *Emma,* Pao thought. *It's not Emma. Please don't let it be Emma.*

"We'll talk to Kit first," she said tersely, and Bruto cocked his head to the side, but wisely, he didn't argue.

They found the girls still huddled in the bleachers, which annoyed Pao, until she realized they were arguing.

"What's going on, Rogues?"

"Nothing!" Kit said in a huff. "Just forget it." She made to storm off, but Emma was up in an instant, grabbing the back of Kit's hood so she couldn't leave.

"Tell her or *I will*," she said in a threatening tone Pao had never heard her use before.

"Tell me what?"

Kit sighed. "Look, it's your stupid key chain, okay? I stole it in the car because I wanted to see how it worked and I knew you'd never let me, but then it turned into this whole big thing, so I tried to ditch it so someone could just, like, come upon it all surprised, like, *Oh, look, it's been here the whole time!*"

"*You* took it?" Pao said, every brain cell aching to jump to the obvious conclusion, to exonerate Emma and finally have someone to blame, some action to take.

But if the Arma del Alma was here, there was no need to jump to conclusions. Finally, she would see for good, and Pao knew exactly what she would see. She could picture it now, Kit stretching taller than her diminutive height, her face twisting and calcifying, her eyes burning green in her skull. A shadow warrior. Proof that Pao's feelings of immense dislike had been warranted all along . . .

"Give it to me," Pao said in a low, even voice. "Now."

"That's the problem," Kit said, exasperated. "I don't *have* it anymore. That's what Goody Two-Shoes over here was getting all twisted up about."

"What do you mean you don't have it?" Pao asked. "Where is it?"

"You tell her," Kit said, rolling her eyes at Emma. "You're obviously *dying* to impress her, so be my guest."

Pao turned to Emma, whose wide eyes were already fixed on her.

"Pao, it's—" she began, but before she could finish, the ground started to shake. "What's happening?" She stepped closer to Pao, who instinctively grabbed her hand as the metal bleachers shook beneath them.

"AN EARTHQUAKE!" Kit cried hysterically.

"It can't be an earthquake," Pao said, eyes scanning for the source of the disturbance. The trembling stopped, but from the office came the sound of an alarm, an old-fashioned, blaring thing that made her stomach clench in fear. "Dad?" she called.

"Here!" he said. "But I don't know what's happening. I need to check the instruments." He dashed toward the office while Pao led Emma down the bleachers to the somewhat safer floor.

The alarm continued to blare. Bruto was whining, pressing close to Pao.

"We should round up the little kids," Pao said, patting him reassuringly. "I need to find Naomi."

"Wait!" Emma cried, pointing past Pao's shoulder to a corner of the room. "It's Dante. He's . . . He's got the Arma del Alma."

TWENTY-FIVE

A Hole in the Sweater Sleeve of the Universe

"Dante?" Pao whirled around to see him up against the wall he'd been staring at for hours, his back to them, looking down at something in his hands.

"He picked it up when Kit tried to leave it in the bleachers," Emma said, near tears as she explained. "I told him we had to give it back to you, and he said he was going to, but then he just walked over to the wall. That's when Kit and I started arguing. I said we had to tell you, and Kit didn't want you thinking she was the bad guy, and—"

"Stay here!" Pao called, sprinting over to the place where Dante stood huddled. He was shaking, she realized, as she drew closer to him. Or was it just another tremor in the floor? "Dante!"

The sound of her voice made him look up. The air was strange over here, Pao thought, the colors all blurring a little at the edges, everything appearing fuzzy, like she was viewing it over a bad internet connection. When he saw her, his face split into a grin that was both like and not like his true smile. Something wider, but also more sinister.

"Dante, give me the arma," she said calmly, only a few feet of space between them now. Bruto was beside her, growling, his hackles up again. Pao slowed down, heeding her pup's warning. "If you just hand it over, everything will be fine."

"You thought you were like us," he said. "You were so *afraid* to be like us. But really you'll never be half clever enough, nor cunning enough, *hungry* enough."

It was the correct use of *nor* that convinced Pao this was not Dante. To make matters worse, as he continued to speak, his voice took on that strange, multilayered quality she had come to associate with void creatures.

Bruto growled again, but Dante paid him no mind.

"You went into the void to rescue *him*," he went on, his eyes darting around wildly. "You didn't even question whether he was the real one. Even after you'd seen the copies. You thought *you* had tricked El Cucuy, stolen a prisoner from him."

The truth of the matter came in like a trickle and then a flood, blotting out everything else. *Dante* had been the copy. The magical signature Franco had picked up when Pao opened the portal.

"But you . . ." she said, the pieces coming together too slowly. "You were the one who asked *me*. About the first time I beat you at *Mario Kart*. How . . . ?"

"You're so slow," he said. "I handed you the answer not an hour ago. The memory was trivial to you, but to *him* . . ."

"It meant something," Pao said in a hollow voice.

The ground was shaking again, and everyone fled the room except Kit and Emma, who huddled against the bleachers waiting for Pao.

"So what you said about Día de los Muertos . . ." Pao went on, needing to keep him talking because she didn't have a weapon to fight him with. She wasn't prepared for this. Not after everything she'd done to find him.

"A ruse," Dante said, his eyes rolling as the ground shook harder. "Luring you into a false sense of security so you wouldn't be ready. It was El Cucuy's original plan, of course, until you showed up full of reckless idiocy, just *begging* to take one of his soldiers back to open the void."

"Where's the real Dante?" Pao asked, finally accepting that this was happening. That she still hadn't seen her friend. That she'd rushed off to help and instead had brought on the destruction of the world ten days earlier than originally scheduled. "Where is he?"

But the Dante copy didn't seem to have heard her. His eyes were all the way back in his head now, and finally Pao could see in his hand the golden glint of her Arma del Alma in its magnifying glass form—the form it had taken in the cornfield when she had needed to see the way forward. He was holding it behind his back, the metal against the wall he'd been staring at since the moment they'd arrived, and at the point where it was making contact, something horribly familiar was happening.

Pao remembered her first experience with a void opening like it was yesterday. It wasn't something you easily forgot, after all. The tiny black hole that had wormed and wriggled like a loose sweater thread pulling open the fabric of the universe.

"No," Pao said. "No, Dante, please."

But this wasn't Dante, no matter how much he looked like him, no matter how much Pao had needed to believe she'd saved him and everything was going to be okay. Everything was definitely *not* going to be okay. The Shadow Dante (one of many,

Pao thought with a sick feeling in her stomach) was using *her* Arma del Alma to open the void right here, and she couldn't let it happen. No matter what she had to do.

So she did the first thing she could think of. She stepped forward and pushed him into the wall, hard, shattering his concentration and forcing his irises back into normal position. Only now they weren't the warm brown eyes of the boy she'd always known—they were a vivid, glowing green, and his teeth were bared in a snarl.

"It's too late," he said in that awful grating voice again. "You won't stop what I've set in motion. But I'll enjoy killing you anyway." And right in front of her, he transformed the magnifying glass into the shining, ruthlessly bladed staff Pao had only ever fought *with*, never against. He was raising it high, ready to slice her in two, and there was nothing she could do. Nothing.

Bruto lunged at him, and Shadow Dante kicked the chupe hard in the shoulder, eliciting a yelp that made Pao's heart skip a beat. Bruto limped away with an apologetic expression, leaving Pao truly alone.

"Help!" she called, even though it went against every one of her instincts. "Someone help me!" She darted to the side, Shadow Dante's blow narrowly missing her skull and clanging against something metal instead.

"You can thank me later," Kit grunted, pulling back her broken-handled rake and flashing a grin at Pao.

"Hero girl, catch!" came Naomi's voice from a few feet away, and Pao spun just in time to catch another staff—wooden-handled, and its blade a little rusty, but it felt at home in her hands as she spun it to ready herself for the next attack. "Just out of curiosity, how many more chances are we gonna give this guy?"

Naomi didn't wait for an answer, just caught his next strike with her double knives, the sharp blades sparking against the staff's handle as they met, separated, and met again.

"It's not him!" Pao said, circling around behind the Dante copy as its attention was diverted. "It's a shadow, like the ones I was telling you about!" She jabbed at Dante's back with the speared end, and he spun, like he could sense her, only to meet Kit's rake again as she brought it down on his head.

"Nice one!" Naomi yelled, ever the fight instructor, even in mortal peril. "Just remember to move your—"

Dante spun with the snarl fixed on his face, features waxen and strange as he swept Kit's legs out from under her and zeroed in on her throat with the blade.

". . . feet," Naomi finished. "Ah well. Beginners, am I right?" She got in close and shoved Dante off Kit, unfortunately turning him straight toward Pao.

He charged at her like a bull, and as she put up her flimsy staff to block his attack, he sliced it clean in two with the superior blade of the Arma del Alma, leaving Pao functionally weaponless again.

"What's our endgame here, hero girl?" Naomi asked, having helped Kit back to her feet and now circling Dante along with Pao as he sized them up, calculating his next move.

"Vaporize him," Pao said. "But, Naomi?" She had just spun to face the wall again, and she pointed to where the wriggling hole was larger now, at least as big as Pao's head. Through it she could see the pulsating fabric of the void, billowing like curtains, waiting for the hand of El Cucuy to part them and wreak havoc on the world of the living.

"Not ideal," Naomi grunted as she swiped at Shadow Dante

again. "The last thing we need is more of these confusing little weasels running around."

"Agreed," Pao said, landing a blow to Shadow Dante's shoulder that made him hiss and whirl to face her. She fought the urge to apologize to him, trying to remember that this copy was no more Dante than her own shadow had been her. Although now her shadow self *was* part of her? She hit Shadow Dante again just to avoid having to make sense of it.

"Do they have one of me in there?" Naomi asked, losing focus for a moment to stare at the hole in the wall, which was growing exponentially now.

"I don't know," Pao said. "Probably. The best thing to do would be to close the hole before we find out."

"Right," said Naomi. "Little as I like to say this, the puffed-up egghead in the office will probably have some ideas. Might as well mine him for all the information we can before we *banish him from Los Niños forever.*" This time, when Naomi struck at Shadow Dante's face, Pao knew she was really picturing Franco's.

Pao looked around for Emma but didn't see her. Maybe she had gone to console Robin?

"I'll go," Pao volunteered. "But that weapon he's using is the only way to identify the shadows, so get it back in one piece. Think you can handle him?"

Naomi scoffed. "One shrimpy void boy? I kicked the real one's butt back in the day—I'll be happy to demonstrate that being pickled in evil hasn't improved his odds. Go, talk to Franco and figure out how to close this thing."

"Coming, Kit?" Pao asked as the other girl walked forward with a slight limp, rake still fiercely brandished in front of her.

"Nah, the kid stays with me," Naomi said. "We'll make a

warrior out of you yet, won't we? Tell you what—you kill him with that rake, and I'll graduate you to a real weapon, hm?"

Pao took off at a run toward the office, leaving Naomi and Kit fighting furiously. Shadow Dante was at least a head taller than them both now that he'd shown his true colors, but there was still so much of the boy she knew in his face. She'd volunteered to get help not just because Emma wasn't handy, or because she couldn't handle the fight, but because when it came down to it, Pao didn't know if she could kill the shadow. Not when it was wearing her friend's face.

She shook herself, calling Bruto to her so she could secure him safely in the office for now. This was no time to be nostalgic about Dante. To wonder what had happened to him, if he was even alive. No time to confront the fact that she had recklessly charged off into the void to rescue him and done nothing but endanger the entire world in the process. If she let herself feel it now, she'd fall apart, and she couldn't afford to do that. Not until *after* she'd fixed her mistakes.

"Dad!" she shouted as she burst into the office. Maria was still in there, glaring at Beto, who had the good grace to look ashamed of himself. Bruto made his way toward her, looking for treats and comfort. Robin and her dads were nowhere to be seen. Neither were Emma, Marisa, and Franco. Pao hoped they were safe, but she didn't have time to stand around catching up.

"What is it, mijita? The tremors seem to have stopped, gracias a Dios. Did you talk to the girls?"

"Things are moving a little faster than that, Dad," Pao gasped. "Dante was the copy. Kit had my arma, and he took it from her, and the void is, like, opening *now* in the training room, and Dante's all freaky-like, and they're fighting him off, but I don't know how long it'll be before that opening is complete, and—"

"We have to close it!" Beto said, his face going white beneath its normal golden brown. "Paola, we cannot let anything come through!"

"I know!" Pao said. "That's why I'm *here*! I was hoping you or Franco knew how to close it, because I've only done it by accident, and—"

"I don't know of any way to close a rift from this side," Beto said, pulling at his hair as he began to pace around the office. "I never learned. And Joaquin was obsessed with *opening*, not closing. . . ."

That's when it occurred to Pao. The secret she knew that no one else could. Shadow Pao's memories had receded since Pao had come through the void, overwhelmed by real experiences that took priority, she guessed. But they were still there, like she'd put them in a box in her closet.

"The words," Pao said, more to herself than her parents. "El Cucuy told Shadow Pao to say some words when she closed them, but I can't . . . quite . . ." It was like trying to remember a dream after she'd woken, the details slipping away. She could picture fighting the ahogados at the lake house, and the avalanche, but whenever she tried to focus on the words themselves, everything got hazy and dim. "Ughhh," Pao groaned. "I can't remember! But there's a phrase, some command he gives to close the doors. We have to try to find out what it is."

"How . . . do you know that?" Beto asked, and for the first time, Pao realized her parents were standing there staring at her like they'd never seen her before.

"When I . . . defeated my shadow self," she said, deciding now wasn't the absolute best moment to describe the whole *fusing in the void pod* phenomenon, "her memories kind of became part of me. I'm not really sure about the logistics, but I can remember things she did as if I did them."

The gaping didn't stop.

"You're just gonna have to trust me, okay?" Pao said impatiently. "There's a command. I don't know exactly what it is, but if we can find out, we can close this one, too, I bet you anything."

"If that's true, there's only one person here who would know it," Beto said, his gaze straying toward the door. "We need to keep Dante's clone alive."

"A little help out here, hero girl!" came Naomi's voice through the door. "It's getting weird!"

"Where's Franco?" Pao asked, already backing toward the door, the pieces of the broken staff in her hands. She knew Naomi wouldn't have called for help unless it was really serious—she had to get back.

"Here," Franco said, stepping out from behind a teetering stack of papers and books. "I'm already looking into alternate ways to close the void, but it's . . . not my area of expertise."

"Great," Pao said. "The one thing we *thought* you'd be good for."

"Paola!" said Beto, but she was already gone, ready to sprint back across the warehouse . . . until she saw something that made her stop in her tracks.

The fight was on hold as Naomi and Kit stood, weapons at their sides, staring. Dante had backed against the wall and was attached to the rapidly opening void mouth like he was a battery charging. His eyes were green floodlights, bathing the whole space in a spooky glow. . . .

But that wasn't even the weirdest thing about it.

Naomi and Kit ran right into Pao, and the three of them stood together, watching as Dante's mouth opened far too wide to be a human mouth, like those videos of a snake's jaw unhinging as it consumed a living mouse. But nothing wriggling disappeared into Shadow Dante's gaping maw—instead, something was streaming *out*. Ribbons of light shot forth, like the time in third grade when Shane Collins had thrown up in the lunchroom, and suddenly the walls were coated in black-and-white pictures that dripped down the walls.

"What the . . ." Kit whispered.

But Pao, who had seen these images before, was the most horrified by far. "It's the nightmares," she said, embarrassed by the shaking in her voice. "El Cucuy's nightmares . . . He's projecting them through Dante."

The Niños who had been sent to the courtyard were now gathered in the doorway, eyes wide, reflecting the pictures that were now beginning to flicker and shift, faster, then slower, like a drunk guy was running the movie projector. Pao could make out familiar images now—the apartment building on fire again, La Llorona's face up close, with her dead eyes and twisted mouth.

Beside her, Kit whispered something that sounded like "Not in my shoes—get them out!" and Pao realized the images were different for everyone, displaying their deepest, darkest fears on every surface they could see. The youngest Niños were crying as the older ones looked stricken, but Pao could barely focus on them, too distracted by the image of her father with Joaquin's cruel eyes, Emma dead on the ground at her feet, Maria and Dante dead, too.

A sob welled up in Pao's throat, and she felt helpless, drained.

Her weapon slid uselessly from her hand. She would never save them. The void would open, and they would all die, and there was nothing she could do to stop it.

Just when she thought she couldn't take any more, the images faded away, leaving nothing but bright white, and everyone began to look around, dazed. Pao saw Emma in the crowd by the door, reassuringly alive, and her heart begin to beat normally again.

Pao was going to run to Emma, take her hand, and try to give voice to all the confusing and scary things she'd started to feel over these past few days, because the future wasn't guaranteed, was it? There was no time like the present. . . .

But then a voice like the screeching metal of two cars colliding rent the air around them, and against the bright white backdrop, there was a sudden shadow. The silhouette of El Cucuy himself, with his amorphous, shifting face, his horrible hands, and his long, billowing cloak. From the intake of breaths around her, Pao could tell she wasn't the only one seeing him this time.

"Children, I speak to you from the haunt of dread, from the place all your fears live. I am coming, and I am coming soon, with an army of shadow souls much more ravenous than the poor runt you see in front of you now. I am coming for your parents, and your friends, and your teachers, and you—yes, you too."

The little Niños were crying harder now, the older ones shushing them, and Pao felt rather than saw her parents take their places behind her, all of them watching as El Cucuy spelled out the end of the world.

"It is not in my nature to be merciful, so I won't promise mercy. What I will tell you is this: Anyone found aiding or abetting Paola Santiago will be last to die. You will watch your families, your friends, your entire world plunged into shadow, and then, finally, I will take you, too. She is not one of you. She is of the void. Think carefully before you choose your side."

On the walls around them, Pao's image flashed, with an expression of fierce concentration that was easy to mistake for anger. For evil. In El Cucuy's rendering, she was sleeker and sharper. She looked like an enemy.

"The world will be mine before long," came the voice again, echoing everywhere, as if it were oozing from the very walls. "The time of the living has ended."

It would have been a relief to have the voice fall silent, but it was replaced by new images. Void mouths opening all over the world. In Santuario, and at the mountain and the lake, but in cities, too. Los Angeles, New York, Tokyo, Mexico City, and more. Pao and the Niños watched in utter terror as El Cucuy showed them his plan. The void mouths widened in every location, and the shadow soldiers streamed out, blending with the populations. Chaos spread as they began to kill the living one by one. The city streets were filled with screaming civilians trampling each other, looking for an escape they would never find.

Then the images abruptly cut off and the bright white disappeared from the walls, leaving the usual patched and faded concrete.

Shadow Dante fell forward onto the floor, his head connecting with a sickening crunch, green ooze spreading like blood from the place where he lay still.

He was gone, and any hope of discovering the phrase to close the void was gone with him. They would have to find another way.

Behind him, the void matter pulsed malevolently. A promise. As soon as it had grown large enough for a soldier to climb through, the battle would begin. At the rate it was going, Pao estimated they only had half an hour. Maybe less.

It wasn't enough time. Not to plan, not to close the mouth, not to save the world.

Still, no one had spoken, but Pao could feel the eyes of the room slowly seeking her out, fastening on her, and she knew they were seeing the sharper, more sinister version of her, remembering El Cucuy's words that she wasn't one of them, that she belonged to the void, that anyone who helped her would have to watch their family die.

She wanted to run, to hide, to give herself up so she'd be spared the agony of admitting who she was, and the fact that she had no idea what to do next. And maybe, once upon a time, she would have. But she wasn't the same girl she'd been when the green mist had taken over Riverside Palace, the same girl who had hidden behind facts and figures and fled from her fear.

"Paola, this is not the time," Beto said as she broke free of their little group and made for the bleachers.

"It's the *only* time," she said, climbing them one by one, not bothering to quiet her footsteps.

TWENTY-SIX

The Beginning of the End of the World

"Excuse me!" Pao called out, making sure she was loud enough to be heard by everyone—the Niños in the courtyard doorway, Franco in the office, even Robin and her dads, if they were still on the property.

"Hi," she said when she was sure all eyes were on her. "I'm Paola Santiago. For anyone who doesn't know me, I'm in eighth grade, I like science and dogs"—Bruto let out a proud bark that echoed through the room—"and also . . . I'm the granddaughter of La Llorona."

There was a collective gasp. Pao was known to most of the Niños, of course, after the events at the Gila River and in the Oregon forest, but she'd asked Naomi to keep Pao's ancestry quiet. Maybe Pao had been ashamed. Maybe she just hadn't understood it well enough to explain. But now it was time to be everything she was, out loud, because if they were going to beat this thing, they were going to have to do it together.

"I know," she said. "It's shocking. I was shocked myself when I found out last summer. In fact, ever since then I've been terrified, running from my shadow, sometimes literally."

There was a loud guffaw from Naomi, but everyone else seemed enraptured, listening.

"El Cucuy is coming," she went on, "because I went into the void to try to take something from him. My best friend, Dante Mata. Instead, he tricked me into bringing back a copy that stole my Arma del Alma and made this opening in the void." She gestured in front at the hole that had grown noticeably bigger since she'd started speaking.

After a deep breath, she said, "I know you guys are here for a reason. You're monster hunters, you fight the creatures of the void, you keep people safe. And maybe some of you are thinking I'm not worth the trouble. That you'd rather make me your enemy because I'm the granddaughter of an evil fantasma who drowned children, or because I make a lot of mistakes, or maybe just because I annoy you. But I'm here to tell you that every part of me—void-born and otherwise—is ready to fight against El Cucuy's invasion. To make sure he can never use the void against us again. To make sure Silver Springs and all those other cities you just saw are safe. Not just for now, but forever."

"How do we do that?" called Sal from the doorway. He looked terrified.

Pao wanted to make something up. She'd never wanted to lie so badly. To say she had a secret plan, that she alone could keep them safe. But she had outgrown that, too.

"I'm not sure yet," she admitted instead. "And that hole is getting bigger all the time. As soon as a shadow soldier can fit through, it'll be time to fight. But being able to travel in the void, having La Llorona's DNA inside me, has given me the ability to think like they think, to see what they see, and I'm betting I can use that to help us defeat this guy. I've been able to defeat other fantasmas without a very good plan—just by fighting, and hoping, and having a little luck at the right time. So, if you'll stick with me, if you'll fight, if you'll help me come up with a plan, I think we can beat him."

She took another deep breath, this one harder to come by, as the anxiety over what she was about to say threatened to squeeze all the air out of her lungs.

"El Cucuy's job is to make us feel fear. Most of us have felt that fear long before today. He wants to make you afraid of me because he knows that we're weaker divided. But all that said, if you want me to leave, I will. So . . . it's up to you."

"But to be clear," Naomi called from beside Pao's parents at the foot of the bleachers, "I go where the pipsqueak goes."

"As do I," came another voice—Marisa's. Her braids were pulled back, her eyes wide and solemn. She drew her Arma del Alma, a water knife that had once slid between Pao's ribs, for extra effect.

"And I," said Beto, his eyes filled with tears as he stepped forward and inclined his head toward Pao. "I've been fighting monsters a long time, both within and without, and I think my daughter is the best chance we have."

Pao was tearing up, too, emotion building in her chest, until she heard a voice that brought her right back to earth with an eye roll of epic proportions.

"The Middle School Champion Boffing Team of the Southwest is with Pao," the girl said in a faux-solemn voice. "Led by me, of course."

"Thanks, Kit," Pao mumbled, wondering for the hundredth time if it wouldn't have been better to leave her in the cornfield.

More people stepped forward—some Pao knew, and some she didn't. It wasn't everyone, but it was enough to make her heart swell. She pressed her hand to her chest and mouthed, *Thank you*, not trusting her voice, but trusting they would all see.

She was about to climb down from the bleachers and get to work coming up with a plan when the office door creaked open and the tall, lanky silhouette of Franco stepped into the room.

"I'm with the kid, too," he said tersely, like it was the toughest pill he'd ever had to swallow. "I wouldn't fight this battle without her."

The rest of the holdouts came forward in a rush as soon as Franco stepped forward, and Pao found she could be grateful even for him. Or at least for Marisa, who had undoubtedly forced him to join her.

"Thank you, all," Pao said, her voice a little wobbly. "Now let's go!" She hopped down the bleachers, her sneakers rattling every bench until she reached the bottom, where Emma was waiting with Bruto.

"Nice speech," Emma said with a shy smile.

"Thanks," Pao said, rubbing the back of her neck, feeling suddenly shy herself. It had been easier to think of the crowd as anonymous when she was addressing it. But now, realizing that *Emma* had heard her say those things . . .

"You know I'm with you, right?" Emma asked, looking at her shoes. "To the bitter end and whatever's past that?"

"I know," Pao said, wrapping her arm around Emma's shoulders. "Sometimes it's the only thing I know."

They would have said more, Pao was sure, and maybe she was even ready for it now, but Marisa, Naomi, and Beto were approaching with—to Pao's enormous surprise—Robin and her dads, and it was time to prepare for war.

"What can I do?" Emma asked, her tone all business, and Pao's arm fell to her side.

"Maybe you could go with my mom and set up somewhere safe for the littlest kids? And we're going to need help from the community, anyone who's willing to take a stand with a bunch of weirdos."

"I'll post it on Nextdoor!" said Jonathan, Robin's witch dad, who was already pulling out his phone.

"Um," Pao said. "I'm not sure that's the best—"

"Oh, don't worry. Recruiting for a shadow-soldier-hunting army will only be, like, the fourth-weirdest thing on there today," Todd reassured her as his husband typed furiously with both thumbs. "Most people will think it's a joke, but a few might show up."

"Try it," Pao said, resigned. "If they don't come to us, there's every chance the shadows will go to them. No point in trying to keep it a secret now."

"I'll get the little ones situated with Emma," Maria said. "Jonathan, you can make your post from the courtyard, where it's safer."

"Sounds good, Ms. Santiago," Emma said, turning away and just as quickly turning back. "Please take care," she said to Pao, her cheeks flushed as she darted in to give her a kiss on the cheek.

Pao stood with her hand against the spot, staring dumbly for several long seconds, until Naomi elbowed her in the side and brought her unceremoniously back to reality.

"Fight now," she said, "swoon later. Oh, and here." Naomi pulled the ornate golden magnifying glass out of her back pocket and handed it to Pao. It was smeared with green goo, but the lens was intact and Pao felt instantly better with it in her hand.

She transformed it into the glimmering staff with its brutal blade just to make sure she still could, and then shrank it back down, scanning the assembled group once, surreptitiously, just to make sure. Everyone was themself, she was relieved to see. No more copies.

Not for another twenty-five minutes or so, anyway.

"I've already sent Emma and my mom to round up anyone too young to fight and find somewhere safe," Pao said without preamble. "Maybe we could have a couple of our more experienced fighters guarding them in case the worst happens?"

"I'll handle that," Marisa said, and Pao couldn't help but feel a little awestruck at the fact that the Niños's leader was following her instruction. But there would be time to get an ego about it later. If they didn't all die first.

"Thanks," Pao said as Marisa walked away. "Naomi, anyone who's in fighting shape should be stationed by the void opening. Shadow soldiers will be coming through in a matter of minutes, and we need to make sure they don't get very far."

"On it," Naomi said, with nary a snarky comment, knives already in hand as she bellowed for fighters to join her.

Pao turned to Franco and her father next, taking a deep breath and swallowing about 90 percent of what she wanted to say to them. Instead, she said, "I know we've all made mistakes these past months. We haven't trusted one another. We've let fear and guilt and resentment get in the way of our working together. But we need to put all that aside now, because"—Pao lowered her voice, looking around to make sure no one outside their little group could hear—"I'm pretty sure we all know we're no match for what's about to be unleashed on this place. On this entire world. Not unless we find some way to stop it for good. From the inside."

"For once, I agree," Franco said, like it was causing him physical pain to admit it. "There has to be a solution. Something we can do to stop it at the source."

"All three of us on the same page," Beto said with a smile. "Alert the presses."

"Let's go into the office," Franco said irritably. "We have about fifteen minutes to figure out how to save the world."

Pao cast one long look over her shoulder at Naomi, who was leading the older Niños through drills, and Marisa, just visible through the courtyard door, barricading the place as best she could. Pao wanted to be with them. To be part of the fight, not the reason for it. But that had never been her role to play.

"Come, Paola," her father said. "We need you."

In the office, Franco pushed a rolling chair toward Pao without looking, and she took it, peering through her magnifying glass. All was as it seemed for now.

"Your main role when the shadow soldiers start coming through," Beto said, "will be to keep an eye out, make sure they don't become confused for the living fighters. You'll be the only one who can tell the difference."

Pao grimaced. It meant she couldn't fight. Her best weapon would have to be a magnifying glass for the duration of the battle. But if it meant keeping their forces from accidentally turning on each other, she knew she had no choice.

"Done," Pao said. "But the people in Tokyo and New York

and Mexico City won't have magic truth-tellers. Silver Springs is only one point of entry."

"Or that's what he wants us to believe," Franco mused, squeezing a rubber stress ball as he stared pensively at the wall.

"What do you mean?" Pao asked.

"This is a fantasma who deals in fear and nightmares," Franco said, like it was the most obvious thing in the world. "They're the source of all his power. If he thinks telling us other cities will be under siege is going to terrify us into spreading ourselves too thin, he will."

But Beto was shaking his head grimly, holding out the smartphone Pao had insisted he get when he reentered society last winter. On the screen was a bold headline reading: *STRANGE ANOMALY APPEARS ON CENTRAL PARK STATUE!* As he scrolled down, other city names appeared, along with grainy black-and-white photos of what were absolutely growing void mouths on hedges, buildings, and even a waterslide in Orlando, Florida.

"So much for that theory," Pao said, fear beginning to twist in her stomach like a nest of snakes. "We can't be everywhere at once. We can't even warn them. What are we going to do?"

"We're going to find a way to shut him down for good," said Franco, clacking away on the old computer with the green-and-black screen like he was going to find the answer there.

Beto, for his part, turned to Pao. "I need you to tell me everything that happened when you were in the obsidian tower," he said urgently. "No matter how small or insignificant it seems. There may be some clue that you didn't have the prior knowledge to decipher."

Pao bristled, but she realized he was trying, so she started at the beginning, describing every detail she could think of, from the empty, lightning-struck field, to the bone warriors, to the empty cages and the endless stairs, until she got to El Cucuy himself.

"We're running out of time," she said, glancing at the office clock. Nine of their fifteen minutes had elapsed. Far sooner than any of them were ready for, the fight would be upon them.

"Keep going," Beto said, his eyes never leaving her face as Franco continued to type furiously.

So she went on, described tricking (or *thinking* she'd tricked) El Cucuy into believing she was Shadow Pao after absorbing her memories, the elevator down into the obsidian mine, the tanks full of clones, and everything she could remember from El Cucuy's description of his process. Then the portal, finding Dante in the cell, expanding her portal range to take him with her through the bars, and their unceremonious arrival back in Santuario.

"He never attacked you directly?" Beto asked after listening to all of this with rapt attention. There were two minutes left.

Pao thought about this. "No," she said finally. "He used his nightmares to try and freeze me up, but he never actually attacked me."

"Was he carrying a weapon?" Beto asked with keen, almost hawklike eyes. "A scythe? A knife? Any kind of weapon at all?"

Pao thought back to the shifting face, the nightmare cloak, the awful hands, even the bright red boots. But there had never been a weapon. She shook her head. "Not that I could see."

The light dancing in her father's eyes at that moment felt

like looking into a mirror. She could almost feel the electricity bouncing around inside his skull as he made connections, formed theories, and dismissed or altered them, trying to find a path forward.

"Pao?" came a voice from outside. Naomi's. Pao's heart began to race. "I think something's happening!"

"Any brilliant insights here, guys?" Pao asked, noticing that her voice was slightly higher and more wobbly than usual. "Because it looks like we're out of time."

Franco was already on his feet, pulling his longsword out of a filing cabinet beside the desk and turning to face the door with a grim expression on his face. Pao's heart sank a little. She'd hoped he had something up his sleeve, something that would prove her wrong about him being a puffed-up know-it-all with a god complex.

There was little comfort in being right this time.

"Dad?" she asked, trying to break his concentration, but he barely looked up.

"I'm close, just let me . . . No, not that, but maybe the other?"

"DAD!" Pao said loudly, still hoping there was a way to do this that didn't involve fighting every single shadow that came through the portal one by one.

"Yes, yes," Beto said, half in and half out of this world, but that was better than nothing. "I have an idea, Paola, but it will take time to solidify my plans. If the others can hold him off for a little while on their own, we may be able to end this thing."

"You got it," Pao said, turning to follow Franco to the door, expecting her father to forbid her from fighting. But he was back in his trance now. He barely even noticed her leaving, which

suited Pao just fine. She didn't want to have to make any promises she couldn't keep.

The warehouse training room had always seemed huge to
Pao, but now, with their modest fighting force crowded around
the length of wall where the void mouth was finally reaching
max capacity, it seemed like far too small a space to wage a war
against the underworld. Pao and Franco joined the rest, a tense,
waiting silence falling over them as the membrane separating
them from the horrors beyond it stretched thinner and thinner
with each passing second.

"Here," Naomi said, elbowing her way over to Pao through
the small crowd. She held out a small tube, and for a wild second, Pao thought it was some cool new gadget that would help
her fight off shadow soldiers. But when she opened it, it was just
black lipstick. Kit's, if she wasn't mistaken.

"Not sure now's the time for a goth phase," Pao said, "but
whatever floats your boat?"

Naomi scoffed, and Pao looked up to see she had an X drawn
on her forehead with the stuff. "It's so we can tell us apart from
them," she said. "Just in case . . . you know . . . he made copies
of any of us."

Pao nodded her approval and drew an X on her own head,
not even caring if it looked ridiculous. She gazed around at the
assembled crowd. Everyone seemed to have followed suit. Pao
privately thought it wouldn't take long for the copies to catch
on, or for the lipstick to sweat off the fighters, but at least it was
something.

"Look," Marisa said, pointing at the opening (as if anyone
was looking anywhere else). But as Pao peered closer, she saw

what the older girl meant. It wasn't just swirling goo anymore. Beyond it she could see the silhouettes of countless shadow soldiers prepared to take them down.

The membrane billowed out, causing several Niños to flinch and step backward. Bruto, returning to Pao's side, growled a low warning.

"The kids?" Pao asked Marisa.

"In the courtyard with your mom and the little blond and the noisy dads."

Pao nodded. Something seemed to be blocking her throat. She knelt down to put her forehead against her pup's. "Buddy, I need you to go to Emma. Protect her and Mom and the kids. You're the only one I trust."

Bruto whined, doing his signature puppy-dog eyes.

"Please," she said. "I have to stay here and help, and I'll have lots of protectors around me. They need you in the courtyard."

After a long look, Bruto licked her hand until it was slimy, and then trotted off, taking a piece of Pao's heart with him.

"Any magical solutions occur during your little brainstorm in there?" Naomi asked Pao.

She just shook her head. "My dad's still in there," she said. "But it's not looking great."

"So we fight," Naomi said. "We've faced worse odds."

Though both of them knew that wasn't true, Pao smiled. "And we're still here."

Another stretching of the void fabric, and a tear, and a collective intake of breath.

"Okay, everyone," Pao said. "These shadows are going to look like regular people. Like people you know. Maybe even yourselves. But trust me, they're not, and they'll kill you the first chance they get, so don't give them that chance."

People nodded as they took their stances, shuffling for position.

"With this magnifying glass," Pao said as the glowing eyes came closer, reminding her of the ahogados that had swarmed her during her first attempt to enter the void, "I can see the truth. If you're not sure whether you're looking at a copy or a comrade, if you feel yourself hesitating, call out, and I'll be the final word. Got it?"

A murmur of assent. The entrance billowed again.

"It's time," Pao said quietly. "You're the bravest people I know. Fight well!"

"Fight well!" they said, almost as one, and then all at once the void membrane burst like a blister, and they were at war.

TWENTY-SEVEN

War

Naomi made the first kill, but Marisa wasn't far behind. The two of them fought back-to-back like a well-oiled machine as the void disgorged one shadow soldier after another. Each time one came through, Pao could see from where she'd backed away to keep an eye on the field through her magnifying glass, the mouth widened a little.

They were dealing with one at a time now, she thought, but it wouldn't be long before it was two, then five, and so on. From what she had seen, El Cucuy had an almost inexhaustible supply of these things, and he cared little if they died in the process.

Pao's mind was whirling at top speed as she monitored the fight, seeing each shadow soldier for what it was—a twisted, gaunt-faced monstrosity, even as the people on the ground saw them as friends or neighbors or even strangers who didn't deserve to die.

Each pool of green goo on the concrete floor of the warehouse told another story.

Already the huge, echoing room was filled with the sounds of fighting, with the Niños doing what they did best. *Maybe we can keep this going until all the copies are gone,* Pao thought with a kind of desperate optimism as Naomi and Marisa struck down shadow after shadow, the rest of the Niños alert and at the ready, but their blades still clean.

It was five whole minutes before one got past them—a redheaded, freckle-faced high schooler Pao thought she'd seen working at the 7-Eleven. He sprinted into the waiting crowd of Niños with startling speed and agility, his feral eyes darting around ceaselessly. Pao wondered what he was looking for until his eyes locked onto her and he snarled, making for her immediately.

"A little help over here?" Pao called, but her voice was swallowed by the echoing din. Gritting her teeth, knowing she only had seconds left, she transformed her Arma del Alma just as the shadow cashier reached her, and she skewered him through with it. His eyes widened in surprise as she withdrew the blade with a truly gross squelching sound, and he sank to the ground, bleeding green.

"Sorry, hero girl!" Naomi called, having just used her knives to take down another soldier. "I'll get the next one, I promise."

"Behind you!" Pao called in response, and Naomi turned just in time to prevent a newly expelled copy from getting its hands around her neck.

The enemy has numbers, Pao thought, watching from the bleachers like a chess player, itching to be part of the action, *but most of them aren't armed.* Apparently, the obsidian staff El Cucuy had given Shadow Pao wasn't a privilege bestowed on all of them. They fought mostly hand to hand, and their tactics seemed to be mostly focused on grappling—strangling, incapacitating limbs, dragging bodies to the ground, etc.

Even with their ragtag weapons stash and their inferior numbers, the Niños de la Luz were holding their own, and Pao—her services not needed so far—spent her time racking her brain for a bigger-picture solution. This obviously wasn't the main assault. El Cucuy hadn't even made a personal appearance yet. But something her father had asked her stuck in Pao's mind.

Did he attack you directly?

El Cucuy was clearly the one powering the charge, and yet he didn't carry a weapon. Didn't make direct attacks. He seemed content to hide behind his monstrosities and his nightmares, controlling but never engaging.

Did that mean that drawing him into the fight, defeating him personally, would stop it all? Or did the shadow soldiers have soul enough to power themselves? Were they a terrible machine set in motion that couldn't be stopped?

She had to find out. But how?

"On your left, Pao!" Marisa's voice rang out across the warehouse, snapping Pao out of her hypothesizing just in time to see another copy of Poppy the chaperone walking up the bleachers toward her.

"Once wasn't enough, huh?" Pao asked, lifting her staff just as Poppy's freckled face began to stretch and morph, her eyes to glow. "Happy to put you in your place again, then."

"You'll never keep them safe," Poppy screeched in that awful, layered voice. *"This is just the beginning. They're going to get tired. They're going to make mistakes. And we will keep coming. There's no end to this, Paola—how long do you really think you can hold us off?"*

Pao felt the familiar stirrings of fear in her belly. The images

El Cucuy had shown her of her loved ones dead, of Silver Springs burning, were all too easy to conjure. But Pao had been mastering her nightmares since she was a little kid. She knew where to put them now.

"Your boss is a coward," Pao said as Poppy drew closer, her poison-green eyes mesmerizing. "He won't even come fight us himself—he just sends all of you to die for him. We *can* and will keep holding you off, but what kind of victory is it if he never defeats a single one of us himself?"

"*We are glad to die for him, to further his cause,*" Poppy said in that awful, grating voice. "*But he is no coward, he is—*"

But what he was, Pao would never find out—at least not from Poppy the Second. Naomi's blade preceded the answer, jutting through Poppy's chest right where her heart would have been.

"It's better if you don't let them talk," she said, her eyes a little distant, and Pao wondered what fears of Naomi's the copies had been preying on.

"Thanks," Pao said breathlessly, transforming the Arma del Alma back into the magnifying glass and scanning the battle, which had picked up significantly in intensity.

"There are so many of them," Naomi said, catching her breath. "But we got this. Just keep your eyes peeled and make sure we don't stab any of our own."

"You got it," Pao said, and she wanted to say something else. Something meaningful, just in case. But she couldn't think of anything that did justice to the moment, and Naomi disappeared into the battle again.

Another five minutes passed, then ten. They weren't killing every soldier as they came out of the mouth anymore, but the

Niños—at Naomi and Marisa's instruction—had developed a new strategy. Three fighters were stationed at the mouth to take as many as they could head-on. There was another ring ten feet back to catch any stragglers, and another beyond that, just in case. Every few minutes or so, Naomi would yell, "Switch!" and the fighters would rotate, the middle ring moving to the front, the overtired first response team taking a break in the back.

It was brilliant, Pao thought, and it was working. The floor was littered with the hollow husks of the copies. The little Niños—along with Emma, Maria, and Bruto—hadn't been touched in the courtyard, and Pao was starting to feel dangerously optimistic again.

The change occurred all at once, when she least expected it. The warehouse was filled once more with bright white light, and knowing what to look for now, Pao's eyes darted to the opening, where another helpless copy was plugged into the void, their eyes streaming green, their mouth a projector for El Cucuy's personal use.

Pao thought she was ready for the onslaught of images, but they were different this time. It was no longer just her loved ones dead or dying, her home in flames. It was worse. So much worse that she fell to her knees, totally lost to the visions accosting her.

Pao was herself but not herself. She was back in Shadow Pao's mind, the parts of herself she most hated and feared pulled to the forefront, overpowering everything else. In the projection, stretched high across the wall and in vivid color, she saw her own face, eyes glowing green, expression feral and sinister. Her staff was black and wreathed in void energy, and she turned, licking her lips, to see Emma, Dante, Naomi, Marisa, Kit, and her parents all lined up, calling for her.

One by one, she killed them all, Emma last, begging and pleading.

"No," she said. "No, please. Please."

It took her several long moments to come back to herself, to realize it was her own voice begging. That she was alone in the bleachers and Emma was safe in the courtyard.

"Get up," said a harsh voice. "Get up, asustada. Are you going to let a bad dream stop you from saving the world?"

"Señora Mata?" Pao said, blinking hard, tearing her eyes away from the images that were still playing across the walls. With more resolve than she'd ever needed in her life, Pao pushed herself up off her knees and descended the bleachers to reach the spot on the floor where Dante's abuela was standing, clutching her walker with gnarled knuckles, a crocheted shawl that looked like one of her horrible afghans draped across her shoulders.

Pao peered at the old woman through the magnifying glass and confirmed that it was her, in the flesh, but still she blurted out, "Is it really you?"

"Yes, yes, it's really me. Don't make a fuss."

"But . . . how did you know where—"

"You think I'm not on El Nextdoor?" she said with a scoff. "How else would I keep up with the neighborhood drama? It's better than mis novelas. Now come here, Paola. There's not much time. The shadows have already escaped—they're heading for the city. The ladies are on their way from the shuttle bus, but we're old—we won't be of much help. And there's a job only you can do."

"No," Pao said. "The Niños are here, they're . . ." But as she looked around the room, she saw the devastation El Cucuy's nightmares had wrought. Almost every single Niños fighter was either on the ground or staring at the walls with a horrified expression, incapacitated by their worst fears.

The few still fighting were no match for the stream of shadow soldiers now pouring from the opening. Some of the enemy had stayed to fight, but the warehouse door was open wide to the outside.

"Silver Springs!" Pao said with a gasp. "They're not ready."

"No one is ever ready for the lord of dread," Señora Mata said. "Did you kids think we were just making up a story to get you to eat your peas? Bah. He's the most powerful fantasma in history, Paola, and he wants the world destroyed. That's exactly what will happen if you sit here with your head in your hands crying over the monster under your bed."

"I *am* the monster under my bed," Pao said, so grateful to have an adult here who understood and could help her. "Señora Mata, what if he's right about me?" She could still see the images flickering on the walls—talking to Dante's abuela the only thing keeping her mind off them. "What if he finds a way to pull the bad out of me and uses me to kill my friends and family . . . ?"

There was a long pause wherein Señora Mata looked shrewdly at Pao, but then her eyes slid out of focus, and Pao's heart sank. "After that, Maria, you'll need to pick up more heavy cream from the bodega. I'll need it for the sauce."

"No, Señora Mata, wait!" Pao cried, her heart pounding. "Don't leave me. Not now. You have to tell me what to do! You can't go yet—please don't go!"

"Settle down, Maria, it's enchiladas suizas, not the end of the world."

"IT LITERALLY *IS* THE END OF THE WORLD!" Pao said, hysteria building in her as she pictured the clones making their way down the highway into Silver Springs. "And I need you to help me!"

Señora Mata blinked hard, taking in her surroundings. "You need to see the truth," she said. "The truth of him. That will show you. He's cloaked, Paola. He's . . . dependent. . . ."

"Dependent on *what*?" Pao asked, frustration and panic mingling until, for the first time in her life, she wanted to physically shake a senior citizen.

"The *cheese*, Maria. Isn't that what I keep telling you?"

"Ughhhh!" Pao groaned. Her heart was truly racing now, and it was getting harder and harder for her to tune out the images, which were now showing the shadow soldiers swarming Silver Springs. Mary at the botánica on Second Street, welcoming them in like customers. Rico at the taquería, asking if they wanted onion and cilantro . . .

They were all going to die, Pao thought desperately. They were all going to die, and it would be her fault.

"Wake them," Señora Mata was saying. "They must fight, but you must go on. My boy . . . my Dante . . . He has been forgotten. . . ."

This time, Pao surfaced from her fear spiral just enough to understand. Marisa, Naomi, Franco . . . all the Niños's best fighters were in thrall to the nightmares. They had to wake up and continue the fight before all was lost. Before Pao could leave to do what she needed to do.

"Thank you, Señora Mata," she said. "Now, please, get back home. It's not safe here. Where's your bus?" But before the old woman could answer, Pao heard the whooping and hollering of at least ten nursing home residents bursting through the door, brandishing walkers, canes, what appeared to be a TV remote, and several lunch trays as they charged into the fray.

The sight of them brought joy bubbling to the surface, just enough to block out the nightmares still playing across the walls. The images weren't real, Pao told herself, but this was. People showing up to help, even when they could have easily sat it out. Even when it was dangerous. Even when nightmares lurked around every corner.

"Come on, you old bag!" called a woman who looked about a hundred and three. "You got us all here—now don't be sitting around letting us do all the work!"

"It's time for me to go, Maria," said Señora Mata with a gleam in her eye. "Don't know whether you've noticed, but the town's under attack."

"Señora, I really think you ought to get your friends home," Pao said, watching as two old men (one in slippers) and a lady in a floral bonnet accosted a shadow soldier by the door. They started whacking it with various non-weapons until it lay still. "It's really not safe, and I'm not sure you're . . . well . . ."

"Cien años slaying fantasmas and you think you can tell *me* what's safe," Señora Mata scoffed. "If you won't help me, at least get out of my way!"

"Onto the next!" yelled Mr. Slippers, and they all charged out into the parking lot.

"Señora, please!" Pao called after her, but it was too late.

Dante's abuela had already started pushing her walker, scream-ing something in Spanish Pao didn't understand but was quite sure she wouldn't be allowed to repeat.

"Don't you have a job to do, Paola?" the old woman called over her shoulder, and Pao shook herself. Señora Mata had made her choice, despite the risks involved. It was time for Pao to do the same.

She climbed the bleachers to where the front line of Niños fighters were either curled up or staring dead-eyed at the walls. Pao focused on their faces instead of the nightmares still being projected and found Naomi.

Pao crouched down and gently shook the girl's shoulder. "Naomi," she said, "the shadows are getting out into the town. It's bad. I need you to snap out of it, okay?"

Her eyes open far too wide, her fingernails digging into the dark skin of her cheeks, Naomi just shook her head unblinking. "No," she said. "Not again, please, no . . ."

Three more attempts to shake her out of her terror didn't help, and Pao didn't know what else to do, so she pulled back her hand and slapped the older girl across the cheek, bracing herself for a return attack. But none came. Naomi's eyes slid back into focus, however, though they seemed to have a hard time landing on Pao's face.

"What happened?" Naomi asked groggily, but then she caught a glimpse of the continually running reel of horrors behind Pao's head, and she began to slip away.

"Stay with me!" Pao said. "Don't make me hit you again!"

"As if . . . you even could . . ." Naomi said, half a smirk lifting her lips.

"That's more like it," Pao said, smiling back. "None if this is real, whatever you're seeing. What *is* real is that the shadows are escaping into town. We need—"

"Into town?" Naomi said, struggling to her feet, though her knees wobbled and Pao had to support her. "But they're unprotected! We need to wake up the rest of these scaredy-cats and get moving."

"That's literally what I was just saying?" Pao replied, but Naomi was already off, slapping Franco to rouse him and clearly not minding the task. Pao made her way to Marisa, who wasn't hard to get moving. Marisa's hand was pressed to her chest, and Pao wondered if she was remembering the live ember she'd had to swallow to become leader of Los Niños de la Luz.

Still more shadow soldiers were making their way out of the void mouth—slower now that the way was partially blocked by the extra bodies, but still faster than Pao would have liked.

"I've got them!" Naomi called. Franco was on her heels, looking pale but alert. "You just wake up the rest of the Niños!"

"On it!" Pao replied, rousing two more fighters whose names she didn't know and sending them to Marisa for instructions. Finally, she came across Kit, curled up in fetal position on the floor, her hands laced around her combat boots.

"Don't go," Kit was whispering, black tear tracks painting lines down her face. "Not again. Don't leave!"

"Kit!" Pao said, not wanting to hear any more of the girl's deepest, darkest fears than she had to. "Kit, you gotta wake up! We need you and your rake, like right now!"

Fortunately (or unfortunately, depending on who you asked), Kit didn't need to be slapped. She sat up warily, casting around until she found Pao's face and locked onto her gaze like it was a lifeline. "It wasn't real?" she asked in a small voice devoid of all her usual bravado.

"No," Pao said, reaching out a hand to help her up. "It wasn't real."

"Ugh, you can let go now," she said, pulling her hand away from Pao's as soon as she was back on her feet. "I was fine, okay? It was just hot in here, and I haven't had water or whatever."

"Totally," Pao said. "Marisa's giving out orders for the next phase. Just don't look at the walls and you'll be fine."

As if rebellion was baked into every one of her neural pathways, Kit's eyes immediately flicked to the walls, and they grew wide again.

"I said *don't* look," Pao said, grabbing her shoulders and turning her toward Marisa. "Now go."

"Bossy," Kit grumbled.

"Brat," Pao grumbled back.

Everyone was off the floor, though some were in worse shape than others. Several skirmishes with shadow soldiers had already broken out in the warehouse, but the real threat was the steady stream of them marching toward town with only a group of (admittedly awesome) octogenarians to stop them from reaching Silver Springs proper.

In the doorway to the courtyard, Bruto stood with his hackles up, growling and snapping at anything that came within reach. Pao's heart strained toward him. She wanted him with her, but he was the closest she could come to protecting Emma herself. He had to stay behind.

"We'll have to split up," Marisa was saying, the black X on

her forehead smudged, shadows under her eyes that hadn't been there before the nightmare interlude. But she was wholly in control in a way that made Pao feel much more at peace. "Half of us into the city to stop these things from terrorizing the town, the other half here to protect headquarters. I'm taking the little kids and the people who can't fight on the viejos' shuttle bus."

"Take them to my place," Pao said, tossing Marisa her apartment key. "My mom will stay with them there, and Emma. Make *sure* they both go—and Bruto, too."

"Done," Marisa said with a respectful nod, pocketing the key.

That was one loose end tied up, Pao thought, her mind already straining toward what was next. "What about her?" she asked, gesturing toward the unfortunate shadow that was projecting the fear machine.

"Leave her," Franco said, his voice a little harsher than normal—which was saying something for him. "She's actually helping to block the void entrance. Now only one shadow can get through at a time. And if we dispatched her, he'd just plug in another."

Given that Pao could see that at least half the Niños here were still visibly shaken by the continuing presence of the nightmare reel, she wasn't sure this was the best course of action, but the clock was ticking, and Señora Mata's words were still ringing in Pao's ears. *There's a job only you can do.* She hadn't known what it meant at the time, but it was all starting to come together.

Marisa was assigning fighters to protect the warehouse and a squad to head into town. People were checking weapons and equipment. A broad-shouldered boy Pao didn't know was guarding the void entrance, where for the moment the shadows had stopped appearing.

"It won't be quiet for long," Naomi said, half to him and half to Pao.

"I know," said Pao.

"You're gonna go do something dumb and heroic again, aren't you?"

"Not sure it's heroic, and hoping it's not dumb, but I have a job to do, yeah."

"And you're not gonna let me come with you?"

"Not this time," Pao said. "But it means a lot that you offered. They need you here. Where I'm going . . . well, let's just say I'm not exactly sure how it's gonna turn out."

"What a novel concept," Naomi said drily. "Nothing at all like destroying an underwater void entrance from inside, or locking yourself in a burning cell with El Autostopisto, or any of the other totally sane things you've done since I met you."

Pao just shrugged. "At least I'm on-brand," she said.

"Be careful, pipsqueak," Naomi said. "I know you have nine lives or whatever, but this place wouldn't be the same without you."

"Take care of Emma, okay?" Pao said on impulse. "And explain . . . why I had to do this. You know, if . . ."

"We're not talking like that," Naomi said fiercely. "Not yet. You go do what needs to be done, and then you get your butt back here, because there's gonna be a hell of a lot to clean up once I'm done with these things."

"I'll bring the mop," Pao said, with a laugh that was more than half sob.

Naomi pulled her in for a one-armed hug that nearly cracked Pao's ribs, and then the silver-haired girl turned away suspiciously fast, dabbing at her eyes.

Pao had so much more she wanted to say—to her mom, to Emma. . . . But the other world was pulling at her, the way it had so many times before—even when she hadn't understood what it meant. She knew it was time to go back in. To see if she could end this for good.

She'd just have to hope she was able to come out again.

TWENTY-EIGHT

Out of the Frying Pan, Into the Void

No one asked Pao where she was going as she crossed the warehouse. They were all so fully present in this world, ready to defend it, while she felt like she was passing through it as a ghost.

There was a job only she could do. Pao was the only person living with a connection to the dead. To the void. The only person who could portal without experiencing punishing aftereffects like the ones that had caused Señora Mata to lose her memory.

El Cucuy would not be drawn out of the void. He had no reason to leave it. Her attempt to lure him by playing to his ego had failed.

He had Dante, whom Pao had spent almost a year of her life searching for. But worse, he now had them all under his thumb. All the people she loved. All the people she *knew*. All these vibrant, passionate, fully *alive* people, including some who were ready to bleed to protect one another. He would wipe them out without a second thought, and why?

That was what Pao had to find out so she could put a stop to it.

The office was the only quiet place in the warehouse now, and Pao made for it, half hoping someone would stop her. She wasn't sure she could keep going if anyone gave her a single reason to stay.

She eased the door open, grateful for the dimness inside, the lack of nightmares playing across the walls. Closing the door behind her, Pao took a deep breath and blew it out noisily like her mom had always told her to do to clear her mind.

It was time. It was—

"AHHH!" She jumped at least a foot when something moved behind the desk. "Who's there?" All she could picture was El Cucuy hiding behind the file cabinet, ready to leap out and kill her before she ever got the chance to stop him.

"Paola?"

"*Dad?* What are you doing?"

"I was just . . . I needed to . . . Oh, it's pointless."

"What's pointless?" Pao asked, stepping closer to where he was crouched amid a pile of books and papers. "What's going on in here?"

"I've failed," he said in a hopeless voice that seemed to echo slightly in the confined space. "I've failed you all, and I'm hiding in here because I can't solve the problem, so what use am I to anyone?"

"Dad, you're not useless," Pao said, taking another step toward her father, who now had his face buried in his hands. "Marisa's delegating tasks to everyone now. I'm sure there's something you can do to help. Better than hiding in here, anyway."

"There's nothing," he said in that plaintive voice. "There's nothing."

Pao crossed the last of the space between them and put a hand on his shoulder, not sure what she should say. If only she'd known him for longer. If she had a lifetime of memories to draw from, maybe she could say the perfect thing to make him realize how much they all needed him. How much *she* needed him.

"Dad," she said, kneeling beside him among the mess. "I don't know what—"

But before she could finish, the door flew open to reveal Franco standing there with murder in his eyes. "Get out of the way, Pao," he said in a low, urgent voice.

"I'm not going anywhere," Pao said, folding her arms. "Aren't you supposed to be with Marisa getting ready to go into town?"

"Not until I resolve this," Franco said, stepping toward them, a little of the nightmare's haunting still lingering around his eyes.

"Whatever you saw," Pao said in as soothing a voice as possible, "it wasn't real. It's just El Cucuy trying to turn you."

"What I saw is none of your business," Franco said. "I know Beto's a fraud."

If it weren't for the smudged X still visible on his forehead, Pao would have thought *Franco* was a copy. As it was, she stayed still, knowing she couldn't discount his theory, but too wary of the way his eyes darted around, the furious set to his mouth, to let him get near Beto.

"He destroyed it," Franco said, his voice wobbling. "Everything. A hundred years of research, gone."

Pao looked again at the mess around her. The papers were torn and wet, ink bleeding freely across the pages, like someone had spilled water on them. For the first time, Pao noticed that the computer was smoking slightly, its screen blank when she had never seen it without its glowing green cursor. . . .

Slowly, carefully, she turned back to her father, who still had his face in his hands. His shoulders were shaking like he was crying.

"Dad?" Pao said. "Do you know what happened in here?"

Before he could answer, three things happened in quick succession. First, the single bulb in the office went out, and the nightmares flared to life on every wall in the tiny, claustrophobic space. Second, Franco shoved Pao aside and lunged for Beto. And third, Pao's father stood up and turned to face them, his eyes glowing green, his mouth open in a silent and perpetual scream so much like his mother's that it turned Pao's heart to ice.

"Get out of the way!" Franco roared, and Pao—with only seconds until she was a goner and no weapon in her hands—did as she was told. She would pull out the Arma del Alma, she told herself. She would transform it, and she would help. . . .

But across the walls came La Llorona's frozen face, the mirror image of her son's, and beside her was Pao, her own mouth twisted and forced open, her eyes spewing green light in every direction.

"No!" she said. "I'm not like them! Please, make it stop. . . ."

Emma appeared in the vision, so real that Pao couldn't help but lose herself in it, and the twisted, waxen Pao on the wall, the product of the nightmares, stepped toward her with her clawed fingers stretched out.

"GET OUT OF HERE!" Franco called, bringing Pao back to reality for a split second. He was engaged in vicious battle with Beto, who was putting up a hell of a fight, and the sight of him here, in person, was so like Pao's nightmare that for a moment she couldn't tell the difference.

"I won't leave you alone," she said, drawing her magnifying

glass at last, hating how weak her voice sounded. "I can do this. . . . I can—"

"Isn't there something more important you were supposed to be doing?" Franco asked with a grunt. "Some kind of big world-saving thing?"

Pao was silent. She'd almost forgotten the reason she'd come in here, to find a quiet space where she could make a portal.

"I . . ." she said. "You can't do this alone. . . ."

"I've been fighting enemies like this for a century," Franco said, his dark hair falling into his eyes as a bookshelf full of ruined volumes crashed onto Beto's back. The shadow let out a terrible roar that filled the space, mixing with the sound accompanying the images on the walls. "You have a job to do. Do it. I can handle him."

Every cell in Pao's body told her not to leave Franco alone. He perpetually underestimated his enemies. She definitely needed to stay. But could she kill her own father, even if he was only a copy? Could she ignore the Dread Lord's visions beckoning her into madness?

Was this her ego again? Telling her no one could do anything without her?

"Are you sure?" she said as Shadow Beto finally fought his way out of the broken shelf and made for Franco again.

"If you don't leave in the next five seconds, I'll kill you instead and tell them I thought you were a copy."

And was there really anything else to say after that?

Pao opened the office's other door, the one that led out into the entryway, and finding it empty (and blessedly free of nightmares), she put her knee to the ground and tried to block out the fear. Still burned into her eyelids were the pictures of herself with La Llorona's twisted face, and of Emma, her eyes full of fear, backing away from the fantasma's murderous claws.

"Good is what you do," Pao told herself once again, holding on so tightly to the belief that it filled all the terrified places in her mind. She would do this good thing. Even if it was the last one she ever did.

Take me to El Cucuy, Pao thought, her eyes on the doorway to the office. *Take me to the place I can end this once and for all.*

As shapes began to rise from the ground, she kept her eyes on Franco and the shadow of her dad until she was seeing them through the green light, which was just beginning to spin around her.

But in the last moment before the world disappeared, Pao saw something that made her cry out and throw herself against the impenetrable boundary of the portal. Her father, his eyes glowing green and his face still horribly distorted, pulled out an obsidian shortsword and plunged it into Franco's chest.

By the time Pao landed in the empty, lightning-struck field again, her face was tear-streaked and her voice was raw from screaming. The portal walls had been indifferent to her pleas to take her back, to her misery over the loss of Franco—who had been a leader of Los Niños de la Luz for a hundred years. Yes, he'd been obnoxious, and occasionally cruel, but his presence had always felt permanent.

And now he was gone at the hands of one of El Cucuy's soldiers, and all Pao wanted to do was portal straight back. But she knew there were fighters in the warehouse who could dispatch the man wearing her father's face. She had offered to help Franco, and he had refused. . . .

You have a job to do, Franco had said. *Do it.* Now that she was here, she had to see it through. For the sake of Franco, and anyone else they had lost or would lose before this was over. To make sure it never happened again, no matter what.

And so Pao turned to the obsidian tower, the place where all this had begun—and the place where it would end, if she had anything to say about it.

The field was deserted, and Pao knew instinctively that the tower's usual guardians were beneath the ground, in the obsidian mines, where shadow soldiers were even now marching toward Pao's world. El Cucuy hadn't expected her to come here, she realized with a surge of pride. He had set them all to guarding the void mouth in case any of the Niños tried to push through.

Drawn to it by the same unknown force that had brought her here, Pao made her way to the tower's entrance, where two massive bone guardians had once stood sentry. The lack of them was almost more terrifying. A green lightning bolt forked down through the violet sky, the air electric and dancing, causing the hair on Pao's arms to stand up as she walked into the entryway, its cages still empty, and began the long climb.

Stairs upon stairs upon stairs, the emptiness almost a physical presence. The closer she got to the top, the slower Pao's feet consented to move. That feeling in her stomach—the sharp, heavy dread she'd felt in the presence of El Cucuy—was stirring again, and the mere memory of it was enough to make her want to turn and flee.

But she had fought the nightmares since then. She could do this. She knew his weakness now—or suspected it, anyway. His only weapon was controlling the minds of others by manipulating their fears. If she could stay strong, remember who she was, and refuse to succumb to his power, she could defeat him. She knew it.

Three more flights of stairs, then two, then one, the dread growing with every step. This time, though, she could tell her trepidation wasn't coming from something on the outside. This was the same feeling that had caused her to draw her Arma del Alma on a roof rat in the Riverside Palace parking lot. The same feeling that had prevented her from portaling for eight months.

The same feeling that had brought her to her knees in Emma's parents' well-manicured yard and led her to break down sobbing because La Llorona was always lurking just behind her eyelids.

It was a fear she had lived with her whole life. And if she didn't conquer it today, the world was going to be lost to shadows and terror for eternity.

"No pressure," Pao grumbled under her breath as at last she reached the top of the stairs. It was pitch black here, before the doorway into El Cucuy's chamber, and she took a deep breath before entering, grounding herself, anticipating the nightmare images. And then she was through the door.

At first, she thought this room was empty, too. But then something moved against the wall. Pao pulled out her magnifying glass—refreshingly heavy and solid in her hand—but didn't transform it. Not before she knew what she was up against, and whether the truth or a blade would be a better weapon.

She crept forward on the balls of her feet, toward the table next to where El Cucuy had sat when Pao first encountered him. On its surface, as she remembered, was the strange Rubik's Cube–looking device that pulsed and swelled with malevolence. Just looking at this object caused a visceral and immediate flee reaction, but Pao tamped it down, breathing in slowly and planting her feet solidly on the ground.

I am not my thoughts, she told herself, and then she stepped closer.

"Don't touch it!" came a snarling voice from behind the desk. "Don't touch it—it's mine!"

TWENTY-NINE

Reconciliation (Remix; Feat. Damaged Dante)

Pao jumped backward toward the door, transforming her weapon and readying herself to fight. Was this who El Cucuy had left to guard this object . . . the whole tower? And if so, why were they hiding behind the table shouting at her instead of . . . well, killing her?

"My name is Paola Santiago," she said, getting right to the point. "I'm here to challenge El Cucuy." It sounded impressive, she thought, standing a little straighter as her words echoed in the room.

"Stay away from the cube!" said the raspy voice, and up stood a boy she recognized but just barely. It was Dante, taller and much thinner than she'd last seen him, and unimaginably filthy. The biggest change was in his manner. The suspicious, darting eyes, the puckered-up mouth that looked braced for pain, the nervous fluttering hands.

She wanted so badly to believe it was him, but she had been burned in this place before. She had to be sure before she did anything.

"Is it really you?" Pao asked to buy some time.

He didn't answer, just returned her gaze warily, and Pao felt a sadness settle in her chest. El Cucuy had done this to them. To *all* of them. Twisted them up so they were suspicious of their loved ones, couldn't trust anything or anyone. This was her best friend, and she couldn't even hug him, let alone save him, until she was sure he wasn't just a lab-grown imposter here to torture her.

"I can prove it's me," she said now. "But you have to promise not to attack me. I won't be able to use my weapon."

"As long as you don't touch the cube, I won't hurt you," he said, his bony chin jutting forward, his eyes moving from her face to the staff in her hands and back again, but never leaving her.

She didn't trust him, of course. Not yet. But he looked so weak. If he lunged at her, she could hold him off for long enough to transform the staff. . . . She hoped.

"Stay right there," she said, tension in her every muscle. "Don't move."

Dante remained still. Feeling absurdly vulnerable and exposed as she did so, Pao shrank the staff back into its magnifying glass form. He didn't immediately lunge at her once she had her guard down, which she figured was probably a good sign.

Slowly, carefully, not taking her eyes off him for a second in case he surprised her, Pao raised the ornate glass to her face. She peered through it at the gangly, filthy boy in front of her, bracing herself for glowing green eyes, the twisted face. . . .

But his eyes stayed brown, his face stubborn and wary, but unmistakably his. Pao let out an involuntary little hiccupping sob as she lowered the glass again, staring at him like he was an oasis in a desert she'd been traversing alone for too long.

"It's really you," she said.

"Of course it is," he snarled. "I'm waiting for *my* proof."

"Ask me anything," Pao said with a horrible sense of déjà vu. "Anything only the real Pao would know."

Dante scoffed. "They always say that. Sometimes they know, and"—he shuddered from head to toe—"sometimes they don't." It started to occur to Pao that whatever imitation of traumatized Dante the shadow version of him had been doing was nowhere close to the real thing.

"This glass," Pao said, holding it up. "Do you remember it? My Arma del Alma?"

He nodded. Short and sharp so his eyes never had to leave her face.

"It shows the truth to anyone who looks through it. That's how I was able to tell you weren't a copy. Would you like to look at me through it, too?" Strictly speaking, Pao didn't think the glass would work for him. It hadn't shown Emma the way through the cornfield, after all. But it would show Dante a vision of her exactly as she was, and if that was enough to get him to trust her, she would have to be okay with a little dishonesty.

"You'd hand over your weapon?" he said suspiciously. "Why?"

"Because I'm here to take you home," she said. "I've been trying for months. And I can't very well take you with me if you think I'm a copy, can I?"

Dante stepped forward, around the desk so Pao could see the sneakers he'd been wearing on their trip north last winter. They were falling apart and filthy with grime and what looked like dried blood, but she was careful not to obey her instincts to flinch, run screaming out the door, or lunge forward and hug him, prisoner stench and all.

Carefully, knowing she was taking a huge risk—one she

probably wouldn't have taken for anyone else in the world—she handed over her sole means of self-defense and allowed Dante to peer through it at her face.

"What does it mean?" he snapped.

"If you look at one of El Cucuy's clones, you'll see them in their true form. Green eyes, twisted, frozen face, the whole deal. If they're not a copy, they just look normal."

For what felt like a silent eternity, Dante said nothing. Then he tossed the glass back to her, throwing her off so much she barely caught it.

"Well?" she said.

"Well, what are you doing here?" he asked. "Because I know you didn't come to rescue me. You just said you're here to fight him. That's not going to work, so you might as well go home."

"He released his shadow army into our world, Dante," Pao said, shocked at his cynicism. "The Niños are barely holding them off, and innocent people are dying. That's why I'm here. To finish this once and for all."

Dante laughed, a high-pitched thing that sounded nothing like the self-conscious chuckle she was used to. "You think you're going to finish him *alone*? You're just as arrogant as ever."

"Shut up!" Pao said, like they were back in the Riverside Palace parking lot and he wouldn't give her a turn on his scooter. "I'm not arrogant. I'm—"

"Heroic, right?" Dante said with a derisive snort. "Well, good luck. Because after however long I've been in here, I've learned a few things about Our Lord and Savior El Cucuy." He stared at her for a long moment, dead-eyed. "There's no point resisting. There's no point fighting, or trying to escape, or even hoping.

If he wants to kill everyone in the world, he will. You're not stopping him, and neither is anyone else. All you can do is die trying."

"So how did you end up in here, then?" Pao asked, her temper still simmering. "If there's no point in escaping? And what did you mean 'it's mine' when I was looking at this cube thing?" She took a step toward it just to see his reaction, and he was between her and the Rubik's Cube faster than she would have thought possible given the state he was in.

"Don't touch it," he snarled again, but this time Pao could hear the panic in his voice, see the hungry yet revolted look on his face as he glanced back at the cube. "I'm here because he left the tower unguarded. The cells were all unlocked. He thought I was . . . broken. He didn't think I'd try to get out."

Useless, came El Cucuy's voice in Pao's memory. *Mind totally destroyed.*

Pao's anger was doused in the flood of her pity. "Let me take you home," she said. "I can come back here after. There are people who can—"

"YOU DON'T UNDERSTAND!" Dante roared, and this time Pao did jump. "There won't be any *home* when he's through with it. All we'll be able to do is watch everyone die before we die, too."

"But we have to try," she insisted. "Don't we have to try to save them?"

"Like you tried to save me?" he asked, and the words were a knife to her chest.

"I *did* try," she said. "You've been in here eight months, Dante, and they were the *worst* eight months of my life. All I've *done* is

try to get you back. I fought with my dad, infuriated Franco—"
Her voice broke on his name, remembering the dagger plunging
in, the surprise on his face. "I made a random girl from school
steal a bus to drive me to a church in the middle of nowhere so
I could fight a clone of myself just to get in here and rescue you."

Now that the details of her escapades were spilling out,
she found she couldn't stop them. She heard her voice getting
higher-pitched and more hysterical as she went, but she went
on anyway, needing him to understand, after all this time, what
she'd been through to find him.

"And I came in here, you ungrateful jerk, and I fooled El
Cucuy—or at least I thought I did. I saw the copies, and I portaled
to what I thought was you and took you back to Silver Springs.
I told you I'd take care of you, and guess what? *You turned out
to be a clone, and you ripped open the void and let shadow soldiers
into the place where we live.* So, I basically destroyed the entire
world trying to get back to you, Dante Mata. You can hate me if
you want, you can think I'm a monster or a fake hero, and you
can fight against me forever, but you *can't* say I didn't try to save
you, because I did."

Her chest was heaving now, and tears were fighting her stub-
bornness for dominance as she waited for him to say something.
Anything. She waited for what she hadn't admitted to herself
she'd wanted all this time, which was for him to take back all
the cruel things he'd said and tell her she was good.

Haven't you learned anything? she asked herself. She knew
Emma would say something like *People can only love you as
much as they love themselves* and pretend that she understood
where Dante was coming from. But the truth was that he had

hurt Pao, and she had needed him, and she just wanted him to be sorry.

"It's connected to the tower," he said finally, turning away from her to look once more at the cube. "The minute you touch it, this whole place will come down around us. We'd die before we ever got it out of here. Even if we did somehow manage to get it out, he would kill us before we got anywhere."

Pao desperately wanted to yell, *Seriously?? That's it??* To force him to acknowledge everything that had happened between them. To apologize. To resolve this somehow. But maybe some of Emma's wisdom *had* rubbed off on her fiery temper because she told herself there would be time for that later. *If* they survived.

"So what are you doing in here, then?" she asked again. "What do you want the cube for?"

"They say most of his power is stored inside it," Dante said, and Pao saw hunger in his eyes. "That whoever possesses it could take his place."

"If it's so important to him, why would he leave it here?" Pao asked, her gaze also straying to it as she pictured herself with powers comparable to El Cucuy's. She could destroy him and his whole creepy corner of the void for eternity.

"He's grown overconfident," Dante said. "He left it here to guard the tower while he supervised the invasion. He killed all the prisoners before he left. All except me. I guess he forgot about me. Either that or I was too pathetic to bother with."

"Dante, I'm so—" Pao began, but he turned away.

"I'm here because I want the cube. I don't care if I die getting it. There are only two ways to be free of him, and right now I don't care which one it is."

"There are other options," Pao said, trying to hold his shifting, darting eyes, sensing the energy in the room shifting. "We've always managed before, as long as we stuck together."

"Yeah, right," Dante scoffed. "That's the Niños, not me. I made my choices, and they led me here." He took a step backward, closer to the cube, and Pao instinctively stepped toward it, knowing that if Dante got his hands on it, all would be lost.

"It's always been you *and* me," Pao said. "Don't do this, Dante. There's still time to fix it."

He was shaking his head, his haunted eyes refusing to meet hers no matter how close she got. "You should go home, Pao," he said. "Whatever happens next, it'll be too much for your delicate hero sensibilities."

"I'm not leaving without you," she said, wondering whether she could really stop him. "I'm not leaving until our world is safe again. That's what I came here to do."

He sized her up, then rolled his bloodshot eyes. "I should have known. At least now you'll get your martyr's death. That's what all you heroes want, isn't it?"

"I don't want to die at all," Pao said fiercely, and it had never been more true. Here, in this lifeless place, all she wanted was to be back among the living, with all their messy entanglements and emotions, with their joys and sorrows living so close to the surface.

She *had* come here knowing she might die and being willing to if it meant keeping them safe. Maybe Dante was right about that. But there was a part of her that would never be that selfless. A stubborn, furious part that would cling to life no matter the cost.

"Too bad," Dante said. "Last chance to go." He reached out for the cube, his hands hovering just above it, his face twisted with fear and revulsion and that awful hunger again.

"You said *you* were the hero," she said desperately, willing to say anything to keep him from grabbing the cube. Goose bumps rose on her whole body, and a bolt of pure terror shot through her every time he got closer to it. "You said you were destined to be. Because of your arma, and the abuela with the ghost-hunting past."

"When you spend a terrified eternity in prison," Dante said, not taking his eyes off the cube to look at her, "you start to realize there is no good. No evil. There's only power, and he who holds it. And I'd rather have all of it, or nothing at all."

"Having power doesn't mean people can't hurt you," Pao said, close enough to grab him now, or to run him through with her Arma del Alma, which she still held as a magnifying glass in her hand. "Nothing can guarantee that. All this will do is hurt other people. Hurt *me* . . ."

She wanted this to be enough of a reason, but of course it wasn't. He wouldn't even look at her.

"I gave you a chance to leave," Dante said, turning slightly, his full attention still on the cube. "Whatever happens to you next is on you."

"Don't," she said, abandoning all pretense now, stepping forward to grab his arms. "Please, don't. We can destroy it. We can destroy it together."

He threw her off with a strength disproportionate to his gaunt frame, turning completely to face her with a murderous expression that scared her even more than the manufactured terror of the cube. "If we destroy it, there'll be no way to be safe from him. And if you try to stop me . . . I'll kill you."

Pao felt tears welling up behind her eyes. She'd been so sure that once she found the real Dante everything would be all right. He'd be grateful to her for saving him, and everything they'd been through would be overshadowed by their need to help each other survive.

"You don't know what it's going to do to you," Pao said, her voice breaking. "Dante, if it makes you like him, how is that worth it? How is that a fitting end to everything you've been through?"

"It won't be the end at all," Dante said. "It'll be the beginning." And then, without another second of hesitation, he turned around and seized the cube with both hands.

THIRTY

The Last Person You'd Ever Expect Your Ex-Boyfriend's Grandma to Be

The floor lurched beneath Pao's feet as Dante's hands closed over the cube, and in that moment, she did the first thing that popped into her head. She seized him around the shoulders from behind and held on tight.

She expected to grapple, to fight for the cube, but instead, when she touched him, the whole world went black. She could no longer feel his bony arms under hers, or the ground beneath her feet. The only thing that seemed to exist in the world was a horrible, writhing, pervasive fear she was sure would drive her out of her mind.

Unable to stop herself, she screamed. Was she dying? Surely this high-pitched keening was a dying sound. And where was Dante? Where was the tower, the world, the light? How was she going to get back to her family? They were most likely dying right now, and it was all Pao's fault. There *was* something bad inside her. Something that had brought her to this place to suffer for everything she had ever done wrong.

"I'm sorry!" she sobbed, her throat raw from the screaming, her body being turned inside out by the terror she felt, the certainty that everything was going to end. "I'm so sorry."

Pao's body, which she could not see, curled in on itself, every muscle tensing, reaching, writhing to escape the feeling of fear and pain that was everywhere and nowhere and inescapable. She had no idea how long she was suspended there, in the empty place with only dread for company. But eventually, out of the darkness came a shape. A human shape, walking toward her.

"Do you see?" it asked, in a voice she knew but did not know. In a voice so familiar and so wrong that it broke her heart into a thousand pieces. "Do you see now why there's no fighting it?"

As Pao wrenched herself out of the quagmire of her nightmares, forcing herself to focus on the haze just clearing in front of her, she saw him. Dante. Only taller now, and older. Sadder and more cruel.

"There's . . . always a way to resist . . ." Pao said, each word, each motion a struggle with the weight of terror pressing down on her from every direction.

"Fool," Dante said, spinning the cube in his hands. "You have to learn to admit defeat."

"Never," Pao said.

"Then I'll show you again."

The sizzling, electric lightning bolt of panic that hit her this time felt as though it would cleave her in two. She was screaming again, though she couldn't feel it, the sound going on and on and on until she felt herself collapse in the emptiness.

"Stop!" she cried when she remembered the word, remembered who she was asking. "Please, why are you doing this to me?"

He was there abruptly, too close, his haunted eyes staring into hers. "Because it's better than being alone in it." His voice echoed around them, plaintive and terrible and sad.

You know this boy, came the small voice in the back of Pao's mind, the inner critic that didn't seem to be bothered by circumstances. The voice that bullied and pushed and cajoled her in both the best and worst of times. And the voice was right—she did know Dante. She latched on to that knowing like a lifeboat in a turbulent sea.

"This isn't you," she said, suddenly aware of the magnifying glass in her hand. And without knowing why, she raised it to her eye and looked at Dante in this strange and terrible place.

Through the glass, she saw the Dante she knew. Thirteen years old, with that proud, jutting chin and those wide eyes, the cheeks still rounded, the hair falling into his eyes. And his face was twisted, but not in the manner of the shadows. It was twisted in fear, screwed up against it like he might start to cry at any minute. And the cube was no longer a cube, but a cage surrounding him—a cage with bars made not of steel, but the flickering images of a lifetime's worth of nightmares.

His hands gripped the bars, and from his white-knuckled fists the images streamed like arrows straight into Pao's stomach. Straight into the place she could feel the bolt of terror striking her every time El Cucuy was near. But not only then . . . Every time she thought she'd hurt her friends and family because of what she was. Every time things were too quiet and she couldn't help expecting a disaster.

Every time she pulled a weapon on a harmless rat in a parking lot.

Dante had been caged here for eight long months, but the bars enclosing him *came from within him.*

"It's okay," Pao told Dante, the one she knew, the one about to cry behind the bars of his own worst nightmares. "We're gonna get through this together."

Meanwhile, her mind was racing ahead. This wasn't Dante's cube. It was El Cucuy's, and it was both power and a prison. Was it possible El Cucuy, Lord of Dread, Shepherd of Nightmares, was held here by his own fear, too? And he projected it out to the people who came near him because he couldn't stand to bear the burden alone?

"What's the antidote to fear?" Pao asked aloud, not sure she expected anyone to answer, but needing to ask anyway.

It wasn't strength, she knew, because some of the strongest people she knew were afraid. It wasn't love, because love made you fear for your loved ones.

Dante screamed, gripping the bars of the cage still tighter, and the intensity of the bolts coming out of his white-knuckled fists toward Pao seemed to double, prompting her to drop the magnifying glass and fall to her knees, as if she could present the fear a smaller target, curl up and hide from it somehow.

"I don't know the answer," she whispered, because every version of her had been afraid. Even when she was trying to hide it, even when she was trying to be brave. Little Pao had been afraid to live without her dad and then afraid of the nightmares she couldn't explain, afraid that she was going to hurt her mom if she didn't find a way to stop screaming all night. She'd been afraid of La Llorona and afraid of the river and afraid of climate change and the police, and then she'd been afraid she wasn't equal to the tasks the world kept giving her.

To find and rescue Emma.

To free Ondina and her grandmother.

To save her father.

To prove to her best friend that she wasn't evil.

To walk down the street without being primed for the next attack, or adventure.

She had found ways, of course, to make her fear smaller. She'd looked away from it, but she'd never been able to beat it. Only to keep it at bay from minute to minute, and sometimes even that hadn't worked. Now she knew why Dante had called her hero's errand hopeless.

Because El Cucuy wasn't the enemy. The enemy was fear itself, and there was no weapon that could vanquish it. And there never would be.

"She's gone!" Dante screamed from behind the bars of his cage. "She's gone and I'm alone. She's gone."

Pao felt every word like an icicle through her chest. She was tired, and she was never going to stop feeling afraid, and she was ready to give up, too. Ready to do anything to stop feeling this way.

"I'm sorry," she said to Dante, barely able to whisper. "I'm sorry I didn't understand."

"She's gone!" he cried again, piercing the darkness with his grief, piercing Pao's heart.

"Don't be ridiculous," said a voice Pao recognized immediately. "Haven't I taught you anything at all? Now get up, mijitos. He's coming back, and this is our last chance to stop him."

"Señora Mata?" Pao said, pushing herself up just a little, feeling fear attack every place she opened up. "How are you . . . ? What are you . . . ?" And then she realized. Dante's screams of *she's gone*. His abuela's sudden appearance here, in the void. The land of the dead.

But did that mean . . . ?

"No te preocupes," the old woman said, kneeling toward Pao and brushing back her hair. "Está bien."

"Wait," Pao said, remembering suddenly. "I need to see. . . ." She groped around on the ground for the magnifying glass, the one that would show her the truth—whether Señora Mata was really here, or whether she was yet another torturous trick being played on them by El Cucuy.

"Looking for this?" the old woman asked, holding up the Arma del Alma with a strange look on her face. "Go on. Take it. I'm dying, not dangerous."

"Dying . . . ?" Pao said, reaching out to take the glass, a strange feeling like static shock zapping her fingers when she touched the señora's hand. "You can't be. I was just with you. You were heading off to fight with those nursing home friends of yours."

"When it's your time to go, it's your time to go," Señora Mata said with a shrug, and Pao sat there with the magnifying glass, not raising it, not transforming it, feeling as though she were on the edge of some understanding she wasn't ready for.

"We're never ready," Señora Mata said gently. "But the time has come."

Pao didn't know how the woman always managed to do that—answer a question that hadn't been asked yet. But there were bigger and worse mysteries to solve, and the first was to make sure Señora Mata was the *real* Señora Mata. So at last, with her hand inexplicably trembling, Pao lifted the glass to her eye.

At first, she was sure the thing was malfunctioning. Maybe she'd broken it when she dropped it. Because the image in the round golden frame wasn't Señora Mata at all. Not the version

Pao had always known. Not the one who had appeared to her an hour ago in the Niños' warehouse, and definitely not the twisted nightmare she would have been if El Cucuy had copied her.

"I don't understand," Pao said, dropping the glass to look again at the familiar abuela in front of her, and then raising it again just to be sure. "Is it broken?" she asked finally, and through the lens she watched her own head shake.

"It's not broken," Pao watched herself say, even as the voice was so clearly Señora Mata's. "All it can do is show the truth. And there are more truths in the void than there were back in our world."

"But . . . how can . . . ? I don't . . ." For the moment, her confusion had overpowered her fear. Even Dante, still sobbing in his prison of memories, seemed far away as Pao looked at a mirror image of herself through the glass.

"There's so much to explain and so little time," the old woman said with Pao's mouth. "I wish I could tell you the whole tale, Paola, because it's a thrilling one. Unfortunately, we are running out of time to save the world, and if I've spent thirteen years in my own past to fix this only to watch it fall apart again . . . Well, let's just say I'd rather not let that happen."

Pao didn't know what to say. She was utterly flummoxed. The connections that usually began to fire in situations like these were fried. Useless. She lowered the magnifying glass, and the Señora Mata she'd always known reappeared before her. But the truth Pao had learned looking through it couldn't be erased.

"So you're . . . me? Or I'm you? Time travel? I just . . . I don't . . ."

"You know I've lived a long time, and the circumstances of

how and when haven't always been clear. I haven't lied outright—
oh, not about anything that matters. But this is it, the reason I
spent a hundred years as a Niña de la Luz, learning everything
I could about the void and its creatures and its portals and our
connection to it all. And then, of course, I had to get old. To
become unrecognizable enough to pull it off."

"Pull *what* off?" Pao said. "You mean we've lived all this
before? That you already know what happens? That you're just
me from the future, come back to fix it all?" She was finding it
hard to take a deep breath now, but her panting was making
her light-headed.

"That's an . . . oversimplified explanation," Señora Mata said.
"But in its essentials, correct."

Pao was definitely dizzy now. Of all the ridiculous things
that had happened to her, all the things she had discovered
about her family and her past and her ancestry, this was *absolutely* the most absurd.

"Are you telling me . . ." she began, her heart beating way
too fast, "that I'm . . . my ex-boyfriend's *grandmother*?"

At this, Señora Mata (which is what Pao would continue to
call her, because anything else was going to completely break
her brain) began to laugh. "No, no," she said, wiping tears from
her eyes. "Dante didn't have any living grandparents, so when
the time came, I stepped into the role. It was so much simpler
that way."

"Simpler?" Pao asked in a daze. *"Simpler?"* She was remembering so many things that didn't make sense, and so many that
did. "What was with the beauty standards thing? And the weird
religion stuff? Please tell me I don't grow up to be out of touch
and closed-minded, because I can't handle that."

Señora Mata guffawed, an old lady's cackle that Pao found infinitely more disturbing than ever before. It was one thing to *know* you were going to get old and quite another to *see* yourself old.

"You had to have something to rebel against!" the old woman said, still laughing. "I was a whetstone to sharpen your commitment to what was right. Lord knows that mother of ours didn't give us much to push back against."

"So it was all an act?" Pao said, a new and more horrible question surfacing to eclipse the rest. "And does this mean . . . ? Do I have to go back in time when I'm old and shepherd child me into the future? Is my entire life already decided? Am I going to lose my memory? *AM I DYING RIGHT NOW?*"

"Cálmate, niña," Señora Mata said. "If what I'm doing here succeeds, it will change our trajectory. And not just ours, but the entire world's. I came back because it was the only way to alter what's to come. If we do alter it, the future—especially your future—is a blank slate. As for my memory—countless trips through the void over hundreds of years take their toll. Even on La Llorona's granddaughter. It'll be worth it, Paola. But when we're done, no more time travel, ¿entiendes?"

At this, Pao nodded, calming down enough to remember Dante in his cage. "He's going to hate this," she said, her face suddenly burning scarlet. Señora Mata—or . . . Pao in the future—had rescued Dante when he was four years old. She'd probably given him *baths!*

"I don't see any reason to tell him, do you?" Señora Mata asked with her owlish gaze on Pao. Were her eyes really going to get so buggy? Was she going to *shrink* that much? "But we're getting ahead of ourselves." She cupped a hand around her ear, like she was listening to something far off that Pao couldn't hear. "If we don't get this next part right, we won't be able to tell anyone anything. Paola, are you ready to do exactly what I say?"

Pao thought about this for a long moment. "If you'll answer the rest of my questions afterward."

A sad smile seemed to light Señora Mata's wrinkled face. "I promise I'll do my best."

"Okay, then, what do we do?"

THIRTY-ONE
Fear Is the Mind Killer

"We won't have much time," Señora Mata said, already checking to make sure Pao had the magnifying glass in hand. She moved toward Dante, who was still imprisoned, holding the cube, and seemingly blind to them in his grief and misery. "El Cucuy will come for the power source as soon as we're out of this limbo. We won't be able to portal from the tower, so we have to get ourselves and the cube back to the field before he catches us. Then you'll have to portal us out."

"Wait," Pao said. "We're taking this thing *back* to our world? Isn't that, like . . . a really bad idea?"

"Not worse than trying to destroy it here on our own, believe me," Señora Mata said, closing her eyes and rubbing her palms together. "Okay, here goes nothing." She reached through the bars and, just like that, pulled the cube from Dante's hands.

Instantly, the tower room rematerialized around them. They had never left. El Cucuy's obsidian edifice swayed and groaned ominously, and Pao had to brace herself to keep her balance.

"Whatever you do, don't panic," Señora Mata said, and Pao noticed that her accent was gone. How much of who she'd been this entire time had been a lie? "And hang on to him. I need to focus on this." Her knuckles were as white on the cube as Dante's had been on the bars. Like she both desperately wanted to and absolutely could not let it go.

"Let's get out of here, right?" Pao said, draping Dante's arm around her and trying to drag him to the door. His eyes were shut, and he was limp and helpless, barely able to hold himself up. It was as if the episode with the cube had robbed him of what little strength he had left.

"No," said Señora Mata, casting around the room with too-wide eyes. "We have to . . . Actually, why not? Let's do it your way."

"Don't you already know what's going to happen?" Pao asked, vaguely panicked at the idea that she was the one calling the shots here.

"Not anymore," Señora Mata said with a grim expression. "From this point forward, it's all brand-new."

There was a horrible cracking sound, stone on stone, like a chunk of the tower had been torn out, and the floor tilted alarmingly beneath their feet. "The stairs are this way," Pao said. Let's go."

She pulled Dante along, trying not to be terrified by his reluctant stumble and lolling head. They could fix him when they got back, she told herself. Señora Mata . . . or future Pao . . . would tell them what to do. All they had to do now was get out of the tower. One step at a time.

"That's right," Señora Mata said, her voice sounding weaker. "One step at a time."

"Let me take it," Pao said, turning around. "The cube. You're more important than me. I can carry it."

"Haven't you learned anything from this?" the old woman snapped. "You're our future, Paola. I didn't sacrifice my golden years so you could give it all up just when we're about to change everything."

"Okay, okay," Pao said, pulling Dante's arm around her shoulder again. "This way."

They made it to the staircase without incident—unless you counted the pained expression on Señora Mata's face as the cube continued to parade her most torturous memories in front of her. *My memories*, Pao realized with a start, suddenly desperately curious about what had befallen her . . . or what would? Time travel was too confusing, and Dante was heavy, and just as they began to descend the stairs, a huge crack appeared in the obsidian in front of them. Before Pao had time to step over it, the section they were standing on started to fall backward.

"Ohhhh, crap," Pao said, adding a silent apology to her mom for the language as she pictured all of them plummeting to the ground, the experiment ruined before it could be completed.

"Jump, foolish girl!" the old woman cried from behind her, and Pao knew she was right. It was now or never. The crack in front of them was widening.

"Come on, buddy," she said, shaking Dante's shoulder until he roused a little. "We gotta jump." She pushed off the staircase just as the whole wall teetered and toppled, leaving them exposed to the open air, the lightning-filled sky. She landed far too close to the edge, hauling Dante up when he nearly slipped, relieved to see the surprisingly sprightly old lady beside her.

"Everyone in one piece?" Señora Mata asked. "Good. Let's keep going."

Down the stairs they went, sidestepping sudden protrusions of stone and gaping holes opening in the floor as the tower continued to crumble. They were halfway down before Pao realized the piercing spear of dread that had been lodged in her stomach since she first set foot here was gone. Her fear was all-natural now. All her own.

She glanced back at the old woman, who was keeping pace even though the cube's effects were clearly draining her. Dante hadn't been able to handle it, the full effect of his fears, and the señora had clearly had more years to rack up nightmares, but she was somehow containing it all, refusing to let it spill over to Pao or Dante as they fled.

I'll have to remember to thank her for that, Pao thought as they leaped over a new crack on the eighth-floor landing and dodged a huge block of obsidian falling from above. They were so close now. Did she dare hope they would make it out before . . . ?

As if in answer to her question, the temperature in the tower fell abruptly until Pao could see her breath. The spike of fear was a hundred times worse than it had been before, a thousand, as in the doorway ahead of them the billowing cloak of El Cucuy obscured the way forward.

"Don't look at his face!" Pao shouted desperately, knowing Dante was on his last legs, and the old woman was already dealing with the effects of the cube in her hands. They couldn't take anymore. This was already too much. . . .

As Pao began to bend under the despair El Cucuy's appearance had caused her, his laugh filled the room, cold and cruel, a nightmare of its own.

"You really thought you could outsmart me this time?" he

asked, his voice a thousand rattlers in tall grass. "That you could take the amplification cube without it destroying you? Well, I'll give you this much, old woman—you're bolder than the last time."

He was speaking directly to Señora Mata, who was still holding the cube like her life—like all their lives—depended on it.

"I know better than to listen to you, Dread Lord," Señora Mata said, her eyes closed, lids translucent and veined. "Stand aside. You will not win this time."

"I have already won," he said. "You should know better than to try to change the past. The outcomes remain the same."

Now Señora Mata laughed, a cackling sound full of joy and secrets. Like she knew something he never would. "That's the beauty of being human. We may not change much on our own— we're stubborn that way—but when we connect with others, when we form bonds, change isn't only possible, it's inevitable."

"*Love*, is it?" sneered El Cucuy. "Love is the constant force for change? You know, as the Lord of Dread, I've heard that a time or two."

"Not love," Señora Mata said. "Love is too personal, too individual. I'm talking about community. Support. Mutual aid and sacrifice. You don't know anything about that. You can't even imagine it, and that is your fatal weakness."

Another laugh, this one the blasts of a gun through a window at night. "Come now, even *love* has a storied history. But *community*? That's what you waited a hundred years to bring to my door?" He seemed to size up Pao and the mostly unconscious Dante. "Let's see what your *community* is worth against the might of the Master of Fear."

Beto had been right, Pao thought from a clinical distance as she watched her own death approach. El Cucuy didn't carry a weapon. Even now he didn't move closer to their little ragtag group. He just held out those horrible pale hands with their filthy too-long nails, and across the cracked and crumbling obsidian walls in the collapsing room, the images Pao knew all too well began to flicker and dance.

Only this time, they weren't fears from her past—they were images of the present. City upon city swarmed with shadow soldiers, newscasters with ashen faces announcing climbing death tolls, and the warehouse of Los Niños de la Luz, where Franco and Señora Mata lay on the ground side by side, shrouded as the remaining fighters clung desperately to life.

They were going to die, Pao knew. All of them. Señora Mata had come back for nothing, put her faith in the wrong community. He would never be defeated. There was no hope.

And then, in the images, she saw frazzled hair and bright blue eyes. Emma was wielding Franco's sword, taking down shadow soldiers alongside Naomi, who was scratched and bleeding but still fighting. Beto—the *real* Beto—was alive and leading the charge. Marisa was still in the fray, too, her braids streaming behind her. Pao's mom was tending to the fallen with Bruto beside her snapping at anything that came close. Kit, teeth bared and makeup smudged, was swinging for the fences with her rake.

As she saw them, Pao knew Señora Mata had been right. Pao's love for these people made her fear for them, but her faith in their community burned bright in her chest. It didn't chase away the fear, but believing in others made it easier to bear.

Señora Mata and Dante had fallen to their knees, powerless against the onslaught of images. With the strength the vision of her home, friends, and family had given her, Pao pulled out her magnifying glass with trembling hands.

She didn't transform it. What she needed in this moment wasn't a blade but the truth. So she turned the lens on El Cucuy, the terrifying lord of the void, who was bringing down his tower of nightmares just to avoid being alone with his own fears.

Through the glass, she saw him clearly for the first time. A stooped, old, mean-faced man, haunted by a life he'd barely lived. His past spooled around him like ribbons, empty of love or care. Devoid of the community Señora Mata had sworn was the antidote to his nightmares. A death unremarked upon, a priest monotonously reading a ritual at a lonely graveside. Then he'd entered the world of the dead, where the spirits around him had moved on to the next phase. To freedom.

But he hadn't wanted to be alone, Pao saw. He began to spin terrifying tales of the beyond so they would stay with him. He'd siphoned his fears into them, finding his well bottomless no matter how many buckets he poured out, no matter how many souls he doomed to linger between worlds forever, victims of the images he placed in their minds.

Centuries passed, his power growing with every soul he kept, but his own fear grew, too, compounding even as he cloaked himself in influence and became the vessel for more fear than one broken spirit could hold. So he created the cube to extend his reach, a kind of external hard drive for the program that would destroy the world.

He couldn't continue without it now, Pao realized. He was

too frail, too eaten away by the terror of centuries of souls. The void had spread from the place where he was stuck, the place between worlds, as he refused to move on and refused to let the others go. The souls became fantasmas in the end, each one driven mad by the nightmares that haunted them.

The shadows, too, belonged to him. El Cucuy was reaching his fingers into the world of the living through bad dreams and trauma to hold a piece of them hostage, dooming them before they'd even walked through the veil.

Just one lonely man. Pao felt the bonds around her fall away as she finally saw the truth of it. He hadn't been able to reach out for support, for help, in life or in death, and all this pain and grief and suffering had been born from that one stubborn seed.

She could free everyone—the dead and the living—if only she could find the strength to do it.

She got up from the ground and straightened her spine, feeling the glow of understanding surround her as she gathered Señora Mata and Dante close. El Cucuy was blocking the door, trying to hold them here with the fear he had used to destroy the will of millions. The tower was crumbling, and he couldn't attack them—not this twisted old man too afraid to strike—but he could hold them until the falling stone did his work for him.

He could always build another tower. He had done it before.

This was why Señora Mata had made her promise to take the cube back to her world. Their community was there, she thought, picturing Emma's face, her parents, the Niños, even the Rogues. She wouldn't have to do it alone.

They were eight stories up, and the floor was falling away beneath them, the wall opposite El Cucuy already gone. She would have to time it perfectly, Pao thought, to leave this place for the last time.

But first, there was something she had to try.

"Just let go!" she shouted at El Cucuy over the sound of the tower crumbling and the lightning storm outside. "Just let yourself move on! It's gotta be better than this!"

"Why would I?" he shouted back, but now his voice wasn't crashing cars, or rattling snake tails, or burning buildings. It was the croak of a stubborn old man who wouldn't let himself accept the love he wanted, the community he needed. "I have all the power here, and you have nothing! Nothing!"

"We'll light candles for you," Pao said. "We'll remember you. Just let them go. Let this place go! Move on!"

"I—I can't," he said, the images flickering and dying. "It's too late."

For a second that Pao knew wouldn't last, all was calm. The tower, open to the sky, the lightning frozen across its canvas. She had freed La Llorona and her last remaining child. She had even freed Joaquin. But this man was beyond her help. It was time to save herself.

"Then good-bye," she said, her voice echoing in the horrible stillness. And Pao, gripping Señora Mata's (still clutching the cube) and Dante's arms as tightly as she could, jumped backward off the tower's edge.

THIRTY-TWO
Together, At Last

El Cucuy's screams followed them down a fall that seemed to last forever, the wind rushing in Pao's ears, the lightning striking again and again all around her.

She couldn't put a knee to the ground right then, but she had never yearned so deeply to reach a different place. And so it was with perfect confidence that she screwed her eyes tight shut and pictured her people. The battle she could not let them fight alone.

The green paper dolls unfolded in midair, embracing the plummeting trio as the cries of the nightmare lord went on and on above them and the tower collapsed once and for all.

We won't let him rebuild it, Pao thought. *Not this time.*

While encased in a bubble of green light, Pao felt the portal erasing the void, heard El Cucuy's screams go silent as they winged their way through the place between worlds toward home. They would destroy the cube there, Pao told herself, her eyes locked on the object in Señora Mata's gnarled hands.

They would destroy it together, and then it would all be over. The threat of the void, the fantasmas, all of it. The spirits would be free to let go of their earthly fears and burdens once and for all and move on. The balance would be restored. . . .

But, as if he had seen her vision of a world that didn't include him, El Cucuy's long-fingered, filthy hand began to reach for Pao. She thought for a wild moment that he was here with her, that she'd accidentally brought him into her portal.

The reality was much worse.

The cube had opened, and El Cucuy was reaching through it right toward Señora Mata's chest.

"Señora . . . PAOLA!" Pao yelled, needing to wake the old woman before the Lord of Dread reached right through her. "WATCH OUT!"

Miraculously, she roused, her filmy eyes casting around the dark, claustrophobic bubble whizzing through space. When they locked on the hand reaching for her, she said, "No, no, not again! It was supposed to be different this time."

"What do you mean? Señora, WHAT DO I DO?" Pao screamed, but the hand wouldn't wait for an answer. It fastened itself around Señora Mata's neck and gripped tightly. Too tightly, until her eyes were bulging and her hands were loosening on the cube. "NO!" Pao screamed. "I NEED YOU! You have to fight!"

But the cube was already falling, and Pao somehow knew that her portal wouldn't stop it, that it would plunge right through the green bubble into the void, where El Cucuy would be free to reclaim it and continue his reign of terror for all eternity.

And everyone she knew and loved would die, fighting, as they waited for her to save them.

And so Pao did the only thing she could. She reached out with both hands and grabbed the metal casing with all its centuries of history and horror. She clutched it to her chest, and this time there were no images—just the long spear of dread that felt buried so much deeper this time, and a horrible nothingness inside her, like the empty sky above the Gila in her earliest dreams, from which she'd woken up screaming.

This time, there was no waking up. There was just fear and pain, so much of it that she couldn't bear the weight alone. So much of it that the only way to hold it would be to siphon a portion into someone else . . .

And there was Dante, barely alive, and such an easy target—the Bad Man Ghost tossing his father out a window, his mother running away, the pervasive fear of being left behind that followed him everywhere, made him lash out, push away first before anyone else could hurt him. It would be so easy to turn up the dial on his inadequacies, just for a little while, to lessen this horrible burden on her heart.

And Señora Mata, with her extra lifetime of waiting for another chance. All the people she'd known and loved were gone now, leaving her with only the fear that even two hundred years hadn't been enough time to get it right. That she was doomed to see the world swallowed up again. To realize that changing the past *was* truly impossible.

And there were more now. More people to choose from as the bubble opened, coughing up Pao and Dante and the old woman like hairballs on the concrete floor of the warehouse.

Naomi, whose mother hadn't known how to love her without hurting her. Marisa, who had endured years of bruises at the hands of her caregivers before finally disappearing into a cactus field, never to return. Sal, watching a van take away the only two people who'd felt like home. Kit, whose house was devoid of anyone to show her love or care.

Beto and Maria, who had loved and lost each other, who had

been tortured by who they were and who they would never be. Whose daughter had disappeared again.

Emma, who thought she could never be good enough. Who might die with the weight of an unexpressed love in her heart . . .

The cube told Pao she could hold them all here, make them suffer so her own suffering felt lighter. She could cloak herself in the feeling of power that came from controlling them. Keeping them small and afraid forever.

From the cube, ribbonlike film strips began to reach forward tentatively, probing through the unfamiliar air toward the beating hearts of all these people, and Pao didn't have the strength to stop them, or to stop the shadows circling them, or the thousands more filling cities across the world. She was just one girl. Just one girl, alone.

And then, like a candle coming to life in an endless cave, Pao remembered what Señora Mata had said atop the lightning-struck tower. The antidote to fear. And she forced her salt-encrusted eyes to open, compelled herself to look at them all. Her family. Her friends.

Her community.

"I can't . . . do it . . . alone," she croaked. "Please, help me." She lifted the cube, hoping they would understand. It was a leap of faith that might end with nothing but another fall, but it was the only move she had left to make, and for an endless moment of fear and pain, her mind half here and half in El Cucuy's ruined tower, she waited. . . .

Until she felt a hand on top of hers, warm, a little clammy. And another on top of that. Hands, reaching out from all around her, arms linking with hers, a group joining together. And she saw, as El Cucuy never would, and as even the old Pao hadn't, the line between punishing others for your loneliness and fear and allowing them to take a piece of your burden. Allowing them to help when you needed it.

With every pair of hands that joined hers, Pao felt the weight on her heart lifting, lightening, until at last she could stand and look at them all, and then at what was happening to the cube that had only caused dread, destruction, and death.

A light, as buttery yellow as the setting sun, was growing brighter inside the object. Its metal casing was shot through with holes as each person present took a ribbon of fear into themselves.

And then, just when Pao thought she could hold it no longer, the empty box crumbled to obsidian dust in her hands. She turned over her palms, and it scattered to the ground at her feet.

Around them, the horde of shadow soldiers that had been on the brink of defeating Los Niños moments ago slumped to the floor, the anger and hatred animating them gone as the hold El Cucuy had placed on them was finally released.

They turned to dust, too, glittering and strange on the concrete as the living began to stagger to their feet, looking around like they'd just weathered a massive storm. Which, in some ways, they had. But Pao's eyes were on the void mouth in the wall. Had the place created by El Cucuy's loneliness and fear survived the destruction of his power? Had Pao done what she had gone there to do? What Señora Mata had waited two hundred years to accomplish?

The mouth had grown in her absence, large enough for five burly adults to pass through shoulder to shoulder, but as she watched, she could see something incredible happening. The perpetual lightning storm in the field around the tower had stopped, and a gentle, cleansing rain was falling in its place. All over, Pao could see fantasmas, shadow soldiers, and bone warriors turning their faces and hands up to it, and then, one by one, they floated into the ether.

Just before the window closed forever, cutting her off from that place, she saw the stooped, frail form of El Cucuy, separated from the mythos of his power. Just an old man crying in the rain, resisting the pull to be free.

Free, Pao thought, with tears running down her face. Because a part of her—the part that had sent her nightmares, the part that had pulled her toward every monster and void entrance in the living world—that was floating up, too.

"Paola!" came her mom's panicked voice. Pao turned just as the mouth closed for good, the wall behind it just a wall again. "Come quick! She's awake, and she's asking for you."

THIRTY-THREE
Good-Bye

Señora Mata, as everyone present knew her, was lying on a pile of blankets in the warehouse's courtyard, her face turned up to the early morning sun.

From a radio nearby came a broadcaster's voice, shocked and crying, saying that the horrible, inexplicable invasion into many of the world's major cities seemed to have come to an end as quickly as it started. The cities would have to rebuild, with communities pitching in time, effort, and money for cleanup, funeral expenses, and reconstruction.

Pao turned it off and then crossed the cobblestones, Bruto limping along beside her. Weeds clung stubbornly to even the smallest strip of earth between them, Pao noticed as she knelt beside the old woman, whose chest was rising and falling too quickly, her breath so shallow. Like a hummingbird's.

"Señora," Pao said, taking her frail, papery hands in her own, careful not to squeeze hard. "You did it."

"No," breathed the old woman. "*You* did it. You did what I failed to do so long ago. You, Paola Santiago, have saved us all."

"You'll be okay," Pao said, the tears flowing freely down her cheeks. "We'll get you to the hospital. We'll . . ."

But Señora Mata only shook her head. "My time has come," she said. "And now . . . there is nothing for me to fear. Now I will get to go on."

Pao remembered the ecstatic looks on the faces of the fantasmas as they floated up into the sky and realized it wasn't Señora Mata who would suffer, but the people here. Like Dante, who was standing, unsteady and ashen-faced, just a few feet away. Pao would miss the woman terribly. But Señora Mata had lived a *very* long time, and she could be proud of her accomplishments.

"Am I really going to marry a guy named Alberto?" Pao blurted out all of a sudden, unable to help herself.

The old woman laughed a breathy, barely there laugh. "Don't you understand, silly girl? We *did* it. We changed the future. What you do now is entirely up to you. You are free."

"Thank you," Pao said, the emotion nearly choking her. "You changed my life. You changed *all* our lives. You believed in us so much you came back just to help us do it."

"I believe," she wheezed, "in *community*. Being a loving grandmother. Being a kindly neighbor who feeds a family when they are struggling. Being a safe place for a mother to send her child when she has to work long shifts. Even showing up for a group of friends who love to play bingo. These . . . are the things that change fates, Paola. If you remember anything I've told you over the years, remember that."

"I will," Pao said, her words mostly lost in a sob as she squeezed the señora's hands. "I will, I promise."

"Now," said the old woman, "send me my boy, and let me go."

Pao nodded, and releasing those comforting hands was the hardest thing she'd ever done. But she obeyed, and with a new kind of weight on her heart, she made room for Dante to approach.

She couldn't hear what the old señora was saying as Dante bowed his head over her, but she didn't need to. There had been enough in what Pao had been told. Enough to change fates—at least she hoped.

It wasn't long enough before Dante wandered back over to her, looking more lost than Pao had ever seen him. "She's . . . gone," he said, and then he plunked himself down on the ground and began to sob. Those full-body, little-kid-scraped-knee sobs that heal as much as they hurt.

Pao wrapped her arms around his bony shoulders, letting herself cry, too. For all the old woman had meant to them. For the gaping hole she left behind.

"She's gone," Dante said again. "And I'm alone."

"You're *not* alone," Pao said, squeezing him fiercely. "You have me. You've always had me."

"After everything I've done to you?" Dante hiccupped, sitting up straight to face her. "Everything I've said? Everything I've ruined? You'll never be able to look at me the same."

Pao thought of all the time she'd known Dante. From four years old until today, when they were mourning the biggest loss they'd ever shared. Their fights and the rifts and the misery. But also the love. The camaraderie. The feeling that she could never be alone in the world because she had Dante.

She'd always had Dante.

"Listen to me," Paola said, looking into the haunted eyes of her first best friend. "We might argue. And we might let each other down. And we might disappoint each other, and make mistakes, and then do it all over again. But you're my family, Dante Mata. I choose you. And *I am never letting you go.*"

"I'm sorry, Pao," he said, the tears starting again. "I'm so sorry. You're my best friend. You're my whole world. I'm so, so sorry."

"I forgive you," she said, hugging him as hard as she could. "And we're gonna get through this, all of this, together."

He was lost to sobs again in a moment, and as Pao held him, she thought of Señora Mata. Pao would never know all that the old woman had been through. But she thought she understood a little part of it now.

"Let me take him," Pao's mom said gently some time later, when Pao's shirt was soaked with tears and Dante's sobs were coming fewer and farther between. "You need to clean up and rest."

"Soon," Pao said, hugging her mom fiercely before handing Dante over. He went willingly, Pao saw, which was a good sign, considering what she was planning next.

Back inside the warehouse, the cleanup had already begun. In the office, a vigil had been set up for Franco, whose arms were folded peacefully over his chest, his eyes closed. He could have been sleeping, Pao thought, the tears coming back again.

"It was my fault," Pao's dad said, coming up behind her and putting a heavy arm on her shoulder. "I can't help but feel responsible."

"Franco was over a hundred years old, Dad," Pao said, sniffling. "He had a long life, and he saved us. The copy of you was here to kill me, and if I hadn't made it into the void . . ."

"I can feel it, you know. The malevolence is really gone this time."

Pao nodded. "I can, too. The void is back to being what it's supposed to be—a way station for souls who are . . . moving on." She thought of Señora Mata again, pictured her joyously ascending into the light.

"Someday you'll have to tell me how you did it," Beto said, half smiling, half frowning.

"Someday soon," Pao said, noticing Emma on the edge of her vision and feeling her stomach do a full-on backflip. "But right now, I gotta . . ." She trailed off, gesturing, and Beto patted her on the back.

"Go," he said. "We have time."

"We do," Pao said, and for the first instance in as long as she could remember, she felt it. Time. Spooling out ahead of her. A glorious, undecided future just waiting for her to shape.

Emma was waiting semi-patiently near the warehouse's front door, leaning forward on her toes and bouncing slightly like she did when she was really nervous. Pao, after her time in the nightmare realm, found the idea of run-of-the-mill excited nervousness so appealing she practically jogged to meet her.

"Hi," Pao said breathlessly when she got there, wishing she'd thought of something cooler.

"Hi," Emma said back, her face already pink.

"Weren't you supposed to be at the Riverside Pal—"

"I'm sorry," Emma interrupted, looking pained. "But can I go first? There's just something I've been trying to say to you for a really, really long time, and I keep being afraid it's too late, and now, even though things *seem* normal, I'm afraid you're just gonna vanish into thin air again any second, and I just, like, *have* to get it out before I lose my nerve permanently."

Pao did her best not to laugh—not mockingly, but purely because of how much she really, really liked this girl. "The floor is yours."

"Okay, thank you." Emma took a breath and blew it out of her mouth like a horse. "Wow, now that I actually *get* to say it, I have no idea what to say. Um . . . it's just that . . . I like you, Pao. I, like, really, *really* like you, and *not* just in a best friend way, and I really thought I was gonna literally die with this secret because I didn't think you felt the same way, but after everything that's happened, I just . . . I *have* to ask if there's any chance that maybe—you know, later, after we've processed all this, which I get might take a long time! But that maybe you might . . . like, ever . . ."

For once, it was Pao saving Emma from the rambling sentence, and instead of doing it with words, she stepped forward and reached out her hand, taking Emma's in hers and intertwining their fingers so Emma's glittery purple nails were on top.

Emma stopped babbling immediately, her face turning several shades pinker. "Really?" she squeaked.

"Really," Pao said emphatically. "And you're right: This *is* a lot to process, and it's probably gonna take a really long time. But I can't think of anyone else I'd rather do it with than you."

They might have stood there beaming at each other for several more hours, but Naomi and Marisa walked up then, shovel and broom in hand. Marisa's eyes were red-rimmed, and Naomi's face had cuts that would definitely become scars, but they were standing and ready to rebuild.

"I wanted to say thank you," Marisa said. "For what you did in the void. And for how you organized things here. El Cucuy's soldiers were everywhere, so I couldn't get people to Riverside Palace, but your offer to hold down the fort was generous, and thinking of the most vulnerable among us in a time of crisis was the action of a leader."

"Oh, well," said Pao, a little embarrassed by the compliment. "It's a good thing everyone was here, anyway."

"A long time ago, I invited you to join the Niños' ranks," Marisa went on, "and I'd like to extend the invitation again now that we've so often found ourselves fighting together. With the . . . losses—" Her voice broke on the last word, and Pao felt a wave of pity for this beautiful girl, who had now lost the boy she loved twice. "With the losses we've sustained, we could use someone like you in our ranks."

Privately, Pao wondered what the Niños de la Luz would have left to do now that all the the void entrances were closed, but they *were* a community, she supposed. They would adapt. "I guess there are always gonna be monsters to fight," she said. "Maybe now that the void's gone you guys can tackle police brutality, or border patrol? Immigrant detention?"

Emma squeezed her hand, and Pao could practically *feel* her glowing with pride.

"We have some ideas I think you'll like," Marisa said, smiling despite the pain in her eyes.

"Plus, you know you're tired of being a tourist," Naomi said with an elbow nudge. "Come on."

Pao thought about it, she really did. After all, in another dimension or timeline or whatever, she *had* joined Los Niños de la Luz and fought with them for a hundred years. . . .

But she had fought hard in *this* life not to have to repeat

Señora Mata's future. Pao found she didn't mind not knowing exactly what was coming next.

"Hey! I'll join!" Kit seemed to materialize out of nowhere. "I mean, I think I've proven myself, right?" Her rake was badly singed, and three or four of its teeth seemed to be missing, along with a chunk of Kit's hair.

Naomi shook her head, laughing, and tossed Kit a broom. "You're an honorary Niña for exactly as long as it takes to clean up this mess," she said. "And then I think you'd better stick to boffering. Whatever that is."

Kit's face fell, but Pao's heart felt somehow more buoyant. Kit had grown on her a *little*, but this was still good news.

Robin and Pops One were helping Pops Two (who seemed to be limping but was otherwise okay) to the door. Pao waved, but Robin was wrapped up in her family. She figured they'd see each other at school. The world of normal civilians was already beginning to break its reluctant truce with the world of the paranormal.

Maybe that was the way it was supposed to be, Pao thought. But which side did she belong on?

Sal wandered up with Bruto at his side, both of them grinning at Pao. "You did it," he said. "You made *all* the monsters go away."

Pao was so touched the little boy had remembered her promise that she hugged him on the spot.

"Are you staying with us now?" Sal asked, wedging himself under Pao's arm as Bruto launched himself up to lick her face.

Naomi and Marisa and even Emma looked at her, waiting for the answer she still wasn't completely ready to give.

"I appreciate the invitation," Pao said, meaning it. "And you know I'll be around. But I think for a while I'm gonna focus on . . . being thirteen?"

"Fair enough," Marisa said.

Naomi rolled her eyes. "I knew you were too chicken."

"Will you settle for some help cleaning up?" Pao asked, feeling lighter than she had in ages.

Marisa tossed her the broom. "You bet."

EPILOGUE

The sun outside the Silver Springs Community Outreach Center was way too hot for fall as Pao, Emma, and Dante made their way toward Riverside Palace. It was the second of November in their ninth-grade year, and they had a celebration to get to.

"How'd it go?" Pao asked Dante, who was wheeling Emma's bike as the girls walked hand in hand beside him.

Dante shrugged. "I don't see the point. It's not like we can tell them anything real."

They'd found Señora Mata's last will and testament among her things at the nursing home after she died. Among the ordinary stuff, there'd been a bit of a shock. It turned out the old woman had been rich. Like, *really* rich. And she'd left very specific instructions for how she wanted her fortune divvied up.

The main thing she'd specified was weekly therapy for Dante, Pao, and Emma until they were eighteen, when—in her words—*they'd be smart enough to continue under their own steam.*

She had also named Pao's parents Dante's legal guardians, which just went to show that Pao and the old lady were really on the same wavelength. It wasn't really a surprise when she thought about it. Or . . . was it? Pao didn't really have a handle on the whole past-and-future-selves thing yet. She probably never would.

"You guys ready for this?" Emma asked, glancing back and forth between the two of them. "Should we grab some flowers or something on the way?"

Dante laughed, and Pao cherished the sound. He was often angry and somewhat lost, still traumatized by everything that had happened to him. But, like her therapist said, everyone moved through suffering and grief in their own way. You couldn't do the work for them, but you could be there for them, and that's what Pao was planning to do for as long as he'd let her.

Therapy seemed to be helping, as well as frequent sparring sessions at the Niños' warehouse. Dante had lost his Arma del Alma to El Cucuy, but Pao didn't mind lending him hers. Ever since their shared grief over the loss of Señora Mata, things were easier between them.

Not the same, as he'd predicted. But all you could do was move forward. Dante was family, and family was forever.

"I think we all know that if Abuela wants anything on her Día de los Muertos altar, it's not foliage," he said now, smiling and shaking his hair out of his eyes in an achingly familiar way.

"Point taken," said Pao, and she turned left instead of right on the next street until they were in front of their favorite taquería.

"Five cheese tamales, please," Dante said, digging into his pocket for a wad of crumpled up cash.

"And a couple spicy chicken, for those of us with taste buds," Pao said, throwing a ten-dollar bill (uncrumpled, from a wallet) on top of his. Whatever the time-travel anomaly was that had made her future self think cheese tamales were good, she was glad it hadn't affected her present.

After a lot of thought, Pao had decided against telling anyone what she'd learned about the old woman. There were a lot of reasons for that, not the least of which was that she knew she'd sound absolutely absurd and no one would believe her. But the biggest one was that she didn't want to complicate Dante's memories of his abuela. He deserved to have that anchor while he waded through all the rest.

With the tamale bag dangling from the handlebars, the three of them approached the Riverside Palace, which was basically a demolition zone. Señora Mata had provided a generous amount of money to Pao's parents for Dante's care (though Pao suspected she'd had other motives, too). It was enough to buy a house—like, a big one in Emma's neighborhood.

But instead, her parents (with some cajoling from Pao) had decided to buy and renovate the apartment complex. For the time being, they were paying for all the tenants' lodging at the fanciest hotel in town. When the tenants returned, their water would run clear, they would have air-conditioning and heating that worked all the time, and their windows would actually let in light.

The Santiagos' one nod to luxury was that they were combining apartments C and K into one unit to make room for their family and anyone else who might need a meal or a place to sleep. Naomi had already called dibs, but Pao had a feeling she was joking—unless, of course, Marisa was already there.

Today, the contractors had been given the day off to celebrate their ancestors and family who had passed on. The town threw a whole parade every year. The Santiagos, however, had decided, given everything, to keep their own celebration small.

Well, the Maria Santiago version of small, anyway.

The entire parking lot had been emptied of cars and filled with tables covered in blankets, and marigolds on practically every surface, including the ground. Candles glowed to rival the sun that was just beginning to set, and the smell of food wafted tantalizingly from the makeshift outdoor kitchen her father had set up.

"Welcome back!" Beto shouted now, as Pao, Emma, and Dante walked up. Bruto bounded over to sniff the tamale bag and lick Pao's hand. "We've been keeping the home fires burning! Come, eat! How were your sessions?"

"Beto, let them breathe," Pao's mom said, approaching with a basket of tortillas and snaking an arm around his waist.

Dante held up his bag. "Cheese," he said. "We thought she'd . . . she'd like them."

"Of course," Maria said. "Put them wherever you like."

Dante went over to Señora Mata's table, which was covered in framed photos of her over the years and several of her crocheted blankets. Maria had even sprinkled it with Florida Water.

Pao's parents stepped forward together to give her a hug.

On Maria's shirt was a print of the Moon tarot card, and Pao smiled, remembering. She'd let her mom read her cards a few more times, and Pao didn't think she'd ever truly understand the appeal.

The Tower card still gave her goose bumps, but that was only to be expected. Pao had actually *fallen* from a lightning-struck tower, after all. Talk about on the nose . . .

"We'll give you all some time with her," Pao's mom said now, sniffling. "She was such a special lady. I don't know how I would have gotten through the past ten years without her."

"Me either," Pao said, squeezing her mom tight, remembering all the nights they'd spent in apartment K, and trying—as she had been ever since she'd learned who the señora really was—not to wonder what the woman's life had been like. What disaster had been so ruinous that she'd spent more than a century trying to change it?

Pao's parents wandered away, and Emma and Pao linked hands again, giving Dante a moment alone before they joined him at the folding table that comprised Señora Mata's first Día de los Muertos altar.

They all stood there silently, looking at her smiling face in all the ornate frames, Pao's mind so tied up in knots that it was hard to mourn properly. She'd told her therapist about it today—in slightly vaguer wording, of course—and her advice came back to Pao now.

She is whoever you need her to be to grieve, the therapist had said. *Don't overcomplicate it with* should*s.*

So Pao decided to keep a Señora Mata in her head and her heart, and not to complicate that image with anything else. At last, remembering the woman who had loved her, the grandmother who had helped raise her, Pao was able to find some peace.

"I'll miss you," she whispered. "Thank you for everything."

"So," Dante said, when enough time had transpired. "No more monsters. No more void. No more creepy fantasmas . . . What are we supposed to do now?"

No one answered right away, but over the cheese tamales, the candle flame danced in a breeze only it could feel. Pao could almost hear Señora Mata whispering, *You go enjoy your lives, idiotas.*

And so they did.